W9-CJC-839

REMINISCING
With
SISSLE
And
BLAKE

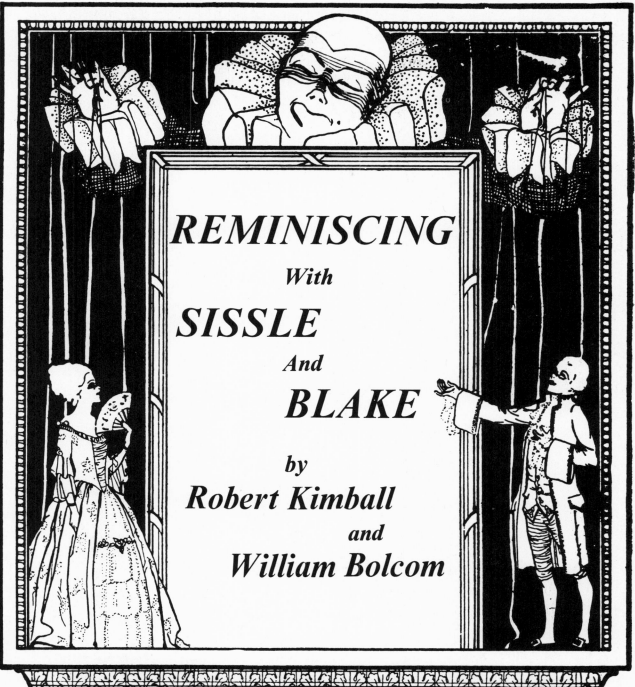

REMINISCING With SISSLE And BLAKE

by

Robert Kimball

and

William Bolcom

The Viking Press
New York

CREDITS AND ACKNOWLEDGMENTS

Culver Pictures: 50, 51; Maryland Historical Society: 36–37; Theatre Collection, The New York Public Library at Lincoln Center, Astor, Lenox and Tilden Foundations: 110, 112–113, 162–163, 164, 169, 170–171, 172–173, 174, 176, 179, 180, 182–183, 185, 188–189, 215, 217, 218–219, 220–221, 222, 223; Wide World Photos: 138; Maurice Zouary, DeForest Collection, Library of Congress: 138–140.

All other photos and exhibits are from the archives of Noble Sissle and Eubie Blake and appear in this book with their permission.

* * *

Grateful acknowledgment is made for permission to reprint reviews and articles that appeared originally in *The Crisis*, published by the N.A.A.C.P., the *New York Post*, the *St. Louis Post-Dispatch*, and *Variety*.

* * *

Special thanks are offered to Irving Brown of Warner Bros. Music for his assistance in obtaining permission to include lyrics of Sissle and Blake songs of which Warner Bros. is the copyright owner.

Warner Bros. Music: *On Patrol in No Man's Land* (Noble Sissle, Eubie Blake, James Reese Europe) © 1919 M. Witmark & Sons, Copyright renewed. All rights reserved. *Love Will Find a Way* (Noble Sissle, Eubie Blake) © 1921 M. Witmark & Sons, Copyright renewed. All rights reserved. *Baltimore Buzz* (Noble Sissle, Eubie Blake) © 1921 M. Witmark & Sons, Copyright renewed. All rights reserved. *In Honeysuckle Time, When Emaline Said She'd Be Mine* (Noble Sissle, Eubie Blake) © 1921 M. Witmark & Sons, Copyright renewed. All rights reserved. *I'm Craving for That Kind of Love* (Noble Sissle, Eubie Blake) © 1921 M. Witmark & Sons, Copyright renewed. All rights reserved. *You Were Meant for Me* (Noble Sissle, Eubie Blake) © 1924 Harms, Inc., Copyright renewed. All rights reserved. *Dixie Moon* (Noble Sissle, Eubie Blake) © 1924 Harms, Inc., Copyright renewed. All rights reserved. *All of No Man's Land* (Noble Sissle, Eubie Blake, James Reese Europe) © 1919 M. Witmark & Sons, Copyright renewed. All rights reserved. All used by permission of Warner Bros. Music

* * *

Noble Sissle and Eubie Blake: *It's All Your Fault* Copyright © 1970 by Noble Sissle, Eddie Nelson, and Eubie Blake. *To Hell with Germany* Copyright © 1973 by Noble Sissle and Eubie Blake. *What a Great Great Day* Copyright © 1973 by Noble Sissle and Eubie Blake. *Have a Good Time, Everybody* Copyright © 1973 by Noble Sissle and Eubie Blake. *The Jockey's Life for Mine* Copyright © 1973 by Noble Sissle and Eubie Blake. *Sons of Old Black Joe* Copyright © 1973 by Noble Sissle and Eubie Blake. Used by permission of Noble Sissle and Eubie Blake.

* * *

First published in 1973 by The Viking Press, Inc.
625 Madison Avenue, New York, N. Y. 10022
Published simultaneously in Canada by
The Macmillan Company of Canada Limited
SBN 670-59388-5
Library of Congress catalog card number: 72-91100
Printed in U.S.A.

Acknowledgments

The authors acknowledge with appreciation all those who helped in the preparation of this book, especially:

Rudi Blesh, teacher and friend, who introduced us, through his book *They All Played Ragtime* (with Harriett Janis), to that basic American music that was the foundation of Sissle and Blake's style.

The late Bert Lahr, whose championing of them was directly responsible for our seeking out his colleagues Sissle and Blake.

Noble Sissle's family: his niece Betty, his late nephew Paul, and his children, Cynthia and Noble, Jr., who gave freely of their time and hospitality as we gathered necessary material for our book.

Carl Seltzer, whose organization of Eubie Blake's music manuscripts was a constant guide to use and whose recent recordings demonstrate not only Eubie's unflagging energy and ability but Carl's devotion to the task of preserving Eubie's inimitable playing style on discs.

Marion Tyler Blake, whose help to us in every way cannot be adequately described or sufficiently thanked.

Richard Buck, Paul Myers, Dorothy Swerdlove, Max Silverman, and Rod Bladel of the Lincoln Center Library of the Performing Arts, for their aid in finding elusive show photographs and unearthing facts and clues to this segment of the theatrical past, so recent and yet so forgotten.

William Hyder, whose extensive and passionate research into Baltimore history saved us from several blunders of scholarship.

Mike Montgomery, whose impressive scholarship was invaluable in the preparation of the list of recordings, piano rolls, and films in the Appendix.

John Hammond, who issued *The Eighty-Six Years of Eubie Blake* on Columbia Records and thus helped rescue Sissle and Blake from obscurity.

Our very special thanks to our dear friends Teresa Sterne and David Hamilton, who helped launch this entire project with their goodwill, encouragement, and very real support; to Norman Lloyd, who may be considered somewhat responsible for the formation of the *ad hoc* writing team of Kimball and Bolcom; to Joan Morris and Abigail Kuflik Kimball, to whom fell the usual unsung and thankless task of keeping us alive and reasonably sane during this book's growth.

To the dedicated and talented people at Viking: Marianne Dormsjo, Shirley Brownrigg, Olga Zaferatos, Barbara Burge, Carol Sue Judy, Linda Yablonsky, and Mary Velthoven Kopecky, whose patience and good humor have sustained us at every phase of this book—but most particularly to our editors Alan Williams and Nicolas Ducrot, who beggar any attempt at thanks, itemized or otherwise, so intimately were they involved with the spawning of this effort.

Finally, to Noble and Eubie we offer this book as a small token of our esteem and affection. We hope we have told enough (no one book could tell all) of their 173 years of life history so that they will be reasonably satisfied with the picture of the performing and writing team, Sissle and Blake, that we have drawn.

Robert Kimball
William Bolcom
September 1972, New York

TABLE OF CONTENTS

Introduction

It is now more than fifty-seven years ago that Noble Sissle, a twenty-five-year-old singer and lyricist from Indianapolis, met Eubie Blake of Baltimore, a thirty-two-year-old ragtime pianist and composer whose great ambition was to write for the stage. Both had been hired for a summer engagement in Baltimore's River View Park. This was 1915, in the days before air conditioning, when the summer heat forced entertainment to move outdoors—from the saloons to the parks, from supper clubs, restaurants, and ballrooms to hotel roofs and gardens. . . . On that May day Noble Sissle and Eubie Blake formed a songwriting partnership that miraculously still endures.

Reminiscing with Sissle and Blake, a story of great musical theater, is about a dream shared by two men who brought their dream to triumphant reality. But anyone looking at these photographs and reading this story today might almost believe that it unfolded on another planet if it happened at all, so great is our ignorance of this essential chapter of American cultural history. For the story of Noble Sissle and Eubie Blake occurred right here, in American cities like Baltimore, Indianapolis, and New York. Had it not occurred our musical theater might well have been very different.

This book is drawn from their own words—but it also contains our commentaries and reflections on what they have told us of their early years, their collaboration, their successful restoration of authentic black artistry to the American stage, and the painful aftermath when they saw what they had achieved against such overwhelming odds destroyed by forces and events beyond their control.

Today our musical theater is nearly moribund, but fifty years ago, when Sissle and Blake performed on and wrote for the stage, Broadway was a vibrant place ablaze with the fires of ambition and aspiration. People came to the Great White Way in quest of the dream of wealth, fame, and personal fulfillment. The shows of the period, marvels full of tunes and talents, pulsed with the excitement of those raw and energetic years. There were really *zany* comedians, *beautiful* showgirls, *lavish* costumes, and many wonderful singers and dancers. The exuberantly talented creations of George and Ira Gershwin, Jerome Kern, Vincent Youmans, Oscar Hammerstein, Lorenz Hart, Richard Rodgers, Irving Berlin, and Cole Porter were aeons away from the depressing and uninspired offerings of most of today's Broadway.

Musical comedy had its greatest flowering during the twenties. As an entertainment form, it was a polyglot embracing many kinds of expression. Perhaps the most all-around successful of all the genres was the revue, as spectacularly produced by Florenz Ziegfeld, George White, Earl Carroll, and the Shubert brothers.

The revue traced its origins at least as far back as the minstrel show.

Beginning as an absurd white parody of black artistry, the minstrel show had evolved into a full-fledged variety show replete with all kinds of novelty acts—singers, dancers, jugglers, contortionists, ventriloquists, and animal acts. Its early headquarters was the saloon, but by the late 1860s the minstrel show had become a "clean," family-type entertainment, ensconced in "opera houses" and given a dignified name: vaudeville. Surviving until its gradual displacement by the motion pictures, vaudeville was organized into circuits, the most powerful of which was the Keith Orpheum Circuit, headed by E. F. Albee. The gargantuan New York revues of Ziegfeld and the others could be seen as really more dressed-up versions of the variety or vaudeville shows.

Burlesque, which is often confused with vaudeville, had its own tradition and line of development. Today the terms "burlesque" and "striptease" have become virtually synonymous in the public mind, but the original stage burlesque was a collection of comedy sketches that either lampooned lofty material or treated banal situations with mock dignity; it was only later that the girlie acts that had been interspersed with the parodies and caricatures would become the bulk of the burlesque evening. Burlesque shows had their own system of organization and booking, usually called "wheels." In general, salaries in burlesque were lower, working hours longer, and working conditions more hazardous and less elegant than on the vaudeville circuits. Where vaudeville might aspire to a higher-class audience and fare, the low-comedy skits of burlesque made no bones about trying to be Art, and it is interesting that some of the more esoteric reaches of modern theater, such as the work of Samuel Beckett, can be traced more directly to the burlesque turns than to vaudeville.

The traditional route followed by many of the most successful performers up until quite recently was to go from burlesque to vaudeville to the revue to the musical comedy. The last-named, the conventional "book show," essentially fitted the variety show into the framework of a story. The growth of this form can be traced from the nineteenth-century farce comedies of Nate Salsbury, Harrigan and Hart, and Charles Hoyt to the Weber and Fields and George M. Cohan shows of the early years of this century.

Cohan especially can be credited for keeping the American vernacular theatrical tradition alive despite the overwhelming influx, in the 1890s and 1900s, of a seemingly endless flood of Viennese operettas, British comic operas, and French *opéras bouffes*, whose principal attractions were their exotic locales and the high sophistication of their music. Against the small-scaled musicals of Bolton, Wodehouse, and Kern, and the syncopated offerings of Irving Berlin, were pitted the huge outpouring of operetta, whose popularity remained high from the first Gilbert and Sullivan operetta performance (in Boston, *Pinafore*, 1878) to Sigmund Romberg's last great success (*The New Moon*, New York, 1928). Operetta's outstanding practitioners on both sides of the Atlantic included Victor Herbert, Franz Lehár, Leslie Stuart, and Oskar Straus. Even today, in the works of Rodgers and Hammerstein and Lerner and Loewe, we find many of the traits of this once-dominant theatrical form.

Burlesque—vaudeville—revue—musical comedy—operetta: all were healthy, alive, and still in the ascendancy when Noble Sissle and Eubie Blake began their careers in the theater.

In a program of a current Broadway musical show, there is a note that its musical supervisor was the first black conductor on Broadway. When we mentioned this to Noble Sissle, he laughingly told us that it was probably correct that the young man may be the first *black* conductor on Broadway, but that there were a few *Negro* Broadway conductors around before him. What interested us about the assertion on the show's program was that it was representative of the kind of error repeatedly made everywhere, in all innocence, because of the widespread belief that blacks have only recently achieved any degree of prominence on the American musical stage.

Many writers who ought to know better proclaim blithely that the Pearl Bailey–Cab Calloway version of *Hello, Dolly!* was the first show on Broadway with an all-black cast. Others who have at least heard of the epoch-making Sissle and Blake musical *Shuffle Along* make all sorts of contradictory and confusing claims about it—it was a revue; it opened in Harlem; it ran for only two weeks; in it Florence Mills introduced "I'm Just Wild about Harry," and so forth. None of the above is true, and every statement there has been gleaned from one of the many and respected histories of the American musical theater. This kind of myth perpetuation is the reason that this book and others on the same subject are necessary.

Not only have there been several black conductors on Broadway over the years but, for more than a century, black Americans have made a rich, exciting, and immensely significant contribution to the musical stage. That these contributors remain so little known is in part a reflection on the failure of theater historians to transcend their customary statistical shell games, all too often consisting of little more than a predictable litany of cast- and song-lists and an equally predictable rundown of the postmortems of the prominent New York theater critics. While there exist several monographs and dissertations which (if read) could enrich our understanding of the contribution of black artists to our musical stage, these works have been almost totally ignored by the historians of the so-called mainstream of American theater. While it is certainly correct to emphasize, as the historians do, the stellar contributions of such men as Rodgers and Hammerstein, Cole Porter, and Irving Berlin, to do so without giving even scant attention to Bob Cole, Will Marion Cook, Scott Joplin, Andy Razaf, Thomas W. "Fats" Waller, and James P. Johnson, all of whom have made permanent donations to our musical theater and all of whom happen to be black, is to commit more than an unfortunate oversight: it is to point up the still prevalent racism in our historical outlook. Worse than that, it is to keep the public uninformed of the provenance of such a large portion of our internationally beloved popular music and musical theater. Many people are more aware that Rodgers and Hart wrote such and such a tune than they are that such standards as "Ain't Misbehavin'" and "Honeysuckle Rose" come from the team of Waller and Razaf, or even that "I'm Just Wild about Harry" was one of the many effusions of the team of Noble Sissle and Eubie Blake.

This book, then, is part of what we hope will be a major and continuing reassessment of our theater history. Noble Sissle and Eubie Blake are among the very few survivors of that golden era of the musical theater of the twenties. They were among the few writers who refused to go along with the crushing stereotype imposed on them by the white man. While others found themselves acquiescently turning out the kind of work black writers were supposed to create (those writers who were still in the running, in areas where white writers had not yet aped and pre-empted them out of business); where Hollywood black actors found work only in ludicrous and shameful travesties of their own art and people (such as the "All God's Chillun Got Rhythm" sequence from the Marx Brothers' *A Day at the Races*, which may have been intended, for all we know, as a horrifying spoof on itself); where black creators and performers everywhere found themselves victims of a new form of yellow-dog contract, this time one perpetrated by their own unions —with all this around them, Sissle and Blake, together and apart, endured these bleak times, still hoping for the day that their work would be accepted on its own merits, still hoping that their love lyrics and waltzes would be given the same place in the sun as the blues and rags white writers were turning out. So much of their excellent work has remained unpublished and unrecognized, yet Sissle and Blake are not angry men—they have not allowed themselves to contract "the disease of hate," as Eubie puts it. They have lived without bitterness or rancor and with the constant hope that they could share their work, their experiences, and their enthusiasm for life with others.

When Bob Kimball first met Noble Sissle in April 1967, the first thing that was to strike him was Noble's continuing optimism. His apartment on St. Nicholas Avenue was filled with memorabilia, some of it dating back to the early 1900s when he was a young singer and reader on the Chautauqua circuit. "You know, I have a lot to tell you," he said to Bob, "enough for several books. People are so ignorant of the Negro's contribution to American music. I think we should talk about it out at Blake's house in Brooklyn, where we can get him to the piano. You ought to hear that boy play."

A few days later Noble stopped by Bob's with his car and they were on their way to Brooklyn, over the Williamsburg Bridge and out along Broadway under the noisy elevated trains, past dingy shops, bleak housing projects, and Spanish movie theaters. On to Stuyvesant Avenue with its potholes and garbage— then suddenly the car came upon an elegant stand of private nineteenth-century town houses, as fine and graceful as any in New York City.

Noble pulled up across the street from the AME Zion Church, and the two entered a handsome four-story dwelling that had been Marion Blake's family home when she and Eubie were married in 1945; it was the second marriage for both of them. "When I got married," Eubie happily proclaimed as they all shook hands, "I got the coop with the chicken." Bob Kimball relates, "That began one of the most memorable afternoons of my life. I entered that town house almost totally ignorant of the black experience in the musical theater. By the time we left that night to begin the long drive home in the rain, I felt that I had been in a time capsule and had been lifted back, through time and space, into the world of song and story that was America embarking on the twentieth century."

As afternoon became evening, for at least five hours Eubie and Noble recounted their adventures in the theater and told stories of the men who had gone before them and had been their idols: Bert Williams, George M. Cohan, Al Jolson, James Reese Europe, and Victor Herbert. Every so often Eubie would dash to the piano and holler to his partner, "Say, kid, do you remember this one?" And Noble did—he sang out clearly, right on pitch, with impeccable diction, while Eubie made the piano sound like several instruments all at once. It was all so good and so thrilling—the past came alive so vividly, with such complete recall—that events of fifty years ago sounded as if they had happened last week. (Eubie was then eighty-four and Noble seventy-eight.)

At one point Eubie rose from the piano bench and beckoned them toward the hallway. "Let me show you some photos of some of the people I've been talking about." They entered a hallway lined with old photos of the artists of that far-off time. When Eubie spotted one faded photograph of a group of men standing, he moved his hand along the row of faces and said simply, "Dead! Dead! Dead! Every one of them. I knew them all, but people don't believe me when I tell how great these men were—and they were giants—because they didn't make any records and you know what kind of chances Joneses had to make movies. No one but Sissle and a few others have heard of or remember them. It's a shame that so much of our heritage is lost. . . ."

There was a time around the turn of the century when the dominant white culture of America appeared ready to accept black artistry on its own terms. Black artists had waged a long, determined struggle ever since Emancipation to break the shackles that had virtually forced them into the ludicrous position of imitating the white man's grotesque parody of themselves. During the 1890s black artists gradually cast off the bonds of minstrelsy and moved slowly toward the presentation of genuine Negro musicals on Broadway. The custom of applying burnt cork to Negro faces began to be discarded, women were introduced into productions, and black musicals entered a new era.

Shows like *The Creole Show, The Octoroons, Oriental America*, and *Black Patti's Troubadours* ("Black Patti" was the opera singer, Sissieretta Jones, for whom Eubie went on ginger snap-buying errands when she lived in Baltimore) led directly to important breakthroughs in the black musical. First, there was Bob Cole's *A Trip to Coontown* in 1898, the first musical, it is believed, to have been owned, operated, and produced entirely by Negroes. That same year composer Will Marion Cook (who had studied in Europe with Joseph Joachim, the great violinist and friend of Brahms, and who would later teach Eubie Blake orchestral conducting) and the revered poet Paul Laurence Dunbar presented their musical comedy *Clorindy, the Origin of the Cakewalk*, which brought black performers to Broadway in a successful show that starred the legendary dancer, songwriter, and comedian Ernest Hogan. (Hogan later worked with the vaudeville comedy team of Flournoy Miller and Aubrey Lyles and founded his own theater company.)

Soon thereafter the Johnson brothers, author James Weldon and composer John Rosamond, teamed successfully with Bob Cole to create the Cole and Johnson Company, which created and produced such melodious operettas as *The Shoo-Fly Regiment* (1906) and *The Red Moon* (1908). Another new company was formed by Bert Williams and George Walker, who joined with Cook, Dunbar, and others to create what at the time would be the most universally acclaimed black theaterpiece, *In Dahomey* (1903). *In Dahomey* was the first black show to penetrate to the heart of Broadway—Times Square. After its command performance in London it would popularize the cakewalk around the

"Bob" Cole
Lester A. Walton
"Sam" Corker
"Tom" Brown
J. Rosamond Johnson
Geo. W.

A. Williams
James Reese Europe
Alec Rogers
Jesse A. Shipp
R. C. McPherson (Cecil Mack)

The Frogs

world. *Abyssinia* (1906) and *Bandana Land* (1908), with book and lyrics by Alex Rogers and Jesse Shipp, were other notable works by the company that starred the incomparable Williams and Walker.

Many of the above-mentioned men were members of a benevolent organization dedicated to the advancement of the Negro in theater and the arts, The Frogs. Few organizations among whites in the American theater can compare in noble purpose and record to what The Frogs (who took their title, incidentally, from the Aristophanes play) were able to accomplish in the group's short lifetime. For about 1909 this great era of black theater artistry began to come to an end. The primary reason was the almost simultaneous deaths of Ernest Hogan, Bob Cole, and George Walker. These men were not only outstanding creators and performers, but also the managers of their respective companies. Without their business acumen it became a struggle just to keep the companies alive, and without other stars of equal prominence to help carry on, their partners (with the exception of Bert Williams, whose famous solo acts enlivened the *Ziegfeld Follies* for some time) abandoned Broadway within two years. Thus began a period of almost total exodus for black performers from the downtown theaters of New York. Those who remained in the entertainment field would play almost entirely to black audiences.

While the deaths of men like Cole, Hogan, and Walker were probably the most important single factor in the loss of Broadway to black theater, there were other reasons. One, unquestionably, was the worsening of race relations in American cities. As long as the urban black population was relatively small and geographically self-contained, racial friction, while always present, seldom broke into open conflict (although there had been several early race riots). But the huge migration of Southern blacks into Northern cities put additional strains on an already uneasy truce. Then, too, Woodrow Wilson, despite his liberal reputation, did more than any other American president to reintroduce segregation into the federal government. The establishment by President Wilson of segregated washrooms in the nation's capital was only one of the many things he did to help engender a deleterious racial climate in the United States. Also, there was widespread public hostility toward Jack Johnson, America's first black heavyweight champion, who had outraged whites not only by his pugilistic prowess but also by his open companionship with white women. Thus the old blackface minstrel tradition would be seen to rise again in a new form; white producers and audiences seemed satisfied anew with black-faced white performers like Al Jolson, Eddie Cantor, and Frank Tinney, and few questioned that their work could stand as a satisfactory representation of black artistry.

Black artists, however, gradually countered this tendency. A primary effort was the work of James Reese Europe, who, as the principal organizer of black musicians into a kind of union, the conductor who transformed W. C. Handy's "Memphis Blues" into the fox-trot for Vernon and Irene Castle, and the leader of society dance bands, was able to meet wealthy industrialists and other prominent social and political figures. It was through these important encounters that Europe was able to garner new sources of support for black artists. It is perhaps no accident then that when black shows did return to Broadway they were billed as "society fads," for indeed it was through the patronage of the wealthy that the closed doors began to open a little in the years after World War I. The war, also, had a temporary salutary effect on race relations, as men who fought together overcame much of the ignorance and mutual suspicion engendered by the long forced separation of the races.

Here, then, was the situation in the theater when Sissle and Blake teamed with Miller and Lyles in 1921 to write and produce *Shuffle Along* and to restore authentic black artistry to Broadway. More even than Cole and Johnson or Cook and Dunbar, Miller, Lyles, Sissle, and Blake were to establish, on the Broadway stage, the humor and music of the American Negro in a pure form. For while there are intimations of ragtime in the work of the earlier men, the overlay of operetta was much stronger there than was to be found in *Shuffle Along*. Eubie Blake had already won fame as one of the principal composers of ragtime, that special American blend of European dance form and African rhythm that would influence the entire spectrum of American theatrical and popular music. Ragtime's principal feature is the pitting of complex African syncopation against a strong, implacable basic beat. Blake was to accompany and abet the rise of this music from the bordellos of America to the vaudeville stage, and with Noble Sissle he would gain theatrical experience on the boards that would prepare them both for the arduous job of constructing a viable theater piece. Miller and Lyles can be credited with the successful launching of authentic Negro folk humor onto the nation's stage, and the fusion of these two vaudeville teams would result in not only a triumphal return of the black man to Broadway, but also an epoch-making stage work without which much that has been individual, original, and viable in American musical theater would probably never have happened.

Beyond its impressive statistic as one of the few Broadway shows of the decade to run more than five hundred performances . . . beyond its impressive array of talented performers that included Florence Mills and Josephine Baker . . . beyond even its achievement in bringing authentic ragtime and jazz dancing to Broadway, accomplishments that radically altered the future direction of musical comedy . . . beyond even its fruitful synthesis of ragtime and operetta, *Shuffle Along* was a dramatic, intensely moving human experience. Its triumph was a clarion call to every talented black artist in America; it was a beacon of hope. It said that the barriers to the black's artistic fulfillment were coming down—at least for a while.

We are too young to have seen the original productions of *Shuffle Along* or any of Sissle and Blake's other shows, but back in Brooklyn that April afternoon and on many days and nights since, we have experienced all the intensity and glory of their memorable songs and extraordinary performing talent. For it should never be forgotten that they did not merely write their shows; they starred in them. They were out there every performance: Sissle as a member of the cast, a kind of cheerleader, Blake leading the orchestra and exhorting the entire company from his place at the piano. Late in the show in the spot next to closing, the top spot on the vaudeville bills that they had occupied so many times, Blake would leave the pit and join Sissle on the stage where they would present in its entirety the act that had brought them to the pinnacle of their profession. In the fusion of creation and performance, there is a realized art in the work of Sissle and Blake that is unsurpassed by anyone who has ever written for our musical stage. This book is a celebration of their achievement.

May 15, 1915. Noble Sissle arrived at River View Park, Baltimore, Maryland, to sing for Joe Porter's Serenaders, a pickup band organized for the summer. His train was late, and he missed his first rehearsal.

Eubie Blake, pianist and composer, had been hired for the same gig.

Sissle, suitcase in hand, arrived at Joe Porter's marble front-door stoop just as Porter's band descended the stairs. "Blake, this is Noble Sissle. He's the new singer who just got in from Indianapolis to replace Frank Brown."

"Sissle? Didn't I see your name on a song sheet?"

"Yes."

"You're a lyricist. I need a lyricist."

They shook hands.

Their first collaboration, and Blake's first song ever, was "It's All Your Fault," written with the help of their friend Eddie Nelson. They asked Al Herman, who was on the same bill as Sophie Tucker at the Maryland Theatre, to see if Miss Tucker would listen to their new song between shows. The word was yes, and Sissle and Blake, song in hand, ink still wet, ran down to the theater to sing it for Sophie Tucker. When they got there, the ink had run so badly that the music was almost unreadable, but, *"bless her heart, she learned it, had arrangements made, and sang it the same week."*

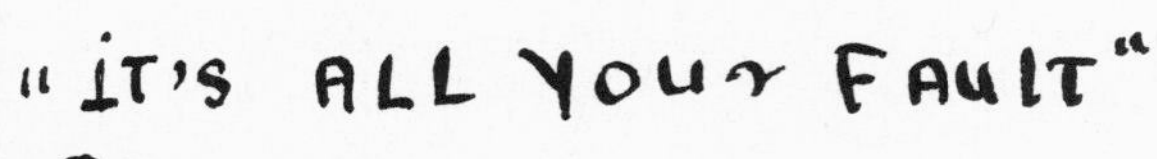

Cho.

All your fault, it's all your fault, you
called me pret-ty names and I told you not to do it, you
prom-ised that you'd love me now I find there's noth-ing to it and it's
All your fault, it's all your fault, one I be—

Noble Sissle, c. 1915

Eubie Blake, 1916

NOBLE LEE SISSLE, BORN JULY 10, 1889, *Indianapolis, Indiana*

Much of Noble's growing-up years reads like any *Penrod and Sam* novel at the turn of the century, even though he attended segregated grammar schools. American cities were more integrated then; the Sissles had both black and white neighbors. It would be twenty years before the great influx of Negroes from the South would result in the huge ghettos of today.

The fights in Noble's early years were rarely because of his race: two of his three best boyhood friends were white. *"As a boy I played baseball, morning, noon, and night, but I never learned to swim—there were no pools and I knew that several boys had drowned in the swimming hole in the creek. . . . I got into the usual amount of mischief, hopping freight trains, raiding the neighbors' peach trees, and breaking my share of windows.*

"But there was always work to do. I had to do housework each Saturday before going to play. I shined shoes, helped in a bicycle shop, and had a newspaper route. Two Negro engineers who were building the sewer on our street gave me a job as a three-dollar-a-week water boy. I had to be careful, for if so much as a drop of water fell on a man working in the sewer he would feel as if hit by a cake of ice. My big ambition as a boy was to have grease on my face like the engine workers who came by our house every night from work. . . ."

"This is home at 1708 Columbia Avenue, Indianapolis. (l. to r.) Brother Richard Longfellow Sissle, my mother, sister Martha Ruth Sissle, brother Andrew Merrill Sissle, and Kidd, our dog. Both Ruth and Andrew were born in this house."

Reverend George A. Sissle

The Reverend George A. Sissle, late pastor of Cory M. E. Church, was born in Lexington, Kentucky, August 28, 1852. His parents were Roman Catholic, and he was converted to the Methodist Episcopal Church at the age of twenty. He devoted several years to teaching school, then became licensed

to preach where his time was much occupied in a traveling connection. He served the church as a minister and elder in Kentucky, Indiana, then Ohio.

He enjoyed the confidence of his brethren, and he shared liberally in the honors that they could bestow upon him. . . . He was cultured, studious, and possessed striking executive ability, while his genial and affable manners, blended with a warm, generous heart, made him a favorite in the conference and parish. Dr. Sissle died Saturday night as the result of an attack of acute indigestion. He leaves six children—three boys and the same number of girls.

Obituary, Cleveland *Gazette*, April 1913

Mrs. Martha Angeline Sissle

Mrs. Martha Angeline Sissle, one of the Cleveland public school teachers, died August 4th after a protracted illness. Mrs. Sissle was born near Lexington, Kentucky, about 1869. When but an infant she was given by her mother to her surviving foster mother, Mrs. Hattie Scott, who moved from Cynthiana, Kentucky, to Springfield, Ohio, where Mrs. Sissle

received her early education. She was appointed to teach in the schools of Springfield and later went to Kentucky where she met and married her husband, a widower with three children, in 1888. Her first son Noble was born in Indianapolis. After the birth of her children, she returned to teaching in the Indianapolis and later the Cleveland schools. Mrs. Sissle was one of the first colored probation officers of the juvenile courts in this country. A temperance advocate and an untiring missionary leader, she was a frequent speaker to the prisoners in jail on Sunday. In evangelistic work among young men and children Mrs. Sissle had few peers.

Obituary, Cleveland newspaper, August 1916

Martha
Noble with mother
Andrew

Noble Sissle, son of godly, strict parents, could have easily become a Methodist minister like his father, George Andrew Sissle. *"I remember him,"* Noble says, *"as a strict but fair man who worked hard and was respected wherever he went. He was away a great deal because as an elder he traveled around the county."* Reverend Sissle played the organ himself, mostly church hymns, and Noble attributes his first interest in music to his father.

(l. to r.) Richard, Mrs. Sissle, Mamie, Lottie, the Reverend Mr. Sissle, Noble

At age four

"My father hoped I would go into the ministry and follow in his footsteps. In fact, my first public performance as a five-year-old was as a minister in a Tom Thumb wedding.

"When we went to church on Sunday mornings, my mother would let me sit on the aisle. I used to get a great thrill when my father or some member of the congregation would lead us in a hymn, reading off the lyrics ahead of us. Then everyone would join in and every foot would keep time, and soon the whole church would be swaying in rhythm or patting their hands and feet. Whenever I sing a rhythm song—even today—I still pat my foot the same way. . . ."

Across the canal behind his father's church in Indianapolis there were circus parades with bass drums, color, and excitement to stir the imagination of a little boy.

"One Sunday in church when I was six years old, I left my aisle seat right in the middle of my father's sermon and went up to the pulpit and climbed in my father's big chair. Then I sat down and crossed my legs just as I had seen him do many times. The congregation roared with laughter, but my father kept on preaching and pretended to be amused too. When I got home my mother gave me such a fanning that I was unable to sit down. But it was all worth it—oh, that audience!"

"It took a long time before I learned that my brother Richard and my sisters Mamie and Lottie had had another mother and were my half brother and half sisters. The boys on the street told me and I fought with them and cried and went home to tell my mother. Then she had to explain it to me. . . ."

"I was expected to be a model student. One day I threw my cap up to catch it in the hall; I caught it, all right, from my mother, and got my first whipping in school."

"My mother stressed the importance of good diction and skill in declamation. Under her guidance I was able to win first prize in an oratorial contest when I was twelve."

"When I was old enough to drive, I worked for Dr. Sumner S. Furniss, our Negro family physician. I was his office boy and was expected to dress up as I drove him to his house calls. He had one of the first automobiles I can remember, an Oldsmobile that cranked up like a coffee grinder, which he had bought from his close friend Carl Fisher, who built the Indianapolis Speedway. . . ."

When the Sissles moved from Indianapolis to Cleveland in 1906, Noble enrolled in Central High School, where there were about 1500 students, six of whom were Negroes. The principal was descended from a family who had operated an underground railroad for runaway slaves in Ohio, and all students were given an equal chance to participate in all school activities. *"In the spring of 1908 I became varsity catcher on the baseball team, and also played football. . . ."*

"I was included in this picture because the team appreciated the fact that, though I was not able to play because of an injury, I had the Rooters' Club out there cheer-

ing them along as I was the Yell Master. After the picture was taken, we all got our dimes together and decided to go to a movie on Erie Street. I was the only Negro in the crowd as Joe Blue, the big fullback, had gone on home. One fellow bought all the tickets, but when we tried to go in, they stopped me and told me I had to sit in the balcony. Well, my friends were even madder than I was, and they stood by me and persuaded me to file a suit against the theater, so with the help of the two NAACP lawyers I won the case and two hundred and fifty dollars in damages. . . ."

With the Central High School Glee Club

Indianapolis *News*

COLORED TENOR AND READER

Noble Lee Sissle, colored, a native of Indianapolis and a former Shortridge student, will appear at Simpson chapel to-morrow evening as a tenor soloist and reader. He has be-come well known in this city and Ohio as a singer and a dramatic reader. He is identified with several of the white musi-cal organizations at Cleveland and was last year elected leader of the Central High School Glee Club. He has appeared before several Chautauquas in Ohio and adjoining states and traveled for a season with the Midland quartet.

Chicago *Defender*

. . . Mr. N. L. Sissle, of Cleve-land, Ohio, sang a very touching solo, "My Mother's Prayer." Many of the men present were seen to use their handkerchiefs in wiping away the tears while Mr. Sissle was singing this song.

From boy soprano in his father's church and various school festivals, Noble, matur-ing, became a tenor in the Central High School Glee Club. Soon he was featured soloist and in his last year was elected leader. In June 1911 he was class vocalist and, at graduation, was given a standing ovation. His first professional singing job had been in 1908, with Edward Thomas's Male Quartett, playing the Chautauqua circuit throughout the Midwest; this was an evangelical circuit, with revivals, spiri-tual- and hymn-singing—Noble had proved himself to be very much his father's and mother's son. *"Mr. Thomas, a Negro, a veteran showman and refined entertainer, took me that one step from the amateur glee club to professionalism. My engage-ment lasted four weeks only, but I learned the lesson of dignity in entertaining."*

With Quartett, 1911

After high-school graduation at twenty-one (Noble had interspersed his education with odd jobs, as he was to do before continuing to college), he rejoined Thomas's circuit with Hann's Jubilee Singers, which took him as far west as Denver and as far east as New York. There, a few years later, he met James Reese Europe, who was to play such an important role in his life. That spring (1913) Noble's father died, and his mother moved back to their homestead in Indianapolis. Noble returned to her, his sister Ruth, and brother Andrew, and stayed long enough to find there was no work that summer. *"I persuaded my mother to let me go to Chicago, where many Negro students got jobs on the Pullman cars and the boats out of Chicago. I even tried a vaudeville act: it flopped—fate was not ready. I could not land any job in Chicago and got so broke that if it had not been for Teddy Bear Jones, a student at Rusk University, who had a big healthy allowance, I would have been in trouble. Neither he nor I wanted to send to my mother for help. But a telegram,* 'COME HOME FOR A PLAYGROUND JOB FOR THE REST OF THE SUMMER,' *saved the day and paved the way for me to go to college, which was my mother's hope and prayer."*

BUTLER PARODIES

By Noble Sissle, '17

1. Tune, "What's the Matter with Father?"

What's the matter with Butler?
She's all right.
What's the matter with Butler?
Out of sight.
From end to end her line is strong,
Her backfield men, they can't go wrong.
What's the matter with Butler?
She's all right.

What's the matter with ——?
She's not right.
What's the matter with ——?
She's not right.
Her line is like a paper wall,
Her backfield men can't gain at all.
What's the matter with ——?
"WOW! GOOD NIGHT!"

2. Tune, "Crooney Melody"

Tia, da, da. Tia, da, da.
Tia, da, da. Tia, da, da.
Rush 'em! Rush 'em! Rush em! boys, clear off the field.
Smash 'em! Crash 'em! Hash 'em! till they yell out, "We yield."
(Skip to last strain.)
Tia, da, da. Tia, da, da.
In the air, anywhere, just simply
Batter them, splatter them. Yea, boys,
Shatter them—and bring us victory.

3. Tune, "Salvation Nell"

We'll keep shouting—"Tear them up, old Butler,"
And we know you'll do it. You always have.
Just keep us shouting, "One more touch down! One more touch down! One more touch down!"
Students, alumni, professors and prexy are rooting for you to win this game.
Play hard and be true to the white and the blue.
And fight for Butler, fight for Butler!
Just to bring more honor to our name.

4. Tune, "E-yip-I-ady-I-ay-I-ay"

E-yip-I-ady-I-ay-I-ay!
E-yip-I-ady-I-ay-I-ay!
Poor old —— your doom is sealed,
You'll be defeated when we leave the field.
E-yip-I-ady-I-ay-I-ay,

Our hearts want to holler "Hoo-
ray! Hoo-ray!"
Sing of touch downs and tricks and
of fancy drop kicks.
E-yip-I-ady-I-ay.

5.

Butler will shine to-night, Butler
will shine.
Butler will shine to-night, Oh,
what a time!
Butler will shine to-night, Butler
will shine.
When the sun goes down and the
moon comes up,
Butler will shine.

YELLS

||:Yea, Butler:||
B-u-t-l-e-r!
Butler!

Oskey Wow Wow,
Skinney Wow Wow,
Wow! Butler! Wow!

Fight, Butler! Fight, Butler!
Fight,
Fight,
Fight,
Fight,
Fight?
Yea, Butler, Fight!

Yea —— —— ——
Bu Bu Rah Rah (5 times)

In the Gallery of Memory

In the gallery of mem'ry there are
pictures bright and fair,
And I find that Butler College is the
brightest one that's there.
Alma mater, how we love thee, with a
love that ne'er shall fade,
And we feel we owe a debt to thee
that never can be paid.

In ev'ry field of action Butler men
have won a place,
Of the schools of Indiana it is Butler
sets the pace;
On the records of the nation Butler
men shall place her name,
And she'll be represented in the nation's hall of fame.

And may ev'ry son of Butler when he
leaves her shelt'ring arm
Feel that he has gained a treasure
that will never lose its charm;
And for Butler's lovely daughters,
they shall never know a care
If they only can be just as fortunate
as they are fair.

"This photo was taken in 1913 when I was on tour with Thomas Jubilee Singers Sextett. There is a note on the back of this card that reads:

Dear Father

Am going into evangelistic work. I sang for Dr. Brooks in New York City last Sunday. I have a fine letter from him. I think I'll attend the Moody School at Chicago.

Yours
Noble."

That fall Noble entered De Pauw University in Greencastle, Indiana, on scholarship, without examination, and out of high school two years; he stayed there one semester. In January 1914 he was back in Indianapolis, at Butler University, where he wrote parodies for the football games and sang, with a megaphone, in a local movie house frequented by Butler students. *"The James Reese Europe I met in New York had been engaged by Mr. and Mrs. Vernon Castle to play his Negro rhythms for them, and they set dance steps that swept the country. The dance craze created by them brought on a great demand for experienced Negro entertainers—the demand was all over the state.*

"I got a job with Harry Farley as vocalist with his dance orchestra. The one-step was just hitting the West. The college kids were dancing till dawn, and I could dance around among them on the floor with my yell master's megaphone and whoop up the dancers. My popularity gained me many jobs on weekends, and I could pay my way through college. It got too difficult to make classes at De Pauw, so I transferred to Butler."

At the Severin Hotel in Indianapolis in early 1915, Noble was waiting tables at lunch for meals and tips. "*One day the manager sent for me—I was frightened, wondering what I had done wrong. He had just returned from New York for Christmas where he said Negro musicians were playing and entertaining in every café.*

"He asked if I would organize an orchestra . . . in ten days I had a twelve-piece orchestra in the same room I'd waited tables in for a dollar a day." Early pictures show Noble holding a bandolin, a hybrid, nearly extinct instrument that combines features of the mandolin, the banjo, and the snare drum. "*I was on the bandstand singing and playing, but I was doing more singing than playing. The bandolin was given to me to hold and make motions until I could learn to play it.*" That spring Noble was hired as vocalist (and bandolin holder) for Joe Porter's Serenaders at River View Park in Baltimore.

Hann's Jubilee Singers

JAMES HUBERT BLAKE, BORN FEBRUARY 7, 1883, *Baltimore, Maryland,*

was the son of former slaves, John Sumner Blake, a stevedore and Civil War veteran, and Emily Johnston Blake, a laundress. He was the only one of their eleven children to reach adulthood; he never knew any of his brothers or sisters. Where Sissle's religious upbringing had been "strict but fair," Blake's, almost uniquely from his mother, was violent in its intensity, as Emma Blake was fanatic in her devotion to a God of terrible and swift punishment. Eubie (in childhood known as Hubie) still remembers her quick darting eyes at moments before she unleashed one of Jehovah's thunderbolts at his sinful head, and even in his twenties he recalls asking her to restrain her vengeance because *"I look so bad up there on stage with all those welts."*

John Blake's most common admonition to his son, as little Hubie hit the streets, was: "Now don't mess with the white folks' business." In the Blake neighborhood in East Baltimore this was sound advice but hard to abide by, as Hubie would have to pass two white schools on the way to his and could count on ambushes laid for "Mouse." Indeed, there was something in the boy that invited trouble from the very earliest; he had earned the nickname "Mouse" through catching the blame for an older boy's prank. *"A doctor on our block had electricity put in his home. There was this boy older than me who decided to pull the power line down with a piece of string tied to a rock. I didn't do anything, I just watched him try several times until he finally pulled the line down and it hit ground. Sparks came out in all directions—I'll never forget it. I just stood there, and the other boy ran away. A lady on the block also watched the whole thing, but when they asked her who did it, she said, 'It was the mouse-faced boy,' meaning me. And that's how I got the name 'Mouse.'"*

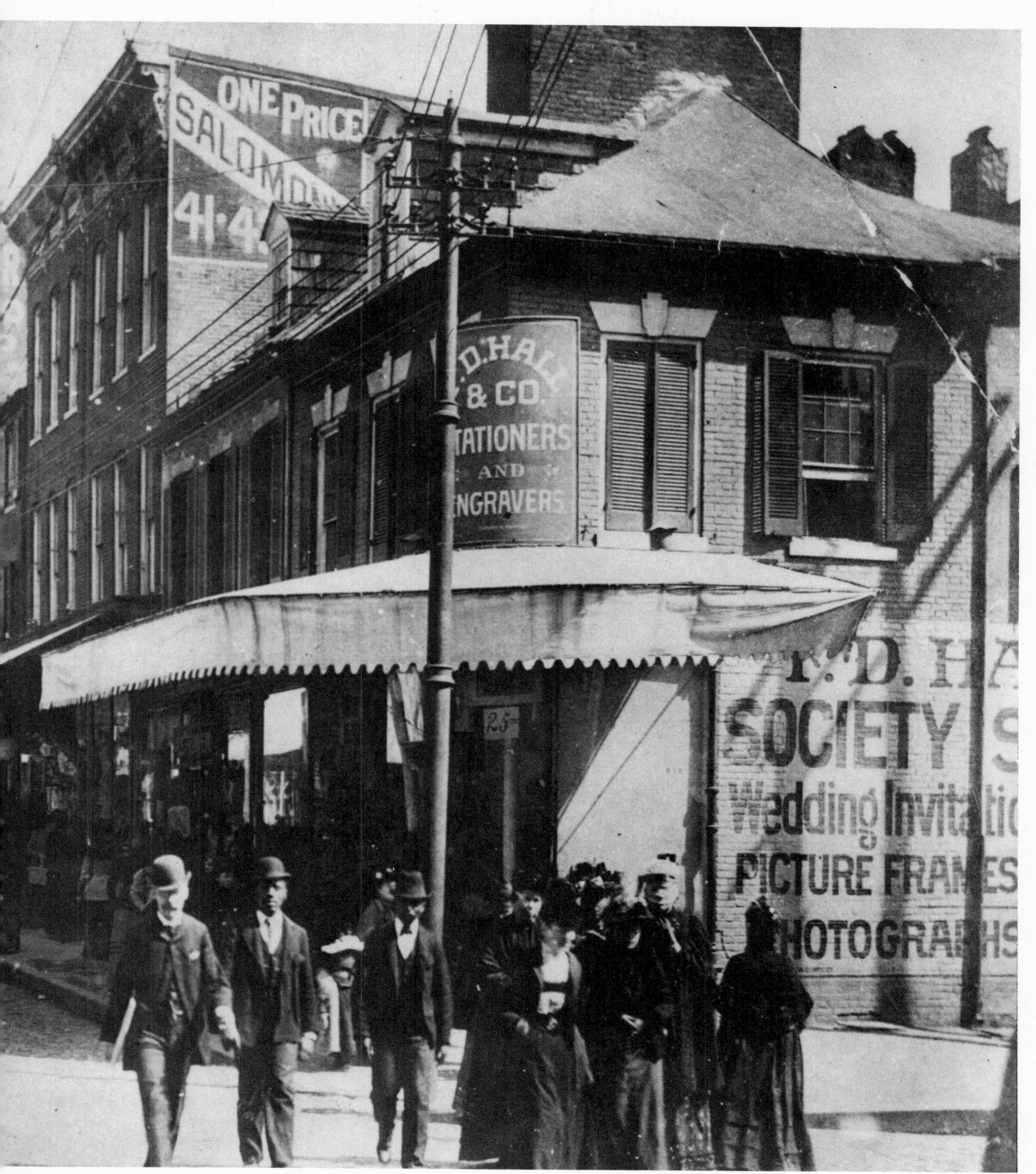

Baltimore, 1890; corner of Lexington and Liberty streets

Emily Johnston Blake

"Mouse" had a technique for self-defense which, he asserted, worked every time: *"They'd come up swinging and trying to get at me. I'd get in close and lean forward, and—*BAM*!—haul off with a hard punch to the solar plexus. They can't stand up, and then I finish them off with my feet."* It was a tough life: if "Mouse" ran home to avoid a fight, his father would send him right outside again.

Once, in an altercation with a much larger white boy, Oakie Witz, over his own two-cent half-moon agate marble, he was chased into his mother's kitchen by his pursuant. *"She beaned him with this wet steel dishtowel ring, and he staggered out in the street and fell down. Years later I was playing in this barrelhouse, and Oakie comes in with a bunch of gangsters and sees me. He's become a small-time prizefighter. 'Don't I know you?' he says. I know him, see, but I don't say anything. 'Ain't you the guy they call "Mouse"?' 'Yeah,' I say. 'Hey, fellas,' he says to his friends, 'this is the guy that killed me in his mother's kitchen when I was a kid!' 'That wasn't just me,' I told him, 'that was me* and *my mother!' "*

Both Blakes could read and write. John Blake had a fine Spencerian hand he had learned as a slave from the plantation owner's daughter, who had taught him secretly and at great peril of discovery. Blake was exactly fifty years older than his son, to the day. *" 'Bully,' he called me, because I was a real boy"*; in American black communities, unlike most white ones, a boy's interest in music raised no doubts as to his eventual manliness.

When Hubie was six years old, he strayed from his mother's side while visiting a downtown department store, climbed up on an organ stool, and began picking out tunes. Over his mother's protests, the store manager succeeded in placing a $75 organ with the Blakes for 25¢ a week, with Emma's unspoken stipulation that only godly music would be suffered from its reeds and bellows. "Mouse," here as elsewhere, could not avoid trouble. The devil had gotten into his fingers, from the music he heard on the street and the rhythms and syncopations in his mother's own Baptist church. "Take that ragtime out of my house!" intoned Mrs. Blake when she heard him syncopating church hymns. "Take it out!" Now at least he knew what it was called: ragtime.

There were piano lessons from the next-door lady, Mrs. Margaret Marshall, organist at Waters' Chapel Church. Hubie and three friends got together a singing quartet that sang outside of the local bars for change—he was twelve then, in short pants, and not allowed inside. *"We sang 'Two Little Girls in Blue,' 'Daisy,' songs like that—not ragtime. The first time I got drunk was on a Christmas morning. I was twelve years old. See, my father used to take me to burlesque shows on Saturday on the sly, for ten cents—if my mother ever knew, she'd throw us both out of the house. We'd get in the last row of the gallery, and I'm sitting on his shoulder. Out on stage comes this drill company, all Negroes. Well, I decide I want to imitate them, so I go over to the Methodist church and get a bunch of guys together and we form a drill team. So when I'm eleven, we get this thing going and we drill Christmas morning, and I win a medal, which is worth two and a half dollars, I don't know what they're worth now—well, this is Christmas morning the next year, and I'm twelve. And I'm going to do the drill again at the Methodist church. At that time my father had a carbuncle under each arm and couldn't work his job, see. So he is coming down the stairs and says to my mother, 'Em, you got anything for that boy for Christmas?' 'I got what you brought in,' she says, which was nothing—he couldn't work. Then he takes her in his arms and kisses her, which is the only time I remember seeing them do that, and he says, 'Em, I'm going out now. I don't know when I'll be back, but if anybody asks, you tell them that I wasn't going to come back until I got food for my family.' So he goes out, and in a few hours he comes back with a side of bacon, a whole turkey, a side of pork chops, cranberries and sweet potatoes, and he gives me twenty-five cents for the first time in my whole life. Then he has seventy-five cents left, and he is going to go down and buy a dram for the boys—see, drinks were a nickle apiece then. . . . Well, I take my twenty-five cents and I go out to the street. I find a bottle and I fill it with water and ashes and rinse it out till it's clean. And I show my twenty-five cents to the boys on the street. They start following me. 'Hey, "Mouse," come on, "Mouse."' And I go down to Orleans Street and Central Avenue, to the back of the barrelhouse. I can still see the copper funnels they used to drain the liquor out of the barrels into your bottle. So I hand the man my bottle and tell him, 'Give me ten cents' worth*

John Sumner Blake

of Overholt whiskey for my father.' He takes my bottle and fills it a little over half full. Then he says, 'Here's a stogie for your father,' because it's Christmas, and he hands me this bent cigar like they used to make. So I go in the alley behind the barrelhouse, and I drink practically the whole bottle of whiskey, just like it was water—I never drink water and never have *drunk water in my life. And I start walking, and the kids are still following me, because I've got fifteen cents left—they want some of the whiskey but I tell them they're too little. Then I look up and I see my father, and he looks twenty feet tall. And I look across the street, and all the houses are leaning and swaying in all directions. And I fall down at my father's feet, and he picks me up and takes me home, drunk. The minute I get home my mother smells whiskey on my breath—she could smell whiskey on your breath if you were in Los Angeles and she was in Baltimore—and I'm dead, see. And she prays over me all night not to die. The next morning at 9* A.M. *I wake up. And she is going to beat the daylights out of me—she* loved me, *but she had such a temper. My father comes downstairs in flannels and has to restrain her. 'John, this boy ain't dead, but I'm going to kill him.'"*

Ragtime was the craze. A moneymaking musician, or someone who just wanted to impress girls, had to know it. There were tricks to learn to do on the piano, just as in playing pool, and players of either game who didn't know them lost. Hubie won at piano, pool, and girls, and kept the street hazards at arm's length. *"Hughie Wolford and I were kids together in short pants and aprons with buttons on the back. He was a great technician and played fast—he was my competitor. Both of us went to Barnes Street School. And I had a girl friend, Miss Teeny Pritchett. She was pretty, she had a hand that never developed properly, but she was pretty—I was about fourteen.*

"Richard K. Fox of the Police Gazette *would sponsor ragtime cutting contests when he came to town. They would get the best buck dancers, singers, bone-players . . . the bones were from animal ribs, and you played two in each hand . . . there*

Hymn-tune by Emily Blake, taken down by her son

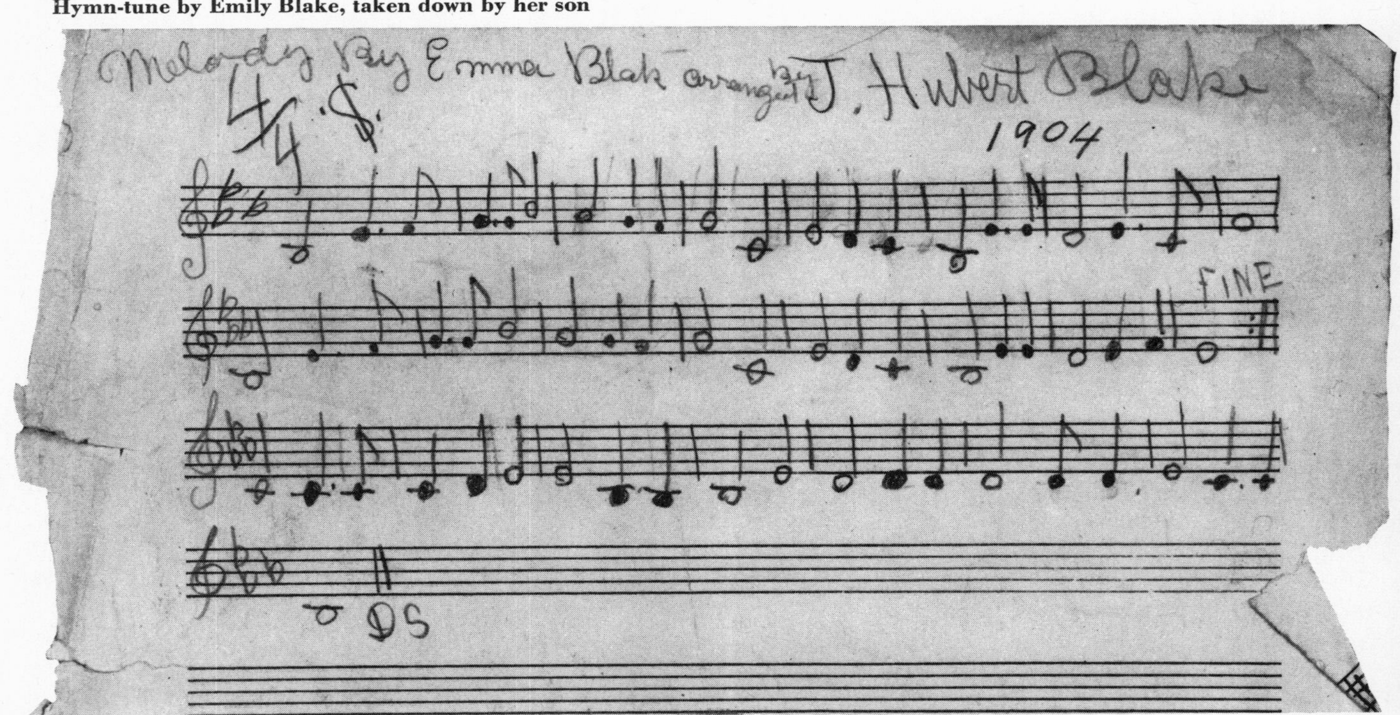

Howard "Hop" Johns and Eubie Blake, c. 1895

were virtuoso triangle players. And a whole lot of pianists. I didn't play in those cutting contests. But Edgar Dowell came down to play from Sand Town, in the Leachville section. He was older than me, handsome, had a burn on the side of his face. Teeny Pritchett's father and mother gave her a lawn party, and they pulled the parlor organ out onto the grass. I was there playing tunes on the organ with my friend Hop Johns, and there was this big sycamore tree in the yard. Anyway, they brought Edgar Dowell out to play, and he cut me so bad. He played the Maxixe, and he played more notes in his left hand than I did. He had this great left hand, wiped me right off the place. Then he took my girl. She had her arms around him. I was so ashamed I hid behind the sycamore tree, and Hop found me. 'Hubie,' he said (he never would call me 'Mouse,' he was my best friend), 'Hubie, come on and play. The girls want you to.' 'No, no, I'm not gonna play.' Well, I finally played, but Edgar Dowell had stolen the show. And my girl too. Dowell killed me, and I didn't play the organ for two years after that."

Eubie Blake's fingers are extraordinarily long and delicate, but strong. It is impossible not to notice them. *" 'Double those fingers up,' my mother would say to me on the streetcar. 'You look like a pickpocket.' "* It was around 1896 or 1897 when he heard Jesse Pickett play his "Dream Rag," a mean and dirty slow drag with a tango bass and the "Spanish tinge." Pickett often called it "The Bull Dyke's Dream" because of its strong impact on the lesbians who worked in sporting houses, who crowded around the piano wherever he went, crying, "Hey, Mr. Pickett! Play 'The Dream.' "

Destined as he was for a life of evil by those long fingers, "Mouse" learned the piece from Pickett, a pimp and gambler, who had brought it to Baltimore. The die was cast. He had been thrown out of school for fighting over a girl, his mother had given up any hope for his soul, and he still wore short pants.

Aggie Sheldon's bawdy house. Or "body house," as he thought it was spelled at the time. . . . In 1898 James Hubert Blake, aged fifteen, took a regular job as pianist at Agnes Sheldon's five-dollar sporting house. He had gotten the tip-off that the job was open from Basil Chase, who was leaving because his father had died and left him money. The job paid three dollars a seven-day week, plus tips, but the tips were lavish. A five-dollar house in 1898 in Baltimore was a palace. Aggie Sheldon's had several parlors and sitting rooms on the first floor up, where the gentlemen callers would indulge in polite conversation with the ladies of the evening, all white, sitting demurely on the elegant settees, before the inevitable climb together up the graceful stairs.

Master Blake, in long pants that came up to his armpits, would play ragtime and also graciously accommodate requests for the popular songs of the day: "After the Ball," "Maggie Murphy's Home," "Hello! Ma Baby," "Goodbye, Dolly Gray," "Any Old Rags?," and, quite appropriately, "A Bird in a Gilded Cage." Very few songs of a prurient nature were to be heard in the better sporting houses of that time, aside from a few with *double-entendre*.

There was much beer and champagne to please the clientele. Master Blake, not having been made aware of the effects of champagne, could consume two quarts a night without apparent discomfort. Occasionally a party of especially distinguished guests would engage the whole house, staff and all, and these would be nights of great revelry. . . . To get to Aggie Sheldon's, "Mouse" waited every evening until his parents' lamp went out and he could hear his father's work boots drop. Out the window he flew, down the shed roof and over the fence, straight to the pool room for the long pants which he rented from Rabb Walker for twenty-five cents a night, then off to Aggie's to play piano. One day a neighbor lady called on Emma Blake. "Sister Blake, I heard someone, sounded just like little Hubie, playing at Aggie Sheldon's the other night. And I *know* it's little Hubie, Em, because of that wobble-wobble in the left hand." The "wobble-wobble," the sort of reverse boogie bass that is still Eubie Blake's trademark, is found in his earliest composition, "Charleston Rag"—here it would get him into trouble.

Home went "Mouse," to be met with a clap of thunder and a bolt of lightning from the Avenging Angel. Then his father came home.

" 'Hi, Bully,' he says. My mother says, 'Do you know what Mr. Blake has been doing?' She always called me Mr. Blake when she was angry. 'Mr. Blake has been playing in a bawdy house.' My father takes me outside. 'All right, how much do you make, Bully?' 'Three dollars a week, but I make extras.' (My father made nine dollars a week when it wasn't raining.) 'How much?' he asks. So I take him upstairs to my room. Under the carpet I have almost a hundred dollars stashed, because I'm too young to spend it, see. My father doesn't say anything for a moment. 'Well, son,' finally he says, 'I'll have to talk to your mother.' "

18 and 99. Eubie Blake composed his "Charleston Rag" in the same year, coincidentally, that Scott Joplin's "Maple Leaf Rag" was published and caused a worldwide sensation. Like Jesse Pickett's "The Dream," "Charleston Rag" is in a mean minor key and breathes a brasher, more urban air than the "Maple Leaf"—a world of pavements and marble doorsteps instead of cornfields and riverboats.

Everywhere, Midwest and East Coast, New Orleans and Chicago, passed an assortment of ragtime pianists, characters the like of which the world had never seen and never would see again, men every bit as colorful as their names: The Shadow, Jack the Bear, Big Head Wilbur, No Legs Cagey, Abba Labba, Cat-Eye Harry, Boots Butler, Sparrow, Seminole, Slue-Foot Nelson, Sheet-Iron Brown, Wild Cat Joe, Black Diamond, Squirrel, John the Baptist. Others less bizarrely named but no less accomplished were the Jimmy Greens ("Big" and "Little"); Hughie Wolford, Blake's long-time competitor; Sammy Ewell; William Turk, who is said to have developed the boogie bass because his left hand could no longer reach past his huge stomach for the ragtime-bass offbeats; and many, many others who lived, bloomed, and faded in Baltimore as elsewhere like exotic, extinct jungle plants. Eubie was to be influenced by nearly every rag-pianist he came in contact with through those years, just as he was to influence many others. His open pair of ears took in and digested much other music, too: Victor Herbert, Franz Lehár, Oskar Straus, and the light classics. Grieg and Wagner were also bouncing around inside his head; it was all music and all fascinating.

After a long tenure at Aggie Sheldon's, in 1901 Professor Blake joined Dr. Frazier's Medicine Show where he played the melodeon, a small reed organ, and buck-danced on the tailgate of the horse-drawn wagon. The next year he signed on as buck dancer for a colored minstrel show, *In Old Kentucky*, playing Colonel Mapleson's Academy of Music on 14th Street in New York. *"We were there two weeks. A wagon pulled up to the theater, unloaded us, picked us up after the show, and took us to a dump on Bleecker Street where we slept. Same thing every day—I never even saw 14th Street."*

Back in Baltimore again, Eubie found a job as relief pianist for Big Head Wilbur at Alfred Greenfeld's saloon, at the corner of Chesnut and Low, for $1.25 a night. The upright piano there was still in the case it was packed in; Greenfeld's had no

Early waltz, probably not in Blake's hand

chairs but had big round iron tables, beer kegs and boxes to sit on, and sawdust on the floor. Hip-swinging whores with green moles on their faces, in starched gingham wrappers, would raunch-dance with the pimps and the male clientele, and the sound of their slow-dragging feet across the sawdust floor haunts Eubie's piano piece "Corner of Chesnut and Low," with its slow walking bass. The pimps dressed to kill—full-back coats, tight-legged pants, Stetson hats, gold watch chains, diamond rings—and there were many fights and much rough language. But whenever a woman of any description entered the main room, the call would go out: "Heads up, men!" and all vile talk would cease instantly. *"I worked from 4 P.M. until midnight. The sawdust was so high it was above the soles of your shoes. When I came home, my mother would say, 'Don't bring that stuff in here. Kick it off.' She'd stay up until I got back, waiting to make sure I kicked off all the sawdust."*

From Greenfeld's Eubie moved on to Annie Gilly's, a dollar-an-hour sporting house at 319 East Street. Unlike Aggie Sheldon's, with its several parlors, piano room, and troweled-on respectability, Annie's was one big, noisy dive of a room with frequent flashes of razors and constant brawls.

After a brief sojourn in New York in 1905, where Eubie lived over a store and played at Edmund's on 28th Street, he returned to Baltimore; at his next job, the Middle Section Assembly Club, he was actually shot at when mistaken for one of the bartenders—a quick duck behind the piano saved his life. At Coots Jones's place he filled in for his friend "Big" Jimmy Green during his illness. When Jimmy died, young and dissipated, Eubie was shocked and saw it as warning to get out of that kind of life.

"I wanted to tell you about the Lyric Theatre fire. Frank Barstock's circus is playing. This is way before the Baltimore fire in 1904. I'm going to see a girl—this is one of the first girls I could go to her house to see. Her name is Edith Buchanan, and she has long, beautiful hair way down her back—I'm crazy about hair—it's a nice night and I'm walking down Pennsylvania Avenue. Her father had a whole lot of dray-wagons. I go by a bar and get a milk punch. And I get to Mount Royal Avenue, where the Lyric Theatre is. There's a park down the middle of the street like Park Avenue. And I've had only one milk punch, mind you! And I see some zebras in the street, grazing. The Lyric Theatre is on fire, and the watchman has let all the animals out. And I am right near the B & O railroad station. And here is this bunch of zebras grazing in the park. And I'm thinking I must be drunk, on one milk punch. . . . And I look and I see elephants, and I see lions. When I see the lions, I tear down Mount Royal Avenue. I could run like a deer then. When I get to Calvert Street, a white man is coming along, and I fell right at his feet. So he says, 'What's the matter with you, boy?' I says, 'I saw a lot of lions up there.' 'What?' 'I saw a lot of lions, elephants, zebras, right up there,' and I pointed. He says, 'Good God A'mighty! The zoo is on fire!' And he lifted me up. I walk down Calvert Street. I can't run no more anyhow. And that's the end of that. . . . And this man, Frank Barstock, he lost every penny."

Eubie had known Joseph Saifuss Butts as a marble shooter on Dallas Street—he was nine years older, and Eubie and his friend Hop Johns used to run errands for him. Joe cleaned fish for a neighborhood market—his employer there was to manage his first professional prizefighting match. Later, under the name of Joe Gans, he became the lightweight boxing champion of the world and perhaps the greatest lightweight who ever lived.

When Gans won against Battling Nelson in the forty-second round in September 1906 and came back to Baltimore $11,000 richer, he built the Goldfield Hotel (named after Goldfield, Nevada, where the fight had occurred) right where Coots Jones's place had stood, at the corner of Lexington and Chesnut streets. The Goldfield opened in September 1907 on a drizzly night, but the place was packed, with whites and blacks alike (one of the first places in Baltimore where such mixing occurred).

Eubie was signed on with Boots Butler to play for fifty-five dollars a week. Boots died a few weeks afterward and was replaced by One-Leg Willie Joseph. Willie had lost his leg in an ice-skating accident, but had gone on to become a prize piano student at the Boston Conservatory; Eubie remembers him as the greatest ragtime pianist he has ever heard. When One-Leg Willie warmed up, he would play the *Poet and Peasant Overture* and Mendelssohn's *Songs Without Words*, but his inventive rag-playing, with its back-basses, sudden shifts of range and tempo, and dramatic loud-and-soft contrasts, was what impressed and influenced Eubie's own playing style so deeply.

The Goldfield was the big-time, and Joe Gans's spirit pervaded the place. He was the first Negro to have a car in Baltimore. *"One night Bates, the Tiffany of Baltimore, and a white girl arrived at the Goldfield. Jack Johnson, the fighter, was there with Alzada Childs, one of the most beautiful women I have ever seen. Bates wanted Alzada, so he arranged through Preston Jackson to get them all together so he could try to trade girls with Jack. Later they all went off in Joe Gans's $5555.55 car. . . . I had this girl. She had long black hair. Everybody knew she was no good. Joe Gans and I were up on the third floor of the Middle Section Club gambling, and he said he had taken my girl away from me. I said I was going to punch him in the nose. Now he could have killed me*—I *was going to try to punch* Joe *in the nose! When I asked him to come outside, he broke into hysterical laughter and got the hiccups. We had to call a doctor to stop it."* One-Leg Willie would stand down at the bar until Eubie would sing "Here Comes Billy Kersands," named after the dancing star of the time. Then Willie would come up, or Joe Gans would get him, to the Kimball upright. Willie would knock out a hammer or a key about once a month with his strong hands. *"I remember the night Willie came to Baltimore. I got Ginger to play for me at the Goldfield, and I took him around to show him Baltimore. He was a heavy drinker. Near the Maryland Theatre he threw his crutch up into the air and it got stuck in the electric wires—it was a broomstick with a cross-piece. We were throwing things to try to get the crutch down. Finally a lineman came along, climbed up the pole to the crossbar, and shook the damned stick down."* One-Leg Willie stayed at the Goldfield one year. Some say he went on to New York for a while, but the only fact known is that he died a few years later, in Virginia, of an overdose of narcotics. His color had blocked him from the career of a classical pianist he had wished for; an angry, embittered man, drowned in alcohol and cocaine, he wrote no music, left no recordings.

Joe Gans was to die soon after also. He had adopted the practice of sweating off excess poundage too quickly and too often to make agreed weights, and when he met Battling Nelson again in 1908 for the second scheduled forty-five-round bout, he had almost certainly contracted tuberculosis. Nelson finished him off in the seventeenth round then, and knocked him out in the twenty-first in a return match two months later. Gans continued to fight, but his health was broken and he died at thirty-six in August 1910, in Baltimore. *"Gans had everything—money, fame, and the rest—but it did not save him from an early death."*

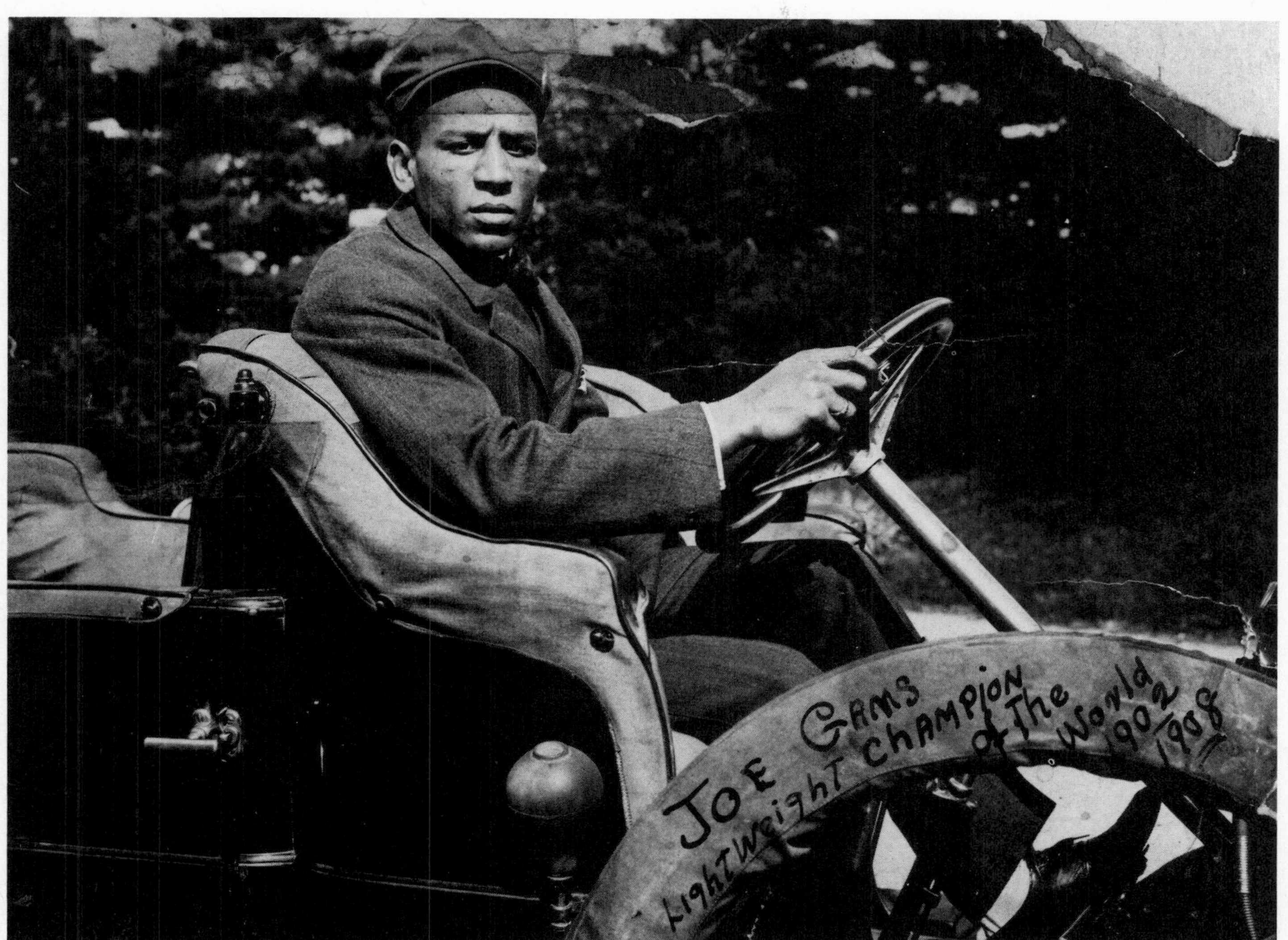

About 1906 or 1907 Eubie began playing summers in Atlantic City, where he met, competed with, and influenced pianists from all over the East. Many are still known and remembered today, and several became Eubie's lifelong friends. Willie "The Lion" Smith, who still plays on occasion, has been one of the most dynamic of all Harlem stride pianists. Charles Luckeyeth Roberts, perhaps Eubie's closest ally in friendship and style over the years, was the composer of "Moonlight Cocktail." It was Luckey who introduced him to his own music publisher, Joseph W. Stern, who then brought out Eubie's first printed rags, "Chevy Chase" and "Fizz Water," in 1914.

Perhaps the greatest of all the Harlem pianists, almost Mozartean in his refinement of detail and constancy of invention, was James P. Johnson. Johnson visited Atlantic City in 1914, and Eubie remembers a young, intent, spindly kid who came to hear him play several nights in a row. It was the custom then for a pianist to start his job in the early evening and play until dawn came, and invention (as well as spirits) might lag in the wee hours—although one imagines that Eubie was one of the few to be able to keep both hands on the piano through the night. One night the kid approached Eubie and said, "I'll take you down," meaning, "I'll spell you." *"Do you play?"* Eubie asked. "Yes, I . . . I play," answered the boy, and immediately sailed into Eubie's own extremely difficult "Troublesome Ivories," with its polyrhythmic basses and superchromatic right-hand passages, taking it about twice as fast as Eubie could. Jimmy nearly lost Eubie his job right there, but the two soon became fast friends and traded many "tricks."

The trick, in piano style of that day, was a device intercalated within the musical texture of a given piece. Luckey Roberts had perfected blindingly fast chromatic scales in the right hand, a trick that no one else could approximate: a few piano rolls bear witness to his style. James P. Johnson, while not well-known for one particular trick, was partial to shimmering passagework in the extreme upper register of the instrument—the recordings that are left to us glow with the lightness and grace that were his trademark. Eubie's tricks were many and from varied sources, as befits his highly eclectic temperament, but the most immediately salient feature of all his playing and composition, without which the particular flavor of his music is lost, is *accent*. Eubie is master of the accent in all its forms: on-the-beat, off-the-beat, in-between. These accents, unlike many of the others' tricks, could be composed into the music, a fact of utmost importance.

James P. Johnson

By Eubie Blake
1908

Blake was developing very quickly but carefully as a composer. His god, Leslie Stuart, English composer of the light opera *Florodora*, infused in him an angular but flowing melodic sense, full of surprising leaps and turns. Franz Lehár's Middle-European insistence on the minor mode found a place in Eubie's harmonic palette: his early written pieces show a strong minorish cast and an almost Russian temperament. For during these years Eubie was learning to write music down on paper, a struggle for those who must master it after early childhood. Gradually, in his early manuscripts, one sees the hand becoming firmer in its control, but even in the scrawls and fragments the marks of a seasoned, sure-handed musician are everywhere present—the basses are always just right and interesting; the rhythms and implied accents are full of character and unmistakably Blake's; in sum, here is a man who knows what he wants. One of the trademarks of the of-necessity simplified piano accompaniments in the sheet music of his songs would be the fullness and imagination of the piano-writing, as will be borne out by comparison with the sheet music of the majority of American composers for the stage; the written accompaniments of most other songwriters simply do not explode off the page as do Eubie Blake's.

In July 1910 James Hubert Blake married Avis Lee of Baltimore, herself an accomplished classical pianist, and schoolmate during Eubie's brief formal education. *"She was one of the ten most beautiful girls in Baltimore,"* Eubie states with

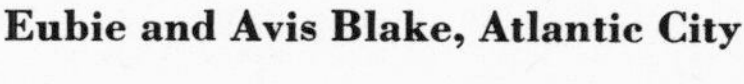
Eubie and Avis Blake, Atlantic City

Piano piece, c. 1908, in Blake's hand

pride. . . . The summers between 1910 and 1915 were spent in Atlantic City—playing at the Boathouse, the Belmont, the Bucket of Blood, Kelly's, and Ben Allen's—and the rest of the year he played at the Goldfield in Baltimore, where he wrote many of his best-known rags and worked as accompanist for the singers Madison Reed, Mary Stafford (a great star of her day), Lottie Dempsey, Big Lizzie, and Alabama Blossom, "*a girl who had never seen snow*." In the back of his mind were the suave, enchanting melodies of his favorite *Florodora* and the image of its composer, Leslie Stuart, whom he hoped to emulate someday.

The Boardwalk at Atlantic City, early 1900s

GREEN'S HOTEL
THE DUNLOP

1915–1916

The Royal Poinciana Sextet: Bob Young (leader), Joe Caulk, Charles Williams, William Carter, Harry Williams, and Noble Sissle

September 1915	Joe Porter's Serenaders disband; Blake forms the Marcato Band and stays in Baltimore, while Sissle, quitting college, performs with Bob Young's group at the Kernan Hotel, Baltimore.
December 1915	Bob Young's sextet, with Sissle as vocalist and bandolin-holder, obtains winter engagement at the Royal Poinciana Hotel, Palm Beach, Florida—the first dance orchestra to play there full time.
Winter 1915–1916	Sissle's introduction to the American social set—Astors, Wanamakers, Warburtons, Harrimans, Dodges, *et al.* Young's group plays in Nora Bayes's Palm Beach Red Cross Benefit show, which is seen by E. F. Albee, head of the Keith vaudeville circuit.
1916	Albee presents Palm Beach Week at his Palace Theatre, New York, starring Nora Bayes and featuring Sissle with Bob Young's sextet, the first Negro act to play the Palace in formal attire—dinner jackets for evening shows, Palm Beach suits for matinees—and without use of cork.
Spring 1916	Sissle takes a letter of introduction from Mary Brown Warburton to James Reese Europe, who invites him to work in his society dance orchestras. Sissle persuades Europe to find a steady job for Blake so that he can leave Baltimore but continue to support his wife and parents. Blake comes to New York and takes a piano job on Long Island.
Summer 1916	Sissle heads ten-man unit at the Bridge Water Inn, Long Branch, New Jersey. Sissle and Blake, reunited as a song-writing team, work as a piano-vocal duo at weddings, debutante parties, soirées, and outings for Jim Europe's most exclusive clients.

* * *

August 4, 1916	After two unsuccessful operations Sissle's mother dies of cancer on her forty-seventh birthday.

James Reese Europe with members of his Society Orchestra, c. 1916; Noble Sissle is directly to Europe's left

Martha Angeline Sissle's last letter to her son Noble

My dear, dear Son.

I am about to be off now to the hospital. You do not know how anxious I am to go. It is my determination to make a good fight & trust the result with our Heavenly Father. I want to live to see you and the rest of the family at ease in Zion, if God wills. If not — Amen.

Do not try to pay your bills so closely that you can not establish the family, should the worst come.

All insurances are up. The endowment I have $500.00 + $50 Sick + Accident has the death benefit of $50 within one year from taking it out, and $100 there after; so we are in for benefit of $50.00 now. Keep cheerful. Count the blessing that God has spared you to so protect and care for me in this hour.

I am going with the blessed assurance that Jesus is mine & that all will be well.

May God bless & keep you. Your brother just made a fervent touching prayer for all, many people here are praying for you especially God will keep you.

Lovingly Mother

TELEPHONE 1930 HARLEM

JAMES REESE EUROPE

SUPERIOR COLORED
MUSICIANS
67-69 WEST 131st STREET
NEW YORK

"Yea Bo!"

THE CLEF CLUB

Of the City of New York, Inc.

PRESENTS

THE CLEF CLUB SYMPHONY ORCHESTRA

COMPOSED OF 150 MUSICIANS.

50 MANDOLINS, 20 VIOLINS, 30 HARP-GUITARS, 10 CELLOS, 1 SAXAPHONE, 10 BANJOS, 2 ORGANS,

10 PIANOS

5 FLUTES, 5 BASS-VIOLINS, 5 CLARINETS, 3 TYMPANI AND DRUMS,

(Under the Direction of JAS. REESE EUROPE)

—IN A—

Mighty Merry Musical Melange and Dancefest

Thursday Evening, Nov. 9th, 1911

The scintillating sensation of the season, the one best beT
Heralded here, there, everywhere, the whole world througH
Everybody, who's anybody will meet and greet you therE

Catchy tunes to "tickle" toes to trip the light fantastiC
Lilting alluring waltzes for his "Lord and Ladyship" as usuaL
Eclipsing all former efforts, everything on a broader scalE
Frolicsome frolics to "frisk" care a far ofF

Chit chat chairs in which to comfortably "catch" the charming cadencing musiC
Lavish expenditure of time, money, merit favorable criticism of the criticaL
Unequalled facilities for dancing, and watching the dancers the evening thrU
Bigger, brighter, better than ever; guaranteed to "tickle" every ri[illegible]

—AT—

MANHATTAN CASINO

155th St. and 8th Ave., New York

ADDED ATTRACTION.—A Select Coterie of Members in a Merry, Marvelous, Mirthful, Minature Cabaret Show. (Under the Direction of WM. PARQUETTE.)
The Cabaret Orchestra, Conducted by WM. H. TYERS.
Caterer Cabaret, ALBER N. BROWN.

GENERAL ADMISSION . . . . 50 CENTS
Private Boxes, 8 Chairs, not Including Admission . . $5.00
Reserved Section, 6 Chairs, not Including Admission . . $5.00
Reserved Seats, Including Admission $1.00

One of James Reese Europe's Clef Club formations. Note the variety of shapes in the mandolins and guitars, especially the large harp-guitars in the third row. In proscenium, percussion and minstrel-group with tambourines.

JAMES REESE EUROPE

THE CRISIS: June 1912

James Reese Europe was born in Mobile, Alabama, February 22, 1881. He descended from a musical family. Both his paternal and maternal ancestors, as far back as is ascertainable by the most diligent research, were musicians.

When he was a child, his parents migrated from Mobile to Washington, D. C., where he was placed under the tutelage of Enrico Hurlei, assistant director of the United States Marine Band, as a student of the violin. At the age of 14 young Europe entered a contest in the national capital in music writing, and while he won only the second prize, the first prize was awarded to his sister, Miss Mary Europe, of whom Coleridge-Taylor said: "She is a genius of dazzling brilliancy."

One of Mr. Europe's distinguishing characteristics is his genius for organization. He is the founder and first president of the famous Clef Club and the organizer of the Clef Club Symphony Orchestra, "one of the most remarkable orchestras in the world," as the *Evening Post* critic called it.

Fully to appreciate the worth of James Reese Europe to the Negro musicians of New York City, one would have to know how the Negro entertainers in cafés, hotels, at banquets, etc., were regarded before the organization of the Clef Club, and how they have been regarded since. Before, they were prey to scheming head waiters and booking agents, now they are performers whose salaries and hours are fixed by contract.

Mr. Europe devoted years of study to the theory and instrumentation of music with such well-known tutors as Hans Hanke, of the Leipzig Conservatory of Music, Melville Charlton and Henry C. Burleigh. His natural talent has been thoroughly trained.

It is as a musical director and composer that Mr. Europe is best known in the country. He toured the country as musical director for the Cole & Johnson and Williams & Walker companies, but recently he has devoted his time exclusively to writing instrumental numbers. Chief among his successes are his marches which are most inspiring. The New York *Tribune*, commenting upon them, said that "All in all they are well worthy of the pen of John Philip Sousa."

THE *EVENING POST*: NEW YORK, FRIDAY, MARCH 13, 1914

New Victor Records of the Latest Dance Music

Tangos, Maxixe and Trots

by

Europe's Society Orchestra

EUROPE

DURING the past three seasons Europe's Society Orchestra of negro musicians has become very popular in society circles in New York and vicinity, and has played for social affairs in the homes of wealthy New Yorkers and at functions at the Tuxedo Club, Hotel Biltmore, Plaza, Sherry's, Delmonico's, the Astor and others. Mrs. R. W. Hawksworth, the famous purveyor of amusements for society, used the Europe players regularly, and they have recently been engaged to play for Mr. Vernon Castle, the popular teacher and exponent of modern dances.

The success of this organization is due to the admirable rhythm sustained throughout every number, whether waltz, turkey trot or tango; to the original interpretation of each number; and to the unique instrumentation, which consists of banjos, mandolins, violins, clarinet, cornet, traps and drums.

Mr. David Mannes says: "Europe has created a new sound in the orchestra world." The Sunday Press, in an article relative to Thé Dansant, speaks of Europe as "the Paderewski of syncopation." Miss Natalie Curtis, in the Craftsman, calls this orchestra an "American Balalaika."

The Victor, in its untiring efforts to give the best assistance to those who have taken up the new dances, has engaged Mr. Europe and his orchestra to make Victor dance records, and now presents the first of the series.

Twelve-inch, Double-Faced—$1.25 each

35359 { Too Much Mustard (Tres Moutarde) One-Step or Turkey Trot (Cecil Macklin) Europe's Society Orchestra
Down Home Rag—One-Step or Turkey Trot (Wilber C. Sweatman) Europe's Society Orchestra

35360 { Irresistible—Tango Argentine (L. Logatti) Europe's Society Orchestra
Amapa—Maxixe Bresilien (Le Vrai) (J. Storoni) Europe's Society Orchestra

NEGRO'S PLACE IN MUSIC

JAMES REESE EUROPE TELLS OF COLORED ORCHESTRA

Conductor Says that Composers of His Race Should Not Try to Imitate White Men—Difficulties Overcome in Finding Musicians—Has a New Kind of Symphony Music

Persons who went to Carnegie Hall Wednesday night to hear the annual concert of the Negro Symphony Orchestra for the benefit of the Music School Settlement for Colored People probably had little idea of the tremendous difficulties which had been surmounted to make any symphonic rendition of negro music possible.

They saw and heard an orchestra of more than one hundred pieces playing works of negro composers in a style and with an orchestration entirely different from those of the white symphony orchestras. But they could not know the toil and planning that had been expended to make such an organization possible. They could not be expected to know that James Reese Europe, the conductor of the Negro Symphony Orchestra, had ransacked the world for colored musicians capable of playing certain instruments.

In some ways, James Reese Europe is one of the most remarkable men, not only of his race, but in the music world of this country. A composer of some note—some of his serious efforts were played the other night, and his dance music is known wherever the Tango or Turkey Trot are danced—he is the head of an organization which practically controls the furnishing of music for the new dances, and at the same time, he is able to expand considerable energy upon the development of the Negro Symphony Orchestra. Unaided, he has been able to accomplish what white musicians said was impossible: the adaptation of negro music and musicians to symphonic purposes.

NEGRO SHOULD NOT IMITATE

And the reason that he has made a success of his musical enterprises, according to Mr. Europe, is that he has recognized the principle that the negro should stick to his own specialties and not try to imitate the white man's work. His attitude is that in his own musical field the negro is safe from all competition, so why should he go to the useless task of attempting to interpret a music that is foreign to all the elements in his character?

"You see, we colored people have our own music that is part of us," he explained. "It's us; it's the product of our souls; it's been created by the sufferings and miseries of our race. Some of the old melodies we played Wednesday night were made up by slaves of the old days, and others were handed down from the days before we left Africa. Our symphony orchestra never tries to play white folks' music. We should be foolish to attempt such a thing. We are no more fitted for that than a white orchestra is fitted to play our music. Whatever success I have had has come from a realization of the advantages of sticking to the music of my own people.

"Now, I have between 150 and 187 musicians I can call on for work in the symphony orchestra, and I am continually adding to their numbers and improving the constituent parts. For instance, I am just sending to South Africa for two French horn players, and to the Sudan for an oboe-player. The British regiments in South Africa and the Sudan have remarkable bands, which receive musicians as young as twelve years and train them rigorously. That is the only way to fit a negro for orchestral work. Our people are not naturally painstaking; they want, as they put it, 'to knock a piece cold' at the first reading. It takes a lot of training to develop a sense of time and delicate harmony.

"Up to now, we have not had the facilities in this country for developing negro symphonic players, but gradually we are finding the men and teaching them. You see, the negro is not able to play every instrument off-hand. And also, some instruments are not exactly suited for our music.

SENDS TO SOUTH AFRICA

"To illustrate my first point, the mouth of a negro is so shaped that it is exceedingly difficult to make him more than a passable player of the French horn. Hence I must send to South Africa, where prolonged training has corrected this handicap, for satisfactory players.

"As for the second point, I can only express it by saying that Walter Damrosch or Mr. Stransky or any white leader of a symphony orchestra would doubtless laugh heartily at the way our Negro Symphony Orchestra is organized, at the distribution of the pieces and our methods of orchestration.

"For instance, although we have first violins, the place of the second violins with us is taken by mandolins and banjos. This gives that peculiar steady strumming accompaniment to our music which all people comment on, and which is something like that of the Russian Balalaika Orchestra, I believe. Then, for background, we employ ten pianos. That, in itself, is sufficient to amuse the average white musician who attends one of our concerts for the first time. The result, however, is a background of chords which are essentially typical of negro harmony.

"Other peculiarities are our use of two clarinets instead of an oboe, because, as I have said, we have not been able to develop a good oboe player. As a substitute for the French horn we use two baritone horns, and in place of the bassoon we employ the trombone. We have no less than eight trombones and seven cornets. The result, of course, is that we have developed a kind of symphony music that, no matter what else you may think, is different and distinctive, and that lends itself to the playing of the peculiar compositions of our race. Naturally, some people have laughed at us, but in answer to this form of criticism what better can I say than to point out the utter futility of any attempt to imitate the methods and organization of a white orchestra? We must strike out for ourselves, we must develop our own ideas, and conceive an orchestration adapted to our own abilities and instincts.

"As yet we have scarcely begun to think of supporting ourselves by symphonic playing. The members of the orchestra are all members of my staff of dance musicians who play at most of the principal hotels and at private dances in this city and out of town. I also furnish the dance music for the resorts at Aiken, Palm Beach, and other places, and frequently send men to play at weekend parties and special dances in country houses.

HAVE GOOD EARS FOR MUSIC

"Our people have a monopoly of this kind of work, for the simple reason that the negro has an inimitable ear for time in dancing. As a matter of fact, this instinct for dancing time in our race is an awkward virtue when it comes to training a symphonic orchestra. You would laugh at some of our rehearsals when, in a moment of inadvertence, the players begin to transpose their parts into ragtime. We get some undesignedly funny effects that way.

"I furnish Vernon Castle's music, and I have also composed most of the pieces for his dances—among others 'The Castle House Rag,' 'The Innovation Trot,' 'Congratulations,' and 'The Castle Walk.' I have just concluded a contract with him to lead a dance orchestra of forty negro musicians, all members of my staff, that will accompany him to Europe next summer. We shall play most of the time in Paris.

"I receive requests for dance musicians from all over, even from Europe, because our men are well trained and instinctively good musicians. The negro plays ragtime as if it was a second nature to him—as it is.

"All of my men are ambitious. They take to the symphonic work with enthusiasm. To give an idea of this, let me say that every member of the orchestra that played at Carnegie Hall the other night had been playing dance music during the afternoon at various places throughout the city, and after the concert was over every man was obliged to hurry back to take up the work of accompanying the tango dancers again. That's the way they make their living, of course; but every man is proud of his part in building up a representative school of real negro music that is worth while. I have at least two violinists and a cellist who, I venture to say, are equal to any in town.

"In playing symphonic music we are careful to play only the work of our own composers. I know of no white man who has written negro music that rings true. Indeed, how could such a thing be possible? How could a white man feel in his heart the music that a black man feels? There is a great deal of alleged negro music by white composers, but it is not real. Even the negro ragtime music of white composers falls far short of the genuine dance compositions of negro musicians.

NOT RIVALS OF WHITE MEN

"But aside from the fact that negro music by white men is not real negro music, I would not permit my orchestra to play the compositions of white men, because I know that my musicians could not begin to rival white men at interpreting the creations of white composers. For example, how could we hope to interpret the works of MacDowell, simple as they are? It is not in us. MacDowell was a white man; his simplicity was the simplicity of a white man; he wrote from the soul of a white man. And in the same way, what white orchestra could render the music of Will Marion Cook or Rosamond Johnson or the old plantation and spiritual melodies, whose composers were workers in the fields? Music breathes the spirit of a race, and, strictly speaking, it is a part only of the race which creates it.

"You are surprised because I have not selected for distinctive mention the name of Coleridge-Taylor, probably the best known of the musicians and composers of our race. But the fact of the matter is, that Coleridge-Taylor, while the greatest musician we have produced, is surpassed as a composer of negro music by several others. Coleridge-Taylor lived too much among white men; he absorbed the spirit and feeling and technique of white men to such an extent that his race sympathy was partially destroyed. His work is not real negro work. It partakes of the finish and feeling of the white man. To write real negro music, a negro must live with negroes. He must think and feel as they do.

"No, the great improvements in higher education for the negro have not developed music as you might think. The schools and colleges for the negro are all of an industrial character. The artistic side has naturally been neglected as of less importance. That is our great difficulty. The people of my race who love music must train themselves. Strictly speaking, I had no musical education myself. I was born in Mobile, Ala., but was brought up in Washington, where I received a high-school education. Music I picked up as I went along. I gained much valuable training during six years I spent on the road as orchestra leader with negro musical comedies, for I was careful to keep always before me the ambition for a higher kind of work, and I was careful not to permit my sense of musical proportion to leave me.

"The great task ahead of us, as I see it, is to teach the negro to be careful, to make him understand the importance of painstaking effort in playing, and especially to develop his sense of orchestral unity."

New Victor Records of the

Sixteen Superb New Dance Numbers

Played by Europe's Society Orchestra and the Victor Military Band

Further Additions to the Victor's List of Dance Records—Now the Greatest in the World

THE ideal place for the new dances is in the home, and here the Victor is absolutely indispensable, as most of this music is extremely difficult and loses much of its effectiveness unless played by band or orchestra.

To its comprehensive and brilliant list of dance records, the Victor now adds four records by the Europe Orchestra, which are described on the last page of this folder, and twelve splendid new selections by the Victor Band, which is now the most widely known and popular organization furnishing music for dancing.

The Tango, Maxixe, Turkey Trot, Hesitation, Boston, One-Step, Two-Step—all are represented, and the selections are those now most in demand in dancing circles. Vernon Castle, Sebastian, Maurice and other celebrated exponents of modern dancing are using many of these numbers, and they will be found ideal for accompanying the new dances.

NEW YORK SUN
April 9, 1914

VERNON CASTLES DANCE BEFORE BIG NEGRO CLUB

Society Tango Favorites Aid Colored Orchestra and Composer

Centered in one of the most picturesque gatherings that New York has ever seen, Mr. and Mrs. Vernon Castle, wizards of the dance, who are to terpsichore what Edison is to electricity, appeared last night before the Tempo Club, one of the leading negro organizations of the city.

In the middle of the great floor of the Manhattan Casino, One Hundred and Fifty-fifth street and Eighth avenue, they danced their latest steps surrounded by 2500 members of the club and more than a hundred white people of fame and fashion.

The entertainment last night, of which the Castles were the chief figures, was for the benefit of the orchestra, which is about to make a tour of Europe—that is, the Continent.

Two of the newest Europe compositions, "The Castle Lame Duck" and "The Castle House Rag," were played for the first time last night by the National Negro Orchestra.

The Castles danced their most noted repertoire—"Half and Half," the Tango, Maxixe and Castle Waltz.

Vernon and Irene Castle

NEGRO COMPOSER ON RACE'S MUSIC

James Reese Europe Credits Men of His Blood with Introducing Modern Dances

The music of the negro like the music of the Indian has caused much ink to be spilled. Some enthusiastic souls have looked to the rhythms of the red man for the melody that is to create American music; in fact, some have gone so far as to declare that the only possible American music can be Indian music. Which is all very interesting and absolutely inconclusive. The fact remains that Indian composers, in any fair sense of the term, do not exist; while we have among us many talented and well trained negro creative musicians. It was with one of these that a Tribune representative talked last week, with a man who has written a very large proportion of the so-called modern dances. The man was James Reese Europe; the composer of all the Castle dances, and the director of Europe's Orchestra, an organization which has all but secured complete control of the cabaret and dance field in the city. Mr. Europe is a well trained musician and a man who has thought deeply on the musical possibilities of his race, and of these possibilities, he has firm and well defined opinions.

"I am striving at present to form an orchestra of negroes which will be able to take its place among the serious musical organizations of the country," said Mr. Europe.

"The Tempo Club now contains about two hundred members, all musicians, and from the body I supply at present a majority of the orchestras which play in the various cafés of the city and also at the private dances. Our negro musicians have nearly cleared the field of the so-called gypsy orchestras. The negro, while not generally equal to the demands of the more sophisticated forms of music, is peculiarly fitted for the modern dances. I don't think it too much to say that he plays this music better than the white man simply because all this music is indigenous with him. Rhythm is something that is born in the negro, and the modern dances require rhythm above all else.

"I myself do not consider the modern dances a step backward. The one-step is more beautiful than the old two-step, and the fox trot than the schottische, of which it is a development. As to the so-called dance craze, it does not appear to be a 'craze.' I have had probably as good an opportunity to observe the various dances as any one in the city, and I have found that dancing keeps husbands and wives together and eliminates much drinking, as no one can dance and drink to excess. However, these are questions for a philosopher and not for a musician.

"There is much interest in the growth of the modern dances in the fact that they were all danced and played by us negroes long before the whites took them up. One of my own musicians, William Tyres, wrote the first tango in America as far back as the Spanish-American War. It was known as 'The Trocha,' and a few years afterward he wrote 'The Maori.' These two tangos are now most popular, yet who heard of them at the time they were written? They were the essentially negro dances, played and danced by negroes alone. The same may be said of the fox trot, this season the most popular of all dances.

"The fox trot was created by a young negro of Memphis, Tenn., Mr. W. C. Handy, who five years ago wrote 'The Memphis Blues.' This dance was often played by me last season during the tour of the Castles, but never in public. Mr. Castle became interested in it, but did not believe it suitable for dancing. He thought the time too slow, the world of today demanding staccato music. Yet after a while he began to dance it at private entertainments in New York, and, to his astonishment, discovered that it was immediately taken up. It was not until then that Mr. and Mrs. Castle began to dance it in public, with the result that it is now danced as much as all the other dances put together. Mr. Castle has generously given me the credit for the fox trot, yet the credit, as I have said, really belongs to Mr. Handy. You see, then, that both the tango and the fox trot are really negro dances, as is the one-step. The one-step is the national dance of the negro, the negro always walking in his dances. I myself have written probably more of these new dances than any other composer, and one of my compositions, 'The Castle Lame Duck Waltz,' is, perhaps, the most widely known of any dance now before the public.

"Yet we negroes are under a great handicap. For 'The Castle Lame Duck' I receive only one cent a copy royalty and the phonograph royalties in like proportion. A white man would receive from six to twelve times the royalty I receive, and compositions far less popular than mine, but written by white men, gain for their composers vastly greater rewards. I have done my best to put a stop to this discrimination, but I have found that it was no use. The music world is controlled by a trust, and the negro must submit to its demands or fail to have his compositions produced. I am not bitter about it. It is, after all, but a slight portion of the price my race must pay in its at times almost hopeless fight for a place in the sun. Some day it will be different and justice will prevail.

"I firmly believe that there is a big field for the development of negro music in America. We already have a number of composers of great ability, the two foremost being Harry Burleigh and Will Marion Cook. Mr. Burleigh is remarkable for his development of negro themes and Mr. Cook is a true creative artist. Then, of course, there was Coleridge-Taylor, the greatest composer of the negro race, although much of his music is not negro in character. What the negro needs is technical education, and this he is handicapped in acquiring. I myself have had to pick up my knowledge of music here and there, and the same holds true of my fellow composers. I do not believe that the negro at present should attempt music distinctively Caucasian in type. The symphony, for instance, he does not really feel as a white musician would feel it. I believe it is in the creation of an entirely new school of music, a school developed from the basic negro rhythm and melodies. The negro is essentially a melodist, and his creation must be in the beautifying and enriching of the melodies which have become his.

"The negro's songs are the expression of the hopes and joys and fears of his race; were before the war the only method he possessed of answering back his boss. Into his songs he poured his heart, and, while the boss did not understand, the negro's soul was calmed. These songs are the only folk music America possesses, and, folk music being the basis of so much that is most beautiful in the world, there is indeed hope for the art product of our race."

"Kicked to France"

Noble returned to New York in September 1916 to resume his career with Jim Europe's orchestra. He and Jim enlisted in the Army, where they organized a regimental band, Sissle helping to recruit band members and eventually becoming drum major. After training at Camp Whitman in Peekskill, New York, the regiment entrained for Camp Wadsworth in Spartanburg, South Carolina, in the fall of 1917. There an incident occurred that nearly precipitated a race riot.

One Sunday night after church services Jim told Noble to "go over to the hotel and get every paper that has the words New York on it." *"When I went to the stand,"* Noble recalls, *"I was roughly grabbed in the collar from behind, and before I realized what had happened my service hat was knocked from my head. A gruff voice roared, 'Say, nigger, don't you know enough to take your hat off?' Well, the first thing that came to me was maybe I was guilty of a breach of etiquette, but a quick glance around showed it was because of my color—every citizen and officer had on his hat. I reached for my hat and as I did so received a kick accompanied by an oath. Lost for words, I stammered out: 'Do you realize you are abusing a United States soldier and that is a government hat you knocked to the floor?' 'Damn you and the government too,' the man replied. 'No nigger can come into my place without taking off his hat.' I left as soon as I could, but not before I received three other kicks. The regiment found out about it quickly enough, as there were several witnesses, and it took the military police and Jim's cool head to prevent a brawl from breaking out. The next day they rushed the regiment north to Hoboken and after several delays we sailed for the front, arriving at the coast of France on New Year's Day 1918—the first American Negro combat unit to set foot upon French soil."*

April 9th, 1918

Hello Eubie:

Your letter received. Gee! I was glad to hear from you. I wrote you 3 letters—this is my fourth. I certainly hope you receive this one. Yes I know business must be dull for I see and hear it from everybody I know over here.

Just stay on the job and take your medicine. If you think of the comforts you are having over there and think of the hardships we are having over here you'd be happy I am sure to go on "suffering." . . . Well, at present Eubie, I am a soldier in every sense of the word and I must *only take* orders and be able to stand all sorts of hardships and make untold sacrifices. At the moment I am unable to do anything. My hands are tied and tied fast but if the war does not end me first as sure as God made man I will be on top and so far on top that it will be impossible to pull me down.

Fitz was kind enough to send me the newspaper clipping of the death of my good friend Vernon Castle. Can you imagine my grief. My one real and true friend gone.

Write me often and tell me all the news. Do not adopt the motto of ones whom I thought unimpeachable—out of sight and out of mind. Remember me to your dear wife and stick to business. I have some wonderful opportunities for you to make all the money you need. Eubie, the thing to do is to build for the future, and build securely and that is what I am doing. When I go up I will take you with me. You can be sure of that.

Your real Pal
Jas. Reese
369th Inf.

Lieutenant James Reese Europe, 369th U.S. Infantry

ST. LOUIS *POST-DISPATCH*, JUNE 10, 1918

Ragtime by U.S. Army Band Gets Everyone 'Over There'

Drum Major Describes Furore Created by the Performances of Afro-American Band Under Colored Leader

Special Correspondence of the Post-Dispatch

WITH THE AMERICAN ARMY IN FRANCE, June 10.—The first and foremost Afro-American contribution to the French fighting line is its band. Subsidized by D. G. Reid with a check for $10,000, and organized by "Jim" Europe, colored orchestra leader, now a Lieutenant in the regiment, the dusky band is fast becoming celebrated throughout France. At the A. E. F.'s chief recreation center a big silver cup and several golden palms were presented to the musicians by the municipality.

Sergt. Noble Sissle, the regimental drum major, has made a study of the effect of Yankee ragtime, as interpreted by his bandsmen, on French audiences. He has addressed the following summary of his impressions to the correspondent of the Post-Dispatch with the American forces:

"After reading so many articles about the American bands and real need of them in France, I thought I would write concerning some of our experiences 'over here.'

"We have quite an interesting time playing our homeland tunes for the amusement of every nationality under the sun. The one interesting thing—to our agreeable surprise—was the enjoyment that all seemed to get out of hearing our ragtime melodies.

"When our country was dance-mad a few years ago, we quite agreed with the popular Broadway song composer who wrote: *(continued on page 68)*

"Syncopation rules the nation,
You can't get away from it."

"But if you could see the effect our good, old 'jazz' melodies have on the people of every race and creed you would change the word 'Nation' quoted above to 'World.'

"Inasmuch as the press seems to have kept the public well informed of our band's effort to make the boys happy in this land where everybody speaks everything but English, I will assume that you know Lieut. James Reese Europe, its organizer and conductor. This Lieut. Europe is the same Europe whose orchestras are considered to have done a goodly share toward making syncopated music popular on Broadway. Having been associated with Lieut. Europe in civil life during his 'jazz bombardment' on the delicate, classical, musical ears of New York's critics, and having watched 'the walls of Jericho' come tumbling down, I was naturally curious to see what would be the effect of a 'real American tune,' as Victor Herbert calls our Southern syncopated tunes, as played by a real American band.

The Jazz Introduced

"At last the opportunity came and it was at a town in France where there were no American troops, and our audience, with the exception of an American General and his staff, was all French people. I am sure the greater part of the crowd had never heard a rag-time number. So what happened can be taken as a test of the success of our music in this country where all is sadness and sorrow. The occasion was at a concert given in a well packed opera house on Lincoln's Birthday, and after the opening address by the Mayor and the response by the American General our band began with its evening entertainment.

"The program started with a French march, followed by favorite overtures and vocal selections by our male quartet, all of which were heartily applauded. The second part of the program opened with 'The Stars and Stripes Forever,' the great Sousa march, and before the last note of the martial ending had been finished the house was ringing with applause. Next followed an arrangement of 'plantation melodies' and then came the fireworks, 'The Memphis Blues.'

"Lieut. Europe, before raising his baton twitched his shoulders apparently to be sure that his tight-fitting military coat would stand the strain, a musician shifted his feet, the players of brass horns blew the saliva from their instruments, the drummers tightened their drumheads, everyone settled back in their seats, half closed their eyes, and when the baton came down with a swoop that brought forth a soul-rousing crash both director and musicians seemed to forget their surroundings; they were lost in scenes and memories. Cornet and clarinet players began to manipulate notes in that typical rhythm (that rhythm which no artist has ever been able to put down on paper), as the drummers struck their stride their shoulders began shaking in time to their syncopated raps.

Whole Audience Catching It

"Then, it seemed, the whole audience began to sway, dignified French officers began to pat their feet, along with the American General, who, temporarily, had lost his style and grace. Lieut. Europe was no longer the Lieut. Europe of a moment ago, but Jim Europe, who a few months ago rocked New York with his syncopated baton. His body swayed in willowy motions, and his head was bobbing as it did in days when terpsichorean festivities reigned supreme. He turned to the trombone players who sat impatiently waiting for their cue to have a 'jazz spasm' and they drew their slides out to the extremity and jerked them back with that characteristic crack.

"The audience could stand it no longer, the 'jazz germ' hit them and it seemed to find the vital spot loosening all muscles and causing what is known in America as an 'eagle rocking it.' 'There, now,' I said to myself, 'Col. —— has brought his band over here and started ragtimitis in France! Ain't this an awful thing to visit upon a nation with so many burdens?' But when the band had finished and the people were roaring with laughter, their faces wreathed in smiles, I was forced to say that this is just what France needs at this critical moment.

"All through France the same thing happened. Troop trains carrying allied soldiers from everywhere passed us en route, and every head came out of the window when we struck up a good old Dixie tune. Even German prisoners forgot they were prisoners, dropped their work to listen and pat their feet to the stirring American tunes.

"But the thing that capped the climax happened up in Northern France. We were playing our Colonel's favorite ragtime, 'The Army Blues,' in a little village where we were the first American troops there, and among the crowd listening to that band was an old woman about 60 years of age. To everyone's surprise, all of a sudden she started doing a dance that resembled 'Walking the Dog.' Then I was cured, and satisfied that American music would some day be the world's music. While at Aix-les-Bains other musicians from American bands said their experiences had been the same.

"Every musician we meet—and they all seem to be masters of their instruments—are always asking the boys to teach them how to play ragtime. I sometimes think if the Kaiser ever heard a good syncopated melody he would not take himself so seriously.

"If France was well supplied with American bands, playing their lively tunes, I'm sure it would help a good deal in bringing home entertainment to our boys, and at the same time make the heart of sorrow-stricken France beat a deal lighter."

Lieut. Noble Sissle
Oct. 14, 1918

Hello Eubie

Well old boy I made it believe me I am now a "shave tail" ha-ha! As you see I am with the old 8th Ill. They have put all the spade officers out of our regiment (15th) but Jim and he's in charge of the band now. He thought he would get the bounce—that's one reason I went to school. Well it will all come out in the wash—you know.

Well on my way here from school I passed thru P_______. I saw Mitchell. He said you wrote him. Well old boy hang on then we will be able to knock them cold after the war. It will be over soon. Jim and I have P_______ by the balls in a bigger way than anyone you know.

Please do this at once. See that Nora Bayes gets "To Hell With Germany." It's a big hit here.

Did you ever get the song I wrote for her—"I Want A Sweetheart in France." I sent you that to put music to—She wrote me she sent to you for music but you never answered her.

Tell Stern that "Camp Meeting Day" is the big hit that runs all thru the Paris Follies of 1918 at Marejin [sic] *Theatre—He had better publish it or give me some kind of answer as I will know what to do. I can get it published here but I would rather it came out there.*

Here is a great song. Write it at

once and get it out for God's sake. Hustle songs. Those dam publishers don't know we can make any song the hit of France. "To Hell With Germany" is the marching song of every regiment in France—Gee that makes me sore to see that money go to waste. I'm tied up in the Army and you can't do nothing there—See if you can get this out.

No Mans Land Will Soon Be Ours

Verse

We are fighting strong, dear
Night and day
And it won't be long, dear
Watch and pray.
Keep your trust in us as we battle for the right
Win this war we must victory's now in sight

Chorus

No mans land will soon be ours, dear
Then I'll be coming back to you—my honey true
Wedding bells in Juney June
All will tell by their tuney tune
That victory's won
The war is over
The whole wide world is wreathed in clover
Then hand in hand we'll stroll thru life dear

TO HELL WITH GERMANY

WRITTEN BY SGT NOBLE SISSLE IN JULY 1918 AS A MARCHING SONG FOR THE
370th. US REGIMENT FROM CHICAGO

(P.S. HE ALSO USED IT AT THE OFFICERS TRAINING SCHOOL IN LANGRES FRANCE)
AS HIS LITTLE SEGREGATED SQUAD ATTENDED
THE OTS.WHERE HE WAS COMMISIONED
OCT 25th 1918 2nd LT.)

"TO HELL WITH GERMANY"

WE RUSHED THEM BACK AT THE MARNE

WE CRUSHED AND HACKED THEM AT CHAMPAIGN

AND EVERY HUN SON OF A GUN

WE MOWED THEM DOWN AT VERDON

WE STACKED THEM IN THE FIELDS OF LORAINE

WE BOTTLED THEM UP AT THE KEIL

WE SUNK THEM TO THE BOTTOM OF EVERY SEA

AND EVERY TIME THEY TRIED TO COME

WE SLAUGHTERED THEM AT THE SOMME

SO TO HELL WITH GERMANY

Just think how happy we will be—I mean we three
So pick our bungalow among the fragrant bowers
And I'll be there to you with the blooming flowers
No man's land will soon be ours, dear.

What a Great Great Day

Verse

Strike boys strike while the iron is hot
We've got the Huns on the run
Strike boys strike hard at every spot
Show them we're sons of a gun
The harder we fight the sooner it will be
We'll have the Kaiser and his gang hung to a Linden Tree.

Chorus

What a great, great day when we get the victory
And it's over over here.
What a great, great day when we sail across the sea
And it's over over here.
When we pass Sandy Hook and steam up New York Bay
When we get one more look up and down old Broadway
Hurrah for the land of the free (Strain of *"Stars and Stripes Forever"*)
You'll hear throughout from the Coast of

Lieutenant Europe and his band playing for a Red Cross hospital, Paris, September 4, 1918

Maine (Strain of "*Yankee Doodle*")
To the sunny shores of Dixie (Strain of "*Dixie*")
When the whole world's at peace again (Strain of "*America*")
And it's all over over here.

Note where I have certain strains I mean those lines are sung to these tunes
Hurrah for the Flag of the Free
Yankee Doodle come to Town
I wish I was in Dixie
My country 'tis of Thee

and then last line.

Noble.

In early 1919, soon after the armistice, Jim and the band returned to America in triumph and began touring the country to cheers and applause. On the night of May 9 of that year, at Mechanic's Hall, Boston, one of the Percussion Twins, Herbert Wright, crazed with anger at what he considered an unfairness, attacked Jim Europe with a knife during the intermission of the band's final concert of the tour. *"Jim wrestled Herbert to the ground,"* Noble recalls. *"I shook Herbert and he seemed like a crazed child, trembling with excitement. Although Jim's wound seemed superficial, they couldn't stop the bleeding, and as he was being rushed to the hospital he said to me: 'Sissle, don't forget to have the band down at the State House at nine in the morning. I am going to the hospital and I will have my wound dressed. Let Felix Weir finish the concert. I leave everything for you to carry on.' The next day the papers carried the headlines: THE JAZZ KING IS DEAD."*

Among the many tributes was one from a gracious lady who knew Jim well.

My Dear Lieutenant Sissle:

. . . During the four years he played for Captain Castle and me, he originated many new "tempos." He was the first to suggest the slow tempo used for the fox trot. . . . No inconsiderable part of our success was due to his wonderful playing and helpful suggestions. . . . I am sure that in his death the colored race has lost one of its most distinguished leaders, the music-loving public one of its most inspired composers, and that a large host of Americans will, like myself, mourn the loss of a generous loyal friend.

Very sincerely yours,
Mrs. Vernon Castle
January 12, 1920

"He was our benefactor and inspiration. Even more, he was the Martin Luther King of music."

Eubie Blake

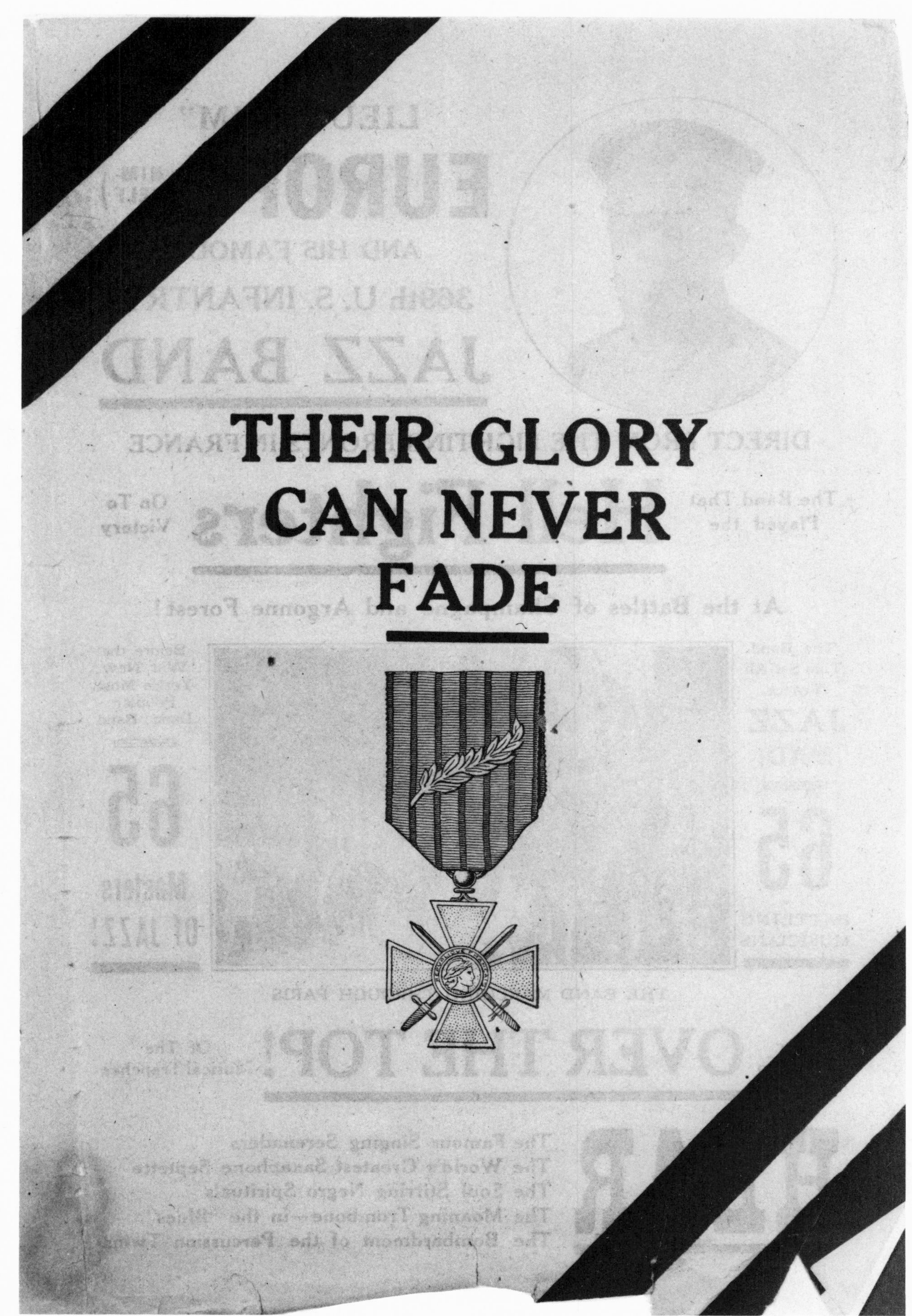

Handbill for Europe's 369th U.S. Infantry Jazz Band, 1919

LIEUT. "JIM"

EUROPE (HIM-SELF)

AND HIS FAMOUS

369th U. S. INFANTRY

JAZZ BAND

DIRECT FROM THE FIGHTING FRONTS IN FRANCE

The Band That Played the **Hell Fighters** On To Victory

At the Battles of Champagne and Argonne Forest!

The Band That Set All France JAZZ MAD!

65 BATTLING MUSICIANS

Before the War New York's Most Popular Dance Band

65 Masters Of JAZZ!

THE BAND MARCHING THROUGH PARIS

Hear Them Go **OVER THE TOP!** Of The Musical Trenches

HEAR

The Famous Singing Serenaders
The World's Greatest Saxaphone Septette
The Soul Stirring Negro Spirituals
The Moaning Trombone—in the "Blues"
The Bombardment of the Percussion Twins

LIEUT. NOBLE SISSLE

The Greatest Singer of his race—formerly Drum Major of the Band—in a repertoire of Original Songs. Acclaimed alike by Press and Public America's Own.

"Young Black Joe"

"The best Military Band in Europe."

IRVING COBB in The Saturday Evening Post.

DON'T MISS THIS!

Watch For Opening of Seat Sale

TRIUMPHANT RETURN MARCH DOWN FIFTH AVENUE

Reserve Your Seats Early—Avoid Disappointment

DON'T MISS THIS!

WATCH The Papers and Billboards for Day and Date---This Band is COMING!!

I'M COMING FOLKS

With the Greatest Bunch of Musicians and Jazz Artists in the World.

WATCH FOR DAY and DATE!!

GOSSLER'S "CAMPUS"

104th Street & Columbus Ave.

Tonight: 7:30—10—11:30 p. m.

"CHUCKLES"

Evan Baldwin's Greatest Mu[illegible]cal Success,

Featuring Miss Marie Boyle, "B[illegible]adway's Own"

TURKEY PLATE DINNER

Roast Vermont Turkey (Stuffed)
with Asparagus Tips and Cranberry Sauce
Hearts of Lettuce, with Russian Dressing
Steamed Soft Clams, with Butter Sauce
Stuffed Celery
Fresh Virginia Crab Meat au Gratin.

DELICIOUS !!! $1.25
IN THE GRILL, $1.10

DANCING

New York's Jazziest Jazz
Broadway Jones
Himself
Assisted by
Merrymakers
of His Own Choice

MIDNIGHT
PRIZE
DRAWING
OF
VALUABLE
SURPRISE
PACKAGES

On the home front

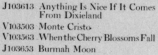

RYTHMODIK RECORD MUSIC ROLLS

POPULAR DANCE AND SONG ROLLS

Some of the artists who play them

MABEL WAYNE

VICTOR ARDEN

HARRY THOMAS

HARRY ARCHER

EUBIE BLAKE

MALVIN FRANKLIN

WM. E. BERGÉ

MARIE COOKE

Latest Popular Hits—All Big Sellers

J103613 Anything Is Nice If It Comes From Dixieland
V103503 Monte Cristo
V103563 When the Cherry Blossoms Fall
J103653 Burmah Moon
J103522 I Found You
J102883 Victory
J103663 Alcoholic Blues
J103473 America Never Took Water
J103633 Music of the Wedding Chimes
J103373 Bluin' the Blues
V103423 By the Campfire
J103343 Don't Cry, Frenchy
J103302 Honeymoon
J103273 How 'Ya Gonna Keep 'Em Down on the Farm
J103453 I'm Goin' to Settle Down Outside of London Town
J103463 Johnny's in Town
J103293 Salvation Lassie of Mine
J103483 That Tumble-Down Shack in Athlone
J103223 You're Some Pretty Doll
X101494 Mickey

MURIEL POLLOCK

LEE DAVID

How is Your Stock on this List?

Send Along Your Orders

We can make quick shipment

RYTHMODIK MUSIC CORPORATION
23 WEST 38th STREET NEW YORK

Vaudeville

Jim's death changed everything. The Clef Club, the big dreams the three had shared, everything seemed to waste away without him.

★ ★ ★

"There was only one Jim Europe, and he had not just been 'made' with that band of his. There was years of experience behind that sweep of his arms, and anyone who tried to follow him would just be out of their mind. . . . I was sure that conducting was not the field in which I was to carry on his life's dreams. In my mind the band should only remain in the memory of those who heard it led by Lieutenant James Reese Europe, and that's how it ended."

Noble Sissle

★ ★ ★

"Jim and I had written several songs during our two years of service. Among them was a song that we had written in France while up in the trenches. It was an experience that Jim had on a patrol in No Man's Land—in fact, Jim wrote the lyrics to the chorus while he was in the hospital following a gas attack.

"I went to the hospital to see him, expecting him to be suffering like many of the other gas patients that were housed there, some of whose eyes were put out, others groaning from severe burns. But when I got to Jim, instead of him being stretched out in pain, there he was sitting up in the bed with a little notebook, writing. What, I said to myself, a last will and testament? 'Hi, Siss,' he said. 'Wait a minute, I'm just finishing a song that is a knockout. I just got a touch of gas on the raid, but listen to this idea for a song, and we can do it in ragtime!' "

On Patrol in No Man's Land

THERE'S A MINNENWURFER COMING—LOOK OUT—(BANG!)
HEAR THAT ROAR, THERE'S ONE MORE.
STAND FAST, THERE'S A VARY LIGHT.
DON'T GASP OR THEY'LL FIND YOU ALL RIGHT.
DON'T START TO BOMBING WITH THOSE HAND GRENADES
THERE'S A MACHINE GUN, HOLY SPADES!
ALERT, GAS, PUT ON YOUR MASK.
ADJUST IT CORRECTLY AND HURRY UP FAST.
DROP! THERE'S A ROCKET FOR THE BOCHE BARRAGE,
DOWN, HUG THE GROUND, CLOSE AS YOU CAN, DON'T STAND.
CREEP AND CRAWL, FOLLOW ME, THAT'S ALL.
WHAT DO YOU HEAR? NOTHING NEAR. ALL IS CLEAR, DON'T FEAR.
THAT'S THE LIFE OF A STROLL WHEN YOU TAKE A PATROL
OUT IN NO MAN'S LAND. AIN'T IT GRAND?
OUT IN NO MAN'S LAND.

On Patrol in No Man's Land

ADDISON AMUSEMENTS Inc. *Presents*

Lieutenant JIM EUROPE

AND HIS FAMOUS

369 *th* U.S. INFANTRY "HELL FIGHTERS" BAND

LIEUT. NOBLE SISSLE

GOOD NIGHT ANGELINE . . .	50
ON PATROL IN NO MAN'S LAND .	50
ALL OF NO MAN'S LAND IS OURS	50

By LIEUT. JIM EUROPE, LIEUT. NOBLE SISSLE and EUBIE BLAKE

M. WITMARK & SONS

New York Chicago Philadelphia Boston San Francisco London

"Well, that song became a big sensation in the band program overseas and especially on tour. We would finish with this 'No Man's Land' number with Jim at the piano and the band making all the sound effects of a bombardment.

"When Jim died, the backers of his band and the agents Pat Casey and B. S. Moss, both top bookers in the Keith circuit, suggested that I take a small 15-piece band in vaudeville, but I suggested they try Eubie Blake and I as a team like Jim and I had worked in the band tour. I was positive that the novelty of the 'No Man's Land' number would get us off the stage, as in those days all any vaudeville act needed was a terrific novelty finish.

"They sent our act up to Bridgeport, Conn., to open and it went so good there that they brought us into the Harlem Opera House to show to the bookers from Keith. To everybody's surprise we were booked into the Palace Theatre, the pride of the Keith circuit, the next week. As the old hams would say, which in our case the records bear out, we stopped every show—and to do that at the Palace meant at least three years' consecutive work from coast to coast. Thus the act of Sissle and Blake was born."

Sissle and Blake, "The Dixie Duo," was one of the first Negro acts to play without burnt cork. To give some idea of what black acts were expected to do in vaudeville of that time, here is Eubie: *"Some agent had a smart idea for an act for us. We were supposed to shuffle on stage in blackface and patched-up overalls. In the middle of the stage there is this big box with a piano in it. The idea was to look at it as if it were from the* moon *and I'd say, 'What's dat?' and Noble would say, 'Dat's a py-anner!' and then we'd do our act. Well, Pat Casey would have none of that. He told the agents that Sissle and Blake had played in the houses of the millionaires and the social elite and they dressed in tuxedos and he'd be* damned *if he'd let us go on the stage in old overalls and act like a couple of ignoramuses."*

Elegantly dressed to the last inch (a trademark that survives with them to this day), Sissle and Blake entered the stage from opposite sides, while the band played their opener, "Gee! I'm Glad that I'm from Dixie." The piano bench would be set at right angles to the piano: Blake on the piano end, Sissle on the singing end, but neither stayed in place very long at a time—the two managed to turn the piano into a trench, a dance floor, whatever would fit the needs of the number. There would be close harmony in "Good Night, Angeline," then a pin spot on Noble for "Pickaninny Shoes." *"Noble talked to those shoes. He made you see them right there in his hands, even when he no longer had prop shoes—somebody'd stolen them as a gag —shoes or no shoes, there wasn't a dry eye in the house when he was through."* Following this, there might be a piano solo by Blake, then the big finale—the Sissle-Europe "Over the Top—On Patrol in No Man's Land," with Sissle sliding across the floor on one shoe to duck the Minenwerfer, dodging the Very light, and hitting the ground with every rocket, bombardment, and fusillade from Blake's piano.

Life on the road was hard; vaudevillians had to be prepared to be away from their families for months at a time. Sissle and Blake had special problems that derived from being black in America. Hotels that would accommodate white performers would rarely take them, so that often it was a problem to find lodging for the night—they had to depend on the kindness of colored families who opened their homes to them during those years. At times service in restaurants was denied them. Once they were refused food at a greasy-spoon in Hartford, Connecticut; a newspaperman who happened to be present wrote a scathing account of the incident, and their friend Al Jolson, who was playing the same town, heard of it and was enraged. *"He sent his chauffeur for us,"* remembers Eubie, *"and told us he wanted to throw a party for us in one of the biggest hotels, just to 'show them.' We urged him to let the matter alone. There's an old saying: when the rabbit bites you the first time, it's his fault, but when he bites you the second time, it's your fault."*

THE PHONOGRAPH AND TALKING MACHINE WEEKLY

NOBLE SISSLE

Famous Colored Vaudeville Headliner

NOW AN EXCLUSIVE EMERSON STAR

(Noble Sissle & His Sizzling Sincopators)

In a few old vaudeville houses that are left intact (such as the Lyric at Allentown, Pennsylvania) one can see the arrangement of dressing rooms that was common to the period: several tiers, with walkways, right behind stage. *"Our dressing rooms were always the worst in the theater—usually on the top floor, a billion miles up from the stage, next to the dog act. Even when we were the most popular act on the bill we were treated that way."* At the opening of a run in a particular house, Sissle and Blake might be placed in the number-two spot (number one was usually an animal act)—this meant that they would warm up the house for the following acts but would just miss the reviewers, who rarely came to the theater until the number-three spot. But by sheer energy Sissle and Blake became one of the hardest acts to follow in show business; the number-three act gave way, then the number-four, till finally by the end of a week's run their act would be next to last because the headliners refused to follow them. (No increase in salary, of course.)

SISSLE-TOYE MARRIAGE

Montclair, N.J.—Mrs. Harriett Toye, widow of the late Patrick E. Toye, former pianist of Boston but who became a member of the United States Navy and died at sea on October 2, 1918, was quietly married on Christmas morning [1919 or 1920] to Lieut. Noble Lee Sissle, former business partner and co-star with the late Lieut. James Reese Europe. Mr. Sissle is now being featured on the Keith vaudeville circuit.

Only the immediate families were present. Miss Martha M. Sissle, the groom's sister, and one of the secretaries of the Y.W.C.A., was the maid of honor, and the groom's brother, Andrew M. Sissle, was the best man.

Mrs. Harriett Toye Sissle is the mother of six-year-old Helen Toye Sissle, who is attending a private school in Philadelphia.

Lieut. and Mrs. Sissle occupied the bridal chambers at the Pinehurst Inn for the weekend and were guests at many social functions. Mrs. Sissle will accompany her husband on his present tour and their mail address will be in care of the Pat Casey Agency, 1493 Broadway, New York.

Toronto, Canada
September 21, 1920

Dear Avis:

I have been waiting to hear if you were in Baltimore or where you were. I don't know where we go from Akron, Ohio. We have no route from there as yet, but I think we will go west as all the acts are going west, but we are trying to keep from going. I'm very tired. I sent my laundry and two suits of clothes from Buffalo—hope you received them. I received my suit. Next week, Hamilton, Canada. I don't know the theatre. . . .

Hamilton, Canada
September 27

. . . Let me know by wire when you leave Baltimore. You have asked me about getting an apartment. Well, you know if I get one we both will have to skin out all the money we can. I think I will get you an apartment when I come home—that is if we can find a nice one. You look around for some nice furniture. I will close now.

Hamilton, Canada
September 29

. . . I accompained Sissle for a Pathé record. He told me he sent you the money which I know he did. I know you're glad to have some money in your pocketbook. They got us on second here where we're playing and you talk about the blues. We're *singing the blues. Well, I don't know where I go from here. We have no route. No one on the bill has any further route than next week. Well, don't let that worry you because they are very short of acts now and we won't lay off. Next week Colonial Theatre, Akron, Ohio, U. S. A.*

Hamilton, Canada
September 30

. . . Just a note to let you know what kind of burg this is. A good place to come and die when you feel like dying alone. You know we're on second this week from splitting honors with Clark and Bergman to second on the bill. Great, eh. Well, we get paid just the same. I suppose you can tell when I am in a slow burg. I write often. Well now I don't mean to be that way but I just hate to write. But here that is all I can do. We have written a very pretty song called "Sing Me To Sleep Dear Mammy." Sounds very good—too good for M. Witmark & Sons. Give my best regards to Mamma.

I am your husband

Eubie Blake

The Dixie Duo, 1919

Along

Sissle and Blake

The team of Sissle and Blake had had remarkably little contact with other Negro performers on the road, as vaudeville managers made it a practice not to bill more than one black act per show. In fact, it was only at an NAACP benefit in Philadelphia in 1920, at the new Paul Laurence Dunbar Theatre, that Sissle and Blake were able to meet the successful comedy team of Miller and Lyles.

Flournoy E. Miller and Aubrey Lyles were a veteran comedy-dancing act who had begun in college theatricals at Fisk University in Tennessee. After a stint in Chicago at Motts's Pekin Theatre and a tour of England, Miller and Lyles had played several years on the Keith circuit. Their blackface act consisted of Southern small-town humor, dance sequences, and a famous fight scene which was imitated by many other vaudevillians for years afterward.

Both acts performed that muggy summer evening, and afterward Miller and Lyles introduced themselves to Sissle and Blake. After a mutual exchange of compliments, Miller and Lyles told them that their songs had the kind of theatrical flavor they had been looking for; perhaps the two acts could join forces to try to put the Negro back on Broadway. . . . Nothing immediate came out of the encounter, but a few months later, by chance, the four met again in New York on the street. They continued their Philadelphia conversation as if no time had passed, but this time Miller had something more concrete: one of their sketches, *The Mayor of Dixie*, about the complicated maneuvers in a small-town mayoralty contest, had, according to him, possibilities of being developed into a full-length musical.

Miller also felt that the only way to put Negro performers into white theaters with any kind of dignity was through musical comedy, where they could run their own show unhampered. Here was the chance to realize Jim Europe's dream: to restore the Negro to the American stage. Sissle, Blake, and Europe had started efforts in this direction before the war, before Europe's murder had thwarted their plans; now Miller and Lyles had come along to provide the frame for the undertaking. The four pooled their meager resources and attempted what few believed possible after George M. Cohan—to write, direct, manage, and star in their own show.

★ ★ ★

Aubrey Lyles and Flournoy Miller

Studio
NY

Shuffle Along was put together quickly. Drawing on their songs and comedy routines, the four assembled a rough sketch of a show that was, in some respects, the fusion of two vaudeville acts—with dancing numbers, a sort of continuous plot, and thrown-in love interest. All over the country black performers responded to the casting notices. Veterans from the old Williams and Walker and Cole and Johnson companies, standouts of the Lafayette Theatre and other black ensembles, and many eager and talented newcomers were assembled for a show that had no money, no sets, or any real assurance of being produced at all.

Miller and Lyles had known Al Mayer, who had formerly worked for E. F. Albee and booked their act on the Keith circuit. Mayer was friendly with the Cort family, father John and son Harry, whose once-gigantic theatrical empire was crumbling as a result of the financial recession of 1921. Everyone was broke just then, including Mayer himself; Miller, Lyles, Sissle, and Blake chipped in $1.25 each so that Al could take Harry Cort to lunch and discuss the new project.

The Cort family agreed to audition the show. *"We ran down a few songs,"* recalls Eubie, *"and Old Man Cort—well, he just sat there with a glum look on his face. When we did our theme song, 'Love Will Find a Way,' the old man didn't say anything. Nothing. He just got up and walked out, saying, 'Thank you, boys. Thank you very much.' I thought we were dead for sure, but it turned out the old man liked the song so much he said he'd help us and give us a theater, sets, some old costumes, if we would just give his son Harry an interest in the show."*

The 63rd Street Theatre was a dilapidated lecture hall, without a proper stage or orchestra pit; the crew would still be building on the stage well into the New York run. The "old costumes" were discards from two flops, Eddie Leonard's *Roly-Boly Eyes* and Frank Fay's *Fables; "they still had sweat-marks under the arms,"* recalls Eubie.

Ideas for a song may come from anything at all—something one's wife said that morning, an unusual gastric disorder, an annoying cigar from the next table in a restaurant—but it must be rare indeed that song ideas come from a particular lot of used costumes dumped on even such a shoestring production as *Shuffle Along*. Sissle and Blake found themselves with a sizable pile of vaguely Orientalish costumes; another lot had clearly been intended for some old-plantation production number. With the Oriental costumes, they were lucky; they had already written an appropriate "Oriental Blues," "*which is neither Oriental nor a blues*," adds Eubie, and it was simply a matter of shoehorning it into the score. What to do with the cotton-pickers' costumes? Simple! They wrote "Bandana Days," which was composed over the phone; Sissle was in Boston, Blake was in New York, and what emerged was a fast, sassy number reminiscent of George M. Cohan.

It might be remembered that, up until rather recently, the usual practice for a Broadway show was to try out on a road tour and then, if the show lasted, bring it into town. The *Shuffle Along* company rehearsed in Harlem in preparation for the tour, but when the time came to go on the road it was discovered that no one had the money to pay the company's train fare to Trenton, New Jersey, their first stop.

Eubie: *"We got down to Penn Station and I was ready to turn around and go straight home, but Sissle wouldn't let me. He said we'd get there somehow, and we did. I think Sissle still felt Jim Europe's hand guiding us. . . ."*

During the rehearsals a shabbily dressed man had hung around the theater. Everyone noticed him and knew him—a Mr. Gasthoffer or something—and assumed he was just a sad old derelict, come to ogle the showgirls. *"But Al Mayer knew him and said we should get him to stay with us on tour. When we were at the station, Al went to him and sold him one-half of his share in the show to get us on the way to Trenton.*

"No one is going to believe the story of what happened to us on the road, but it's all true!"

Center: Al Mayer, the manager of *Shuffle Along*

The *Shuffle Along* itinerary traced a helter-skelter course, jumping and doubling back over town, hamlet, theater, auditorium, barn, and movie house throughout New Jersey and Pennsylvania. *"We'd play one-night—if we were lucky, two-night—stands. No one knew us, so they'd only book us for a short time. We'd get good reviews in one town, but before they could do us any good we'd be on to another town—that is, if we had the money. One night Sissle and I were sitting on the steps of a building, and Sissle was writing out checks. They weren't any good until we could wire the box office receipts into the New York bank—we were always one day behind at the very least. I looked up. 'Sissle,' I say, 'do you know where you're sitting?' 'No,' he said, and looked around. We were sitting on the steps of the jailhouse, writing bum checks! We broke up in a fit of laughing and couldn't stop."*

In one town the four found, to no one's surprise, that they were flat broke—no money to stay the night. Lyles, a consummate bluffer, found a cabdriver at the station, began talking, and somehow convinced the young cabbie that, if he was willing to advance them the cash for a night's lodging, Lyles's company would forward it to him later. The driver took the group to a seedy rooming house. *"There were five of us. Miller and Lyles slept in one bed, Sissle in another; Paul Floyd, who was in the show, was in the bed with me. All night long the chinches had a picnic, and Paul kept waking me up, slapping the chinches."*

The next morning they got up and tried to sneak down the stairs, Lyles, big cigar in mouth, leading the way. The proprietor, a huge black man, was ready for them, blocking the door and hollering for his money. "I didn't trust you minstrel niggers! You're all no good!" "Sir," Lyles answered mildly, "the boy will be here with the money very soon," all this said with the five men struggling unsuccessfully to get past the owner. Incredibly, the cabdriver did show up with the money and bailed them out. . . . In Washington, D. C., it was discovered that one of the cashiers had been using the company's money to play the horses; the man was summarily fired, and again some Maecenas was found to make good the losses.

Certainly the tallest of the road stories happened in Burlington, New Jersey. Eubie again: *"You know what I'm going to tell you—no money for train fare. Al Mayer is down at the station, walking up and down the platform wondering what to do. Up walks this man and says:*

" 'Say, did you see that nigger show here in town last night?'

" 'Yeah,' said Al.

" 'That was the best thing I ever saw, that nigger show. Yes, sir!'

" 'Yeah,' said Al. 'It's my show. I'm the manager.'

" 'Well, you've got a gold mine there.'

" 'Yeah,' said Al. 'Well, sir, that's nice to hear, but we don't even have enough money to get to the next town.' So the man said he'd be right back, walked into the ticket office, and talked to the station master.

"It turns out that man was one of the owners of the railroad, for when he came back he had tickets for the whole company." Saved again!

White Studio
N.Y.

Opening Night, 63rd Street Theatre, New York City, May 23, 1921

Riding into town with an $18,000 deficit, *Shuffle Along* began preparations for its New York opening. The show was tight and ready, but there were worries.

One day Eubie ran into Jesse Shipp, a writer for the old Williams and Walker shows, and told him he and Sissle had written a song called "Love Will Find a Way." "You're crazy," Shipp told him, and walked off, shaking his head. For honest, unburlesqued romantic love interest in a black show was dangerous ground: white audiences might be expected to boo the show off the stage.

Noble: *"On opening night in New York this song had us more worried than anything else in the show. We were afraid that when Lottie Gee and Roger Matthews sang it, we'd be run out of town. Miller, Lyles, and I were standing near the exit door with one foot inside the theater and the other pointed north toward Harlem. We thought of Blake, stuck out there in front, leading the orchestra—his bald head would get the brunt of the tomatoes and the rotten eggs. Imagine our amazement when the song was not only beautifully received, but encored. During the intermission we told Blake what we had been doing, and he came near to killing us.*

"But the biggest moment of all came near the end of the show, with a number called 'The Baltimore Buzz.' I sang it while Blake and the orchestra played like fury and the girls danced up a storm. People cheered. I almost fell off the stage when I looked out into the auditorium—there was old John Cort dancing in the aisles! His faith in us had been borne out. That night it looked like we were home."

Love Will Find a Way

LOVE WILL FIND A WAY
THOUGH SKIES NOW ARE GRAY
LOVE LIKE OURS CAN NEVER BE RULED
CUPID'S NOT SCHOOLED THAT WAY
DRY EACH TEAR-DIMMED EYE
CLOUDS WILL SOON ROLL BY
THOUGH FATE MAY LEAD US ASTRAY
MY DEARIE, MARK WHAT I SAY
LOVE WILL FIND A WAY.

Shuffle Along opened to generally favorable reviews, but they were slow in coming. Many of the first-line critics passed up the show's première and sent the second-stringers—for the production was indeed something of a sleeper and had come to New York largely unheralded by advance ballyhoo. A few reviewers, notably of the *Globe* and the *Morning Telegram*, offered mixed appraisals. Some criticism was made of the flimsy book and staging, and of the generally amateurish quality of the production. But the great majority of aisle sitters was captivated by the show; Burns Mantle and Heywood Broun were especially warm in their praise.

Evening Journal: "A breeze of super-jazz blown up from Dixie!"

Mail: "The principal asset of the new entertainment is the dancing and the jazz numbers."

Evening Post: "A good deal better than a number of the musical plays offered this season—it's well worth hearing."

Daily News: "Interesting as a novelty, the song numbers are full of melody, and everybody dances." BURNS MANTLE

Billboard: "Real, wholesome and filled with a spirit of liveliness and good humor which amazes anyone who has endured the languid efforts of ordinary Broadway musical affairs."

FIRE NOTICE

Look around NOW and choose the nearest Exit to your seat. In case of fire walk (not run) to THAT Exit. Do not try to beat your neighbor to the street.
THOMAS J. DRENNAN, Fire Commissioner.

WEEK BEGINNING MONDAY EVENING, MAY 23, 1921
Matinees Wednesday and Saturday

NIKKO PRODUCING CO., INC.

Presents

A Musical Melange

SHUFFLE ALONG

Conceived by Miller and Lyles
Music and Lyrics by Sissle and Blake
Staged by Walter Brooks

Cast of Characters
(As They Appear)

At the Piano....EUBIE BLAKE
JIM WILLIAMS, Proprietor of Jim Town Hotel....PAUL FLOYD
JESSIE WILLIAMS, His Daughter....LOTTIE GEE
RUTH LITTLE, Her Chum....GERTRUDE SAUNDERS
HARRY WALTON, Candidate for Mayor....ROGER MATTHEWS
BOARD OF ALDERMEN....RICHARD COOPER, ARTHUR PORTER, ARTHUR WOODSON, SNIPPY MASON
MRS. SAM PECK, Suffragette....MATTIE WILKS
TOM SHARPER, Political Boss....NOBLE SISSLE
STEVE JENKINS, Candidate for Mayor....F. E. MILLER
SAM PECK, Another Candidate for Mayor....AUBREY LYLES
JACK PENROSE, Detective....LAWRENCE DEAS
RUFUS LOOSE, War Relic....C. WESLEY HILL
SOAKUM FLAT, Mayor's Bodyguard....A. E. BALDWIN
STRUTT, Jim Town Swell....BILLY WILLIAMS
UNCLE TOM....CHARLES DAVIS
OLD BLACK JOE....BOB WILLIAMS
SECRETARY TO MAYOR....INA DUNCAN
JAZZ JASMINES—Misses Goldie Cisco, Mildred Brown, Theresa West, Jennie Day, Adelaide Hall, Lillian Williams, Beatrice Williams, Evelyn Irving.
HAPPY HONEYSUCKLES—Misses Ruth Seward, Lucia Johnson, Marguerite Weaver, Bee Freeman, Marion Gee, Mamie Lewis, Marie Roberts.
SYNCOPATING SUNFLOWERS—A. E. Baldwin, Charles Davis, Bernard Johnson, Robert Lee, Snippy Mason, Miles Williams, Arthur Woodson and Bob Williams.
MAJESTIC MAGNOLIAS—Misses Edna Battles, Ina Duncan, Lula Wilson, Hazel Burke and Paula Sullican.

Critical approval came in also from Gilbert Seldes, George Jean Nathan (who saw the show five times), and other theatrical pros. Especially helpful were a perceptive, intelligent review by "IBEE" (Jack Pulaski) in *Variety* and the enthusiastic paean of veteran critic Alan Dale in the *American*, a man not notably fond of musical comedy.

Eubie: *"It was Alan Dale's review that really made people want to see the show.*

We were afraid people would think it was a freak show and it wouldn't appeal to white people. Others thought that if it was a colored show it might be dirty. One man bought a front row seat for himself every night for a week. I'd noticed him—down in the pit you notice things in the audience—and finally, after the whole week was past, he came up and told me that now he could bring his wife and children because there was no foul language and not one double-entendre."

A few days after the opening and the reviews, *Shuffle Along* ran its first ads and

TIME—Election Day. PLACE—Jimtown in Dixieland.

ACT I.

Scene 1—Exterior of Jimtown Hotel.
Scene 2—Possum Lane.
Scene 3—Jenkins' and Peck's Grocery Store.
Scene 4—Public Square.

ACT II.

Scene 1—Calico Corners.
Scene 2—Possum Lane.
Scene 3—The Mayor's Office.
Scene 4—Saunders Lane.
Scene 5—Ball Room of Jimtown's Hotel.

During the action of the piece, the following numbers will be rendered:

ACT I.

(Orchestra Under Personal Direction of Mr. E. Blake)

Opening Chorus....................By Entire Company on Election Day
"Simply Full of Jazz"......Gertrude Saunders and Syncopation Steppers
"Love Will Find a Way"—Duet..............Miss Gee and Mr. Matthews
"Bandana Days"..............................Arthur Porter and Company
"Sing Me to Sleep, Dear Mammy".Roger Matthews and Board of Aldermen
"Honeysuckle Time"..Noble Sissle
"Gypsy Blues"..................Misses Gee, Saunders and Mr. Matthews
Grand Finale.........................By Entire Population of Jimtown

ACT II.

"Shuffle Along"................By Jimtown Pedestrians and Traffic Cop
"Wild About Harry"..................Miss Gee and Jimtown Sunflowers
"Jimtown's Fisticuffs"...................................Miller and Lyle
"Syncopation Stenos"...................................By Mayor's Staff
Selections...By Board of Aldermen
"If You Haven't Been Vamped by a Brown Skin, You Haven't Been Vamped at All"................Miller and Lyle and Jimtown Vamps
"Uncle Tom and Old Black Joe".......................Davis and Williams
"Everything Reminds Me of You"—Duet.....Miss Gee and Mr. Matthews
"Oriental Blues"........................Noble Sissle and Oriental Girls
"I Am Craving for That Kind of Love" and "Daddy"......Miss Saunders
A Few Minutes with.......................................Sissle and Blake
"Baltimore Buzz"............Noble Sissle and Jimtown's Jazz Steppers
"African Dip"...Miller and Lyle
Finale by Entire Outfit....................................Including You

Musical arrangements by William Vodery.
Production built by J. Van Sickler.
Piano furnished by Aeolian Co.
Typewriter used in Second Act furnished by Oliver Typewriter Co.
Draperies by Beaumont.

For Nikko Producing Co., Inc.

Al. Mayer ....Manager
Estelle Nolan.....................................Wardrobe Mistress
William Cripps...............................Press Representative

Evening World: "*Shuffle Along* is well worth your attention. . . . No musical show in town boasts such rousing and hilarious teamwork. . . . We don't suppose the members of the cast and chorus actually pay for the privilege of appearing in the performance, but there is every indication that there is nothing in the world which they would rather do. They are all terribly glad to be up on the stage singing and dancing. Their training is professional, but the spirit is amateur. The combination is irresistible." HEYWOOD BROUN

Opening night program, New York

inaugurated the policy of special midnight performances on Wednesday nights. This proved a splendid innovation, as it drew many theatrical people who quickly spread the word of the show's many attractions. Within a matter of weeks the show was New York's biggest hit and soon became the rage of society, who flocked to the 63rd Street Theatre to watch (and try to learn) the jazz dancing that *Shuffle Along* had introduced to Broadway.

MID-WEEK
PICTORIAL
War Volumes.
CHINA

Broadway and 43rd Street, 1921

Variety, May 1921

SHUFFLE ALONG

The 63d Street Theatre, acquired by John Cort interests some months ago, stepped into the theatre division Monday with the first all-colored show that has got close to Broadway since Williams and Walker. "Shuffle Along" is programmed as presented by the Nikko Producing Co., of which Harry L. Cort is said to be one of the principals. The house was formerly used mostly for recitals and special performances, having practically no stage. For this attraction the apron has been extended outward, taking in the first box on either side. By use of drapings the stage can be closed in by pulley lines and a similar arrangement for "one" is provided. The orchestra takes up the space occupied by the first three rows, the first row now being D. This is supposed to be a temporary device. In the fall the house is to be given a regular stage. With the present extension the depth is under 20 feet.

"Shuffle Along" is a lively entertainment. It has an excellent score supplied by Eubie Blake and Noble Sissle, both members of the late Lieutenant Jim Europe's band that won admiration abroad during the war. The musical numbers are worthy of a real production, which "Shuffle Along" lacks entirely. Whatever book there is and the comedy business came from F. E. Miller and Aubrey Lyles. Both these players are from vaudeville, which field further contributed with the staging, done by Walter Brooks.

A private showing was given the piece Sunday night. Song writers who were not present then came Monday for the premiere, for there appears to be a hearty respect for Sissle's [*sic*] ability as a composer, and wiseacres predicted that some of the big shows downtown would receive a suggestion or two.

Broadway may not know it, but the fashion of wearing the feminine head with the bobbed hair effect has more fully invaded the high browns of the colored troupes than in the big musical shows. All the gals in "Shuffle Along" showed some sort of bobbed hair style, principals and chorus alike. It wasn't so successful with some, but they tried just the same. The feminine contingent was probably recruited from the colored organizations that have entertained the uptown colored populace in the shows at the Lafayette.

Miller and Lyles handled the comedy entirely and they worked up some laughs away from anything they offered in vaudeville. There was a grocery store bit, that suggested the old afterpiece idea. Both boys are partners and both are tapping the till. One of the richest lines came when Lyles was told that a detective was coming to catch his partner, the informant saying that he sure was done stealing now. Lyles inquired: "When did he die?" The humor of the situation was that neither wanted the "bull," fearing he would catch the wrong man first. The partners are rival candidates for mayor of Jimtown. Miller in making a speech to the citizens said he "had no idea there was going to be a dark horse, but you ain't going to be no black mayor." The team inserted their boxing bit in the second act, and it was the comedy hit of the show.

Dancing started in the second act, but there was comparatively little of it. The song numbers had the call all evening. Gertrude Saunders, the ingenue, and Lottie Gee, prima donna, together with Roger Matthews, juvenile, handled most of the songs, and all showed good voices. The show opened with "Simply Full of Jazz," handled by Miss Saunders, and it went for three encores. Miss Gee proved herself a few minutes later while the two girls and Matthews scored with "Gypsy Blues," a tricky melody that caught on quickly.

The melody hit came at the finale of the first act. It was "Love Will Find a Way," probably the same number first handled by Miss Gee. Repetition brought the air out to its true value. It is a peach. "Shuffle Along," from which the show takes its name, was led by Matthews, it opening the second act. Matthews is a neat worker, sings well and delivered in duets with Miss Gee several times. Miss Saunders was alone for "I am Craving That Kind of Love," another tricky number. She had a number called "Daddy" for encore, which was well liked. "Oriental Blues," sung by Sissle, was perhaps the only number where half a dozen show girls bloomed out in anything like a costume flash. The number was delivered in "one."

The actual song hit score came near the close. Here Blake, who directed the orchestra from the piano, went to the stage for a specialty with Sissle. Their first number was "Low Down Blues." The other songs were out of the team's vaudeville routine, taking in "Pickanniny's Shoes" and "Out in No Man's Land," Sissle announcing the number coming from "our benefactor, the late Jim Europe." But the playing of the "Love" melody won out so strong Sissle used it also to Blake's smiling accompaniment.

Immediately afterwards the show went into the finale with "Baltimore Buzz," another number that stood out and should have been earlier. For that song the only flash of "shimmy" was present.

"Shuffle Along" played Philadelphia for a week, repeated three weeks later, then came into New York to rehearse a week before opening. In Quaker Town the show had a $1 top, including war tax, and grossed around $8,000 for its first engagement there. At the 63rd Street the top is $2 for half the lower floor, the price for the other downstairs rows being $1.50. Colored patrons were noticed as far front as the fifth row on the opening night when the upper floors did not sell out. The house has a balcony and gallery, seating around 1100.

The production cost looks close to the minimum. Costume outlay was not a heap more, some of the outfits appearing to have come from the wardrobe of another show, perhaps one of the elder Cort's productions. The show therefore stands a good chance to grab a tidy profit, unless the scale is too high. The 63rd Street is around the corner from the Century. A few blocks to the westward is a negro section known as "San Juan Hill." The Lenox Avenue colored section is but 20 minutes away on the subway, so that "Shuffle Along" ought to get all the colored support there is along with the white patrons who like that sort of entertainment.

Some day Sissle and Blake will be tendered a real production and they deserve it.

IBEE

Shuffle Along 1921 Review by Alan Dale (New York *American*)

"SHUFFLE ALONG" FULL OF PEP AND REAL MELODY

Colored Troupe Gives Entertainment That Might Well Be Copied by Downtown Managers for Its Music and General Worth

By ALAN DALE.

SEVERAL highly important Broadway shows in the suave vicinity of Forty-second street might send their stage managers and high cockolorums up to the little Sixty-third Street Theatre, there to see a "darky" musical comedy entitled "Shuffle Along." With no ostentation of scenic effects and no portentous "names" and no emphasized "sensations," this jolly evening's entertainment manages to lift the drear from your entity and to liven up your disposition.

Act, and the audience acts with you. This seemed to be the motto of the "troupe" at the Sixty-third. How they enjoyed themselves! How they jigged and pranced and cavorted, and wriggled, and laughed. It was an infection of amusement. It was impossible to resist a jollity that the company itself appeared to experience down to the very marrow. Talk of your pep! These people made pep seem something different to the tame thing we know further downtown. Every sinew in their bodies danced; every tendon in their frames responded to their extreme energy. The women were wreathed in smiles that did not suggest the "property" brand; the men simply exuded good nature.

And yet "Shuffle Along" is a darky show that has lost most of its darkiness. The men "black up" just as though they were tintless; the women rouge up, very much as they do in non-colored performances. One expects to see an essentially colored aggregation, but it isn't that by any means. It is a semi-darky show that emulates the "white" performance and—goes it one better.

Some of the voices were excellent in quality and in cultivation. Miss Lottie Gee, for instance, has a singularly pure soprano and knows how to use it. Downtown, where they don't want voices and rarely suffer from them, Miss Gee would be quite a novelty. In her vocal equipment there is none of that jellified consistency that wobbles and quavers and makes you nervous. She sings with taste, discretion and distinction. The same may be said for Roger Matthews, who also boasts a voice that musical comedy managers would say was too good for the business.

But they are not ashamed of their voices, and the damsels of the chorus are almost equally disposed to warble. They were billed last night as the Jazz Jasmines, the Happy Honeysuckles and the Majestic Magnolias, whilst the chorus men did duty as Syncopating Sunflowers. The reigning spirits of the show were Miller and Lyles, who "conceived" it, according to the programme. This twain did a musical fight called "Jimtown's Fisticuffs" that brought down the house. Probably it has been seen elsewhere in vaudeville. But as I never sample vaudeville, it was perfectly new to me. The music was by Noble Sissle and Eubie Blake, and it had considerable melody. It was not at all pretentious, but it had simplicity and charm. It lacked the molassesian consistency of many of your musical shows. It also lacked their primitiveness. In nearly every number there was some phrase, some twist, some kink that gave it a semblance of novelty.

The "book" was devoted to darky politics, but it had some humor. There was one scene with a cash register in a grocery store that was most hilarious. It was very quietly and funnily acted. It was in fact done with the unctuous humor of a Lew Fields, and if poor Lew had been given anything half as droll in this last enterprise, he might have looked upon himself as a lucky chap.

Some of the ditties in this comedy were "If You Haven't Been Vamped by a Brown Skin, You Haven't Been Vamped at All," "Sing Me to Sleep, Dear Mammy," "Shuffle Along," "I'm Wild About Harry," "Bandana Days," "Gypsy Blues" and "Everything Reminds Me of You."

At times it seemed as though nothing would stop the chorus from singing and dancing except ringing down the curtain. They revelled in their work; they simply pulsed with it, and there was no let-up at all. And gradually any tired feeling that you might have been nursing vanished in the sun of their good humor and you didn't mind how long they "shuffled along." You even felt like shuffling a bit with them. All of which I admit isn't usual in dear old Forty-second street.

The show was staged by Walter Brooks, who was evidently able to give the pep full scope. As a matter of fact there was enough pep for two average musical comedies.

Center: Miller and Lyles

A Musical Melange

Shuffle Along arrived in New York during a period of transition in American musical theater. European operetta, which had been the inspiration and touchstone for the works of Victor Herbert, Sigmund Romberg, and even Jerome Kern, was losing some of its grip on the American style. The minstrel and variety shows had fused with burlesque to create the large-scale revue, and the farce-comedy was giving way to a more urbane and unified plot form as the city and the city style became the dominant force in American life.

Yet the style barriers were still intact—city slicker and country cousin still eyed each other with suspicion. The novelty of *Shuffle Along* was that it mixed the urban with the rural, the old with the new, in a

way that cut across all boundaries. *Shuffle Along* returned the Negro to the stage after an absence of ten years—more than that, this show was willing, on the one hand, to speak of his agrarian roots in earthy humor and sentimental song; on the other hand, to speak of the urban setting of his present hopes and struggles, in the blues, shouts, and jazz dancing that were to sweep Broadway in so many pale imitations. Finally, the show dared to reach out to European operetta and present again, electrified, the love ballad as a universal statement.

Taken in its entirety, *Shuffle Along* cannot be more accurately described than by the words the company chose themselves: "a musical melange." For it is a melange of temporal values, past, present, and future, musical styles, and cultural influences. Raunchy, delicate, romantic, syncopated, it is all of these things in part. It is a series of fragments, bits, individual varied moments, each valid, brief, and pointed. But the unity is something like the unity in plurality of America itself—held together by its very disparateness and many-faceted character, in a way that any hierarchical order would violate. In short, there is no reason at all that *Shuffle Along* should have worked—and that is evidently just why it did.

Front: Adelaide Hall and Arthur Porter in "Bandana Days"

"Jimtown's Fisticuffs" (l. to r.) Richard Cooper, Arthur Porter, Snippy Mason,

Baltimore Buzz

THERE HAVE BEEN A THOUSAND RAGGY DRAGGY DANCES
THAT ARE DANCED IN EV'RY HALL
AND THERE HAVE BEEN A THOUSAND RAGGY DRAGGY PRANCES
THAT ARE PRANCED AT EV'RY BALL
BUT THE BESTEST ONE THAT "WUZZ"
IS CALLED THE BALTIMORE BUZZ
SO

FIRST YOU TAKE YOUR BABE AND GENTLY HOLD HER,
THEN YOU LAY YOUR HEAD UPON HER SHOULDER,

F. E. Miller, C. Wesley Hill, Aubrey Lyles, Arthur Woodson

NEXT YOU WALK JUST LIKE YOUR LEGS WERE BREAKING,
DO A FANGO LIKE A TANGO,
THEN YOU START THE SHIMMY TO SHAKING.
THEN YOU DO A RAGGY DRAGGY MOTION
JUST LIKE ANY SHIP UPON THE OCEAN
SLIDE
AND THEN YOU HESITATE
GLIDE
OH, HONEY, AIN'T IT GREAT!
YOU JUST GO SIMPLY IN A TRANCE
WITH THAT BALTIMORE BUZZING DANCE.

Honeysuckle Time

IN HONEYSUCKLE TIME
SWEET EMALINE
SAID SHE'D BE MINE
AND IN THE WEDDING LINE
THERE'LL BE NO HESITATING
FOR THE PREACHER WILL BE WAITING
WHEN THE KNOT AM TIED

WITH "EM-Y" BY MY SIDE
ALL THE FELLOWS WILL BE JEALOUS AND FEELING KINDA ROUGH,
WHEN I COME ALONG WITH EMALINE A-STRUTTIN' MY "STUFF,"
HOT DOG, MY SOUL, GOIN-A KNOCK 'EM COLD,
WHY, I'LL BE WORTH MY WEIGHT IN GOLD
IN HONEYSUCKLE TIME
WHEN EMALINE SAID SHE'D BE MINE.

Noble Sissle and Allegretta Andrews

Sissle, Blake, Miller, and Lyles

Shuffle Along had just about every current dance step—except the waltz. Given Blake's propensity for waltzes from the very earliest, this seems odd; in fact Eubie had planned a waltz for the show, an elegant one in the suavest English style that he had written in 1920.

One day he played it for Lottie Gee, the leading lady, for whom he intended the number. Miss Gee had been in several Williams and Walker and Cole and Johnson productions, and her backlog of experience was as impressive as her beauty. "How can you have a waltz in a colored show?" she asked when he had finished playing.

Eubie recalls, *"I reminded her of a waltz 'When the Pale Moon Shines,' which had been in a colored show. Lottie answered, yes, she had been in that show, and the song wasn't a hit. Well, she had me there. 'Make it a one-step,' said Lottie. A one-step! That cut me to the quick—she was going to destroy my beautiful melody! I* loved *that waltz!*

"Then Sissle went along with her. He was always more commercial than I was. All right, I said, I'll make it a one-step."

The new one-step was not a particular hit in the show, even with Lottie Gee singing it with a background of six dancing chorus boys. Noble: *"Something seemed to just miss in its presentation, and we were about to throw the song out of the show in Philadelphia, where we were playing prior to taking it into New York.*

"One night one of the chorus boys was sick, and Bob Lee, a member of the singing ensemble, was drafted to replace him in the number. Bob couldn't dance very well, so we sent him on stage leading the line so that he would be the last off and not in the way of the others when they made their exit.

"Miller and Lyles and myself were making a change and Blake was in the pit, conducting, when all of a sudden we heard a roar of laughter from the audience. Lyles said, 'I bet Bob Lee fell down.' Then there was terrific applause and we all three ran to the wings to see what happened. Blake flew up out of the pit, wild-eyed: 'Keep him in! Keep him in!' he yelled, and disappeared. We thought he had gone nuts, but by then the encore was on. Then we saw. Bob Lee could not do the steps the other fellows were doing and couldn't get off the stage, so he dropped out of line and with a jive smile and a high-stepping routine of his own stopped the show cold."

In New York "I'm Just Wild about Harry," the song they had almost thrown out, became a sensation, Bob Lee taking nine to ten encores a night.

BALTIMORE BUZZ

SHUFFLE ALONG, Inc. *Presents*

THE NEW YORK MUSICAL NOVELTY SUCCESS

Shuffle Along

Book by Flournoy Miller and Aubrey Lyle

Baltimore Buzz	60
Bandana Days	60
Daddy Won't You Please Come Home	60
Everything Reminds Me of You	60
Gypsy Blues	60
Good Night, Angeline	60
Honeysuckle Time	60
I'm Just Wild About Harry	60
If You've Never Been Vamped By a Brown Skin	60
I'm Craving for That Kind of Love	60
I'm Just Simply Full of Jazz	60
Kentucky Sue	60
Love Will Find a Way	60
Liza Quit Vamping Me	60
Low Down Blues	60
Old Black Joe and Uncle Tom	60
Oriental Blues	60
Pickaninny Shoes	60
Shuffle Along	60
Vision Girl	60

Lyrics & Music by Noble Sissle and Eubie Blake

Theatrical and Music Hall Rights of these Songs are fully protected by Copyright and MUST not be used for public performances without permission.

M. Witmark & Sons
New York

OPERATIC EDITION

Printed in U. S. A.

AMERICAN SOCIETY OF COMPOSERS, AUTHORS AND PUBLISHERS

AS OF CAP

1922

FIFTY SIX WEST FORTY FIFTH STREET
NEW YORK CITY

EUBIE BLAKE

WHOSE SIGNATURE IS AFFIXED HERETO, IS A MEMBER IN GOOD STANDING, FOR THE YEAR SHOWN.

Eubie Blake
MEMBERS SIGNATURE

SECRETARY

From an unknown New York newspaper, 1921

Eubie Blake Gives His Best Recipe for Sure-Fire Song Hit

"It's the song that makes a fellow want to get right up, no matter where he is, and begin whistling and dancing all over the place, that makes a hit these days."

This is the opinion of Eubie Blake, composer of "Shuffle Along," the All-Colored Musical Melange at the Sixty-third Street Music Hall.

"A modern song," declares Mr. Blake, "to make any kind of a hit at all, must have 'pep' to it, and also must have a 'catchy tune' that unconsciously sticks to the mind of the hearer. I have made it a point to study the audiences at every performance of 'Shuffle Along' in order to note whether my songs have produced the results which I have first mentioned. I have found that such songs as 'Love Will Find a Way,' 'Bandana Days,' 'Low Down Blues,' 'Baltimore Buzz' invariably set a large part of the audience, particularly the younger members, to beating with their feet and swinging their shoulders rhythmically. Also, I have never failed to hear after the performance and between the acts a number of men whistling snatches from 'Gypsy Blues,' 'Shuffle Along,' 'Full of Jazz' or any one of the songs of the play.

"These facts tell me that I have succeeded in accomplishing in my songs just what I strove for, namely, to produce in the audience the desire to dance and whistle these songs as they are coming out of the theatre and teach me that these songs have stuck with them and possess the essential elements of 'catchiness.'

"The successful song writer of to-day must be something more than a mere juggler of harmonious sounds. He must be a student of what the public wants—a sort of psychologist. The mushy, sobby, sentimental love songs of twenty or more years ago would not be at all popular to-day. Nor would the semi-martial music of songs popular during the United States' participation in the war make a hit now.

"What the public wants to-day are lively, jazzy songs, not too jazzy, with love interest, but without the sickly sentimentality in vogue a generation ago."

* * *

In 1922 Julius Witmark, of the music publishing house, entered Eubie Blake and Noble Sissle into ASCAP, which at that time rarely admitted Negroes to its ranks. The gesture has assured both Sissle and Blake a measure of security from their works, "I'm Just Wild about Harry" still being their principal source of income.

I'M JUST WILD about HARRY

FOX-TROT NOVELTY SONG

from the

SENSATIONAL MUSICAL COMEDY SUCCESS

SHUFFLE ALONG

BY

NOBLE SISSLE &

EUBIE BLAKE

Writers of All the Lyrics & Music in This Successful Production

M. WITMARK & SONS

NEW YORK

OPERATIC EDITION 60¢ NET

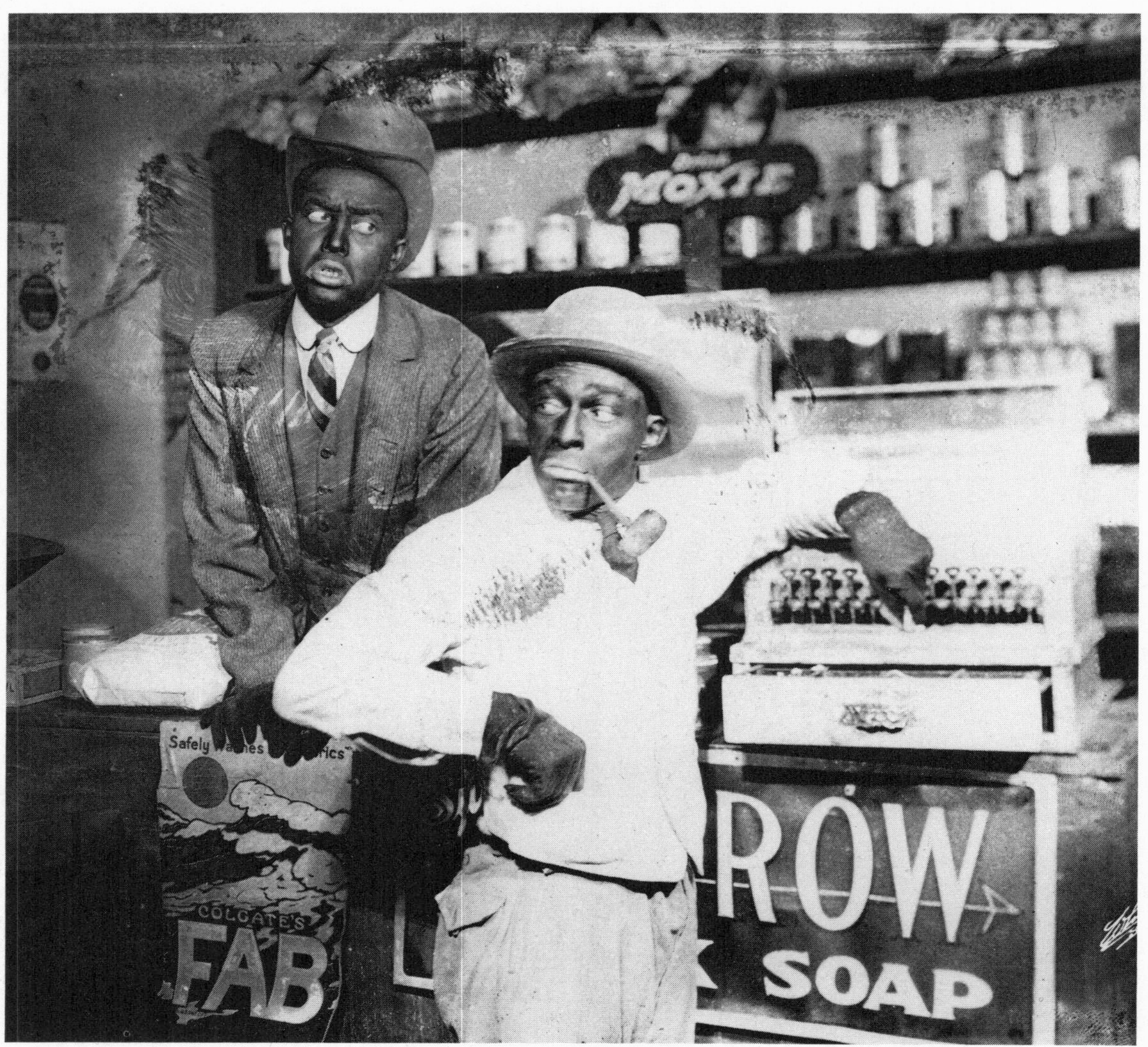

Miller and Lyles in grocery-store scene

Shuffle Along's plot concerns a three-cornered mayoralty race among Miller (Steve Jenkins), Lyles (Sam Peck), and Roger Matthews (Harry Walton, to whom "I'm Just Wild about Harry" is sung during the campaign). Jenkins and Peck are partners in the grocery business as well as rivals for Mayor of Jimtown. Each promises the other that, if elected, he will name him chief of police. Both are inveterate crooks: each steals from the cash register to finance his campaign; each engages a detective, from his stolen funds, to check up on the other (it's the same detective, of course). Steve Jenkins wins the election with the help of an unscrupulous campaign manager (Tom Sharper, played by Sissle), while Sam Peck, whose chances were hurt by his driving suffragette wife (Mattie Wilks), becomes chief of police, to find that his chief and practically only duty is to "salaam the mayor." Finally he *slams* the mayor, and a fight occurs. Meanwhile, a movement led by the reform candidate, Harry Walton, unseats the crooked pair, and justice triumphs.

Those who remember the early *Amos 'n' Andy* radio programs will have some idea of the dialogue written for the Miller and Lyles routines in *Shuffle Along*; Flournoy E. Miller was, in fact, one of the principal writers for that show in the early thirties. Many of the tortured forty-dollar words like "regusting" and "reliver," that made a whole generation of Americans guffaw, were collected assiduously by Miller, who haunted poolrooms, taverns, and general stores for the most recondite verbal forms he could find, then inserted them into his comedy sketches.

Mayor and Chief of Police

ICE COLD
Coca-Cola
SOLD HERE
CLASSIC
ASK FOR
DEMONSTRATION
Swift's Premium
Oleomargarine
Labor Light
Clothes White
ARROW
BORAX SOAP
Swift's Premium
Frankfurts
Silverleaf
Brand Pure Lard

Finale, Act 1

Vanity Fair
BEAUTY SOAP
ICE COLD
Coca-Cola
SOLD HERE
ST EACH OTHER,
TRUST YOU?
Swift's
ARROW
BORAX SOAP
ARROW
BORAX SOAP
MOXIE

Shuffle Along orchestra. Back row (l. to r.): Williams, Ricks, Jones, Smith, Hicks. Front row (l. to r.): Reeves, Yarborough, L. Johnson, Jeter, Still, H. Johnson, Blake (at piano), Carroll. Some members of the orchestra were not present for the photograph.

Mr. J. HUBERT BLAKE,

Dear Sir:---

We, the undersigned members of the Orchestra feel very greatful to you for the interest you took into our affair on last Sunday Eve. and wish to express our many thanks to you.

We know that words alone will not be the real sincere proof of our gratitude and that money such as we may be able to get together could not pay you for your valuable service, so we do hope that you may accept our diligence, efficiency and loyalty to you speak and voice our sentiments.

Yours most respectfully,

T. T. Ricks. S. W. Yearwood
W. H. Hicks Felix F. Weir
R. T. Smith Lorenzo Caldwel
Cal B. Jones. Clarence Harris
Geo. Reeves H. Lemar Jeter
Edgar O. Campbell Hall Johnson
Wm. G. Still

SHUFFLE ALONG
WITH
EUBIE BLAKE
and his
Shuffle Along Orchestra

Mr. Blake and his Orchestra are at your disposal to furnish you music for all occasions.

NO JOB TOO SMALL OR TOO LARGE

Write
EUBIE BLAKE
236 West 138th Street
Phone Aud. 1087 **New York City**

"To our dear friends"
Sincerely
(4) Harmony Kings
London
England
1926

Charlie Davis, the superlative dancer of *Shuffle Along*

Mattie Wilks, who performed for the Czars

Four Harmony Kings

U. S. Thompson (Slow Kid)

The pit band of *Shuffle Along* always drew comment because it played without using music, having committed the entire score to memory. *"We did that because it was expected of us,"* remembers Eubie. *"People didn't believe that black people could read music—they wanted to think that our ability was just natural talent."* Talent there was aplenty in the orchestra, but hardly raw or unschooled. Each member of the *Shuffle Along* orchestra was as skilled a musician as Blake; several had concert careers. Two were later prominent figures in the history of American music. Hall Johnson, the violist, was the founder of the Hall Johnson Chorale and a prolific composer of large-scale choral works. The oboist, William Grant Still, is considered the dean of black American composers; his *Afro-American Symphony* is a staple of the symphonic repertoire.

Whereas in American white musicals it has not been uncommon for relatively untrained performers to be successful, in this black musical a great number of performers were already trained and sophisticated beyond the usual scope of white musical comedy singers, dancers, and instrumentalists before being hired. Denied work in the white theater because of their color, here they found a job and a chance to show their considerable virtuosity—small wonder that the critics and public found the level of performance in *Shuffle Along* so much higher than what they were used to!

The list of performers who went on to later success is long and impressive; Josephine Baker, Florence Mills, and Paul Robeson are just a few examples. Robeson, the bass-baritone, had just finished Rutgers College and had begun studying law when William Hann (the same man who had headed Hann's Jubilee Singers, of which Noble Sissle had been a member as a boy) had to drop out temporarily of the Four Harmony Kings when his mother died. Robeson was put in to replace Hann as bass in the singing quartet during his absence, and when Hann returned to his post, Will Vodery, one of the orchestrators of *Shuffle Along* and choral master of Lew Leslie's *Plantation Revue*, took Robeson on to sing in the chorus in the Leslie show. Noble: *"Robeson has always felt this was the beginning of his singing career."*

Probably the most famous performer to emerge from *Shuffle Along* at the time was Florence Mills. Noble relates: *"We gave her her big chance, and she saved us*

Florence Mills

one of our biggest headaches. The first soubrette we had was Gertrude Saunders, for whom 'Daddy, Won't You Please Come Home' *and* 'I'm Craving for That Kind of Love' *had been written. She was the sensation of our show—stopped it cold every night. But like so many artists in show business who had become a sensation overnight, Gertrude, in spite of our efforts at persuasion, left the show, and we had just got started! She was our next-to-closing big smash. . . .*

"Florence and her husband, U. S. (Slow Kid) Thompson, were always together in the same shows. Slow Kid was a dancer, and they were both in the Keith circuit in an act called 'The Tennessee Ten.' *I only knew her slightly as the singer in a little gingham dress who made a sensation in* Swanee River *with her birdlike voice. The four of us ate together that night at our boarding house, and when Florence and Kid left the dining room, my wife Harriett said, 'Why don't you give Florence a chance to replace Gertrude?' I smiled and said, 'Why, she's a ballad singer. Gertrude's part calls for dancing and singing blues.' Harriett told me Florence was singing* 'I'm Craving for That Kind of Love' *at Baron Wilkins' nightclub, and at her insistence I went to see her without saying anything to my partners. The next night I told them we were saved, but Lyles, in his dry way, said, 'She* ought *to sing—she has legs like a canary.'*

"She was Dresden china, and she turned into a stick of dynamite." Florence Mills was hardly the earthy creature "I'm Craving for That Kind of Love" had been written for, but she gave to the part, by all accounts, an ingenuousness that added greatly to the ensemble. Noble Sissle has called her "*lovable*," and not many performers can project such a feeling on stage.

If we have been favored with a few recordings of Bert Williams, George Walker, and some of the other early figures of the Negro theater, we have not the luck to possess a single recording of Florence Mills. By the time she left *Shuffle Along* for the *Plantation Revue* and international stardom, it was already clear that her delicate constitution was being strained. On November 2, 1927, she died in the hospital of appendicitis. Her funeral was the occasion of the greatest outpouring of grief Harlem had ever known; more than 250,000 people lined the streets, many fainting as the cortege passed by. Only in her early thirties at her death, she was probably the most beloved performer of her race. Those of us who never heard her will never know what it was in that birdlike voice that endeared Florence Mills to so many and made her an enduring legend.

Florence Mills
-1927-

NASIB
STUDIO

The Gypsy Blues: **Florence Mills, Roger Matthews, and Lottie Gee**

I'm Craving for That Kind of Love

I'M WISHING AND FISHING
AND WANTING TO HOOK
A MAN KIND LIKE YOU FIND
IN A BOOK
I MEAN A MODERN ROMEO
I DO NOT WANT A PHONEO
HE MAY BE THE BABY
OF SOME VAMP, OH, BABE!
AT VAMPIN' AND LAMPIN'
I'M THE CHAMP.
AND IF I ONCE GET HIM
WHY, I'LL JUST SET HIM
BENEATH MY PARLOR LAMP, AND LET HIM

KISS ME, KISS ME,
KISS ME WITH HIS TEMPTING LIPS
SWEET AS HONEY DRIPS
PRESS ME, PRESS ME,
PRESS ME TO HIS LOVING BREAST
WHILE I GENTLY REST
BREATHE LOVE TENDER SIGHS
GAZE INTO HIS EYES
EYES THAT WILL JUST HYPNOTIZE
THEN I KNOW HE'LL
WHISPER, WHISPER,
WHISPER TO ME SOFT AND LOW
SOMETHING NICE, YOU KNOW.
HONEY, HONEY,
HONEY, WHEN THERE'S NO ONE NEAR
MY BABY DEAR WILL
HUDDLE ME
CUDDLE ME
SING TO ME
CLING TO ME
SPOON TO ME
CROON TO ME
SIGH TO ME
CRY TO ME
I'M CRAVING FOR THAT KIND OF LOVE.

The rewards of a successful show are many and varied, and Sissle and Blake received the benefits of large sheet-music royalties and other spin-offs through recordings, many of their own making. Sissle and Blake recorded for Pathé, Emerson, Regal, Victor, and other labels, sometimes using pseudonyms (a commonplace in the industry at that time), while many of the show's songs, especially "Gypsy Blues" and "I'm Just Wild about Harry," were recorded by well-known dance bands of the day. Eubie remembers Paul Whiteman with special fondness: *"Every time 'Harry' would die, 'Pops' would get Roy Bargy to make another arrangement."*

TWO SUPER-HITS

From the musical show of the year that is simply chockful of melodious tunes:

LOVE WILL FIND A WAY

GYPSY BLUES

Some sensational, syncopated selections from the seasons best bet.

NOBLE SISSLE and EUBIE BLAKE
Author and Composer

Not since the days of Williams and Walker has there been such a stupendous musical success. This show is being accorded a most overwhelming reception and at the rate it's going (it is in its seventh month at the Sixty-third Street Music Hall now) it should play to packed houses for at least another year before it goes on tour.

You can readily imagine what difficulty we had in selecting the two most popular numbers when you've undoubtedly heard of the unsurpassed excellency of them all.

Here they are — ***SHUFFLE ALONG'S*** extra special best.

LOVE WILL FIND A WAY AND GYPSY BLUES

These numbers are **NOT** a success.——They're a **CRAZE**

Hear PAUL WHITEMAN
and His Orchestra
Play
GYPSY Blues
THE FOX TROT HIT
From SHUFFLE ALONG
VICTOR RECORD No 18839
"DA-LITE" ELECTRIC DISPLAY CO. TOLEDO, OHIO.

Cort Theatre

48th Street, East of Broadway
New York
Direction of John Cort

Box Office Statement

Performance of Shuffle Along

Date Aug 13 1921

Weather Warm

NO. SOLD		PRICE	AMOUNT
	Box Seats	$3.50	
	Box Seats	3.00	
	Box Seats	2.50	
	Orchestra	3.00	
	Orchestra	2.50	
242	Orchestra	2.00	484.00
60	~~First Balcony~~	~~3.00~~	90.00
	First Balcony	2.50	
24	First Balcony	2.00	48 00
101	First Balcony	1.50	151.50
122	First Balcony	1.00	122 00
53	Second Balcony	1.00	53 00
83	Second Balcony	.75	62 25
25	Second Balcony	.50	12 50
	Admission	1.50	
	Admission	~~1.00~~	114 80
	Exchanges	2.50	
	Exchanges	2.00	
	Exchanges	1.50	
15	Exchanges	1.00	15 00
2	Exchanges	.75	1 50
3	Exchanges	.50	1 50

$1156.05

Treasurer of Theatre

Manager of Company

All too often the economics of theatrical production remain the carefully guarded secret of a show's producer. Fortunately, because Sissle and Blake were in effect co-producers of their show as well as creators and leading performers, we have the benefit of the financial data they have preserved in records of daily receipts, weekly balance sheets, and company salary lists. These data tell their own story.

The economics of *Shuffle Along* were simple enough. It was a show with eight principal beneficiaries: Miller, Lyles, Sissle, and Blake owned half of the show, while the other half was the joint property of Harry Cort, John Scholl, an associate of the Cort family; Al Mayer, the company manager; and the show's surprise "angel," the mysterious Gasthoffer.

With only an 1100-seat house to fill, a low salary scale, and reduced ticket prices (the scale for John Cort's own theater confirms this), *Shuffle Along* was able to meet its weekly expenses with a gross of just over $7500 a week; in time, with three companies touring the country, it would make its creators wealthy men.

No._____ Statement of Receipts and Expenditures of

Month	Day	Town or City	Share %	Performances	Gross	Co. Share
				Sunday Matinee		
				Sunday Evening		
				Monday Matinee		
May	22	63d Street Theatre		Monday Evening	839.20	
		53d Week		Tuesday Matinee		
	23	60/40		Tuesday Evening	1107.05	
	24			Wednesday Matinee	1177.85	
	"			Wednesday Evening	514.00	
				Thursday Matinee		
	25			Thursday Evening	1158.10	
				Friday Matinee		
	26			Friday Evening	1204.05	
	27			Saturday Matinee	673.55	
	"			Saturday Evening	980.80	
					7654.60	4592.76

Other Earnings:

Railroads		
Fines		
House Share, Co. Musicians		
Total Cash Receipts or Gross Earnings for Week		4592.76
Less Vouchers Paid in Cash, as per List		4576.22
Cash Balance for the Week Carried Down		
Add Unpaid Vouchers as per List		
~~Loss or~~ Earnings for Week		16.54

Summary of Earnings:

Net ~~Loss or~~ Earnings as Shown on Last Weeks Statement	8174.74	
Net ~~Loss or~~ Earnings on This Week's Statement	16.54	
Net Earnings for Season Ending This Week	8191.28	

I hereby certify the above statement is correct

.... Manager.

SHUFFLE ALONG Co. for Week Ending MAY 27 1922

	Vouchers Paid No.		Vouchers No.	Unpaid	Remarks
...ting					
...wspapers	1	124.11			
...s Billposting	2	69.24			
...er Advertising					
XXX Lunches	3	15.00			
XXX Photos	4	6.75			
...nt's Expense Press	5	10.40			
XXXX Expense Baum	6	2.65			
...ress and Freight Advance L.Gee Jun 3	7	150.00			MEMO.
...npany Salaries	8	3247.50			Due from No.2 4392.64
...re, House Musicians	9	379.50			Checks No 1 1360.95
...perty Department	10	6.25			Bank Balance 2437.69
...trical Department Calcium 13.50 Operator 34.50	11	48.00			8191.28
...penter Department					
...rdrobe Laundry 7.85 " 16.09 Shoes 12.00	12	35.94			Received A/c One Night Stand Rights 2500.00
...ce Expense					
...egrams and Telephone	13	2.85			
...alty %	14	76.54			
...me.Havestock	15	300.00			
...Lee Back salary	16	25.00			
...Y.Cal.Light Co	17	20.75			
...ent Uptown Office	18	55.00			
		4576.22			

EXAMINED AND FOUND CORRECT
Robeu Walker
Auditor

...r's Statement of Cash Receipts and Disbursements:

...er's Cash Balance From Last Week

...alance, This Week

...eceived from .... at ....

—Vouchers Unpaid—Paid This Week, $.. Week

" " " " " $.. "

" " " " " $.. "

" " " " " $.. "

...mitted to

" "

Cash balance carried to next week

John Cort's Enterprises

SALARY LIST

RECEIVED from the management of Shuffle Along Co. Company, the amount set opposite our respective names, in full payment and satisfaction of any and all claims which we have against said management, and we do hereby release the said management of any and all claims of whatsoever name and nature which we have against them to date.

Dated .... Week ending April 29/22 192 ......

No.	Name	Amount	No.	Name	Amount
1	Miller & Lyles	425.00	26	" M. Weaver	30.00
2	Sissle & Blake	425.00	27	" Jennie Day	30.00
3	Lottie Gee	150.00	28	" Lydia Webb	30.00
4	Eva Spencer	75.00	29	" Happy	30.00
5	Roger Mathews	75.00	30	" Ina Duncan	30.00
6	Harmony Kings Quartette	275.00	31	" M. Lewis	30.00
7	A. Porter	50.00	32	" M Odlum	30.00
8	J.H. Woodson	45.00	33	" Ruth Walker	30.00
9	E.H. Cooper	40.00	34	" Lulu Wilson	~~[illegible]~~
10	Snippy Mason	30.00	35	" H. Mitchell	30.00
11	Paul Floyd	55.00	36	" Goldie Cisco	30.00
12	Jeffroy & Wife	80.00	37	" H. Yarborough	30.00
13	Mattie Wilkes	60.00	38	" Emma Thomas	30.00
14	Davis & Williams	107.50	39	" Sally Irving	30.00
15	C.W. Hill	45.00	40	Mr. Ralph Bryson	40.00
16	Carl Johnston	50.00	41	" B. Andrews	30.00
17	Eva Taylor	45.00	42	" R.B. Johnson	30.00
18	Miss E.V. Nolan	35.00	43	" B. Lee	35.00
19	" B. Rickson	30.00	44	" Miles Williams	30.00
20	" A. Hall	30.00	45	" W. Shepherd	30.00
21	" M. Caldwell	30.00	46	" Billie Moore	30.00
22	" L. Williams	30.00	47	" H.L. Cort	200.00
23	" M. Brown	30.00	48	" Al Mayer	150.00
24	" A. Andrews	30.00	49	" W. Cripps	40.00
25	" Fanning	30.00	50	" R. Walker	25.00
					3307.50

John Cort's Enterprises

SALARY LIST

RECEIVED from the management of SHUFFLE ALONG CO...No 2 Company, the amount set opposite our respective names, in full payment and satisfaction of any and all claims which we have against said management, and we do hereby release the said management of any and all claims of whatsoever name and nature which we have against them to date.

Dated ______ Week ending April 22/22 192 ____

No.	Name	Amount
1	Lucille Hegeman	125.00
2	Mazoon sipp	125.00
3	Lew Peyton	100.00
4	Fred Bonny	75.00
5	Lena Roberts	75.00
6	Quintard Miller	60.00
7	James Burris	50.00
8	Thomas Woods	50.00
9	Theo McDonald	45.00
10	Al Watts	42.50
11	Claude Lawson	42.50
12	Fred Robinson	45.00
13	Roy Holland	40.00
14	Al.Baldwin	35.00
15	Archié Cross	30.00
16	C.Caldwell	30.00
17	James Jackson	30.00
18	C.Carpentier	30.00
19	Dan Small	30.00
20	Geo Shields	30.00
21	J.Dean	30.00
22	Sterling Grant	30.00
23	Mrs C.Lawson	45.00
24	Madiline Pearman	30.00
25	Ethel Taylor	30.00
26	Maude Ward	30.00
27	Barbara Perkins	30.00
28	Berenice Capers	30.00
29	Nettie Davis	30.00
30	Ethel Jones	30.00
31	Helen Deas	30.00
32	Byrdie Hall	30.00
33	Josephine Baker	30.00
34	Susye Brown	30.00
35	Carrie Edwards	30.00
36	Willimina Bernardo	30.00
37	Helen Dunmore	30.00
38	Barrington Carter	75.00
39	Lawrence Deas	75.00
40	Luckyth Roberts	125.00
41	Douglas Johnston	70.00
42	Al Legare	70.00
43	Jose Laverazzi	70.00
44	Francisco Tizol	70.00
45	Walter Porter	70.00
46	Carmela Jari	70.00
47	L.Daroe	70.00
48	H.D.Collins	100.00
49	J.H.Diehl	100.00
50	J.O'Hara	62.50
	Harry Cooke	62.50
	Thos Shea	62.50
		2780.00

Chorus girls in *Shuffle Along*; Josephine Baker is the sixth from the right (above) and the ninth from the right (below).

On the preceding page, in the salary lists, the name of Josephine Baker appears as a chorus girl, at thirty dollars a week.

Noble: *"We had turned her down when she tried out for us in Philadelphia because she was not yet sixteen. We had wanted to hire her but by law we couldn't. She was heartbroken."* In fact it appears that Josephine Baker was either fourteen or fifteen years old when she tried out for *Shuffle Along*. The daughter of an East St. Louis washerwoman, she had quit school to join the company.

"We produced a number-two company to play one-nighters through New England while we were still in New York. Word got back to us that a comedy chorus girl had joined the company after we had rehearsed it and sent it out on the road—it was Josephine. She had slipped out on the road to join that company because she thought we didn't like her or want to hire her. How glad we were to get her back."

Josephine Baker joined the number-one company in Boston in August 1922, clowning her way to stardom as the cross-eyed, out-of-step whirling dervish at the end of the chorus line. *"Every place we went, people buying tickets asked: 'Is the little chorus girl here who crosses her eyes?' In time she became the highest-paid chorus girl of her day and the most acclaimed. She had a wonderful disposition and kept us in stitches off the stage as well as on."*

SUSSMAN
MPLS.

SELWYN THEATRE
Miller & Lyles..........
All-Around the Wor
Musical Knock-Out.."
at the Selwyn Theatre

ssle & Blake and their
Company in their....
uffle Along" Now Playing
..... Boston.

SHUFFLE ALONG
MILLER · LYLES · SISSLE · BLAKE
THE HIT
OF THE SEASON
SELWYN · THE
MILLER AND LYLES
SISSLE AND BLAKE

Boston

After the triumphant New York run of 504 performances (one of the longest of its time), the *Shuffle Along* company decided to begin a national tour, against the advice of skeptics who were sure that, while it might do well in New York, the rest of the country would have trouble buying an all-black show. In late July 1922 producer Arch Selwyn offered his theater in Boston to the company for two weeks, on the condition that they vacate at the end of that time for the Shakespearean team of Sothern and Marlowe, who had already engaged the Selwyn.

When the box office opened in Boston, Sissle and Blake were amazed to find a practically all-black line for tickets. In New York mostly whites had attended the show. Upon questioning the ticket buyers, they found that in fact these people were primarily maids and chauffeurs, buying tickets for their employers. . . . Once again

The STEINERT Piano

Indispensable to

"Shuffle Along"

Wanted in London by Sissle and Blake

In extending our appreciation for the brilliant success of "Shuffle Along" on the occasion of our 100th performance in Boston tomorrow night, it gives us pleasure to recommend the wonderful playing qualities and brilliancy of tone of the Steinert Piano, which we feel has materially helped our success.

In a few weeks' time we are going from here to Chicago and then to London, England, which will be the first stop on our tour of the world.

We desire to have you securely crate and ship *two Steinert Pianos to accompany us,* such as we have been so satisfied with during our engagement here in Boston.

Sincerely yours,

Noble Lee Sissle
Eubie Blake

M. STEINERT & SONS

Steinert Hall 162 Boylston St.

Noble Sissle, Lottie Gee, Jack Dempsey, Aubrey Lyles, Eubie Blake, and Edith Spencer, who had replaced Florence Mills in New York

Shuffle Along was a sensation, running for fifteen weeks instead of the contracted two. This resulted in a lawsuit threat from Sothern and Marlowe, which finally ended the Boston run in November.

At the time Jack Dempsey, the boxing heavyweight world champion, was in Boston involved in a controversy concerning Harry Wills, considered by many the logical contender for the crown. Dempsey had wanted to fight Wills, his manager Tex Rickard refused to let him, and the rumor was about that Dempsey wouldn't fight Wills on racial grounds. One night after a *Shuffle Along* performance, Dempsey showed up backstage. "Can I talk to you fellows?" he addressed Sissle and Blake shyly. "People are saying that I won't fight Harry because he's black. I swear to you, and I want you to know, that's not true. I'll fight anybody. Tex just won't let me." When the troupe was to go out to do one of their many benefits, Dempsey asked if he could accompany them, and they all went off together.

As a publicity stunt, the manager of the Selwyn Theatre arranged a meeting of the *Shuffle Along* four with the colorful mayor of Boston, James Michael Curley. Miller demurred from the meeting, suspecting trouble, but Sissle, Blake, and Lyles, dressed in what they thought correct attire for the occasion, went to visit Curley. "Where's the Mayor?" asked the Mayor, disappointed, for the whole gimmick rested on the fact that *Shuffle Along*'s plot concerned a mayoralty contest. The other three made excuses for Miller and were photographed with Curley anyway. When the picture was printed in the papers and no trouble had occurred, Miller, on second thought, went down to City Hall by himself, where, as Mayor of Jimtown, he received the key to the city from the Mayor of Boston, a stunt that would be repeated with other mayors in other cities. (It is interesting to note that Curley would much later become theatrical material himself as Skeffington in *The Last Hurrah.*)

While rehearsing new songs one day at the Selwyn Theatre, Sissle and Blake tried out one that producer André Charlot liked so well that he bought it for his forthcoming London revue. The song, "You Were Meant for Me" (not to be confused with the later film song of the same title, by Nacio Herb Brown and Arthur Freed), was introduced in *London Calling* in 1923, the first song Noël Coward and Gertrude Lawrence ever sang together on the stage. It became an American hit when sung in *Charlot's Revue of 1924* by Miss Lawrence and Jack Buchanan.

(5)
VERSE YOU WERE MEANT FOR ME
IN THIS WORLD EACH ONE IS MEA
FOR SOME ONE

AND WHEN THOSE ONES MEET THEY
NEVER PART

OUR ACCIDENTAL MEETING ~~MAY~~
MAY SEEM QUITE UNREHEARSED
BUT DESTINY MARKED US
FROM THE FIRST

CHO
YOU WERE MEANT FOR ME
AND I WAS MEANT FOR YOU
TOGETHER ON LIFES TEMPESTUOUS
SEA
WE PADDLE OUR LOVE CANOE
WE'LL OFTEN DISAGREE
TRUE LOVERS ALWAYS DO
IT WONT MATTER YOU SEE
IF YOU LOVE ME
AND I'LL ALWAYS LOVE YOU

Sissle's manuscript

Gertrude Lawrence

If all the show is as good as "You were meant for me" which has been such a winner for me in the "Charlot Revue" then you have some show and I am going to enjoy myself tonight. Gertrude Lawrence

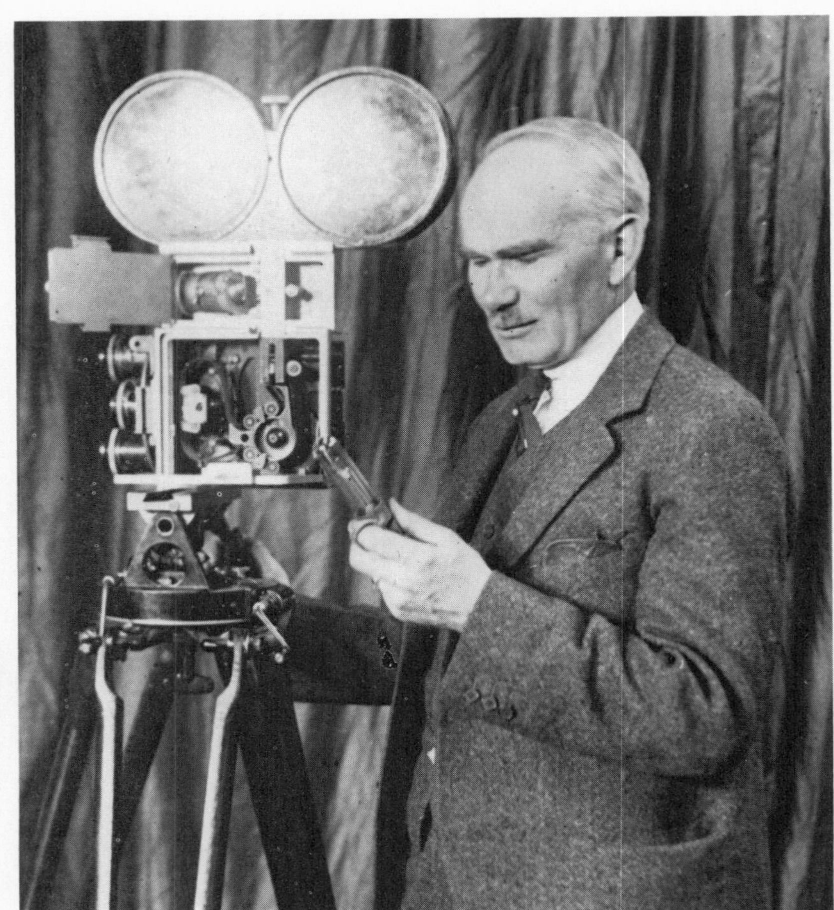

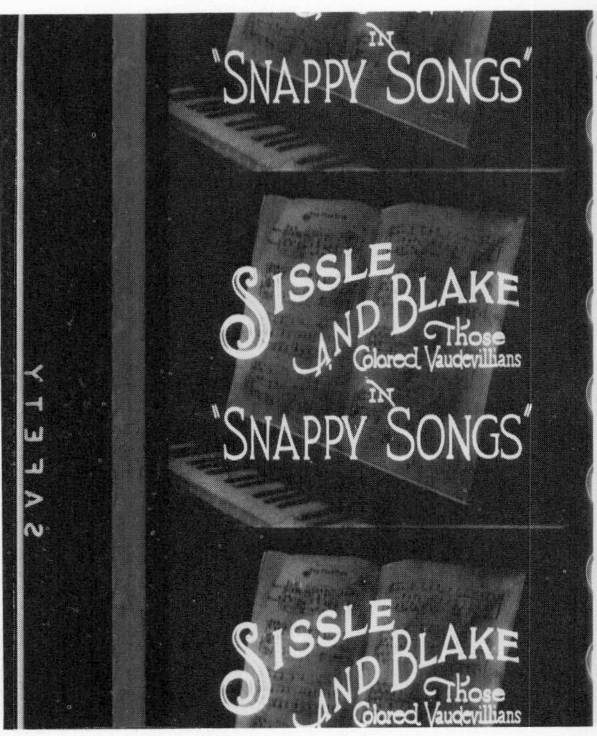

Lee DeForest

Film clips from DeForest's sound film, *Sissle and Blake's Snappy Songs, 1923*

Most people still believe that *The Jazz Singer* (1927) was the first sound film made in America; in fact, the talking picture, in various primitive forms, is almost as old as the silent film. The usual effort was toward synchronizing a phonograph record with a moving picture reel, with frequently hilarious results. Some attempts had been made to record directly on the film itself, but the usual problem was the conversion of sound into electricity and the reconversion of that electrical impulse back into sound (it must be remembered, by the way, that until about 1925 most phonograph records were made by purely acoustical means).

On June 25, 1920, working alone, Lee DeForest, the famed inventor of the vacuum-tube amplifier, patented the Phonofilm system, a method of recording sound synchronously on the film stock, that could, DeForest boasted, be understood, "every word, first time through." As well as making sound-on-film recordings of speeches by President Coolidge, Robert La Follette, and other notables, DeForest produced short films of a number of theatrical personalities. Sissle and Blake were the first black performers to participate in DeForest's historic undertaking, and *"although,"* as Eubie recalls, *"we didn't get as much money as Eddie Cantor did, still it was big money for those days."* Their film was first shown at New York's Rivoli Theatre in April 1923; surprisingly, these early efforts attracted little attention. The big silent-movie makers, still suspicious and afraid of talking pictures, thwarted DeForest's attempts at distribution and cost him his fortune.

Almost fifty years later, for perhaps the first time since 1923, the film was shown again publicly by Maurice Zouary (whose DeForest Collection is at The Library of Congress), on the Joe Franklin television show, with Sissle and Blake in the viewing audience. The film, featuring the two in animated performances of their own "Affectionate Dan" and the spiritual, "All God's Chillun Got Shoes," is a delightful memento of Sissle and Blake in their vaudeville days.

NOW BOOKING

A SENSATIONAL TWO-HOUR SHOW

DE FOREST PHONOFILMS VAUDEVILLE PICTURES

Films that actually talk and reproduce music without the use of a phonograph

Presenting

The greatest cast ever assembled on one program, including

WEBER and FIELDS
SISSLE and BLAKE
PUCK and WHITE
EDDIE CANTOR
PHIL BAKER
CONCHITA PIQUER

FOR PARTICULARS WRITE

DE FOREST PHONOFILMS, Inc. 1560 Broadway, New York City

OLYMPIC MATINEES WED. AND SAT.

EVERY EVENING

After Two Seasons in New York and 4 Months in Boston, Chicago puts its Stamp of Approval upon the Sensational Knockout

Shuffle Along

(THE SOCIETY FAD)

and Acclaims it the Greatest Musical Comedy Produced in Years.

Consensus of Opinion of Chicago Critics:

"As clean as a hound's dentistry—the fastest and most melodious musical comedy of several seasons."
—*Ashton Stevens–Herald Examiner*

"A splendid show—every ballad and ragtime swing is a gem."
—*Amy Leslie in the News*

"'Shuffle Along' is the Negro 'Lightnin'!"
—*Charles Collins in The Post*

"Any Caucasian producer who achieves an ensemble of such spirit and abandon would regard it as a triumph."
—*Sheppard Butler in The Tribune*

"Shuffle Along is a series of hits."
—*Journal*

"'Shuffle Along' is distinctly an innovation—it should become a theatrical institution."
—*Journal of Commerce*

"'Shuffle Along' is jazzy, tuneful—full of pep."—*American.*

TURN OVER—
OLYMPIC
TO-NIGHT AT 8:15 SHARP
"The SPEEDIEST. PEPPIEST. BREEZIEST. FUNNIEST. MUSICAL COMEDY CHICAGO HAS SEEN IN YEARS"—
EVERYBODY'S VERDICT
"SHUFFLE ALONG"

THE WORLD'S GREATEST DANCING SHOW

BY AND WITH

MILLER AND LYLES | SISSLE AND BLAKE

IT'S THE BIGGEST HIT IN TOWN

PRICES

NIGHTS. (EXCEPT SAT.) 50c TO $2.50

WED & SAT. MATINEES 50c TO $2.00

This Is the Original Long Run New York Cast—Production Intact and Goes Direct to London from Chicago for a Tour of the World.

Avis Blake

Chicago *Herald and Examiner*

In the Spotlight With ASHTON STEVENS

Our colored brothers at the Olympic, who sing and dance in "Shuffle Along," have eleven limousines and their own chauffeurs. It is easy come, easy go with them. "What's money for but to spend?" is their slogan, and they live up to it in union suits that cost $40.

* * *

The company was shuffling along in the small towns of Pennsylvania a couple of years ago when Al Mayer—a connection of the Guggenheims—saw a performance and said, "Come with me to Broadway." Not a scratch of the pen was heard, nor has been heard to date. "Al's" word "went" with the shufflers and is still going strong. Last season he and Harry Cort and the teams of Blake and Sissle and Miller and Lyles subdivided more than a quarter of a million dollars. And just before they came to Chicago Mr. Eubie Blake, the Paderewski of the production, bought himself a raccoon overcoat, taking the same almost off the shoulders of Mr. Jack Pickford, a competitor for the purchase.

* * *

The raccoon coat followed Mr. Blake to the Olympic by parcel post and was diverted in transit. That is, Mr. Aubrey Lyles got to the expensive parcel first. In the layers of Alice blue tissue paper that lined the box he substituted for the raccoon masterpiece an ancient and mangy garment that had been discarded by his chauffeur. And when this spurious package was delivered to Mr. Blake in his dressing room, there was an off-stage roar which is not written in the libretto. Mr. Blake's rightful raccoon coat had to be restored before the show could go on.

* * *

Mr. Lyles is not a frugal person, either. His waistcoat is attached to a platinum watch trimmed with diamonds that cost a thousand dollars. Mr. Mayer carries the only Ingersoll in the organization.

Eubie's comment:

"It's not true about the coat. Lyles never pulled that stunt. But it's a good story—print it anyway."

John Scholl, who had been one of the original backers of the show, asked Sissle and Blake to write a dozen songs for a new white show, *Elsie*, to add to music by the team of Carlo and Sanders. *Elsie* played Chicago during the run of *Shuffle Along*, and because the two shows were playing simultaneously Sissle and Blake were able to see *Elsie* only at a special performance arranged for them in Indianapolis.

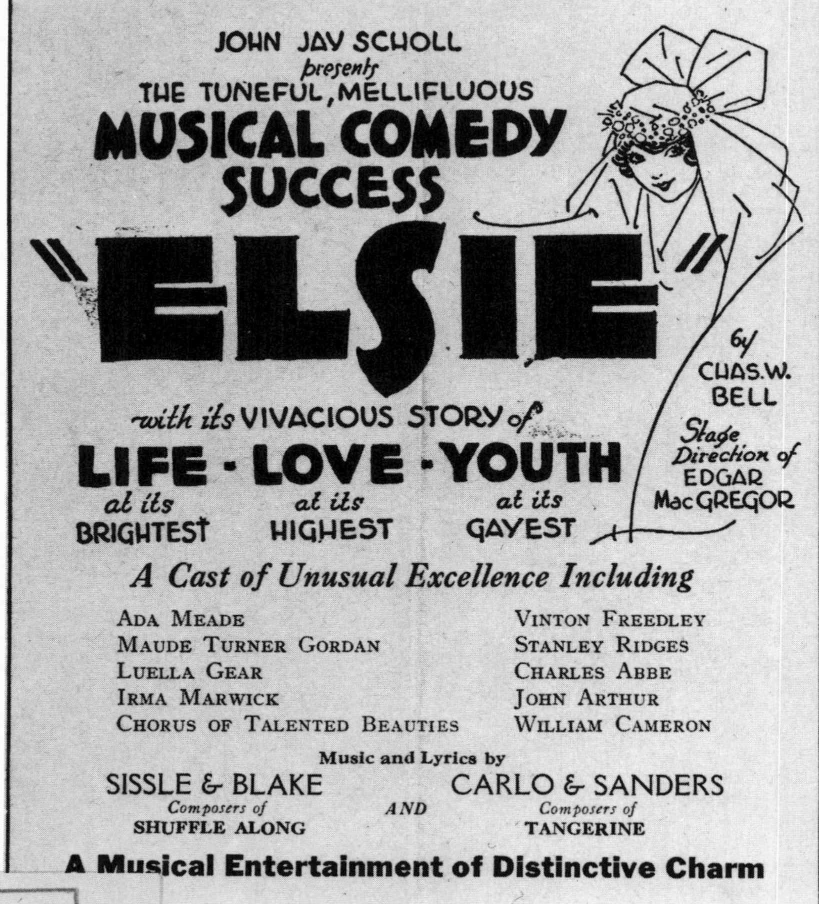

Everybody's Struttin' Now

John J. Scholl
Presents
the novel musical comedy
Elsie

Numbers by
SISSLE & BLAKE

Baby Buntin'	60
Elsie	60
Everybody's Struttin' Now	60
I Like to Walk With a Pal Like You	60
Jazzing Thunder Storming Dance	60
Jingle Step	60
Lovin' Chile	60
My Crinoline Girl	60
Regular Guy, A	60
Sand Flowers	60
Two Hearts in Tune	60
With You	60
Selection	1.00

Book by
CHAS W. BELL

Stage Direction
EDGAR
MACGREGOR

Lyrics and Music by
NOBLE
SISSLE
&
EUBIE
BLAKE
AND MONTE
CARLO
&
ALMA
SANDERS

OPERATIC EDITION

M. Witmark & Sons
New York

PRINTED IN U. S. A.

Freddie Washington

Luella Gear was advanced toward stardom by the show; it was during the run of *Elsie* that Vinton Freedley, also of the cast, met Mrs. Freedley. Other than that *Elsie* was, by most critical accounts, unremarkable, except for some fine songs by Sissle and Blake.

The showgirls were to Noble *"the heart of* Shuffle Along," and its life also. Besides Josephine Baker, several went on to further careers. Freddie Washington became famous as an exotic dancer and as lead actress in *Imitation of Life*. Elida Webb became a choreographer and director of Broadway musicals and floor shows, black and white. Katherine Yarborough went to study opera abroad and was apparently the first black artist to appear with a white opera company (in *Aida*, Chicago, 1933).

APEDA
N.Y. 34.

Freddie Washington

Ruth Walker

Dorothy Irving

Bernice Rickson

Elida Webb

Marion Gee

Jean Kane

Mae Fanning

Eunice Yancye

Katherine Yarborough

New York . . . fourteen months.
Chicago . . . fifteen weeks.
Boston . . . fifteen weeks.

Then Milwaukee, Des Moines, Peoria, Indianapolis, St. Louis, Toledo, Grand Rapids, Detroit, Buffalo, Rochester, Philadelphia, Atlantic City—all across America until the summer of 1923, playing white theaters to mixed audiences, *Shuffle Along* broke ground Williams and Walker had never tested.

What *Shuffle Along* meant, as a human experience to all the company, was the opening of doors that had been tightly closed to most of them. From this distance it is probably impossible to gauge the enormous impact the show had on the American musical theater on all levels, but it was certainly the first and most telling example of Negro influence on American show business at large.

The jazz dancing introduced in *Shuffle Along* had an immediate effect on white shows. Florenz Ziegfeld and George White opened special studios and hired show-girls from *Shuffle Along* to teach the white girls the jazz dance steps. There was seldom a night that the *Shuffle Along* orchestra, or Sissle and Blake as a duo, were not hired to entertain after the show in the homes of the rich.

The show opened doors to further efforts by black writers, including James P. Johnson (*Runnin' Wild, Keep Shufflin*), his protégé Thomas W. "Fats" Waller (*Hot Chocolates*), Andy Razaf, Maceo Pinkard (*Liza*), Creamer and Layton, Luckey Roberts, and Donald Heyward. A few of their shows ran two hundred performances, many of them much less—but all of them were training ground and exposure for a whole generation of black performers, many of whom, like Ethel Waters, are still known and loved today. It can be said that the renaissance of the black performer in the twenties is directly traceable to the success of *Shuffle Along*.

Perhaps its most pervasive (though least acknowledged) influence has been felt in American popular music. One only has to listen to a few minutes of any Broadway show music written before, then after *Shuffle Along*, to sense the emergence of something faster-paced, more syncopated, more American. From it the explosion of the black American musical style was to fan out in all directions beyond Broadway to permeate the spirit of the Jazz Age.

Helen Mitchell

ST. AGNES CHAPTER OF ST. AUGUSTINES EPISCOPAL CHURCH

MRS. WM. NOTTINGHAM, Pres.

PRESENTS

Prof. EUBIE BLAKE

AND HIS WORLD FAMED

"SHUFFLE ALONG" ORCHESTRA

......IN A. ....

MONSTER BENEFIT

Friday Evening, August 17th, 1923

WALTZ DREAM ACADEMY, ARCTIC AVE., NEAR OHIO

DANCING 9 to 2

Admission, = = 75 Cents

Velvet
THE SMOOTHEST
SMOKING TOBACCO
PARIS
GARTERS
No metal
can touch you

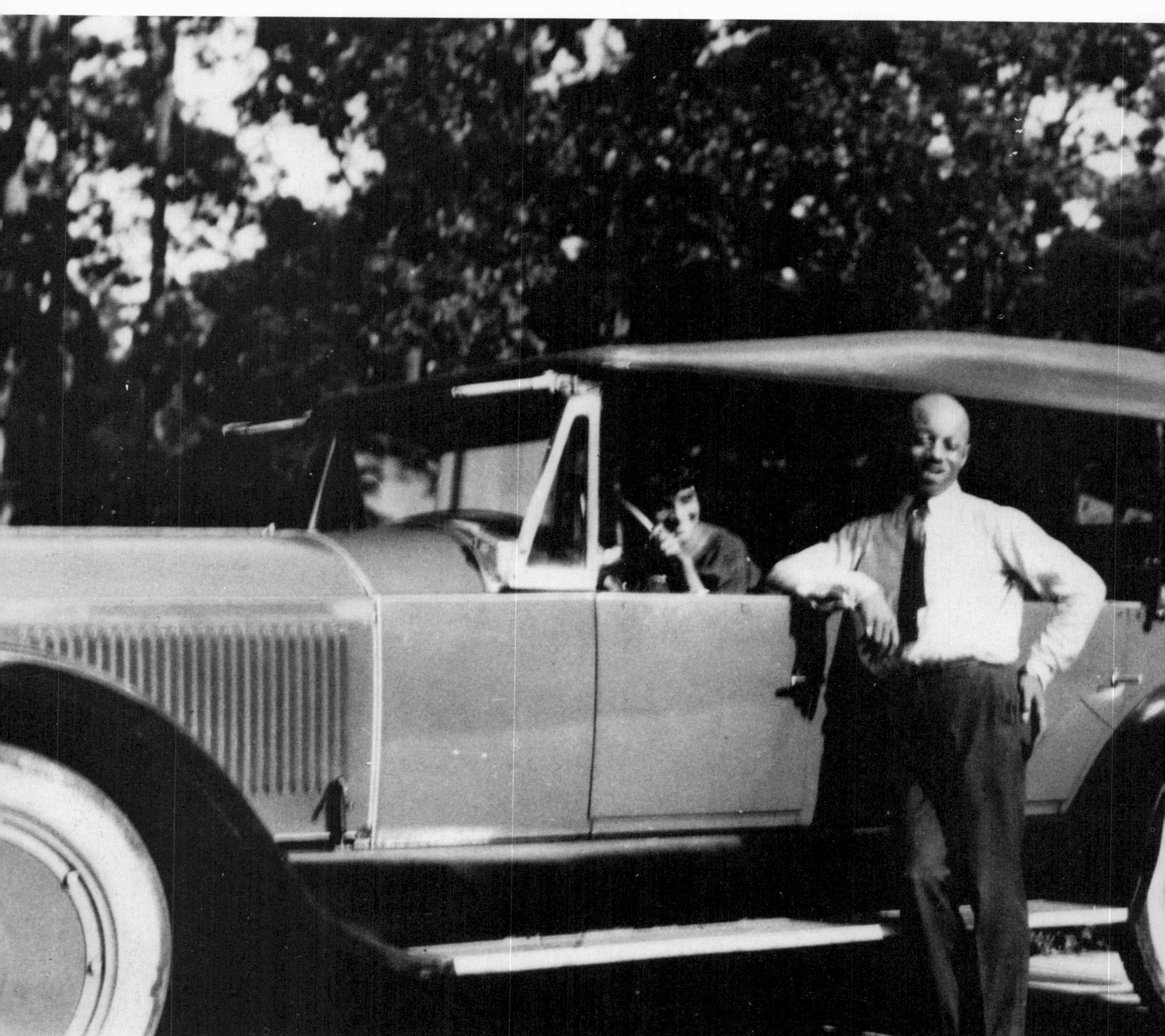

Eubie with his new Paige; Avis at wheel

Summer 1923

Eubie with Ivan Harold Browning

The summer of 1923 had given the members of the *Shuffle Along* company their first vacation since the show's opening. They had achieved a significant breakthrough and fulfilled what was for many of them the great dream of their lives.

Yet, underneath the general sense of well-being, there were restlessness and differences of opinion on what should come next. While Blake and Lyles enjoyed their good times to full measure, Sissle kept pounding at Miller to finish the book

Noble, at the corner of 138th Street and Seventh Avenue, New York. Blake's house is down the street.

of a new show he was projecting for the company. Miller kept his own counsel. While the four had shared equally in the profits of the show, Sissle and Blake had garnered the lion's share of the acclaim. Their songs were bringing in royalties; they were the successful recording artists; they were the ones who performed at the private parties, while Miller and Lyles felt overshadowed and perhaps a little resentful of the other team's better fortunes.

Finally, a rift came when Miller told the two that he and Lyles had signed a contract with producer George White to present their own show in the fall of 1923. With them they took half of the *Shuffle Along* company to produce what was to become *Runnin' Wild*. While the separation was in one sense a cruel blow to the ensemble, in another sense it afforded an opportunity to form two companies out of one—thus creating twice as many jobs for black performers.

Miller and Lyles and Sissle and Blake had constituted a well-balanced team: while Miller and Lyles provided the kind of ethnic humor that was to prove a staple in American theater for so many years afterward, Sissle and Blake had provided the class, elegance, and refinement of detail that had lifted the show out of the minstrel category. Without the comedy team, Sissle and Blake were to strike out in a different direction.

Al Mayer had stayed with *Shuffle Along*, lending his good sense and vast experience. The show was still Sissle and Blake's property, and in August 1923 they

In Harlem

would take it back on the road to play to even larger audiences than on their earlier tour. Meanwhile, through their newly formed and vast society connections, the pair gained access to the powerful producers B. C. Whitney and Abraham Lincoln Erlanger, once the czar of Broadway. Enlisting the aid of comedian Lew Payton to help on the book, Sissle and Blake began the creation of a new musical show, *In Bamville*, writing and rehearsing the show at the same time they were still performing *Shuffle Along* eight to ten times a week. With Whitney as producer, *In Bamville* opened at the Lyceum Theatre, Rochester, New York, on March 10, 1924, less than two months after the final closing of the old show.

MOST GORGEOUS, MOST STUPENDOUS
MUSIC PRODUCTION EVER!
"WHEN IT COMES TO SHUFFLIN' FEET
THESE CHOCOLATE DANDIES CAN'T BE BEAT."

4 HARMONY KINGS

SISSLE
AND
BLAKE
SYMPHONY
ORCHESTRA

METROPOLITAN THEATRE

ST. PAUL, MINNESOTA

Week of **MARCH 1st**

Matinees Wednesday and Saturday

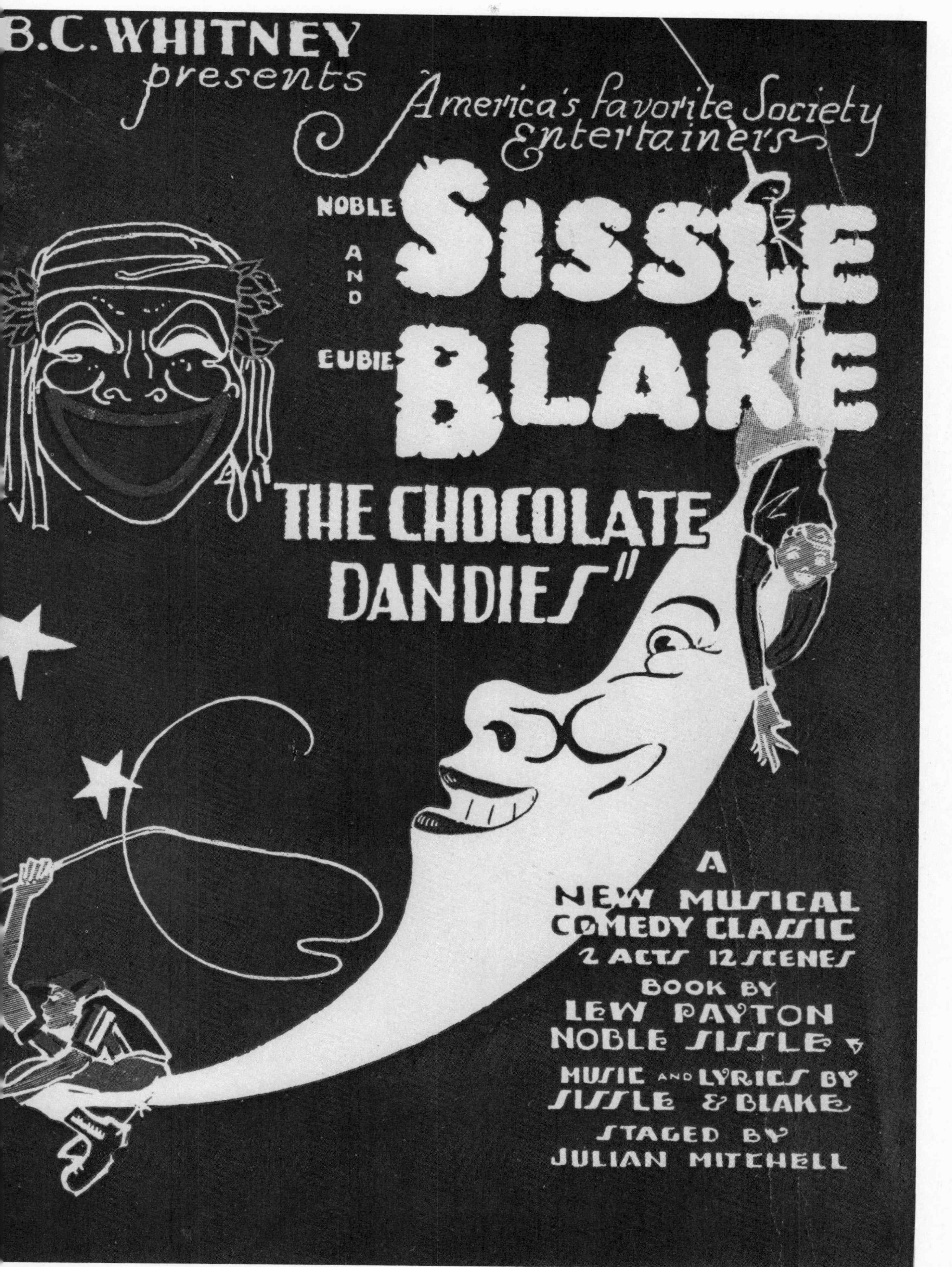
B.C. WHITNEY
presents
America's favorite Society Entertainers
NOBLE SISSLE
AND
EUBIE BLAKE
"THE CHOCOLATE DANDIES"
A
NEW MUSICAL
COMEDY CLASSIC
2 ACTS 12 SCENES
BOOK BY
LEW PAYTON
NOBLE SISSLE
MUSIC AND LYRICS BY
SISSLE & BLAKE
STAGED BY
JULIAN MITCHELL

J. Mardo Brown and the Bamville Opera House Band

"Last day at the Bamville Fair and Races. A drum rolls offstage and there comes the crash of a band coming down the street.

"Then comes quick action! Windows fly up, heads pop out, clerks, bankers, deacons, barbers come out of stores and shops, yelling and waving hands, following the band. The band then stands in the middle of the street in concert formation. The whole company assembles onstage and sings 'Have a Good Time Everybody.' "

Have a Good Time Everybody

HAVE A GOOD TIME EVERYBODY
LET'S ENJOY OURSELVES
HAVE A GOOD TIME EVERYBODY
LAY YOUR TROUBLES ON THE SHELVES
LAUGH TILL YOUR SIDES ARE SHAKIN'
KICK YOUR HEELS UP MIGHTY HIGH

EAT DRINK AND BE MERRY
FOR TOMORROW YOU MAY DIE
HAVE A GOOD TIME EVERYBODY
CAUSE I'M FEELING MIGHTY FINE
HAVE A GOODY GOODY GOODY GOOD
HAVE A GOODY GOODY GOOD GOOD TIME.

(This, and the subsequent excerpts, are from the script of *The Chocolate Dandies* by Noble Sissle and Lew Payton.)

The Jazzy Jassamines

Their old friend and star dancer, Charlie Davis, choreographed the new show. Julian Mitchell was brought in, however, at Sissle's behest, to give it "the Broadway touch." Mitchell, who had staged for Ziegfeld, was one of the most respected directors in the business, and he could be counted on to give *In Bamville* all the polish one could hope for. (Visual polish, that is: Mitchell was reportedly so deaf at the time that the only way he could hear the musical numbers during rehearsals was to jam his ear up against the piano.) With its lavish sets, elaborate costumes, and a cast of 125, *In Bamville* strove for a level of opulence equal to the gala presentations of Ziegfeld and George White. Sissle and Blake had been hugely successful with *Shuffle Along*, and they finally felt able to put on the show they had always wanted to write. *In Bamville* would be that show.

Their week in Rochester had gone well, and the *In Bamville* company traveled immediately to Pittsburgh. Within a week the company experienced a profound shock: Al Mayer, who had been ill with cancer for some time, expired at the age of forty-five. Sissle and Blake rushed back to New York by midnight train for the funeral. They had lost an old friend, but also they had lost their manager, and

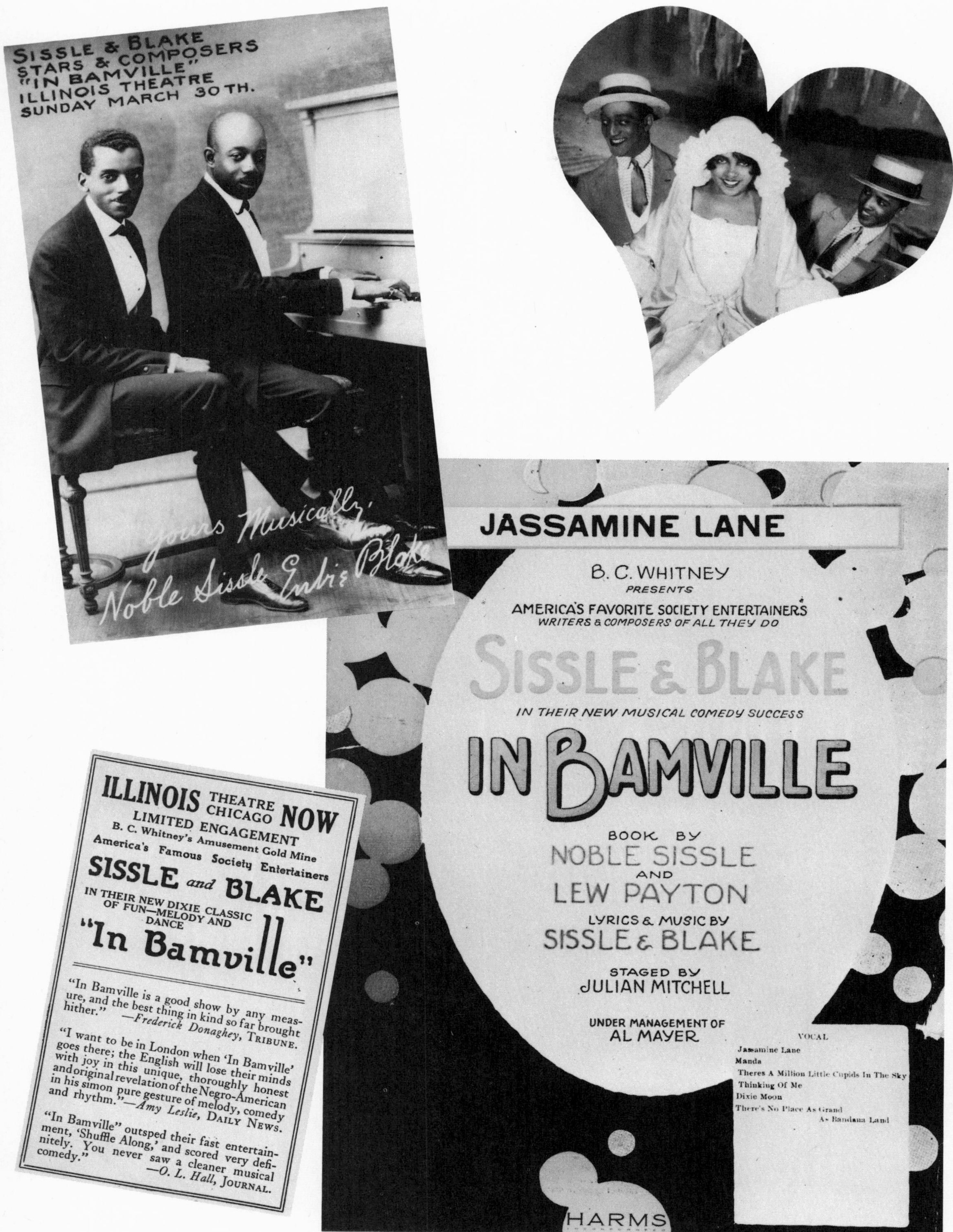

SISSLE & BLAKE
STARS & COMPOSERS
"IN BAMVILLE"
ILLINOIS THEATRE
SUNDAY MARCH 30TH.
Yours Musically
Noble Sissle Eubie Blake
JASSAMINE LANE
B. C. WHITNEY
PRESENTS
AMERICA'S FAVORITE SOCIETY ENTERTAINERS
WRITERS & COMPOSERS OF ALL THEY DO
SISSLE & BLAKE
IN THEIR NEW MUSICAL COMEDY SUCCESS
IN BAMVILLE
BOOK BY
NOBLE SISSLE
AND
LEW PAYTON
LYRICS & MUSIC BY
SISSLE & BLAKE
STAGED BY
JULIAN MITCHELL
UNDER MANAGEMENT OF
AL MAYER
VOCAL
Jassamine Lane
Manda
Theres A Million Little Cupids In The Sky
Thinking Of Me
Dixie Moon
There's No Place As Grand As Bandana Land
HARMS

ILLINOIS THEATRE CHICAGO **NOW**

LIMITED ENGAGEMENT

B. C. Whitney's Amusement Gold Mine

America's Famous Society Entertainers

SISSLE *and* **BLAKE**

IN THEIR NEW DIXIE CLASSIC OF FUN—MELODY AND DANCE

"In Bamville"

"In Bamville is a good show by any measure, and the best thing in kind so far brought hither." —*Frederick Donaghey*, TRIBUNE.

"I want to be in London when 'In Bamville' goes there; the English will lose their minds with joy in this unique, thoroughly honest and original revelation of the Negro-American in his simon pure gesture of melody, comedy and rhythm."—*Amy Leslie*, DAILY NEWS.

"In Bamville" outsped their fast entertainment, 'Shuffle Along,' and scored very definitely. You never saw a cleaner musical comedy." —*O. L. Hall*, JOURNAL.

there was to be considerable difficulty in finding a new one. Finally the Erlanger office appointed Jack Yorke, and the show went on to Detroit, toured twenty-four weeks on the road, experiencing financial difficulties, and, renamed *The Chocolate Dandies*, opened in New York on September 1, 1924.

If *Shuffle Along* had been folk-comedy interlaced with vaudeville, *The Chocolate Dandies* was pure fantasy. Most of the plot happens during a dream in a never-never land peopled by some very earthy characters. The setting is a Southern plantation town constructed totally out of thin air: "Bamville" is a Negro folk expression for a place-name roughly equivalent to "Podunk," and this particular Bamville is a structured society of barbers, bankers, plantation owners, deacons, clerks, even "town flappers." In the center of the town are the bank and the Bamville Opera House. But the hub of Bamville's entire economy and activity is the racetrack, and here the owners of the horses can be found, merrily fixing races, doping horses, and arranging bets.

Mose Washington (Lew Payton), the owner of the horse Dumb Luck, falls asleep before the race and dreams he has won a huge amount of money. In his dream Mose becomes bank president and the most respected member of Bamville. Fantastic musical-comedy confusion occurs during his tenure, and there is a run on the bank. During the madcap dénouement, Mose wakes up to find that he has not won the horse race after all. It has been won by Dan Jackson (Ivan Harold Browning), the owner of Rarin'-to-Go, who gets to marry Angeline (Lottie Gee), the daughter of Mr. Hez Brown (William Grundy), who is the manager of the Bamville Fair, which is in its last day at the opening of the play. Angeline and her beau are, depending on which script one reads, married either on the stage of the Bamville Opera House or up in Chocolate Land, among a "million little cupids," and go off to live happily ever after in Jassamine Lane. Hardly a searching "war drama" (see page 175), but *The Chocolate Dandies* nonetheless shows off the foibles of the American Dream through the prism of a black show gently laughing at itself, and this is a highly ambitious undertaking on any scale.

The *In Bamville* baseball team outing, Boston, 1924. "*The Van and Schenck team killed us.*"

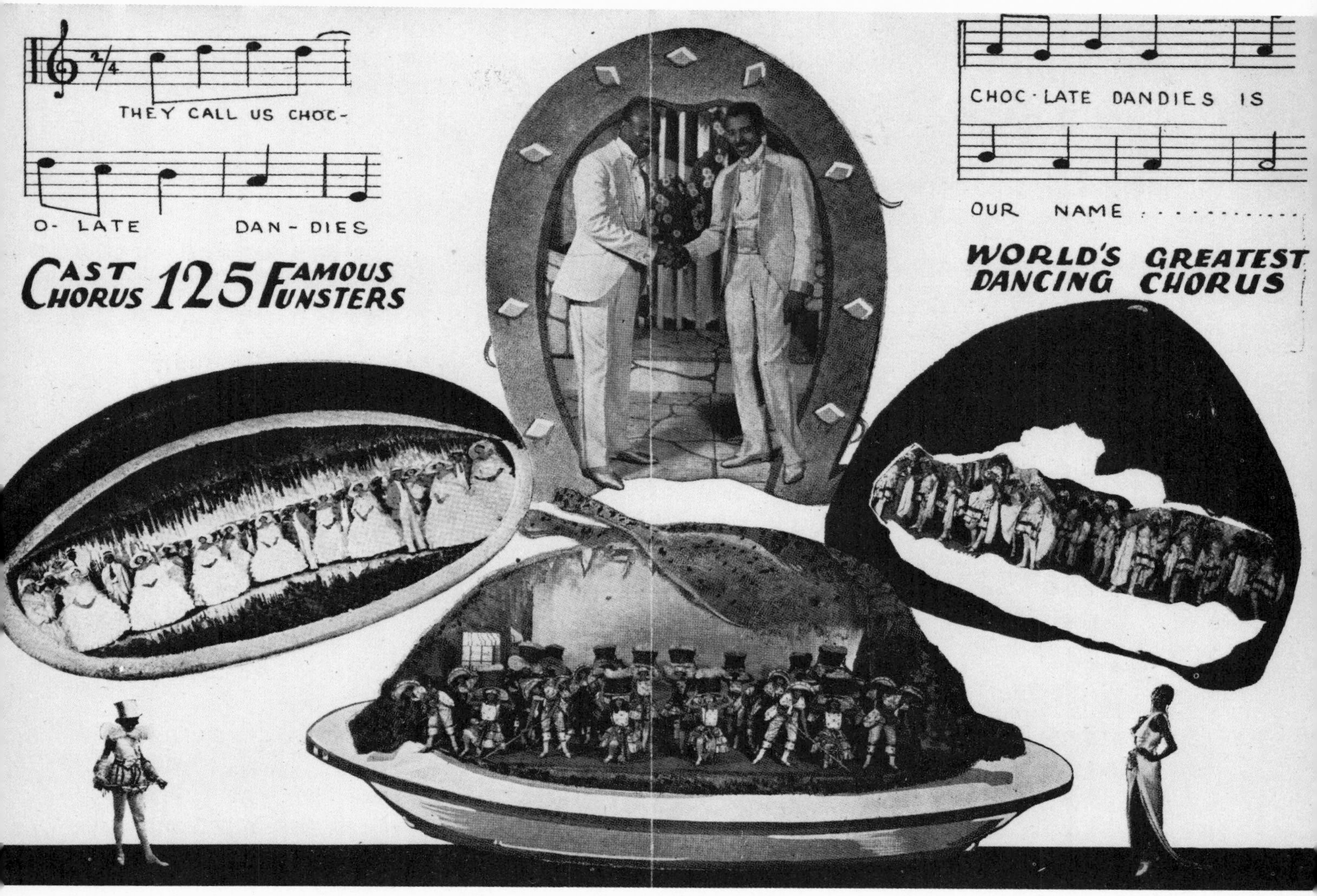

THEY CALL US CHOC-

O- LATE DAN - DIES

CAST CHORUS 125 FAMOUS FUNSTERS

CHOC-LATE DANDIES IS

OUR NAME

WORLD'S GREATEST DANCING CHORUS

At the station

Sons of Old Black Joe

THOUGH WE'RE A DUSKY HUE LET US SAY TO YOU
WE'RE PROUD OF OUR COMPLEXION
WE BLUSH WITHOUT DETECTION
BUT HOW SERIOUSLY SURPRISED YOU'LL BE
WHEN WE TELL YOU 'BOUT OUR PEDIGREE.

NEW AMSTERDAM THEATRE
NEXT SUNDAY AT 2.15 AND 8.15
B. F. KEITH'S
CELEBRATED SUNDAY CONCERTS
By Arrangement With Erlanger, Dillingham & Ziegfeld

Popular Price

Matinees— 25c to $1.00

Nights— $1 to $2.50

★ ★ ★

Same Superb Keith Show Afternoon and Evening

Twice — Sunday, October 26 — Twice

SMASHING BILL OF SENSATIONALLY SUCCESSFUL STARS

MADAME SOPHIE TUCKER & CO.
In New Songs and Comedy

SISSLE & BLAKE
Stars of "CHOCOLATE DANDIES"

BOBBY O'NEIL & 4 QUEENS

RATH BROTHERS

KLEIN BROTHERS

WILLIAM J. KENNEDY

ELMER CLEVE

TORINO & COMPANY

OTHERS

THE CREAM OF CURRENT SHOWS ASSEMBLED AT THE NEW AMSTERDAM

Sissle and Blake often shared Sunday night bills with their benefactress, Sophie Tucker, who had started them on their career with "It's All Your Fault."

FOR WE'RE THE SONS OF OLD BLACK JOE
AND WE WANT YOU TO KNOW THAT WE'RE PROUD OF
OUR DEAR DADS
AND THOUGH HIS HEAD IS BENDING LOW
WHY TO US HE'S GROWING DEARER AS THE YEARS COME AND GO
HE'LL NEVER BE FORGOTTEN LONG AS FIELDS OF COTTON DOWN
IN SUNNY DIXIE GROW
THAT'S WHY WE WANT THE WHOLE WORLD TO KNOW
THAT WE'RE THE SONS OF OLD BLACK JOE.

The Jockey's Life for Mine

FOR JUST TO SIT ASTRADDLE OF MY LITTLE SADDLE
WITH MY WHIP READY TO SWING
RIGHT AND LEFT AGLANCING AS MY HORSE IS PRANCING
TILL THE BARRIER THEY SPRING
IT GOES! WE'RE OFF!
AND THEN TO TAKE THE LEAD AND HOLD IT
DOWN THE HOMESTRETCH TO THE FINISH LINE
THE THRILLS OF CROWDS ACHEERING
AS THE WIRE I'M NEARING
MAKES THE JOCKEY'S LIFE FOR MINE.

A feature of *The Chocolate Dandies* that elicited much comment was the staged race, on a treadmill, between three actual live horses. "*They were a lot of trouble,*" Eubie remembers.

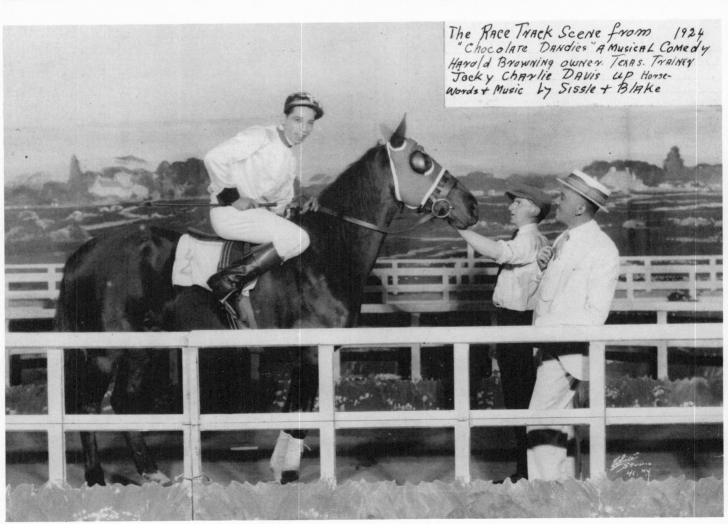

The Race Track Scene from 1924 "Chocolate Dandies" A Musical Comedy Harold Browning owner. Texas. Trainer Jocky Charlie Davis up Horse- Words + Music by Sissle + Blake

White Studio
27.

To Dear Little Aves with
a Sweet Disposition
and wonderful personality
From Valada Snow
In Bamville 1924
White Studio NY

(Patter)

OUR ENTRY'S PAID AND WE'VE BEEN WEIGHED
AND OUR VALETS ARE STRAPPING THE SADDLES
AT OUR MOUNTS WE KNOW, AT THE BUGLE'S BLOW
TO THE PADDOCK WE'LL ALL SKEDADDLE
WE'LL MOUNT OUR STEED AND INSTRUCTIONS HEED
AND WHEN THE ESCORTS LEAD 'FORE THE JUDGES
WE'LL TAKE THAT CHANCE OUR MOUNTS TO PRANCE
THOUGH THEY REAR AND KICK THEY'LL NEVER BUDGE US

NEW YORK *TRIBUNE* REVIEW, SEPTEMBER 2, 1924

'Chocolate Dandies,' Colored Show, Better Than 'Shuffle Along'

New Sissle and Blake Musical Melange Full of Snappy Tunes, Clean Comedy and Excellent Dancing

If "Shuffle Along" set New York's feet dancing to a dozen jazz hits, "The Chocolate Dandies," Sissle and Blake's latest contribution to Broadway musical melange of the negro variety, will go still further. New York never has seen a colored show to compare with the rip-roaring revue which the dusky Van and Schenck brought to the Colonial Theater last night. With the thermometer soaring upward and the big company of nearly 100 singers and dancers working as though they just had to exercise or freeze, the new show sped along without an interruption in its pace.

If the songs of "Shuffle Along" were hummed all over this country and

TO THE POST WE'LL TROT AND WHEN OUR PLACE WE'VE GOT
THE STARTER WILL BEGIN TO YELL AND HOLLER
AND AS THE CROWD GROWS STILL OUR BLOOD RUNS CHILL
AND IT WILL SEEM AS THOUGH OUR HEARTS WERE 'BOUT TO SWOLLER
BUT THOUGH THE WAIT IS TENSE AND THE STRAIN IMMENSE
AND THE DANGERS OF THE TRACK ARE MANY
YET, FOR ANOTHER GAME THAT WE'D LOVE THE SAME,
REALLY, WE DON'T THINK THERE IS ANY.

played abroad, "Slave of Love," the melody theme piece, should prove even more popular, and such numbers as "D-i-x-i-e," "Manda," the lovely "Thinking of Me," and "Jassamine Lane" will score with the man who whistles as he goes along. Eubie Blake, with his dexterous fingers, has turned out melodies which fit every sort of theme and which will keep dancing feet stepping for a year to come.

"The Chocolate Dandies" was far and away ahead of "Shuffle Along" in every respect, and despite the fact that the production was done in the most elaborate fashion as to costumes and sets, B. C. Whitney, the producer, wisely kept all of the native humor and clever touches in the new production, which were responsible for the success of the other piece.

We have rarely seen any company work as hard as does the happy ensemble at the Colonial. To begin with, even the orchestra, directed by Blake, uses no sheet music, knowing every quirk of the score by heart. From the very first scene, when Amanda Randolph, with a gorgeous voice, sang "Mammy's Choc'late Cullud Chile" until a remarkable cornetist played an encore to the finale, the show traveled at breakneck pace.

While the show lacks a Florence Mills, it has a comedian in Johnny Hudgins that is the nearest thing to Bert Williams we ever saw. The show was staged by Julian Mitchell, of many Broadway productions, and the chorus did everything from acrobatics to ensemble work which compares well with the precision of John Tiller's minions. There is plenty of good, clean comedy, good dancing, remarkable music and more pep in two hours than any show has brought to this town in many, many months.

M. V. O'C.

Noble Sissle and Russell Smith

John Alexander

DOBBY HICKS (Noble Sissle):

There's positively no way for you to lose, absolutely impossible; so brace up, poke out your chest, don't be a quitter! I told you to put your money on Jump Steady and you can bet your last dollar. You simply can't lose. I'm telling you to go hook, line, and sinker on this because he's a fifty-to-one shot, and now is your chance to make a killing. Remember what Shakespeare said, "Where there's a will, there's a way."

JOHNNIE WISE (Russell Smith): I've got the will, but if you keep relieving me this way I ain't gonna weigh so much. . . .

DOBBY: Now listen, you've just got a few more minutes. You'd better let me lay fifty dollars more on Jump Steady. Come on now and you'll be the richest man at this racetrack tomorrow.

JOHNNIE: Tomorrow? Today is the last day of the races.

DOBBY: Oh, don't get technical. Give me the money.

(JOHNNIE gives him the money and DOBBY goes over to the betting booth, switches the fifty, and lays a dollar bet on Jump Steady. The bookie marks down "One" on the slip and DOBBY hands it back to JOHNNIE, who looks at the "One" and says:)

JOHNNIE: Hey—I gave you fifty dollars and you only bet one.

DOBBY: Say—don't be dense. How much is Jump Steady quoted at?

JOHNNIE: Fifty to one!

DOBBY: That means for every one there's fifty.

JOHNNIE: Yes.

DOBBY: How many fifties did you give me?

JOHNNIE: One.

DOBBY: And there's the one, ain't it?

Speedy Comedy

"The Chocolate Dandies" Is a Dancing Carnival.

COLONIAL—"The Chocolate Dandies," a musical comedy; book by Noble Sissle and Lew Payton, music and lyrics by Sissle and Blake, produced by Bert C. Whitney.

THE CAST.

Sissle and Blake, Johnny Hudgins, Lew Payton, Lottie Gee, Four Harmony Kings, Josephine Baker, Valada Snow, Mildred Smallwood and Inez Clough.

Not just another war drama. Nothing of the tedious, flag waving and cheering marking earlier efforts at war plays. A story of what the war did with human feelings. A tale of man turned primitive, friend against friend, thoughtless love-making, the elemental let loose. Consequently, decidedly serious, but decidedly worth while.

—H. C.

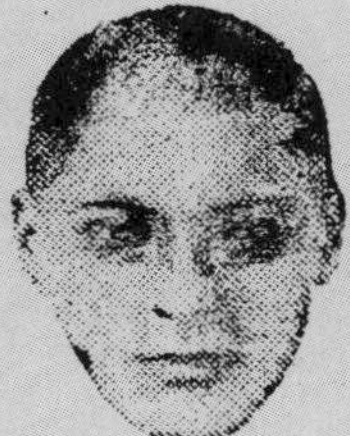

Ralph Forbes.

New York *Mirror*, Sept. 2, 1924

Valada Snow, one of the singing stars of the show, was an immensely talented girl, able to play every instrument of the orchestra well. She possessed a form of absolute pitch which sounds impossible to believe: pitch memory within the space of a few frequencies.

Eubie Blake always used an A-440 tuning fork for his orchestral tune-ups. One day on the train Valada heard him strike the fork and said, "Mr. Blake, your tuning fork's flat." Blake looked at her incredulously—how can a tuning fork be flat? "I say your tuning fork's flat," she insisted.

At the next town Blake grabbed Valada by the arm and ran off to the nearest music shop. The music dealer listened to the story and got a tuning fork off his shelf, struck the two forks together on his counter, and winced. Then he struck one, then the other. Finally he took Blake's fork and sighted down its side. "She's right," he said; "it's a tiny bit bent." Evidently Blake's tuning fork, jostling about in his metal trunk, had gotten slightly out of true, but the difference in pitch could only have been extremely slight.

Johnny Hudgins, the dancer, who worked with Lew Payton in the show, had a phenomenal memory. Johnny, known in his heyday as "The Wow Wow Man," could not read or write, but he made up for it. Whenever a review appeared of a show he was in, he would buy a paper, accost a passerby, and ask him if he found his name in it. If the passerby said yes, Johnny would ask: "Please read it for me." Having heard his review read, Johnny arrived at the theater and, ostentatiously pulling out his paper, would declare, "Ahem! I see by the papers that"—and then proceed to "read" his review, almost verbatim, to anyone who would listen.

Lew Payton (l.), Josephine Baker (r.)

To Dear little
Cives. Wishing
more Luck
Success
Valada Snow
In Barnville
1924

Valada Snow

Eubie: *"Let me tell you about 'Dixie Moon.' It was at the opening of the second act, at night with the moon rising very slowly while the string section played the melody; then George Jones and the Harmony Kings sang it. It was a beautiful scene, with jack-o'-lanterns and moss hanging from the trees. The men were in pongee suits like any Southerner would wear. The girls wore white dresses, with* hoop skirts.

"Now when the audience saw that scene they would oooh and aaah until they saw the girls—then they would stop dead. The applause would just die. It was the hoop skirts. It happened night after night; I see it because I'm out front conducting.

"So I went to B. C. Whitney, our producer. I said, 'Mr. Whitney'—he loved me—'Mr. Whitney, I didn't come to tell you how to run the show. I just know how to write music and conduct the orchestra, but everywhere we play, the audience stops dead when they see the girls in the hoop skirts. The scene is too beautiful *for a colored show.* Our *girls wouldn't wear hoops in their dresses—it's just not the way they would dress.' He heard me out. Then he answered, 'Eubie, this is* not *a colored show. This is Sissle and Blake's show for Broadway. . . .' "*

NEW YORK CITY *TELEGRAPH*, SEPTEMBER 2, 1924

NEW ALL-COLORED SHOW AT COLONIAL

It Is Called "The Chocolate Dandies" and Is the Work of Noble Sissle and Eubie Blake

PRODUCTION IS PRETENTIOUS

By JAMES P. SINNOTT.

Eubie Blake at the piano is all that this writer needs to insure a night of enjoyment in any kind of weather. And Eubie Blake was at the piano last night at the Colonial Theatre, where B. C. Whitney offered the latest Sissle & Blake colored musical melange entitled "The Chocolate Dandies."

When Eubie Blake plays, the piano sings. He writes great popular music, too, as all who remember "Shuffle Along" will attest to.

There never was a colored show like "The Chocolate Dandies." It is the "Ziegfeld Follies" or "Music Box Revue" done in brownskin.

Williams & Walker never knew as pretentious a production. It has everything.

The girls and boys of the chorus can dance. The music is tuneful. It is very funny, and there is Eubie Blake at that piano. Don't overlook Eubie. I never can, and never want to.

He has a piano up on the stage in the second part of the show and does a specialty with his partner, Noble Sissle. They are a good team. Sissle writes the lyrics for Blake's score and plays in the shows that they do together. He has the good sense to know his vocal and acting limitations and always gives a creditable performance.

Julian Mitchell staged "The Chocolate Dandies." After years of toil with the white pampered dolls of Broadway it must have been a pleasure for Mr. Mitchell to direct these brownskin gals, who just love to dance and show it in every move.

They reflect credit upon this veteran of the musical comedy arena, and he has done well for them.

A brownskin chorus does a number after the manner of the Tiller Girls of London, and it is not too much to say that they do it quite as well as these famous girls could put it over.

It is impossible to describe "The Chocolate Dandies." Go and see it.

There is not a dull moment in the entertainment. It is at least 50 per cent better than "Shuffle Along." That's high enough praise for any show.

"Dixie Moon" and "Thinking of Me," struck this writer's fancy as the best tunes that Eubie Blake has written. But there's not a bad one in the lot.

Go to the Colonial and laugh with Lew Payton and Johnny Hudgins. There's a team of Negro comics for you! Listen to Joe Smith the jazz cornetist. He's there forty ways!

And Eubie Blake is at the piano! Enough said!

OUR MELODIES IN MINOR KEYS WERE FIRST ORIGINATED
UNDER THE DIXIE MOON
THOSE MELODIES IN MINOR KEYS WERE FIRST SYNCOPATED
UNDER THE DIXIE MOON
THERE'S A RHYTHM SWINGING WITH 'EM THAT MAKES LIFE SEEM
DEARER
UNDER THE DIXIE MOON
SWINGING WITH 'EM IN THAT RHYTHM MAKES PARADISE SEEM
NEARER
UNDER THE DIXIE MOON

GOD BLESS THE
DIXIE MOONLIGHT
YOUR BRIGHT BEAMS GLOWING
KEEPS THE WORLD WITH JOY O'ERFLOWING
DIXIE MOONLIGHT
GOD MADE THE NIGHT FOR YOU
TO EVERY SOUL WITH SORROW PINING
YOU SHOW A SILVER LINING
KEEP SHINING
DIXIE MOONLIGHT
NEXT TO THEIR MOTHERS, SISTERS AND BROTHERS*
LOVE THE DEAR OLD DIXIE MOONLIGHT.

Dixie Moon

* Alternate reading: "Each Sue and Sammy/Next to their mammy,/Loves . . ."

WHITE ART RATHER THAN BLACK MAGIC, SAYS STEVENS

Sissle and Blake's "In Bamville" Has Not the Razor-Edged Originality of "Shuffle Along," Critic Says

BY ASHTON STEVENS.

If I hadn't recently gone to see "Plantation Days" at a South Side theater I should be inclined to the opinion, after seeing Sissle and Blake's "In Bamville," at the Illinois last night, that "Shuffle Along" was an accident rather than a masterpiece. But my faith in our colored brother as a song and dance entertainer is still firm. I just don't think that "In Bamville" shows him at his happiest.

This show seems to suffer from too much white man; it is both sophisticated and conventional. You feel that the colored folk have been encouraged to go their own way only in the talking scenes, where, save for the miraculous exception of "Shuffle Along," they are habitually dull.

You feel the arresting, the civilizing hand of Julian Mitchell in the direction. Nobody seems to go out of his head. Where we used to have splendid barbarians we now have splendid barbers.

* * *

It is, I felt last night, the fatal influence of the white man that makes the show seem second rate for all its costly costumes and sceneries. There is too much so-called politeness, too much platitudinous refinement and not enough of the racy and the razor-edged. There is, in a word, too much "art" and not enough Africa. Yes, even in the music of that gifted melodist, Eubie Blake.

He might now be Professor

ASHTON STEVENS' REVIEW, CHICAGO *HERALD AND EXAMINER*, MARCH 31, 1924

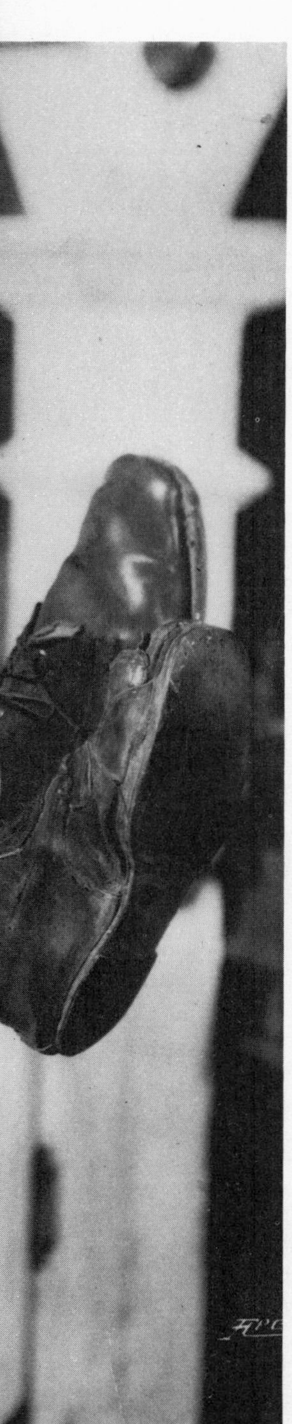
Johnny Hudgins

Blake, Doctor of Music Blake, for all the real Blakiness of his music in the first act. Not bad music, mind; not stupid stuff. No; lots of action; lots (as I heard a lady behind me say) of pep. But no stab of originality. No feeling within you that Victor Herbert couldn't have composed it on a bet.

* * *

Blake was Blakier in act two. "Dixie Moon" was a delightful choral. "Manda" was a moving affair. And moving and interesting was the quaint face of Valada Snow, who warbled the melodic line of "Manda." Nor was "Land of Dancing Pickaninnies" anything but second to "Shuffle Along's" immortal "Harry" number. (I won't say how second.)

And I daresay that Sissle and Blake's teamed appearance in their "studio" scene turned up something good—time called me before they came to it. Anyway, there was life in the second half of "In Bamville," even if there were oodles of civilization and commonplace too.

And there were, unforgettably, the Four Harmony Kings, as good as their title was bad; making the welkin resound with close and distant concord; making a male quartet something that you did not want to quarter and hang. Civilization had touched, but spared them.

But it had not got within a hundred generations of the comic little chorus girl whose very gaze was syncopation and whose merest movement was a blues. I don't know her name, but that wild baby took me many miles away from Jackson Blvd., and made me wish that the whole show was like herself.

Ashton Stevens voiced the opinion of several important critics of *The Chocolate Dandies*: it wasn't their idea of a colored show. Eubie: *"Friends had encouraged us, and so Sissle and I felt that after* Shuffle Along *we could write any show we wanted. We were wrong. People who went to a colored show—most people, not* all *people expected only fast dancing and Negroid humor, and when they got something else they put it down."* Powerful stereotypes had been created that would not be easily broken. Curiously, some critics welcomed *The Chocolate Dandies* for the same reason that others denounced it.

But the relative failure of the show is almost as readily attributable to unnecessary extravagance in the production. In New York *Shuffle Along* could turn a profit with a cast of 60, drawing \$3700 a week in salaries, with a \$7500 weekly gross; on the road its typical salary "nut" was \$4500, with a similar cast count, but with a \$12,000 gross. But the "nut" of *The Chocolate Dandies* simply did not allow as much margin. With a cast always of more than 100 people (and three horses), drawing \$7500 in salaries, the show would have to have earned at least \$16,000 a week to break even. This meant that capacity houses *everywhere it went* would be mandatory, and no show could "go clean" all the time in those days any more than now. With fewer than six profitable weeks, *The Chocolate Dandies* lost more than \$60,000 during its sixty-week life span. It remains a monument to the ambitiousness of its creators; Noble's conception had been grand to the extreme. But to Eubie, no matter what the critics felt then or what history's verdict would be of the show, it is the score of which he is most proud.

"That's the score. I know the world thinks Shuffle Along *was the best, but that is more because it was such a novelty when it came out. It was the first, and it left an indelible mark on people's minds. But I have never written a score to compare with* The Chocolate Dandies. *I know there is nothing in* Shuffle Along *anywhere near the melodies of 'Dixie Moon' and 'Jassamine Lane.'*

"I know what people say, but I still fight the world on it. You know, you have to have a lot of nerve to tell the whole world off, but that's how I feel."

White
Studio
52. N.Y.

Form No. 2 B. & F. 11-25-19

SALARY LIST

$ ....

Received of .... Company

Salary in full to Date, and in full of all claims and Demands for week ending ....

	Is	Was		Is	Was
Noble Sissle	300	500	Ruby Barbee	35	35
Eubie Blake	300	500	Carson Marshall	35	40
Lew Payton	250	300	Amie Bates	35	40
Johny Hudgins	150	150	Rose Young	35	40
Lottie Gee	150	200	Thelma McLaughlin	35	40
Valada Snow	100	125	Howard Elmore	35	40
Josephine Baker	100	125	Lloyd Keyes	35	40
W.A.Hann	125	150	Willie Sheppard	35	40
I.H.Browning	125	150	Ruth Walker	35	40
Russell Smith	75	100	Earl Crompton	35	40
Ines Clough	75	100	Bournis Brown	35	40
Geo Jones Jr	75	95	Mae Cobb	35	35
Wm H Berry	75	95	Marie Fraine	35	35
Chas Davis	75	75	~~Mae Fortune~~		
Amanda Randolph	60	75	~~Rose Gillard~~		
Elizabeth Welsh	60	75	Marion Gee	35	35
Wm Grundy	65	70	Lolita Hall	35	35
J.W.Mobley	65	70	Viola Jackson	35	35
Ferd Robinson	65	65	Helen Mitchell	35	35
Lee J Randall	65	65	Catherine Parker	35	35
Joe Smith	65	65	Mabel Nichols	35	35
R Cooper	50	60	Jennie Salmon	35	35
P Colston	50	60	Clara Titus	35	35
M Smallwood	40	50	Doris Mignotte	35	35
Fred Jennings	40	40	Frankie Williams	35	35
G Lawson	50	50	Jacqueline Williams	35	35

“That Comedy Chorus Girl”

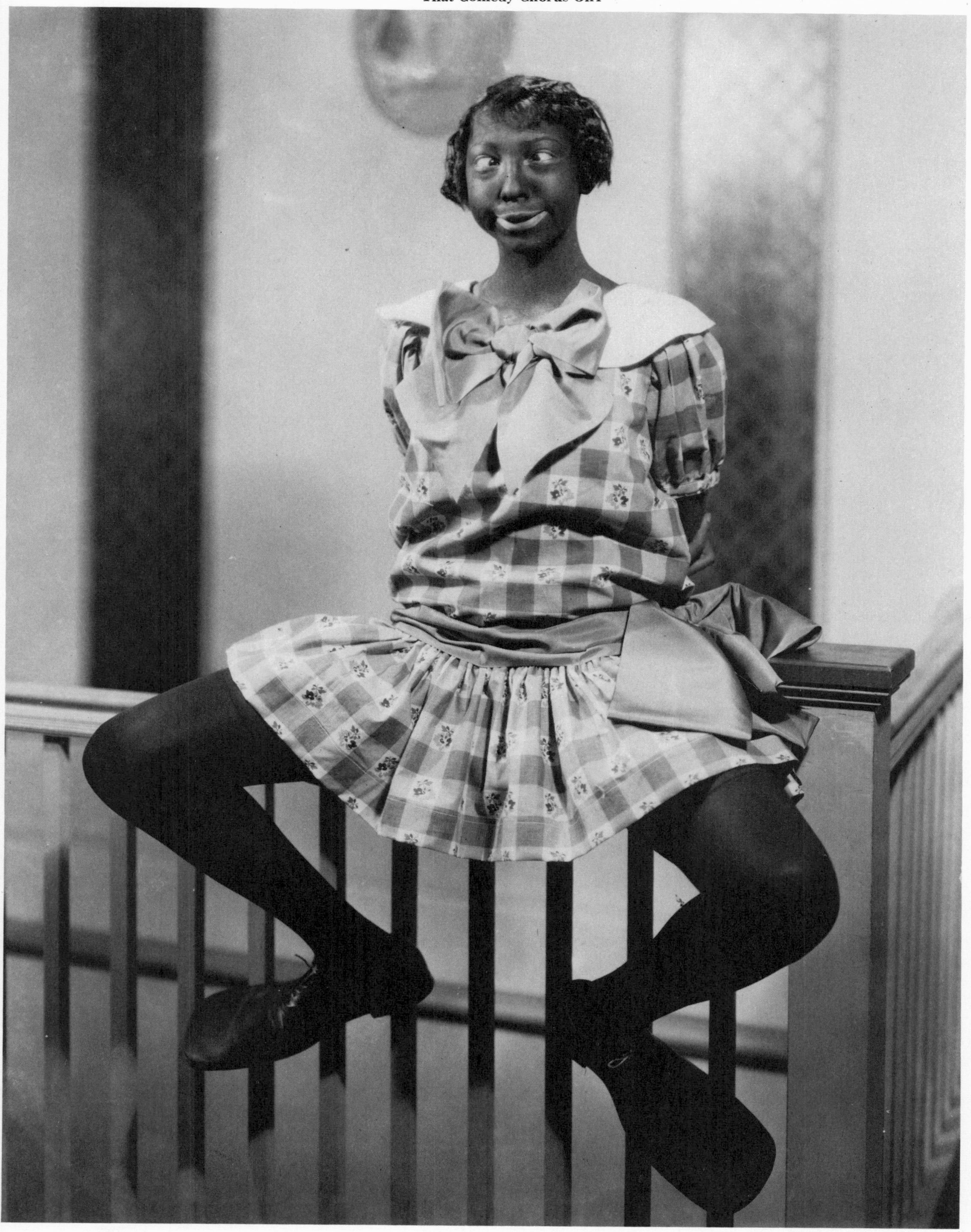

tbacks on weekly salary list, *The Chocolate Dandies*

SISSLE AND BLAKE ARRESTED IN TORONTO

EUBIE BLAKE CHARGED WITH MAKING HIGHBALL

Toronto, Canada. —(Special)—A party given by Fay Bainter, white, who was appearing in the "Dream Girl" at the Royal Alexandra Theatre in this city, last Friday resulted in the death of Carl Lynn, white, and the arrest of Sissle and Blake, who were appearing at the Princess Theatre with the "Chocolate Dandies" for the illegal purchase of liquor.

The party was given at the King Edward Hotel in celebration of the 100th performance of the white company. Blake and Sissle were alleged to have been engaged as entertainers. An officer is said to have noticed a suspicious bulge in the clothes of the artists, and on examining them found three bottles of whiskey.

Pair Arrested

They were taken to the Court Street Station where it is said that they stated that they had been given the liquor for entertaining. The officer stated that he followed the pair from the King Edward Hotel.

When arraigned in the police court they were charged with the illegal purchase of liquor. Noble Sissle was fined $50 and costs by the magistrate and Blake was dismissed.

Blake Made High-ball

Blake's statement at the trial was that they were present at the party solely as entertainers and not as guests. After the close of the affair he and Sissle were invited to a room on one of the floors where Miss Bainter was entertaining friends. He noticed a bottle of whiskey on the table and not being invited to have a drink, helped himself.

Were Not Guests

The musician further stated that aside from Miss Bainter he was not acquainted with any other of the guests. Blake when asked at the trial where Sissle obtained the whiskey replied that he thought the bottles were handed Sissle as he left the room. He also said that their services were gratis.

Sissle Drank Ale

Noble Sissle was under the impression that the liquor had been given him by a man in one of the rooms used for cloaks and that he had not knowledge of the identity of the donor. He also stated that he was not a drinking man. He acknowledged drinking two glasses of ale, and it did not appear to have any "kick." The man who presented the whiskey was masked and in costume.

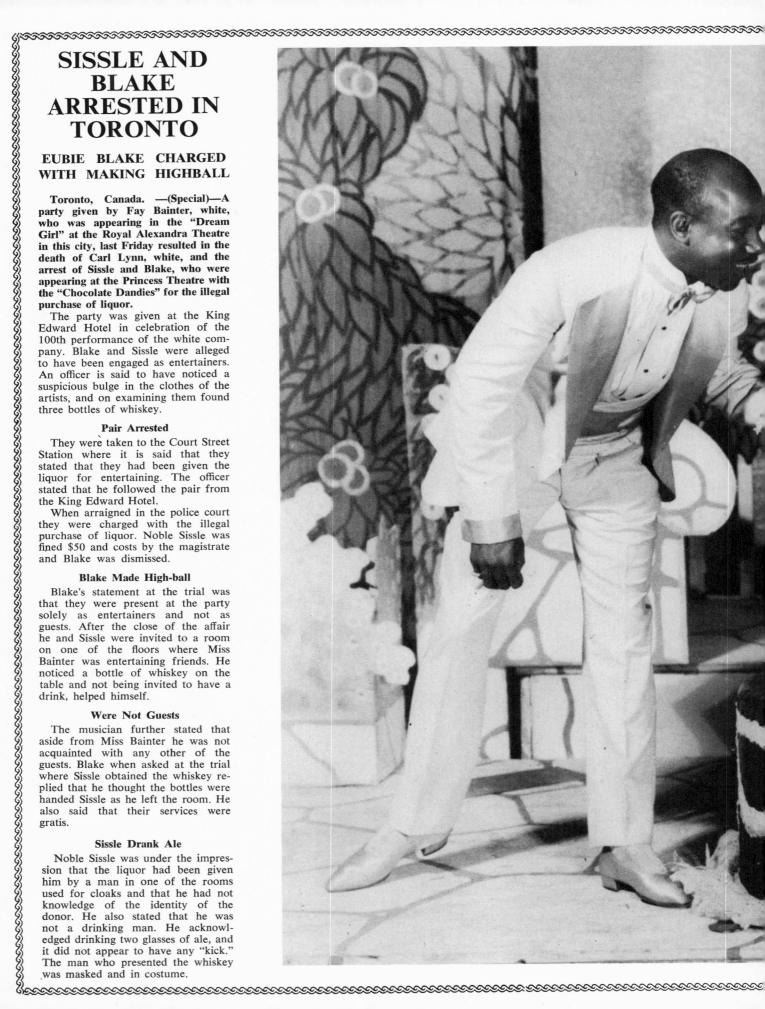

White
Studio
59. N.Y.

58 VARIETY Wednesday, November 18, 1925

CONCLUSIVE PROOFS!

NOBLE EUBIE

SISSLE AND BLAKE

"AMERICAN AMBASSADORS OF SYNCOPATION"

Originally booked in London for eight weeks, now featured floor entertainers at the KIT-CAT CLUB and doubling at the PICCADILLY, to be followed by BLANCHARD'S CLUB and CARNIVAL CLUB, while playing London's leading music halls, VICTORIA PALACE, COLISEUM and ALHAMBRA

SISSLE and BLAKE'S new scenic song creation, "Lady of the Moon," to be featured in Charles Cochran's edition of "On with the Dance"

Management A. J. CLARKE

Booking Representatives: WILLIAM MORRIS and FOSTER AGENCY

The Chocolate Dandies closed in May 1925. Noble Sissle and Eubie Blake returned to vaudeville, this time as a presentation-house act in theaters that also showed full-length silent films. After a few successful months at this, William Morris presented them with an opportunity to tour abroad, and in September 1925 Sissle and Blake sailed on the *Olympic* to Europe, where they were to spend eight months, along with their wives, in England, Scotland, and France.

In England they were commissioned to write songs for Charles B. Cochran's *Revue* of 1926, two of which, "Tahiti" and "Let's Get Married Right Away," were sung with success by Basil Howes and Elizabeth Hines. Cochran was the greatest theatrical impresario in England, the Florenz Ziegfeld of London. He had brought Florence Mills to England in a show, *Dover Street to Dixie*, in 1922, and had planned to bring *Shuffle Along* also until the break with Miller and Lyles made the enterprise too touchy. This was a curious loop in the line of Sissle and Blake's life his-

Compliments of the Season.

NOBLE EUBIE

SISSLE *and* **BLAKE**

American Ambassadors of Syncopation

Now playing at THE COLISEUM

Sissle and Blake, as new-comers, are deeply appreciative of the wonderful reception they are receiving in London.

With a past record of having written and starred in two of the most famous coloured musical shows the world has ever seen, "Shuffle Along" and "The Chocolate Dandies," with -uch song hits as "I'm Just Wild About Harry," "Love Will Find a Way," "Bandana Days," "Manda," "Slave of Love," etc., etc., Sissle and Blake are creating in new fields new friends with new inspirations as evidenced by the Fox-trot ballad "WHY," just published by Keith Prowse, and the recent song success "LADY OF THE MOON," featured in Charles B. Cochran's "Still Dancing,' also "THERE'S ONE LANE THAT HAS NO TURNING" (Feldman), "WONDER WHERE MY SWEETIE CAN BE" (Lawrence Wright), "YOU OUGHT TO KNOW" (Chappell).

Sissle and Blake wish Everybody A Prosperous and Happy New Year

Representatives - - FOSTER AGENCY

SUSSMAN
MPLS.
Sissle & Blake

tory: they had been booked for an English tour in 1920 which Miller and Lyles had dissuaded them from in order to write *Shuffle Along*, and now they were back almost where they started, in vaudeville, but much richer and more famous by far than they had been in 1920.

Their vaudeville act played to great acclaim in London, and from all indications they could have stayed there much longer. Charles Cochran had even asked them to write the entire score for his 1927 revue, and thus their long-range success in England was practically assured.

Off to Europe

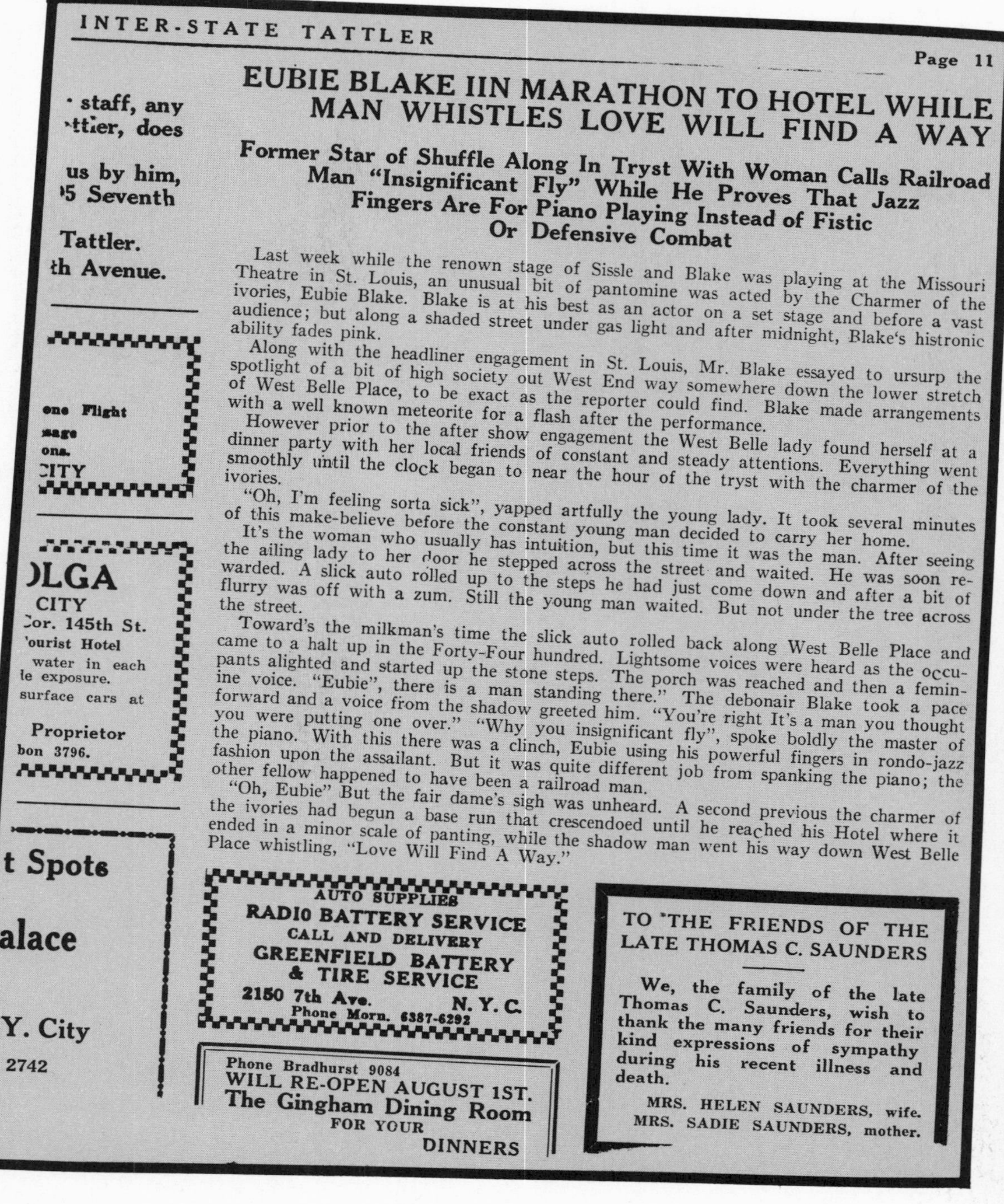

INTER-STATE TATTLER

Page 11

· staff, any
·ttier, does

us by him,
·5 Seventh

Tattler.
th Avenue.

EUBIE BLAKE IIN MARATHON TO HOTEL WHILE MAN WHISTLES LOVE WILL FIND A WAY

Former Star of Shuffle Along In Tryst With Woman Calls Railroad Man "Insignificant Fly" While He Proves That Jazz Fingers Are For Piano Playing Instead of Fistic Or Defensive Combat

Last week while the renown stage of Sissle and Blake was playing at the Missouri Theatre in St. Louis, an unusual bit of pantomine was acted by the Charmer of the ivories, Eubie Blake. Blake is at his best as an actor on a set stage and before a vast audience; but along a shaded street under gas light and after midnight, Blake's histronic ability fades pink.

Along with the headliner engagement in St. Louis, Mr. Blake essayed to ursurp the spotlight of a bit of high society out West End way somewhere down the lower stretch of West Belle Place, to be exact as the reporter could find. Blake made arrangements with a well known meteorite for a flash after the performance.

However prior to the after show engagement the West Belle lady found herself at a dinner party with her local friends of constant and steady attentions. Everything went smoothly until the clock began to near the hour of the tryst with the charmer of the ivories.

"Oh, I'm feeling sorta sick", yapped artfully the young lady. It took several minutes of this make-believe before the constant young man decided to carry her home.

It's the woman who usually has intuition, but this time it was the man. After seeing the ailing lady to her door he stepped across the street and waited. He was soon rewarded. A slick auto rolled up to the steps he had just come down and after a bit of flurry was off with a zum. Still the young man waited. But not under the tree across the street.

Toward's the milkman's time the slick auto rolled back along West Belle Place and came to a halt up in the Forty-Four hundred. Lightsome voices were heard as the occupants alighted and started up the stone steps. The porch was reached and then a feminine voice. "Eubie", there is a man standing there." The debonair Blake took a pace forward and a voice from the shadow greeted him. "You're right It's a man you thought you were putting one over." "Why you insignificant fly", spoke boldly the master of the piano. With this there was a clinch, Eubie using his powerful fingers in rondo-jazz fashion upon the assailant. But it was quite different job from spanking the piano; the other fellow happened to have been a railroad man.

"Oh, Eubie" But the fair dame's sigh was unheard. A second previous the charmer of the ivories had begun a base run that crescendoed until he reached his Hotel where it ended in a minor scale of panting, while the shadow man went his way down West Belle Place whistling, "Love Will Find A Way."

TO THE FRIENDS OF THE LATE THOMAS C. SAUNDERS

We, the family of the late Thomas C. Saunders, wish to thank the many friends for their kind expressions of sympathy during his recent illness and death.

MRS. HELEN SAUNDERS, wife.
MRS. SADIE SAUNDERS, mother.

The *Inter-State Tattler*, a midwestern gossip newspaper, consisted of juicy tidbits concerning the famous; whether the stories were true or not was evidently of no great importance.

VICTORIA PALACE

Victoria Station, S.W. | Victoria Station, S.W.

Managing Directors - - ALFRED BUTT and R. H. GILLESPIE | Manager - - - J. A. WEBB

6.15 | TWICE NIGHTLY | 8.50

MONDAY, OCTOBER 12th, 1925

Composers of "I'M JUST WILD ABOUT HARRY"

In a Repertoire of their own Compositions

NOBLE SISSLE AND EUBIE BLAKE

From the Piccadilly Cabaret

ETHEL LEVEY

The Celebrated Revue Star in Selections from her Repertoire

In their Musical Super-Sketch "IN THE CABARET" AND THE SENSATIONAL PRIZE FIGHT

WILLY PANTZER

And his World-Renowned Company

Comprising Four of the Smallest People on Earth

LA ZEPHYR

Original and Novelty Dancer

GUDRUN AND GALLOWAY

In STEPPING HIGH

Latest Events on the Bioscope

DAVE LEE

& COMPANY

In a Comedy Interlude, "OH, HAROLD"

Written by R. P. Weston and Bert Lee

WILLY GARDNER

The "Skate Specialist"

AMBROSE BARKER & PEGGY WYNNE

In Song Impressions and "Fowl" Language

TIMES OF PERFORMANCES: FIRST HOUSE, Open 6; Commence 6.15 SECOND HOUSE, Open 8.35; Commence 8.50 EARLY DOOR, Balcony 8.30

BOXES	Fauteuils	ORCH. STALLS	DRESS CIRCLE	STALLS	FAMILY CIRCLE	BALCONY
21/- & 18/-	3/6	2/3	2/3	1/6	1/3	9d.
Plus Government Tax 4s. Plus Government Tax 3s. TO HOLD FOUR Extra Seats 4s. 6d. and 3s. 6d. Tax 9d. Tax 9d.	Plus Government Tax 9d.	Reservable in Advance 2s. 6d. Plus Government Tax 6d.	Reservable in Advance 2s. 6d. Plus Government Tax 6d.	Reservable in Advance 1s. 9d. Plus Government Tax 4d.	Plus Government Tax 3d. Reservable in Advance 1s. 6d. Plus Government Tax 4d.	Plus Government Tax 2d. Early Doors 1/- Plus Government Tax 2d.

BOX OFFICE open from 10 to 9.30. TELEPHONES 5282, 5284, 7358 Victoria. Seats Booked by Telephone will not be kept after 6 p.m. and 8.30 p.m. unless previously paid for.

NO RE-ADMISSION. All Children to be Paid for.

But Eubie was unhappy in England. Somehow his rough-and-tumble upbringing on the streets of Baltimore had left him unprepared for the more gentle, sophisticated life of England's capital. In the large American cities he had found an accord with his nature in the bustling, energetic give-and-take of a growing country. He had come far in status from the saloons and sporting houses of his youth. But something about England was too tame, too well-bred for him; always a man of perfect manners, he was at the same time of an informal, relaxed demeanor, and the apparent rigidity of the British temperament made him nervous. He longed to go back home.

Noble, on the other hand, was something of an elitist. From the earliest society-orchestra days with Jim Europe he had had visions of attaining social status through association with the rich and great. In England, it seemed, he had found a spiritual haven.

Naturally, some tension was bound thereby to develop between Sissle and Blake. When Eubie urged Noble to come back to America with him to continue their vaudeville tour, Noble grudgingly assented. They very likely picked the wrong moment to leave, for leaving when they did meant turning down Charles Cochran's important offer. (In their place, a team of young writers, Richard Rodgers and Lorenz Hart, took the assignment Sissle and Blake decided to refuse.) Eubie denies that he ever knew about the Cochran deal, but the whole affair led to the only serious quarrel the team of Sissle and Blake ever had had—one which would lead to consequences later.

ALHAMBRA

LEICESTER SQUARE, W.C.2.

Chairman & Managing Director Sir OSWALD STOLL · General Manager GEORGE F. REYNOLDS

Week commencing MONDAY FEB. 15

DAILY 2.30—6.10—8.45

PROGRAMME CHANGED WEEKLY

HARRY WELDON
THE GREAT "S'NO USE" COMEDIAN

LITTLE TICH
THE GREAT LITTLE COMEDIAN

NOBLE SISSLE & EUBIE BLAKE
AMERICAN AMBASSADORS OF SYNCOPATION
IN A REPERTOIRE OF THEIR OWN SONGS

MAIDIE SCOTT
PRESENTS "WOMAN"
VICTORIAN ERA—PRESENT DAY—FUTURE
BY PETER CHANEY MUSIC BY S. W. RICHARDSON

SCALA
MASTER OF HIS BANJO

TEDDY BROWN
(THE "GREAT" XYLOPHONIST)
AND HIS CAFE DE PARIS BAND

NEWS VIEWS
ON THE SCREEN

TOM CLARE
AT THE PIANO—IN ENTIRELY NEW SONGS

SHISHTL'S COMICAL WONDERETTES

GILLIE POTTER
IN HIS USUAL GOOD FORM

NATIONAL SUNDAY LEAGUE CONCERT EVERY SUNDAY at 7 p.m.

Musical Director, GEO. SAKER · Asst. Manager, F. G. BROOKS · Manager, Press Intelligence Dept., ARCHIBALD HADDON · Stage Manager, A. CROCKER · Advertising Manager, W. ROBERTS

PRICES AS USUAL

PHONE GERRARD 5064

ADVANCE BOOKING OFFICE, CHARING CROSS ROAD, OPEN 10 a.m. to 10 p.m. DAILY
NO HALF PRICE—CHILDREN IN ARMS NOT ADMITTED
The Management Reserve the Right of Refusing Admission
UNDERGROUND STATIONS LEICESTER SQUARE, PICCADILLY & TRAFALGAR SQUARE

5065 PHONE GERRARD

HAYCOCK, CADLE & GRAHAM L^TD, CAMBERWELL, S.E.5

Walery
Paris

On their way to America the team capped their eight-month European tour with a visit to Josephine Baker in Paris. She had come over with a Lew Leslie revue, *La Revue Nègre*, which opened in October 1925, and her jazz dancing became an overnight sensation. Josephine became the darling of Paris; within a few months she left Leslie's show and joined the Folies-Bergère. Her antics became legendary—one day she would stroll down the Champs-Elysées with two cheetahs on a leash, another day with two swans. Her always flamboyant personality had found freedom in Paris, where the restrictions and racial tensions of home were suddenly lifted off her shoulders. Now she had money to buy herself a menagerie of boa constrictors, cheetahs, and monkeys, which she kept in her apartment. (Eubie remembers *not* going too deeply into that part of her apartment, although invited by Josephine.) Forty thousand fan letters were addressed to her within her two years, thousands of proposals of marriage were tendered and refused, and at least two attempted suicides were attributed to unrequited love for the girl from East St. Louis. Much had happened to Josephine Baker since she had sneaked into the company of *Shuffle Along*.

Much had happened to Sissle and Blake, too, in the ten or so years of their collaboration. Sissle's marriage, unlike Blake's, seemed to be a source of constant tension to him. With this and the memory of their show's recent failure fresh in their minds, it is not surprising that the fissure in their relationship, formed in England, would widen. When Noble told Eubie he wanted them to go back to Europe to work in the music halls, feeling that this was their best hope for the future, Eubie simply would not go.

Noble walked out.

Sissle and Blake were no longer together.

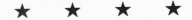

It was only after Eubie's return to America that he learned that his early idol, Leslie Stuart, had died several years earlier in England. *"They threw him into Potter's Field. If I'd only known! I had all the money in the world then, and I could have given Leslie Stuart a proper grave."*

EUBIE BLAKE BACK FROM FOREIGN TOUR

Sissle And Blake Scored Hit In London And Ireland With Act

ARTIST HERE SAYS DON'T VISIT EUROPE

Bread Lines, Poverty, Poor Housing, Queer English Baffle Americans

Eubie Blake member of the team of Blake and Sissle which has just finished an eight months tour of Great Britain visited his mother, Mrs. John S. Blake, 915 Rutland avenue, on last Friday.

Eubie Blake

Eubie, as the pianist, is known to his friends was well, and showed few effects from his ocean voyage. He landed in New York from the French liner Paris on Wednesday night.

The team opened at the Piccadilly in London soon after landing, and were almost an instant hit. From the famous establishment they were booked into the Kit Kat Club, one of the smartest places in the British capital. Out of many acts that were offered the patrons of the latter Blake and Sissle received the most votes and were engaged. Followed dates at the Victoria Palace, and at the Alhambra and Coliseum music halls. The Englishmen were particularly enthusiastic in their reception of "Pickninnny Shoes" and "Why" both numbers composed by the team.

"My playing of Jazz," said Eubie, "seemed particularly astounding to the English musicians. They tried to classify it according to musical form, but failed. Yet when each measure would come out even' as the schoolboy says of his sums; they were further nonplussed. However our audiences in the clubs and theatres fell a victim to syncopation as my partner and I played and sang it, and we were called upon to play many repeat dates.

Wrote Three Hits

One outcome of our appearances was an order from Charles B. Cochoran, the Ziegfield of London, to write a number for his musical, "Still Dancing." We wrote "Lady of the Moon" which was placed in the production, but suffered because the soloist seemed to miss the musical point of the number. Subsequently, however, we wrote "Tahaiti," a South Sea Island number and "A Wedding Song" both of which "clicked" as the English say. Both soon became the rage of London. Out of five numbers that the act wrote three became monumental hits and have been recorded.

Layton And Johnson

Blake says that next to Scott and Whaley, Layton and Johnson are the biggest attractions in London, and that Carpenter and Hatch are also unusually popular. Lottie Gee is appearing in the music halls, (establishments similiar to our vaudeville theatres) but will return home soon he understands. After London the act opened in Manchester, England and then went to Belfast and Dublin, Ireland, repeating their conquests."

Poverty Appaling

"In Europe, said the artist," a man or woman is either rich or poor. Poor boys don't grow to be rich men over there there's no chance. The class system consigns one to the estate in which he was born until death. There is a caste system as strong as there is in India.

"My advice to all American Negroes is to stay away from Europe. Particularly is this so if you are poor. No matter what happens or what the conditions may be in America, they can be nothing like the deplorable conditions that exist in London. I have seen thousands sleeping in the streets, bread lines with human beings standing four abreast and other distress that I hate to remember."

English Customs

The English customs of all tarffic turning and keeping to the right, the absence of baths and steam heat, and English as it is spoken in Great Britain all seemed to puzzle and be distasteful to Blake. Thetreatment of the team was spoken of, however, as being courteous and entirely gratifying in a financial sense.

Returning on the Paris the act was requested to participate in the ship's concert. The distinguished actress, Amelia Bingham was a passenger, and participant in the concert which was managed by Winchall Smith the distinguished playwright and producer, who also acted as master of ceremonies.

Eubie Baltimore Boy

The pianist began his public career as pianist at the famous Goldfield Hotel conducted in this city by the late Joe Gans. His first vaudeville engagement was at Daly's Theatre on Pennsylvania avenue. Several years ago he and Sissle collaborated with Miller and Lyles on "Shuffle Along," and later with Lew Peyton he was co-star and writer of "The Chocolate Dandies."

At the close of the latter, the team was tendered an engagement in the Famous Players (Publix) picture theatres, and only interrupted the tour to fill the European engagement. The team will shortly complete their tour of the picture houses.

Back home with mother

Dear Grandmother

This is the first time a Negroes name ever blazed forth in lights on a white show over here— One of the Duncan Sisters was sick and I went in as an added attraction to off set her absence I was quite a success.

Yours,
Noble

London

The Ace of Syncopation an
his Ambassadeurs Orchestr

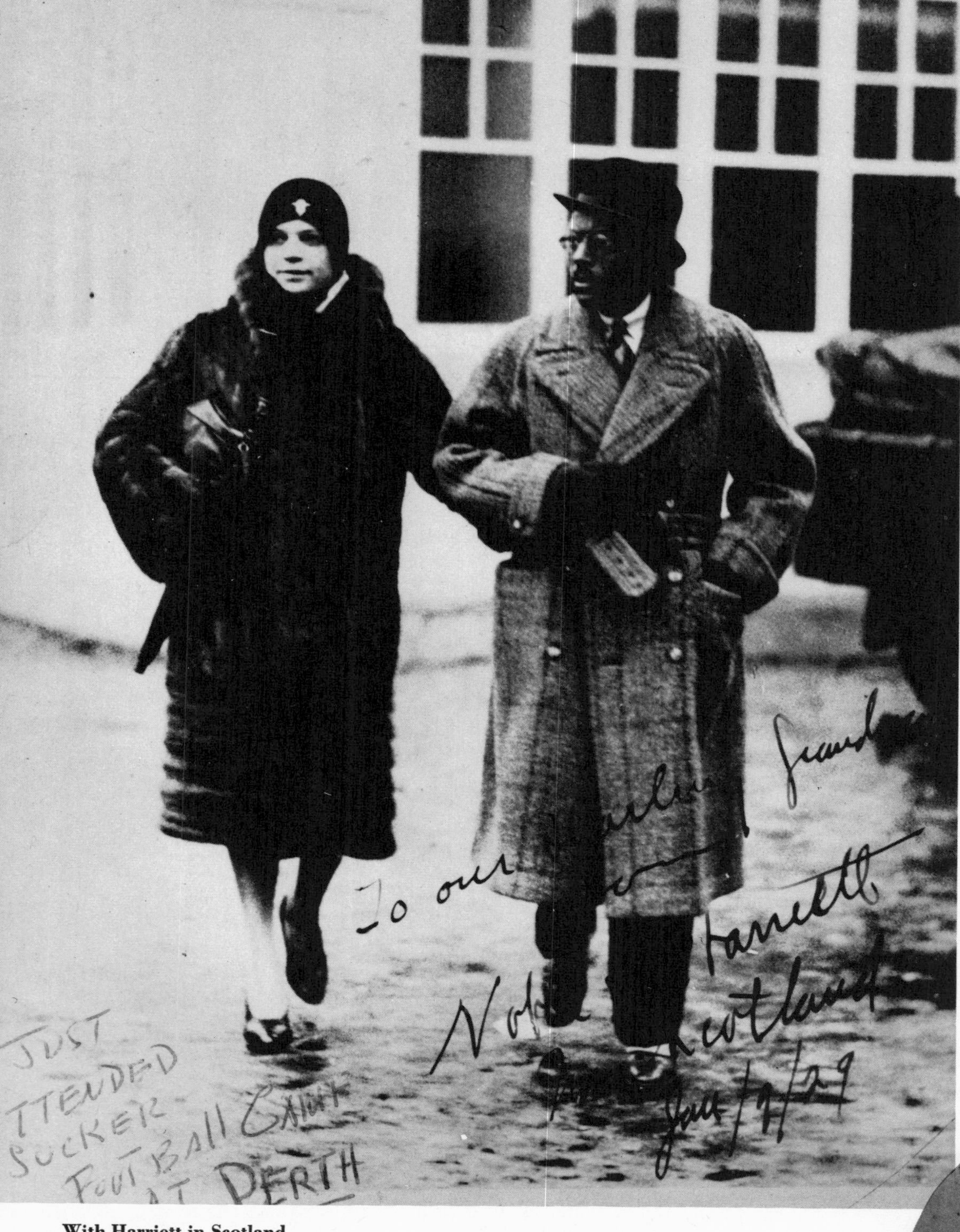

With Harriett in Scotland

1926–1932

With the death of his mother in 1916, Sissle had become an orphan, a blow for someone as family-oriented as he. His "grandmother," Hattie Scott, who had reared Sissle's own mother, became his devoted second mother and correspondent.

Summer 1927 Sissle returns to France for American Legion convention.

1927 Blake, remaining in United States, teams with lyricist Henry Creamer to write floor shows.

1928 Sissle performs in English music halls and theaters with composer-pianist Harry Revel, and helps Revel to migrate to America. (Revel later teams with Mack Gordon to write "Did You Ever See a Dream Walking?" and other hits.) Sissle is signed by French agent Henri Lartigue to replace Morton Downey as an intermission vocalist at Edmond Sayag's Paris café Les Ambassadeurs. Instead, he is hired at the urging of Cole Porter, who had written the score for the floor show, to replace Fred Waring with an orchestra of his own. With Porter's help, Sissle finds expatriate black musicians in Montmartre (including Sidney Bechet) and is successful as a bandleader.

1928–1929 Blake rejoins singer Broadway Jones and with cast of eleven they put on *Shuffle Along Jr.*, a headline attraction on the Keith-Albee Orpheum Circuit. The show tours America, featuring Marion and Dade, Dewey Brown, Katie Krippen and The Seven Panama Pansies.

1929–1930 Sissle's orchestra plays several engagements in Europe, including Monte Carlo, Deauville, Ostend, London, and Glasgow.

1929–1930 Blake and Jones work as vaudeville team with Fanchon and Marco shows.

1930 Blake contributes songs to Will Morrisey's *Folies-Bergère* at the Gansevoort Theatre, and to *Hot Rhythm* for Broadway.

September 1930 Blake teams with lyricist Andy Razaf to write the score for *Lew Leslie's Blackbirds of 1930*.

December 1930 Sissle plays for British Royal Family at Ciro's in London; Duke of Windsor sits in as drummer with Sissle's orchestra.

1931 Blake conducts Broadway musical *Singin' the Blues*, performs in hotels, vaudeville, and motion picture shorts.

1931 Sissle's orchestra performs in Paris and New York. In the fall, Sissle opens at the Park Central Hotel and begins nationwide broadcasts on the CBS network.

* * *

1932 Aubrey Lyles dies of tuberculosis. Sissle and Blake are reunited with F. E. Miller, and together they write *Shuffle Along of 1933*.

NOBLE SISSLE IN A RECORD FLIGHT

Noble Sissle, the celebrated theatrical star, who has recently startled the musical world by putting a first class Race orchestra in the Ambassadeurs, the smartest night club in Europe, was called to London by his managers concerning his compositions and records.

Mr. Sissle left Le Bourget flying field, Paris, in the morning. On arriving at Croydon field, London, he was met by his representatives, who speeded him to their office. After negotiating his several appointments, he again boarded a plane at Croydon field at 4:30 p. m. and arrived in Paris at 7 o'clock. The famous star of "Shuffle Along" always travels by way of Imperial Airways Limited.

At 10 o'clock that night when seen by a representative of this journal at the Ambassadeurs, he was directing his Sissling Syncopators before a large crowd, composed of the cream of society throughout the world. He was delighted with his trip, which, according to officials of the Imperial Airways, is exceptional even in this flying age.

Mr. Sissle stated that the air was so "bumpy" that it was necessary to fly at an altitude of 4,000 feet. The view of the pure white clouds as far as one could see was one of the most beautiful sights he has ever witnessed.

This celebrated star-director with personality plus, is the talk of Paris. His orchestra is creating a furor here, where they replaced the famous Waring's band. It is the first time that a Race orchestra has been engaged as the feature attraction at this chic rendezvous of royalty and multimillionaires. This master organization also plays for the revue composed of white stars from Broadway.

M. EDMUND SAYAG
PRESENTS

NOBLE SISSLE & HIS BAND

At the famous society rendevous

" LES AMBASSADEURS "

AVENUE DES CHAMPS-ÉLYSEES - PARIS

SOME FAMOUS AUTOGRAPHS !

" I like your band better than any I have ever heard-and when I said it was popular, I meant it !
MAY BIRKHEAD.

" It reminds me of " Jim " Europe and 1913 "
— IRENE CASTLE MC LAUGHLIN.

" To the first man I ever saw " hold " a hungry audience, despite the fact that they were hungry for food-as well !
— ERSKINE GWYNNE.

" I think your band is marvelous "
— LADY DUDLEY (GERTIE MILLAR)

" Noble you're living up to your name "
— FRANCIS J. HUNTER.

A most marvelous conductor of a band that plays divinely "
— PEGGY HOPKINS JOYCE.

" I have yet to think you could do bétter "
GEO. A. DIXON JR.

" A fine band-unequaled "
JASCHA HEIFITZ.

" The best in Paris "
BEATRICE LILLIE.

" I think it's " jazz Grand "
— TALLULAH BANKHEAD.

A few Noted Persons who have Thoroughly enjoyed this band at

" LES AMBASSADEURS "

HENRY BERNSTEIN
ALMA GLUCK.
AMBASSADOR HERRICK
LORD NORTHESK
DOLLY SISTERS
GANNA WALSKA
BARON ROTHSCHILD
PRINCE TUMANOFF
JOHN A. RIGGIN
MARGERY DE FONTANA
PRINCE AND PRINCESSE LOTFALA
M. BOKANOWSKI
DODGE TWINS
WILLIAM TILDEN

APPEARENCES IN EUROPEAN SOCIAL COLONY SPONSORED BY

MISS ELSA MAXWELL M. ANDRÉ DE FOUQUIÈRES

In our autograph book
FAMOUS NAMES
WHO CAME-HEARD AND PRAISED
NOBLE SISSLE'S BAND

LORD AND LADY LOUIS MOUNTBATTEN
H. R. H. MAHARASAH OF KARPARTHULA
ANTHONY J. DREXEL
LORD AND LADY DUDLEY
IRENE CASTLE MCLAUGHLIN
LOUISE HAVEMEYER
BARCLAY WARBURTON
LEE SHUBERT
POLA NEGRI
FRANCIS J. HUNTER

BARONESS EUGENE DE ROTHSCHILD
Desse DE TALLEYRAND
DUDLEY FIELD MALONE
LADY PEEL (BÉATRICE LILLÉE)
JASCHA HEIFETZ
COLE PORTER
GEORGES CARPENTIER
GEORGE DODGE
ELSA MAXWELL
INA CLAIRE

Broadway Jones, born Henry Jones in Florida, was a drummer and baritone with whom Eubie had worked at Gossler's Campus, New York City, about 1918. With him Eubie put together *Shuffle Along Jr.*

Broadway Jones, Jessie Wilson, and Eubie, c. 1918

Shuffle Along Jr. with the Panama Pansies

Miller and Lyles and chorus girls of *Keep Shufflin'* (1928): Marion Tyler, in white dress, is kneeling next to Lyles's left hand.

Marion Gant Tyler is the granddaughter of Hiram S. Thomas, a famous chef and inventor of the Saratoga chip. In the late 1920s she was a showgirl in several black musicals; later she was to become Eubie Blake's second wife.

ROYALE THEATRE

SHUBERT THEATRE CORPORATION, LESSEE
DIRECTION MESSRS. LEE AND J. J. SHUBERT

PROGRAM · PUBLISHED · BY · THE · NEW · YORK · THEATRE · PROGRAM · CORPORATION

FIRE NOTICE: Look around now and choose the nearest exit to your seat. In case of fire, walk (not run) to that exit. Do not try to beat your neighbor to the street.
JOHN J. DORMAN, Fire Commissioner.

BEGINNING WEDNESDAY EVENING, OCTOBER 22, 1930

MATINEES WEDNESDAY AND SATURDAY

THE WORLD'S FUNNIEST AND FASTEST REVUE

Glorifying the American Negro

1930 EDITION

LEW LESLIE'S BLACKBIRDS

THE CAST

ETHEL WATERS — FLOURNEY MILLER
Mantan Moreland — Blue McAllister
Broadway Jones — Minto Cato
Marion Harrison — Neeka Shaw
BERRY BROTHERS
Cecil Mack's Blackbird Choir
EUBIE BLAKE AND HIS BLACKBIRD ORCHESTRA
and
BUCK AND BUBBLES

PROGRAM SUBJECT TO CHANGE OWING TO MAGNITUDE OF PRODUCTION

ACT I

1. *Scene: The Levee on the Mississippi*
Cotton pickers and levee workers. Cecil Mack's Blackbird Choir.
Deacon Brown . . . . . Howard Johnson
River Jordan . . . . . Broadway Jones
Sunshine Susie . . . . . Neeka Shaw
Mammy Jones . . . . . Minto Cato
Mississippi Steppers . . . . . Blackbird Beauty Chorus
Mississippi Beauties . . . The Misses Ulma Banks, Blanche Dunn, Mary Bethune, Estelle Bernier, Emma Jones, Dorothy Kennedy, Ionya Hayes and Dolores Blaine
Amos and Andys . . . . . Al Richards, Crawford Jackson, Bill Bailey and Roy Atkins

(Program Continued on Second Page Following)

Song, "Roll, Jordan,"
Sung by Broadway Jones and Cecil Mack's Blackbird Choir.
Song, "Cabin Door,"
Sung by Neeka Shaw and Blackbird Beauty Chorus.
Song, "Memories of You,"
Sung by Minto Cato and Entire Company
Cabin Door Ensemble by Entire Company.

2. *A Charleston Honeymoon*
Train Announcer . . . . . J. Lewis Johnson
Steve . . . . . FLOURNEY MILLER
Caesar . . . . . Mantan Moreland
Hannah . . . . . ETHEL WATERS
Diploma . . . . . Marmetta Newton
Liza . . . . . Marie Robinson
A Stranger . . . . . Estelle Bernier
Ticket Agent . . . . . Jimmy Baskette

3. *Song, "Mozambique"*
Sung by Marion Harrison.
Scene: An African Jungle.
Song, Jungle Moon,"
Sung by Minto Cato and Cecil Mack's Blackbird Choir.

4. *Shadow Dance* . . . . . BERRY BROTHERS

5. *A Dark Triangle*
Hannah . . . . . ETHEL WATERS
Caesar . . . . . Mantan Moreland
Henry . . . . . JAMES BERRY
Steve . . . . . FLOURNEY MILLER
Mandy . . . . . Louise Uggans
Her Husband . . . . . Blue McAllister

6. *My Best Gal*
Two Pals . . . . . BUCK AND BUBBLES
Melinda . . . . . Neeka Shaw
Song, "Lucky To Me,"
Sung by Neeka Shaw and BUBBLES.
Reprise by ETHEL WATERS, Minto Cato and EUBIE BLAKE and HIS BLACKBIRD ORCHESTRA.

7. *Boy Wanted*
Boss . . . . . Jimmy Baskette
Steve . . . . . Mantan Moreland
Boy . . . . . FLOURNEY MILLER

8. *Song, "Lindy Hop"*
Sung by ANANIAS BERRY and Neeka Shaw, assisted by Blackbird Beauty Chorus.
Specialty: Lindy Hop Dancers

9. *A Harlem Restaurant*
Bus Boy . . . . . FLOURNEY MILLER
Waitress . . . . . ETHEL WATERS
Customers . . . . . Crawford Jackson, Emma Jones, Bill Bailey and Estelle Bernier
Song, "We Belong Together,"
Sung by ETHEL WATERS and FLOURNEY MILLER.

10. *Somewhere in Harlem*
Bub . . . . . BUBBLES
Buck . . . . . BUCK
Caesar . . . . . Mantan Moreland
Officer . . . . . Blue McAllister
A Friend . . . . . Howard Johnson
A Stranger . . . . . Crawford Jackson
Another Stranger . . . . . Roy Atkins
A Dummy . . . . . Bill Bailey

11. *Green Pastures*
A travesty based on the famous book and play, with apologies to Marc Connelly and Roark Bradford.
The Lord . . . . . Broadway Jones
An Angel . . . . . ETHEL WATERS
Satan . . . . . Jimmy Baskette
A Harlem Midnight Rounder . . . . . BUBBLES
She Devils . . . . . Southern Beauties
Harlem Steppers . . . . . Blackbird Beauty Chorus
Angels in Heaven . . . . . Cecil Mack's Blackbird Choir
Scene based on three episodes: Heaven, Earth and Hades.

Lew Leslie was one of the more fascinating characters of a colorful period of Broadway history. Once a vaudeville performer with Belle Baker and, he claimed, Walter Winchell, he rose to prominence as a musical comedy producer at a time when the fortunes of Earl Carroll and George White were ebbing. The irascible White was tied up in marital troubles. Carroll had his problems too: as a publicity stunt, he had had a nude showgirl sit in an enormous bathtub filled with champagne and was arrested, not for any affront to public decency, but for the champagne—this was Prohibition—and incarcerated in the Atlanta Federal Penitentiary for one year.

It was not uncommon for Leslie, an eccentric producer if there ever was one, to jump into the orchestra pit, oust the conductor, and take over—even though he knew nothing about music. His habits of changing the running order of his shows, hiring and firing his performers on a whim, and changing costumes and scenery for no apparent reason during a run were legendary—in fact, on his printed programs it was not uncommon to find his *nota bene*, PROGRAM SUBJECT TO CHANGE OWING TO MAGNITUDE OF PRODUCTION.

Leslie lined up Flournoy E. Miller and Andy Razaf to write the book and lyrics for a new show, *Lew Leslie's*

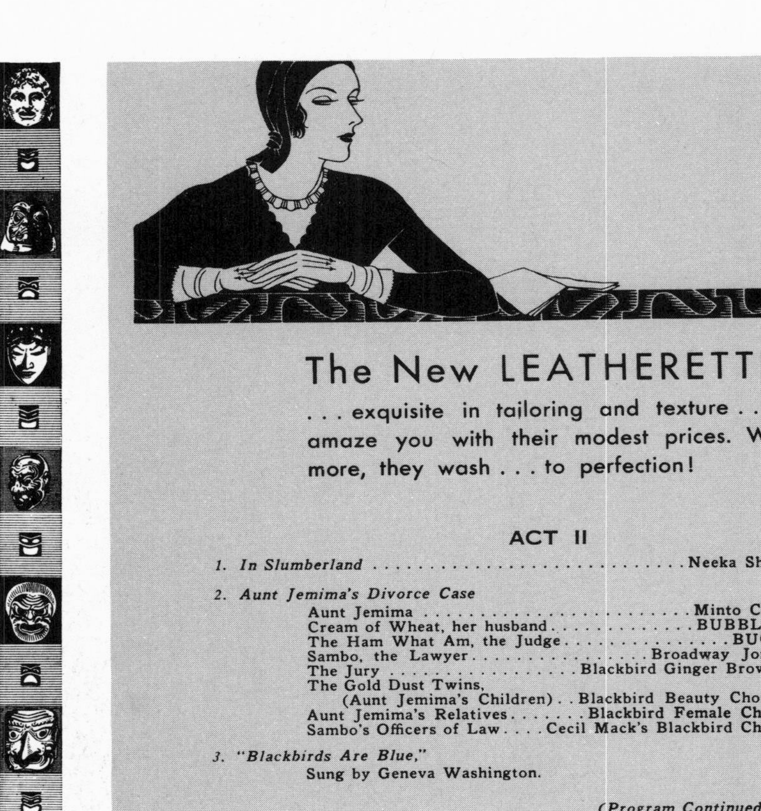

The New LEATHERETTES*

. . . exquisite in tailoring and texture . . . will amaze you with their modest prices. What's more, they wash . . . to perfection!

ACT II

1. *In Slumberland* . . . . Neeka Shaw

2. *Aunt Jemima's Divorce Case*
   Aunt Jemima . . . . Minto Cato
   Cream of Wheat, her husband . . . . BUBBLES
   The Ham What Am, the Judge . . . . BUCK
   Sambo, the Lawyer . . . . Broadway Jones
   The Jury . . . . Blackbird Ginger Browns
   The Gold Dust Twins,
   (Aunt Jemima's Children) . . Blackbird Beauty Chorus
   Aunt Jemima's Relatives . . . . Blackbird Female Choir
   Sambo's Officers of Law . . . . Cecil Mack's Blackbird Choir

3. *"Blackbirds Are Blue,"*
   Sung by Geneva Washington.

(Program Continued on Next Page)

Bill Robinson and Adelaide Hall in *Lew Leslie's Blackbirds of 1928*

Blackbirds of 1930, and then approached Eubie to write the music. When Leslie arrived at the Blake home on West 138th Street and offered him the commission to write the score, Eubie answered, "I'll be glad to. Who is your publisher?" (In those days impresarios were commonly connected with publishing houses, who forwarded advance money to composers and lyricists through the producer.) "Shapiro and Bernstein," was the answer; this was fine, as Eubie had already had several numbers placed there, and the deal was closed with a three-thousand-dollar advance, with the stipulation (usual at that time) that twenty-eight songs would be delivered by a certain date.

Andy Razaf, born in Madagascar as Andreamenentania Paul Razafinkeriefo, had first been known to Eubie as a brilliant soapbox orator for the rights of the Negro; later Andy had written lyrics with Fats Waller and Harry Brooks, having become famous for his *double-entendre* numbers, especially "My Man of War."

Composer and lyricist went to work. *"Andy's working method,"* remembers Eubie, *"is like no one else's I have ever seen. He will hear a tune once through, sit right down, and write out the lyric in one sitting. In all the time we worked together—and we wrote four shows together—once he wrote a line it was* down *there. I never saw him change a line with me."* Except once. Razaf wrote a lyric for *Blackbirds on Parade*, a march with a strong Victor Herbert flavor, that Blake was worried about. It told of the history of the black man in America, from the first violent incidents to the indignities of the present. "*That song, and the other one, We Are Americans Too'—well, they gave the white people hell. I was sure that people who had paid twenty dollars for seats didn't want to hear that, even though it was all true. But Andy was adamant. 'I won't change a word,' he said. And our deadline was tomorrow! 'You write the music,' said Andy, 'and I'll write the lyrics.'*

"The next day Lew Leslie arrives at my house to hear the score. When he heard these songs, he was ecstatic. Now Lew was eccentric, and he'd had even less education than I've had, but he was a damn good showman. So he said again how much he

liked the songs—Andy is looking at me as if saying, 'See? I told you!'—then Lew said: 'But how can you tell people things like that when they are paying you twenty dollars?' . . . 'I'm not going to change a line,' said Andy.

"So out we go to Englewood, New Jersey, where Andy lives. Once in the house, it starts all over again: I'm telling him to change the words, and he won't change. His wife is sitting on the couch, reading a magazine, and she waits for Andy to calm down a little. Then she goes over to the desk, takes a paper and pencil, takes it to Andy, and asks him to write a new lyric for Blackbirds on Parade. *Damned if he didn't, perfect rhythm and all!"*

Lew Leslie's Blackbirds, "Glorifying the American Negro," opened September 1, 1930, at the Majestic Theatre in Brooklyn, with a cast including Buck and Bubbles, F. E. Miller, Mantan Moreland, Broadway Jones, the Berry Brothers, Jazzlips Richardson, Minto Cato, and Ethel Waters. As was Leslie's habit, the lineup and personnel changed every week throughout the show's run; later the comedian Jimmy Baskette would be added, and several others in the cast would be fired.

The two hits of the show were "You're Lucky to Me," sung by Ethel Waters, and "Memories of You." Eubie wrote "Memories of You" especially for Minto Cato, who had a larger voice-range than most theater singers; the span of the tune, an octave and a fifth, made it a test (if not a performance) piece for many auditioning singers, but it owes its perennial popularity to Benny Goodman, who championed it as a jazz tune in the late thirties.

The show's lineup included parodies of current Broadway hits. In the one on *Green Pastures*, Eubie wrote a choral number, "Heaven, Earth, and Hades," in which the tenants of each sing a tune in counterpoint with the other two groups. Since Eubie would not have time to make the choral arrangements, Leslie hired a Professor Chambré, from St. Louis, to come do them. The good professor arrived at the rehearsal hall at the Alhambra Theatre (at 126th Street and Seventh Avenue) and was introduced to Blake, who never let Leslie know that he had recognized Professor Chambré as Ulysses Chambers, a musician from Baltimore, and a classmate of his in Llewellyn Wilson's harmony class many years before.

Lew Leslie, who was often found on Broadway standing outside Lindy's with spats and cigar, always carried a roll of several hundred dollars in his pocket. His cast members learned that they could put a touch on him if he was standing where others could see him, whereas Leslie unobserved would not lend money. His ostentation and grand gestures were eventually to cost him dear. When he brought the famous Spanish dancer Argentinita to New York to dreadful reviews, he was forced to shell out $10,000 to salve her wounded pride. This happened only months before the *Blackbirds of 1930* opening.

Evidently, especially at the opening, *Blackbirds* was an excellent show. Miller's routines were as funny as ever; a week later in Boston a man swallowed his false teeth while laughing at one. At the Brooklyn showing the critic from the *Eagle* expressed pity for those who hadn't seen *Blackbirds* opening night, for he knew Lew Leslie would be sure to mess around with it. *"Sure enough, he did,"* remembers Eubie. *"When that asbestos curtain came down he called a rehearsal at one* A.M. *in the morning, threw this out, changed that—tore the whole show apart."*

After a six-week tour the show opened on Broadway and lasted sixty-two performances, then went to Newark where it got stranded. Magnanimous Lew Leslie was nowhere to be found, and all cast members, crew, and orchestra had to get home under their own power. Fortunately Newark was close. Some of the showgirls sent for their benefactors' limousines; Ethel Waters got home in a broken-down car. Some may have walked—this was already 1930, money was scarce, and the Jazz Age was over.

Minto Cato introduced "Memories of You."

Elite
Studio N.Y.
10074-2.

YOU'RE LUCKY TO ME
LEW LESLIE'S BLACKBIRDS of 1930
book by FLOURNOY E. MILLER
lyrics by ANDY RAZAF
music by EUBIE BLAKE
ENTIRE PRODUCTION CONCEIVED AND STAGED BY
LEW LESLIE
Published by Shapiro, Bernstein & Co.
MUSIC PUBLISHERS
COR. BROADWAY & 47th STREET
New York

Ethel Waters and Eubie Blake in "You're Lucky to Me"

Aunt Jemima's Divorce Case: seated, Broadway Jones (Sambo, the Lawyer), Minto Cato (Aunt Jemima),

Buck (The Ham What Am, the Judge) and Bubbles (Cream of Wheat, Aunt Jemima's husband).

Mozambique

Studios N.Y.
10074-49.

Shuffle Along of 1933

In the heart of the Depression, from mid-December 1932 to the summer of 1933, only eight musicals reached Broadway, and all eight, including shows by such luminaries as George and Ira Gershwin, Lew Brown and Ray Henderson, Sigmund Romberg, and Kurt Weill, were early failures.

With millions out of work, money scarce, banks closing every day, and faith in America tested as it had not been since the Civil War, the times were unpropitious for unbridled expressions of euphoria. Even people who could afford a night on the town to escape momentarily the harsh realities of their lives found it difficult to forget their troubles and indulge themselves in a show. Musical comedy at its best had always been a manifestation of confidence in the hopes and dreams of the American middle class, black and white, but in that winter of discontent such optimism was in short supply and sadly inappropriate. There was too much pain, despondency, and starvation to laugh, sing, dance, and be happy.

In the aftermath of Aubrey Lyles's death in 1932, Sissle, Blake, and Miller, reunited in tragedy much as they had been divided by success, valiantly mustered the talents and energies that had brought them wealth and fame a decade before.

Yet it was not enough. For *Shuffle Along of 1933*, one of the ill-fated eight (it ran fifteen performances in New York), good as it appears to have been, was simply out of joint with its time.

After New York, *Shuffle Along of 1933* began a cross-country tour as a tab show, in a shortened form. A tab show, it might be remembered, was a theatrical presentation tailored to fit on the same bill with a movie. Sissle stayed with the troupe until late February 1933, then left to pursue his bandleading career.

The black lyricist and composer had influenced a whole generation of musical comedy. White writers had already begun to learn the Negro style and usurp the field; subsequent *Blackbirds* would hire black casts (at low salaries) and white writers to write ersatz black music. Meantime, the real thing was having trouble surviving: *Shuffle Along of 1933* broke up on the road, leaving young Nat King Cole, among others, stranded in Los Angeles. Then known as a pianist (he was to make excellent recordings in this connection later with Lester Young), it was about this time that Cole began to discover he had a voice.

James Hubert Blake was having a tough time. Once on top of the world, he now found himself walking the streets, not knowing what to do next. But just as important in his life as the need to succeed was the need to keep writing. And, with young Joshua Milton Reddie, a talented lyricist with a flair for alienating the Brill Building types, he began writing a series of shows, of which one, *Swing It*, was pro-

duced by the WPA in New York in 1937. The Blake and Reddie songs are less exuberant than the Sissle and Blake songs, less theatrical than the Razaf and Blake output. Eubie did all he could, as he has always done, to catch the spirit of his collaborator, and with Reddie his music is muted, more pastel in color—but this is not to deny that the pair wrote some beautiful songs indeed, notably "Green and Blue" (for *Swing It*), "You Were Born to Be Loved," and "I Can't Get You out of My Mind." In the mid-thirties Eubie began writing again with Andy Razaf, and they were able for a time to make a living writing floor shows and "industrials." The latter were events sponsored by big companies to promote products while incidentally entertaining prospective customers; Razaf and Blake wrote several of them, including one for Pabst Beer.

But the biggest blow for Eubie was the death, in early 1939, of his beloved wife Avis. She had stuck by him from the early days when she had helped him with his homework, and now Eubie, childless, was alone. Despite his grief Eubie completed, with Andy Razaf, the most important stage-piece of these bleak years, *Tan Manhattan*. Except for "We Are Americans Too" (resuscitated from *Blackbirds of 1930*) nothing has been published of this excellent score, although it was presented successfully in a floor show at the Ubangi Club, New York, in 1943, after a prior theater presentation at the Howard in Washington. Both the music and lyrics are first-rate, on a par with the Sissle and Blake shows. There are several numbers that should be reheard, but one especially, "I'd Give a Dollar for a Dime," is of hit quality. Eubie had not lost his touch, despite economic pressure, personal loss, and the perhaps now oppressive ghost of his early success.

Marion Tyler

In the 1940s he worked U.S.O. shows and kept writing songs with other collaborators, Grace Bouret and Bob Riley; despite the fact that he was at the low point of his life, Blake kept working on a high level. His spirits were to improve when he met Marion Gant Tyler and married her shortly after, on December 27, 1945. Both moved to her father's old house in Brooklyn, and a new cycle began in the life of Eubie Blake.

This would be a time of consolidating his earlier gains by study. He wrote out by hand many of his earlier piano pieces; he studied the Schillinger system with Professor Rudolf Schramm, which enabled him to work out his own orchestrations; he continued collaboration with Reddie until the latter moved to Mexico.

Life became quieter, though economically shaky at first. The Blakes soon gained greater financial security when Marion checked his ASCAP rating, learning that Eubie had been classified at an absurdly low level and was due much more money in royalties than he had been receiving. ASCAP complied in stepping up his rating, and Eubie could relax a little for the first time in twenty years.

Milton Reddie

Edith Wilson starred in *Shuffle Along of 1933*

The sound films were to bring the death knell of vaudeville, although it was to be a series of long, convulsive death throes: vaudeville would survive in the outer reaches of the country till the early fifties, till certain television programs, such as *The Ed Sullivan Show*, would displace the few live acts then still found.

But if there were few live shows for black (or white) performers, the situation in films was not much better. Here most black artists were barred entirely, and the racism always latent in American show business practice began to come more and more to the surface. Times were hard, so black performers everywhere were the first to go jobless.

Despite overt efforts from the musicians' union to keep black players from getting engagements, Noble Sissle, with the band he reconvened in 1933, was able through sheer doggedness to get jobs on the circuit, playing college proms and one-nighters. An engagement at the Park Central in New York City revived that hotel's flagging fortunes for a time; Noble could still use his name to pave footpaths, though the superhighways were harder now.

In 1934 a pageant, *O, Sing a New Song,* depicting the Negro experience in America, was staged at Soldier Field, Chicago; Noble helped write and assemble the show, and it was there that a young choreographer, Katherine Dunham, came to his attention. Noble's patronage helped to start her career. On the M.C.A. tour in 1935, playing amusement parks, resorts, country clubs, and the like, Noble was put in touch by F. E. Miller with a young singer, Lena Horne, who, it turned out, was able to substitute as vocalist *and* conductor when Noble and his regular singer Billy Banks were hospitalized after an auto accident. In 1938 Noble Sissle and his band had a

Nina Mae McKinney, featured in the Blake-Razaf *Tan Manhattan*, first achieved stardom in the King Vidor film *Hallelujah* (1929).

long-term engagement in Billy Rose's Diamond Horseshoe that lasted until 1942. And it was during this time that he met and married a second wife, Ethel, who bore him two children, Cynthia and Noble, Jr. The war took him into the U.S.O., where with Miller and Ivan Browning he staged another modernized version of *Shuffle Along*; after 1945 Noble was back at the Diamond Horseshoe with his band.

More and more active in civic duties, Noble Sissle, who had helped found the Negro Actors' Guild and was its first president, established a concert varieties program for young performers. These were but a few of the accomplishments and activities that were to distinguish Noble's career in these long years away from the theater;

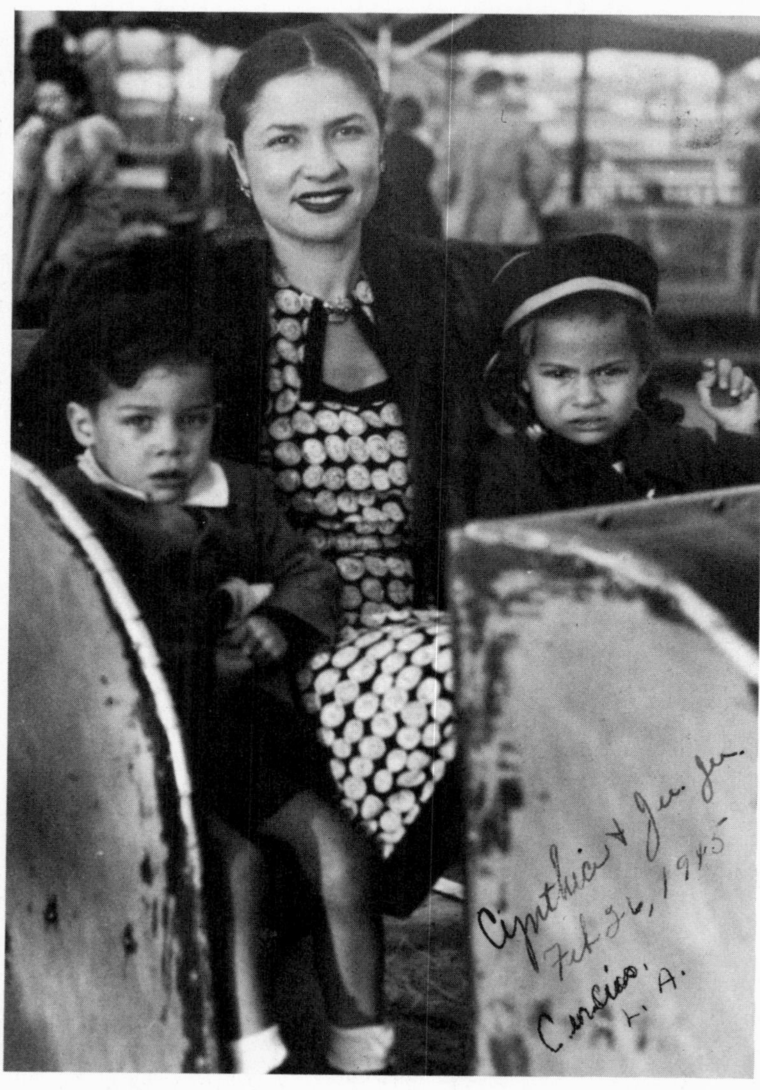

At the circus, Los Angeles, 1945: Ethel Sissle, Noble, Jr., and Cynthia

eventually they would lead to his election as Mayor of Harlem, an honorary post, in 1950. The post had been vacated by the death of Bill (Bojangles) Robinson the year before; one of the greatest and most beloved of all American dancers, his funeral marked the end, not only of his career, but of his era. It would be some time before a new generation of black artists would regain a significant foothold in this country.

In 1948, like a gentle bolt from the blue, came a new lease on the life of the Sissle-Blake partnership. Truman ran against the Governor of New York State, Thomas E. Dewey, for President. The race would be close, so close that a few newspapers were to print double editions on the day after elections, some with Dewey's picture on the front page as the President-elect. As it happened, Truman's first name,

I'M JUST WILD ABOUT HARRY

Hit of "SHUFFLE ALONG"

Words and Music by
NOBLE SISSLE
and
EUBIE BLAKE

Souvenir Edition

M. WITMARK & SONS, NEW YORK

NOBLE SISSLE and EUBIE BLAKE, Sole Selling Agents for this Edition

Funeral procession, Bill "Bojangles" Robinson, Times Square, November 28, 1949

RKO PALACE
WORLD FAMOUS Since 1827
BUITONI
The Spaghetti with less starch
NEW YORK PARIS ROME
USE Gillette Blades IN YOUR GILLETTE
DUST
MAYFAIR THEATRE
PARISIAN DANCING
GIRLS
DANCE
FRESH FRUIT DRINKS
FRANKFURTERS
NOW! 8 BIG ACTS 8 VAUDEVILLE FEATURE PICTURE
8 BIG ACTS VAUDEVILLE THE DALTON GANG
SO LONG BILL ROBINSON
LATE SHOW Tonite
EMBASSY Quartet
BRILLIANT EXQUISITE WORLD-TELE NEWS

Harry, spurred a revival of the old hit from *Shuffle Along* as a campaign song (a coincidence, as "Harry" had been a campaign song in the show), and soon "I'm Just Wild about Harry" flooded the airwaves. It cannot be claimed that the Sissle and Blake song was the deciding factor in that neck-and-neck election, but "Harry" did revive an incidental interest in the show it came from, and suddenly once again there was talk of reviving *Shuffle Along*. London wanted to import the show again; several movie producers wanted to film it. But in the end (about 1951) the decision was made to return *Shuffle Along* to the Broadway stage in an updated version.

The Broadway Sissle and Blake were returning to was a far different place from the one they had left. The Great White Way, no longer "white" as before, had suddenly become very like the multicolored chaotic blaze of movie theaters, "adult" magazine shops, and penny arcades it is today. For the movies had made serious inroads in the attendance figures there as well as in national-circuit vaudeville. Where in the twenties it was not unusual for sixty different attractions to be playing simultaneously in the Broadway houses, in the thirties more and more theaters closed, and the postwar theatrical scene was never to regain its former bustle and energy. Moreover, a significant change in managership and personnel had occurred—where, in the days of George M. Cohan and for several decades afterward, the writers and performers had a hand in mounting their own shows, drawing from their own experience, now the age of the nonperforming specialist had dawned. People who had never trod the boards in their lives suddenly became full-fledged directors; the artistic decisions, once handled in a hierarchic manner and with a unified concept, were now relegated to committees. Broadway was scared, in very much the same way it is still scared, and it needed (or thought it did) the counsel of so-called experts to assure success. From here on, producers played safe.

And it was also about this time that the method the movies had used and used again to box-office success, the star vehicle, began to tyrannize the stage. The star, not the show, it was thought, would lure ticket buyers away from the film emporia into the theaters, and *Shuffle Along* was recast for Pearl Bailey. In the same desperate frame of mind the producers of *Shuffle Along 1952* felt it necessary to recast the plot, scene, time setting, in fact the entire shape of the show, in an effort to reach modern audiences. New, jazzier arrangements were made to replace the tiny pit band of 1921; monster production numbers were substituted for the modest but witty vaudeville turns of Miller and Lyles; the show was cast and recast time after time by all the visiting experts then—and now—to be found in great numbers hanging around Broadway. Sissle and Blake's vaudeville background was looked on patronizingly by the new *cognoscenti*, who of course knew that all vaudevillians are low comics and second-class performers. The Sissle and Blake vaudeville act did not include, however, Sissle's falling into the orchestra pit, which happened during rehearsals; Noble was injured, and ever since then has had bad luck with his health. Pearl Bailey, for whom much care had been lavished on vehicalizing *Shuffle Along*, left the show before opening, and more rewrites were called for. *"They threw my music out of* Shuffle Along," grumbles Eubie, and well may he grumble, for in their efforts to modernize

Ethel Waters, Adelaide Hall, Noble Sissle, and Eubie Blake watch the demolition of the 63rd Street Theatre

and "improve" the show, the geniuses of the modern stage succeeded only in denaturing it completely. One has only to read George Jean Nathan's acerbic review to glean what an intelligent critic could see in the situation; his words apply as well today as they did then to the great majority of efforts presented on Broadway to an ever-dwindling audience.

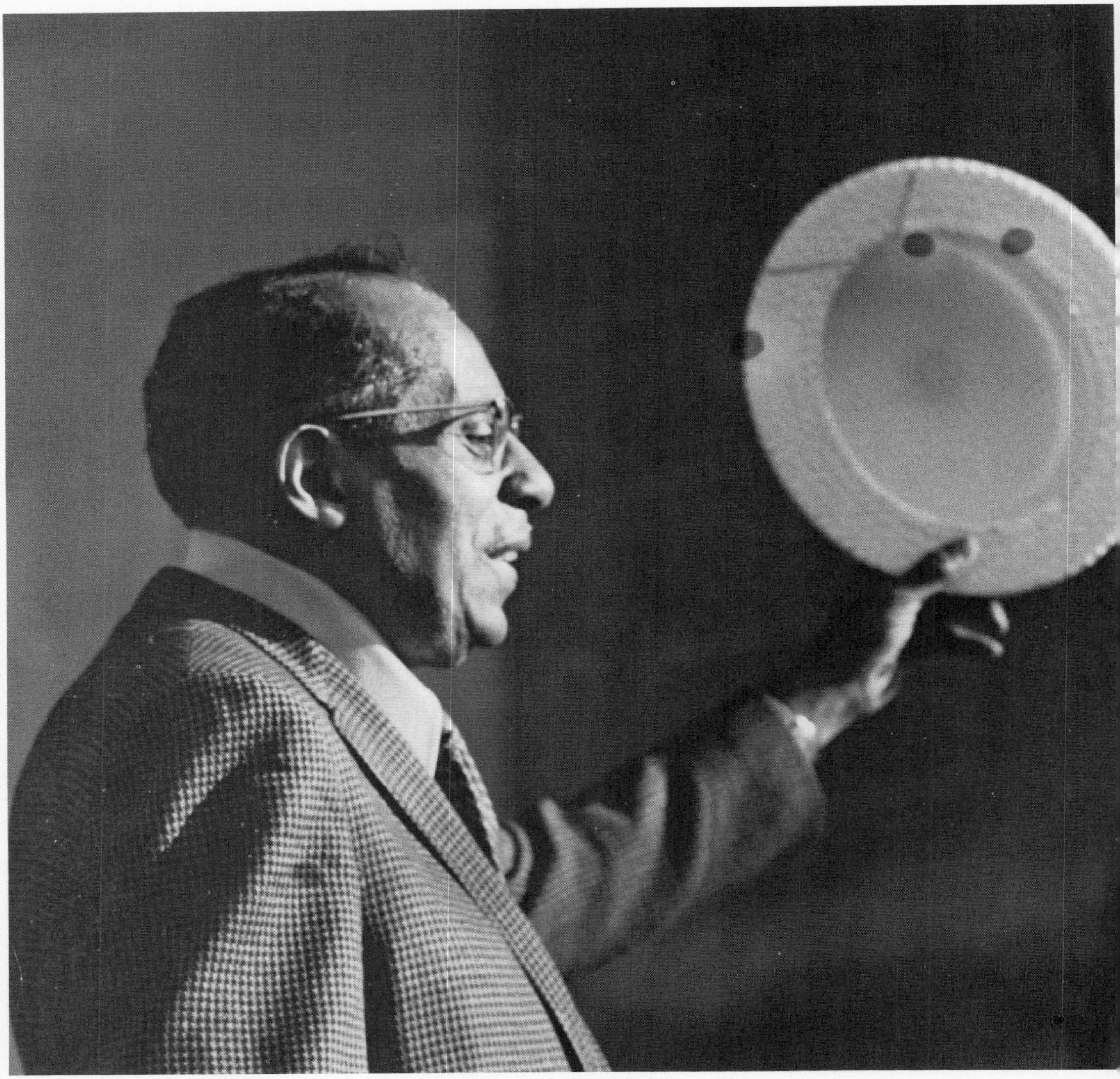

Sunday, May 25, 1952 New York *Journal-American*

GEORGE JEAN NATHAN

The Lesson of Another Failure

CHARLES SPURGEON, the English curate, once remarked, "Alteration is not always improvement, as the pigeon said when it got out of the net and into the pie." Which text I borrow for my today's own sermon.

The inspiration, so to speak, for my discourse is the recent revival of that grand show of the early 1920's, "Shuffle Along," now a catastrophic failure for, among other things, the reason the Rev. Charles pointed out to his parishioners some seventy years ago. Operating under the delusion, increasingly noticeable among our producers, that if theatregoers loved a show when they first saw it they will not love it any longer unless all sorts of alterations are made in it, the present sponsors monkeyed the revival out of any public acceptance and right into the can. The producing gentry, it seems, won't let even the more or less classic drama alone and bring the creditors down on their heads by incorporating hula-hula dancers into "Peer Gynt," transplanting "An Enemy of the People" in an American setting, not to mention adding Damon Runyon lingo to it, and converting "The Cherry Orchard" into a magnolia garden. And, to paraphrase the old French saying, the more things change the less of it there is in the box-office till.

In their zeal to bring shows up-to-date the producers succeed not only in diminishing their original values but in making them even more out-of-date, like women's knee-length skirts supposedly made à la mode by sewing two feet of lace onto their bottoms. Thus, the squirting of Stassen gags, Truman sports shirts and the like into "Of Thee I Sing," far from acceptably modernizing it, only makes an audience doubly conscious of its age, as artificially colored hair and face enamel accentuate a woman's. And thus, when about a half dozen years ago its producers sought to liven up "The Merry Widow" by inserting a banana-eating comedian, not only did they murder the excellent operetta's chances on the spot but caused the people seeing and hearing it for the first time seriously to doubt whether it had ever been what earlier audiences properly appreciated it was.

As I write this, the sponsors of "Shuffle Along" have miraculously admitted they made a mistake in changing what was originally a gala show and announce they are withdrawing it temporarily until they can rectify their blunder, which cost them the favor of the few paying customers and a pile of money. If by any remote chance they ever put the show on again, what they had best do is throw away all the many variations and present it exactly as it was in 1921. It is, if anything, a nostalgic show, and you can't work up any nostalgia by dressing up a favorite old aunt like a bobby-soxer. It isn't enough to keep in just two of the spirited old songs that in their day set Scott Fitzgerald to dancing in the aisle with one of the girl ushers, nor is it enough to preserve a single hot dance number in which the dusky belles perform as if they were afflicted with particularly acute cases of hydrophobia complicated by mariacal chorea. All the original stuff should be retained.

Even if some of this original stuff might now seem a bit old-fashioned, it would not seem nearly as old-hat as the substitutions involving a sand-dance, which goes back to 1895, a succession of senescent, gooey music hall ballads titled "Give It Love," "Farewell With Love," etc., a 1904 vaudeville act in which a comedian on a mountain-top accidentally drops over the edge his sole remaining provisions, and a scene in a dressmaking salon with its parade of models which was already obsolete when Clara Lipman introduced it into a show at the old Herald Square Theatre back in the era of the free lunch and Bonnie Maginn.

It was, as I have said, a wonderful show those thirty-odd years ago—I went to see it no less than five times—and it might still seem at least a good show if they left it alone with its story of small town politics instead of its altered one about an army post in Italy, with its imbecile Negro humors instead of its changed sentimental nonsense, and with its wild instead of politely tamed stage action. Audience excitement cannot be generated, as the producers thought it could, merely by instructing the brass in the orchestra to blow the roof off the theatre, nor can audience laughter be stimulated solely by having a woman appear in a ridiculous dress and agitate her bustle.

Such producers bedazzle themselves out of their and their backers' money with their belief that the new generation of theatregoers is not interested in the past and must be catered to with stuff of the moment. The belief is faulty on two counts. First, present-day audiences are composed not of these younger folk but largely of their elders; the proportion of customers under twenty-five to their elders is overwhelmingly in favor of the latter. And, secondly, both the younger theatregoers and the older often indicate as great an interest in the past as in the present, indeed an even greater. Otherwise how account for the popular success of plays like "Life With Father," "I Remember Mama," "Years Ago," and the kind? And how account for the enduring popularity of such old-timers as the remotely laid "Fledermaus," under whatever name it is produced, or "Show Boat," or the before-mentioned "Merry Widow," provided only yes, we have no bananas?

But still the producers insist upon going broke by taking the originally delightful "Music In The Air" out of Germany and quartering it, heaven and they alone know why, in Switzerland, by converting "The Beggar's Opera" into an up-to-date gangster whatnot called "Beggar's Holiday," and by dressing up the originally comical Negro yokels in "Shuffle Along" in wiseguy military garb. The few more intelligent producers, like those of "Pal Joey," cash in handsomely by keeping the materials of the show intact and simply improving the scenery, costumes, and one or two of the dance numbers.

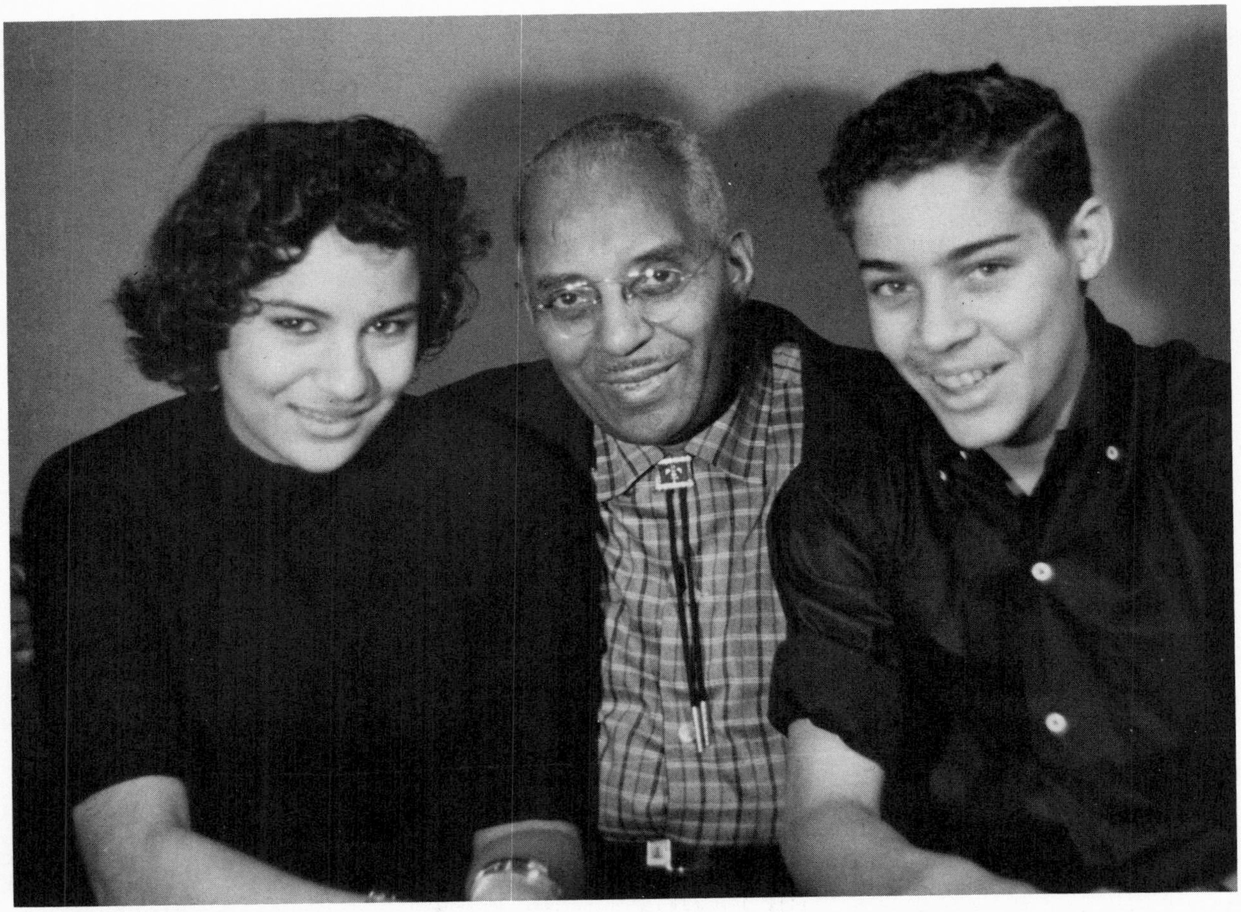

Noble with Cynthia and Noble, Jr.

Eubie and Marion

Conclusions and Questions

Shuffle Along was the most successful, influential, and widely disseminated work of musical theater ever written and performed by American blacks. The Williams and Walker and Cole and Johnson musicals, while important, never got comparable exposure to *Shuffle Along*. The operas of Harry Ward Freeman and Lucien Lambert, though performed in their day, have not been remembered; Scott Joplin's *Treemonisha* is currently experiencing more of a rebirth than a revival, as it was never professionally produced during the composer's lifetime. Thus, in 1921, the Sissle and Blake work may be said to have broken new ground, charted new territory, in bringing the music of the American black to the musical theater at large.

It should have led to much more than it did. No subsequent black theatrical work, even by such redoubtable composers as James P. Johnson, Fats Waller, and Duke Ellington, ever attained a measure of *Shuffle Along*'s success. One is hard put to believe that, with such musical genius, paired with writers such as Langston Hughes and Andy Razaf, these works failed because of overwhelming intrinsic weakness in the writing. Why, then?

Inspired by the Sissle and Blake breakthrough, black writers wrote shows which would need financial backing. At best hard to find for a black enterprise, legitimate backing became well-nigh unobtainable after the 1929 crash, and black writers often had to turn to shady sources to find money. Even then, such efforts were shoestring enterprises, deficient in many of the accouterments that could make a show successful with the general public.

But this is skirting the issue. It is incontestable that in America of the twenties and thirties racial lines were hardening with at first imperceptible speed; later the drift became impossible to ignore, and today the situation between blacks and whites has hardened into a cold war. The reasons for this are many and outside the scope of this book. But some of its causes and effects can be viewed clearly if the treatment of the black musician in this country can be taken as an example.

Sissle and Blake, to this day, persist in the beliefs of the Old American Dream, chief among them that any man can rise to great heights in this country by dint of sheer hard labor, no matter what his race or creed. So many other blacks, in the years that followed *Shuffle Along*, were to try their luck elsewhere: Josephine Baker, Sidney Bechet, Dean Dixon, Bud Powell, Paul Robeson, and so many other excellent performers cannot be chastised for not sticking it out in their own country, for their own country was to prove more and more inhospitable to them as the years passed.

The discrimination against black artists was even to become legalized in some cases, just as the treatment of the Jews during the Third Reich was vindicated by

then-current German law. This, added to the aforementioned economic prejudice, was to make life close to intolerable for Negroes in those years. The 1954 Supreme Court decision led to the repeal of many of these discriminatory laws—but the underlying hostilities and stereotypes remain, even though often the perpetrators of such daily insults may do so unconsciously or unintentionally.

In the performing arts the stereotype has strait-jacketed the American black man since the earliest times, and it continues the same today. The Negro is still thought of as some sort of brilliant performing monkey, who can sing and dance, and who is incapable of deep affection or feeling. If he is taken seriously, he is still expected to act in a certain set way, either as a performing clown (from Fats Waller to Flip Wilson), or as a perpetual angry-man (from "Ol' Man River," all the way to much of today's white-foundation-sponsored black theater): in either case, he is not supposed to understand, love, or be conversant with any part of the general Americo-European culture, except that part thought to belong to the ghetto. It would be wonderful to relate that this latter part of the prejudicial system of the United States were on the wane; unfortunately, it is not, and the prejudice is leveled from both sides of the racial fence.

This is a touchy part of this book, for neither of the writers of this book is black. We cannot feel firsthand any part of the weight of prejudice a black person feels, and we have intentionally underplayed to an extent the larger racial issues that surround this story. We did this for two reasons: one, that the problem is too all-pervasive and familiar to need reiteration here; two, because we felt that emphasis on it would tend, both for guilt-ridden white and anger-ridden black readers, to blur the clear and individual pictures we are trying to draw of two absolutely unique men. As Noble once said, *"We've been banged around so much, and enough has been said about it, that we needn't print any more stories,"* and we hope that we are honoring both his and Eubie's express wish in our choice of emphasis.

But to return to our earlier point: one of the subtlest forms of race prejudice is the insistence, on the part of both blacks and whites, to expect the Negro to create a *certain kind* of music or lyrics, one that would in part reflect the stereotype inflicted on him by both sides of the racial fence. Apropos of this point, here is an excerpt from a four-way conversation among Eubie Blake, Noble Sissle, and ourselves, on May 22, 1972:

ROBERT KIMBALL: When you wrote music and lyrics for the stage, did you make concessions for the fact you were singing for white audiences?

EUBIE BLAKE: *Yes. The lyrics and music would have to be equally applicable to white and black audiences. You see, Sissle went to white schools, Central High, then Butler, and he had a different slant on a lyric than the average Negro person. I wrote*

(PHOTOGRAPHS BY MARY VELTHOVEN)

waltzes. The reason I did that is because I was exposed to them; these were great writers, Victor Herbert, Franz Lehár, Leslie Stuart.

NOBLE SISSLE: *When Mr. Wanamaker took us in his house he asked us to write a song in honor of his daughter. That kept us going for a long time.*

EUBIE BLAKE: *You see, we were very lucky, Bill, that we were with a master thinker, James Reese Europe.*

WILLIAM BOLCOM: Was part of his plan getting into the homes of the rich?

EUBIE BLAKE: *Yes. It was his idea for us three to be able to write a Broadway Negro show, and only the rich could help us. We had no money of our own.*

NOBLE SISSLE: *It was his dream to have a Negro symphony orchestra. He almost had it, before he was killed.*

EUBIE BLAKE: *Paul Whiteman—and I love him, Sissle and Blake love him, we got a right to—was* not *the first man that put jazz into Carnegie Hall. It was James Reese Europe.*

WILLIAM BOLCOM: You both had the drop on most of the white writers. You could write for the white and black stage equally well.

EUBIE BLAKE: *That's because we were exposed to it* all. *It was* all *part of our heritage.*

And that it was. Eubie Blake has always loved to write waltzes. Today, at eighty-nine, he is writing a set of them, full of all the rich Middle European harmony one could ask for, played by him with the same accent and power he brings to all his work. His musical ear, always quick, had picked up and digested the ragtime syncopation of his era; why shouldn't it have also digested and accepted music by white composers? Noble Sissle's lyrics are equally influenced by African rhythms and models from English poetry; does that mean he is not giving his racial background its due? No: it is *we* who are being racist, in our unwillingness to allow *anyone* to play, sing, write, paint anything that person chooses. Sissle and Blake synthesized Afro-American and Euro-American elements in their work, at the same time retaining clear lines of influence—in such a polymorphous country and culture as ours, that is an almost impossible achievement, and yet they did it. In the end that achievement is of even more far-reaching importance than the fact that Eubie Blake and Noble Sissle, two immensely talented performers and writers who happen to be black, were able to carve, for such a tragically short time, a space for the black man in American musical theater.

(PHOTOGRAPH BY MARY VELTHOVEN)

APPENDIXES

The following is an attempt to catalogue the immense output of Sissle and Blake, as a team, separately, and as collaborators with other writers. We make no pretense to a definitive listing. There are two reasons: 1. some material is not yet catalogued or uncovered; 2. one has to stop somewhere. This listing can, however, be valuable as an aid to ongoing research and as a rallying point for future contributions by others.

I

CHRONOLOGICAL LIST OF SISSLE AND BLAKE SONGS AND PRODUCTIONS

EARLY SONGS AND VAUDEVILLE

1915
With Eddie Nelson:
IT'S ALL YOUR FAULT
SEE AMERICA FIRST
1916
AT THE PULLMAN PORTERS' BALL
MY LOVING BABY
WALKING THE DOG
1917
GOOD NIGHT, ANGELINE
MAMMY'S LITTLE CHOC'LATE CULLUD CHILE
1918
AFFECTIONATE DAN
TO HELL WITH GERMANY
WHAT A GREAT GREAT DAY
With James Reese Europe:
GOOD-BYE MY HONEY I'M GONE
I'VE THE LOVIN' ES' LOVE FOR YOU
MIRANDY
1919
BALTIMORE BLUES
GEE! I WISH I HAD SOMEONE TO ROCK ME IN THE CRADLE OF LOVE
AIN'T CHA COMING BACK, MARY ANN, TO MARYLAND
HE'S ALWAYS HANGING AROUND
GEE! I'M GLAD THAT I'M FROM DIXIE
YOU'VE BEEN A GOOD LITTLE MAMMY TO ME
MICHI MORI SAN
I'M JUST SIMPLY FULL OF JAZZ
With James Reese Europe:
ON PATROL IN NO MAN'S LAND
ALL OF NO MAN'S LAND IS OURS
1920
ORIENTAL BLUES
PICKANINNY SHOES
FLORODORA GIRLS
MY VISION GIRL
1921
CLEO ZELL MY CREOLE BELLE
GOOD FELLOW BLUES
KENTUCKY SUE

SHUFFLE ALONG

A "Musical Melange" presented by the Nikko Producing Co., Inc. (Headed by John Cort, Harry Cort, John Scholl, Gasthoffer, Al Mayer, F. E. Miller, Aubrey Lyles, Noble Sissle, and Eubie Blake.) Book by Miller and Lyles. Music and Lyrics by Sissle and Blake. Staged by Walter Brooks. Dances by Lawrence Deas and Charles Davis. Musical Arrangements by William Vodery. Company Manager: Al Mayer. Orchestra "Under personal direction of Mr. E. Blake."

Tryout: One-night stands in New Jersey and Pennsylvania beginning in late February 1921. Two weeks at the Howard Theatre, Washington, in late March, and two weeks at the Dunbar Theatre, Philadelphia, in April.

New York: 63rd Street Theatre May 23, 1921—504 performances. Cast featured, in addition to Miller and Lyles and Sissle and Blake, Lottie Gee, Roger Matthews, and Gertrude Saunders.

MUSICAL NUMBERS

OPENING CHORUS: ELECTION DAY
I'M JUST SIMPLY FULL OF JAZZ
LOVE WILL FIND A WAY
BANDANA DAYS
IN HONEYSUCKLE TIME
GYPSY BLUES
SHUFFLE ALONG
I'M JUST WILD ABOUT HARRY
IF YOU'VE NEVER BEEN VAMPED BY A BROWNSKIN
UNCLE TOM AND OLD BLACK JOE
EVERYTHING REMINDS ME OF YOU
ORIENTAL BLUES
I'M CRAVING FOR THAT KIND OF LOVE
DADDY, WON'T YOU PLEASE COME HOME
SISSLE AND BLAKE—INCLUDING
  GOOD NIGHT, ANGELINE
  LOW DOWN BLUES
  AIN'T CHA COMING BACK, MARY ANN, TO MARYLAND
  ON PATROL IN NO MAN'S LAND
BALTIMORE BUZZ

Article from *Variety* April 22, 1921

CORT COLORED SHOW "A RIOT" IN PHILLY
Draws $9000 on week at 90¢ top Phila., April 20

Shuffle Along, the all-colored show produced by John Cort, is a "riot" at the Dunbar, a colored theatre where it is now completing its second week. The piece will be brought into New York as soon as a theatre is assigned to it.

With a top price of 90 cents the attraction played to a gross of $9000 last week. Matinee business was not as heavy, but the demand was so great that a midnight performance was held last Friday.

J. J. Shubert came here to see *Shuffle Along*. Two patrons were requested out of the boxes (which hold 30 persons) and the manager, accompanied by his nephew, remained throughout the performance.

1922
SERENADE BLUES
1923
DEAR LI'L PAL
DON'T LOVE ME BLUES
YOU WERE MEANT FOR ME

Sissle and Blake wrote the following songs for *Elsie,* a musical comedy that opened in New York on April 2, 1923, after a lengthy tour:
BABY BUNTIN'
ELSIE
EVERYBODY'S STRUTTIN' NOW
I LIKE TO WALK WITH A PAL LIKE YOU
JAZZING THUNDER STORMING DANCE
JINGLE STEP
LOVIN' CHILE
MY CRINOLINE GIRL
A REGULAR GUY
SAND FLOWERS
TWO HEARTS IN TUNE
WITH YOU

1924 THE CHOCOLATE DANDIES

B. C. Whitney presents Sissle and Blake in *The Chocolate Dandies*. Book by Noble Sissle and Lew Payton. Music and Lyrics by Sissle and Blake. Staged by Julian Mitchell. Entire production under personal direction of Sissle and Blake. Cast included Lottie Gee, Ivan Harold Browning, Valada Snow, Elizabeth Welch, Lew Payton, Russell Smith, George Jones, Jr., and Josephine Baker.

Tryout: Lyceum Theatre, Rochester, New York, March 10, 1924; show had extensive tours both before and after its New York performances that lasted a total of over 60 weeks.

New York: Colonial Theatre, September 1, 1924—96 performances.

MUSICAL NUMBERS

Under the Direction of Eubie Blake

MAMMY'S LITTLE CHOC'LATE CULLUD CHILE
HAVE A GOOD TIME EVERYBODY
THAT CHARLESTON DANCE
THE SLAVE OF LOVE
I'LL FIND MY LOVE IN D-I-X-I-E
THERE'S NO PLACE AS GRAND AS BANDANA LAND
THE SONS OF OLD BLACK JOE
JASSAMINE LANE
DUMB LUCK
JUMP STEADY
BREAKIN' 'EM DOWN
JOCKEY'S LIFE FOR MINE
DIXIE MOON
DOWN IN THE LAND OF DANCING PICKANINNIES
THINKING OF ME
ALL THE WRONGS YOU'VE DONE TO ME
MANDA
RUN ON THE BANK
CHOCOLATE DANDIES
Added after New York opening:
YOU OUGHT TO KNOW
JAZZTIME BABY
Dropped from show before New York opening:
THERE'S A MILLION LITTLE CUPIDS IN THE SKY
1925
AL-LE-LU (OLD NOAH'S ARK)
I WONDER WHERE MY SWEETIE CAN BE
LADY OF THE MOON
THAT SOUTH CAR'LINA JAZZ DANCE
THE THREE WISE MONKEYS
WHY DID YOU MAKE ME CARE?
1926
LET'S GET MARRIED RIGHT AWAY
MESSIN' AROUND
TAHITI
THERE'S ONE LANE THAT HAS NO TURNING

1932 SHUFFLE ALONG OF 1933

Sissle and Blake joined F. E. Miller to create a new musical that eventually became *Shuffle Along of 1933*. Opening at the Mansfield

Theatre, New York, on December 26, 1932, the show played 15 performances and had a short road tour. The cast was headed by Miller, Sissle and Blake, Mantan Moreland, and Edith Wilson; the orchestra was conducted by Eubie Blake.

MUSICAL NUMBERS

LABOR DAY PARADE
SING AND DANCE YOUR TROUBLES AWAY
CHICKENS COME HOME TO ROOST
BREAKING 'EM IN
BANDANA WAYS
IN THE LAND OF SUNNY SUNFLOWERS
SUGAR BABE
JOSHUA FIT DE BATTLE
SORE FOOT BLUES
GLORY
SATURDAY AFTERNOON
HERE 'TIS
FALLING IN LOVE
DUSTING AROUND
IF IT'S ANY NEWS TO YOU
HARLEM MOON
YOU GOT TO HAVE KOO WAH
Dropped from show before New York opening:
YOU DON'T LOOK FOR LOVE
KEEP YOUR CHIN UP
WAITING FOR THE WHISTLE TO BLOW
LONESOME MAN
WE'RE A COUPLE OF SALESMEN
ARABIAN MOON

1933–1951
Some of the many songs Sissle and Blake wrote during this period:
ALONE WITH LOVE, *c.* 1950
BOOGIE WOOGIE BEGUINE, *c.* 1945
A NATIONAL LOVE SONG, *c.* 1950
SWINGTIME AT THE SAVOY (written with Langston Hughes), 1948
SYLVIA, *c.* 1950

SHUFFLE ALONG OF 1952

Miller, Sissle, and Blake headed the cast of this four-performance debacle that Eubie always refers to as "The Turkey." The show opened in New York on May 8, 1952, and also featured in its company Delores Martin, Napoleon Reed, Hamtree Harrington, Eddie Rector, Mable Lee, Avon Long, and Thelma Carpenter. The show was staged by many, but in the end only George Hale allowed his name to be listed in the program. The score, which featured songs of other composers, included the following numbers that are attributed to Sissle and Blake, in addition to numbers that had been written for their earlier shows:

MUSICAL NUMBERS BY SISSLE AND BLAKE

JIVE DRILL
CITY CALLED HEAVEN
BONGA-BOOLA
SWANEE MOON
THE RHYTHM OF AMERICA
IT'S THE GOWN THAT MAKES THE GAL THAT MAKES THE GUY
(with Joan Javits)
FAREWELL WITH LOVE

1953– Recent songs:
CASTLE OF LOVE, *c.* 1960
DON'T MAKE A PLAYTHING OUT OF MY HEART, *c.* 1958
IT'S AFRO-AMERICAN DAY, 1969
MARTIN LUTHER KING (DIDN'T THE ANGELS SING), 1968
THEY HAD TO GET THE RHYTHM OUT OF THEIR SOULS, *c.* 1958

II

ALPHABETICAL LIST OF SELECTED SISSLE AND BLAKE SONGS

Below song title: first known performer(s) and performance. An asterisk (*) after the title indicates publication, if known; most are out of print. (Same policy for categories III–V.)

A

AFFECTIONATE DAN
Sissle and Blake, vaudeville, 1918,
and in the DeForest film, *Sissle and Blake's Snappy Songs, c.* 1923

AIN'T CHA COMING BACK, MARY ANN, TO MARYLAND*
Sissle and Blake, vaudeville, 1919,
and in *Shuffle Along,* 1921

ALL OF NO MAN'S LAND IS OURS*
(Written with James Reese Europe)
Sissle and Europe's Orchestra, 1919

ALL THE WRONGS YOU'VE DONE TO ME
Lew Payton and Johnny Hudgins,
The Chocolate Dandies, 1924

AL-LE-LU (OLD NOAH'S ARK)*
Sissle and Blake, England, 1925

ALONE WITH LOVE
Unused, *Shuffle Along of 1952*

ARABIAN MOON
Unused, *Shuffle Along of 1933*

AT THE PULLMAN PORTERS' BALL
Lou Clayton, vaudeville, 1916

B

BABY BUNTIN'*
Luella Gear and Stanley Ridges, *Elsie,* 1923

BALTIMORE BLUES*
Sissle and Blake, vaudeville, 1919

BALTIMORE BUZZ*
Sissle and ensemble, *Shuffle Along,* 1921

BANDANA DAYS*
Arthur Porter, Adelaide Hall, and ensemble,
Shuffle Along, 1921

BANDANA WAYS
Edith Wilson, *Shuffle Along of 1933*

BONGA-BOOLA
Mable Lee, *Shuffle Along of 1952*

BOOGIE WOOGIE BEGUINE
Sissle and Blake, 1945

BREAKIN' 'EM DOWN
Valada Snow, Joe Smith, and ensemble,
The Chocolate Dandies, 1924

BREAKING 'EM IN
F. E. Miller, Edith Wilson, Bill Bailey,
Shuffle Along of 1933

C

CASTLE OF LOVE
c. 1960

CHICKENS COME HOME TO ROOST
George Jones, Jr., Fay Conty, and Lavada Carter,
Shuffle Along of 1933

CHOCOLATE DANDIES
Sissle, Blake, and ensemble,
The Chocolate Dandies, 1924

CITY CALLED HEAVEN
Laurence Watson and ensemble,
Shuffle Along of 1952

CLEO ZELL MY CREOLE BELLE
Sissle and Blake, vaudeville, 1921

D

DADDY, WON'T YOU PLEASE COME HOME*
Gertrude Saunders, *Shuffle Along,* 1921

DEAR LI'L PAL*
Sissle and Blake, 1923

DIXIE MOON*
George Jones, Jr., and ensemble,
The Chocolate Dandies, 1924

DON'T LOVE ME BLUES*
Sissle and Blake, 1923

DON'T MAKE A PLAYTHING OUT OF MY HEART
Written for unproduced musical *Happy Times,* 1958

DOWN IN THE LAND OF DANCING PICKANINNIES
Charlie Davis and ensemble,
The Chocolate Dandies, 1924

DUMB LUCK
Lew Payton, *The Chocolate Dandies,* 1924

DUSTING AROUND
George McClennon, *Shuffle Along of 1933*

E

ELECTION DAY
Ensemble, *Shuffle Along,* 1921

ELSIE*
Unused, *Elsie,* 1923

EVERYBODY'S STRUTTIN' NOW*
Luella Gear, Stanley Ridges, and ensemble, *Elsie,* 1923

EVERYTHING REMINDS ME OF YOU*
Lottie Gee and Roger Matthews, *Shuffle Along,* 1921

F

FALLING IN LOVE
Fay Conty and Clarence Robinson, *Shuffle Along of 1933*

FAREWELL WITH LOVE
Delores Martin, *Shuffle Along of 1952*

FLORODORA GIRLS*
Written for a Shubert revue, 1920

G

GEE! I WISH I HAD SOMEONE TO ROCK ME IN THE CRADLE OF LOVE*
Sissle and Blake, vaudeville, 1919

GEE! I'M GLAD THAT I'M FROM DIXIE*
Sissle and Blake, vaudeville opening, 1919

GLORY
Sissle, *Shuffle Along of 1933*

GOOD FELLOW BLUES
Sissle and Blake, vaudeville, 1921

GOOD-BYE MY HONEY I'M GONE*
(Written with James Reese Europe, 1918)

GOOD NIGHT, ANGELINE*
(Written with James Reese Europe)
Sissle and Blake, vaudeville, 1919, and in *Shuffle Along,* 1921

GYPSY BLUES*
Gertrude Saunders (later by Florence Mills), Lottie Gee and Roger Matthews, *Shuffle Along,* 1921

H

HARLEM MOON
Lavada Carter, *Shuffle Along of 1933*

HAVE A GOOD TIME EVERYBODY
Ensemble, *The Chocolate Dandies,* 1924

HERE 'TIS
Lavada Carter, Mantan Moreland, and ensemble, *Shuffle Along of 1933*

HE'S ALWAYS HANGING AROUND*
Sissle and Blake, vaudeville, 1919

I

I LIKE TO WALK WITH A PAL LIKE YOU*
Irma Marwick and Stanley Ridges, *Elsie,* 1923

I WONDER WHERE MY SWEETIE CAN BE*
Sissle and Blake, England, 1925

IF IT'S ANY NEWS TO YOU
Edith Wilson and Mantan Moreland, *Shuffle Along of 1933*

IF YOU'VE NEVER BEEN VAMPED BY A BROWNSKIN*
F. E. Miller, Aubrey Lyles, and ensemble, *Shuffle Along,* 1921

I'LL FIND MY LOVE IN D-I-X-I-E
Sissle and ensemble, *The Chocolate Dandies,* 1924

I'M CRAVING FOR THAT KIND OF LOVE*
Gertrude Saunders (later by Florence Mills), *Shuffle Along,* 1921

I'M JUST SIMPLY FULL OF JAZZ*
Sissle and Blake, vaudeville, 1919,
Gertrude Saunders in *Shuffle Along,* 1921

I'M JUST WILD ABOUT HARRY*
Lottie Gee and ensemble, *Shuffle Along,* 1921

IN HONEYSUCKLE TIME*
Sissle and ensemble, *Shuffle Along,* 1921

IN THE LAND OF SUNNY SUNFLOWERS
Clarence Robinson, Fay Conty, and ensemble, *Shuffle Along of 1933*

IT'S AFRO-AMERICAN DAY
Sissle and Blake, 1969

IT'S ALL YOUR FAULT*
(Written with Eddie Nelson),
Sophie Tucker, vaudeville, 1915

IT'S THE GOWN THAT MAKES THE GIRL THAT MAKES THE GUY
(Written with Joan Javits)
Shuffle Along of 1952

I'VE THE LOVIN'ES' LOVE FOR YOU*
(Written with James Reese Europe, 1917)

J

JASSAMINE LANE*
Lottie Gee and Ivan Harold Browning, *The Chocolate Dandies,* 1924

JAZZING THUNDER STORMING DANCE*
Unused, *Elsie,* 1923

JAZZTIME DANCE
Valada Snow, *The Chocolate Dandies,* 1924

JINGLE STEP*
Unused, *Elsie,* 1923

JIVE DRILL
William Dillard, *Shuffle Along of 1952*

JOCKEY'S LIFE FOR MINE
Charlie Davis and ensemble, *The Chocolate Dandies,* 1924

JUMP STEADY
Lee Randall, *The Chocolate Dandies,* 1924

JOSHUA FIT DE BATTLE
Edith Wilson, *Shuffle Along of 1933*

K

KEEP YOUR CHIN UP
Unused, *Shuffle Along of 1933*

KENTUCKY SUE*
Unused, *Shuffle Along,* 1921

KOO WAH (YOU GOT TO HAVE KOO WAH)
Noble Sissle, *Shuffle Along of 1933*

L

LABOR DAY PARADE
Ensemble, *Shuffle Along of 1933*

LADY OF THE MOON*
Cochran's London Revue, *Still Dancing,* 1925

LET'S GET MARRIED RIGHT AWAY*
Elizabeth Hines and Basil Howes, *Cochran's Revue of 1926*

LONESOME MAN
Unused, *Shuffle Along of 1933*

LOVE WILL FIND A WAY*
Lottie Gee and Roger Matthews,
Shuffle Along, 1921

LOVIN' CHILE*
Unused, *Elsie,* 1923

LOW DOWN BLUES*
Sissle and Blake, *Shuffle Along,* 1921

M

MAMMY'S LITTLE CHOC'LATE CULLUD CHILE*
Sissle and Blake, vaudeville, 1919;
Amanda Randolph, *The Chocolate Dandies,* 1924

MANDA*
Valada Snow and ensemble,
The Chocolate Dandies, 1924

MARTIN LUTHER KING (DIDN'T THE ANGELS SING)*
(Written in 1968 in memory of Dr. King)

MESSIN' AROUND
Sissle and Blake, vaudeville, 1926

MICHI MORI SAN*
Written for a Shubert revue, 1919

MIRANDY*
(Written with James Reese Europe, 1918)
Sissle and Europe's Orchestra, 1919

MY CRINOLINE GIRL*
Vinton Freedley and Irma Marwick, *Elsie,* 1923

MY LOVING BABY*
Written in 1916

MY VISION GIRL*
Helen Bolton, Eddie Cantor's *Midnight Rounders,* 1920

N

A NATIONAL LOVE SONG*
Written *c.* 1950

O

ON PATROL IN NO MAN'S LAND*
(Written with James Reese Europe, 1919)
Sissle and Blake, vaudeville, 1919,
and in *Shuffle Along,* 1921

ORIENTAL BLUES*
Sissle and ensemble, *Shuffle Along,* 1921

P

PICKANINNY SHOES*
Sissle and Blake, vaudeville, 1920

R

A REGULAR GUY*
William Cameron and ensemble, *Elsie,* 1923

THE RHYTHM OF AMERICA
Delores Martin and ensemble,
Shuffle Along of 1952

RUN ON THE BANK
Ensemble, *The Chocolate Dandies,* 1924

S

SAND FLOWERS*
Irma Marwick and ensemble, *Elsie,* 1923

SATURDAY AFTERNOON
Ensemble, *Shuffle Along of 1933*

SEE AMERICA FIRST*
(Written with Eddie Nelson, 1915)

SERENADE BLUES*
Sissle and Blake, 1922

SHUFFLE ALONG*
Charlie Davis and ensemble, *Shuffle Along,* 1921

SING AND DANCE YOUR TROUBLES AWAY
Lavada Carter and ensemble,
Shuffle Along of 1933

SING ME TO SLEEP DEAR MAMMY*
Roger Matthews and ensemble,
Shuffle Along, 1921

THE SLAVE OF LOVE*
Lottie Gee and Ivan Harold Browning,
The Chocolate Dandies, 1924

THE SONS OF OLD BLACK JOE
W. A. Hann and ensemble, *The Chocolate Dandies,* 1924

SORE FOOT BLUES
George McClennon, *Shuffle Along of 1933*

SUGAR BABE
Sissle, Lavada Carter, and Vivienne Baber,
Shuffle Along of 1933

SWANEE MOON
Thelma Carpenter, Eddie Rector,
Shuffle Along of 1952

SWINGTIME AT THE SAVOY
(Written with Langston Hughes, 1948)

SYLVIA
Sissle and Blake, 1950

T

TAHITI*
Elizabeth Hines and Basil Howes,
Cochran's Revue of 1926

THAT CHARLESTON DANCE
Elizabeth Welch, *The Chocolate Dandies,* 1924

THAT SOUTH CAR'LINA JAZZ DANCE*
Sissle and Blake, 1925

THERE'S A MILLION LITTLE CUPIDS IN THE SKY*
Unused, *The Chocolate Dandies,* 1924

THERE'S NO PLACE AS GRAND AS BANDANA LAND*
Lee Randall, Russell Smith, and ensemble,
The Chocolate Dandies, 1924

THERE'S ONE LANE THAT HAS NO TURNING*
Sissle and Blake, England, 1926

THEY HAD TO GET THE RHYTHM OUT OF THEIR SOULS
(Written for unproduced musical *Happy Times,* 1958)

THINKING OF ME*
Lottie Gee and Ivan Harold Browning,
The Chocolate Dandies, 1924

THE THREE WISE MONKEYS*
Sissle and Blake, England, 1925

TO HELL WITH GERMANY
Sissle and Blake, 1918

TWO HEARTS IN TUNE*
Vinton Freedley and Irma Marwick, *Elsie,* 1923

U

UNCLE TOM AND OLD BLACK JOE
Charlie Davis and Bob Williams,
Shuffle Along, 1921

W

WAITING FOR THE WHISTLE TO BLOW
Unused, *Shuffle Along of 1933*

WALKING THE DOG
Unused, *Ziegfield Follies of 1916*

WHAT A GREAT GREAT DAY
Sissle and Blake, 1918

WHY DID YOU MAKE ME CARE?*
Sissle and Blake, England, 1925

WITH YOU*
Unused, *Elsie,* 1923

Y

YOU OUGHT TO KNOW*
Valada Snow and Russell Smith,
The Chocolate Dandies, 1924

YOU WERE MEANT FOR ME*
Noël Coward and Gertrude Lawrence, *London Calling,* 1923;
Gertrude Lawrence and Jack Buchanan, *Charlot's Revue of 1924*

YOU'VE BEEN A GOOD LITTLE MAMMY TO ME*
Sissle and Blake, vaudeville, 1919

III

SELECTED LIST OF EUBIE BLAKE'S RAGS AND SEMICLASSICS

Title and Approximate Date of Composition	
THE BALTIMORE TODOLO	1908
BLUE CLASSIQUE*	1939
BLUE RAG IN TWELVE KEYS	1969
BLUE THOUGHTS*	1936
BRITTWOOD RAG	1911
BUTTERFLY	1936
CAPRICIOUS HARLEM	1937
CHARLESTON RAG	1899
CHEVY CHASE*	1914
CLASSICAL RAG	1972
CORNER CHESNUT AND LOW	1903
DICTY'S ON SEVENTH AVENUE*	1955
EUBIE DUBIE (Blake and Guarnieri)	1972
EUBIE'S BOOGIE	1904
FIZZ WATER*	1914
HIGH MUCK DI MUCK	1972
KITCHEN TOM	1908
MELODIC RAG	1971
MOODS OF HARLEM*	1937
NOVELTY RAG	1910
POOR KATIE RED	1910
RAIN DROPS	1924
TRICKY FINGERS*	1908
TROUBLESOME IVORIES*	1911
VALSE AMELIA	1972
VALSE EILEEN	1972
VALSE ERDA	1968
VALSE ETHEL	1972
VALSE MARION	1972
VALSE VERA	1972

IV

BLAKE SONGS WITH ANDY RAZAF

Beginning in 1930, Eubie collaborated with Andy Razaf on more than eighty songs for at least three shows: *Blackbirds of 1930,* a Pabst Blue Ribbon Beer industrial show, and a floor show, *Tan Manhattan* (1940). Their songs include:

From *Blackbirds of 1930:*
MEMORIES OF YOU*
YOU'RE LUCKY TO ME*
BLACKBIRDS ON PARADE
MY HANDY MAN AIN'T HANDY NO MORE*

From *Tan Manhattan:*
TAN MANHATTAN
A DOLLAR FOR A DIME
A GREAT BIG BABY
DIXIE ANN IN AFGHANISTAN
MAGNOLIA ROSE
WEARY
WE ARE AMERICANS TOO*

BLAKE SONGS WITH JOSHUA MILTON REDDIE

During the 1930s and 1940s Blake wrote more than a hundred songs with Joshua Milton Reddie for several musicals; only one, *Swing It* (1937), was produced on Broadway. The Reddie-Blake songs include:
AIN'T WE GOT LOVE (with Cecil Mack) *Swing It,* 1937*
GREEN AND BLUE (with Cecil Mack) *Swing It,* 1937
I CAN'T GET YOU OUT OF MY MIND
JUBILEE BRAZILIAN
MY LITTLE DREAM TOY SHOP
TROUBLE SEEMS TO FOLLOW ME AROUND
YOU WERE BORN TO BE LOVED

V

OTHER COLLABORATORS WITH BLAKE AND SISSLE

Among Eubie's other collaborators were:
Grace Bouret (at least thirty songs in the early 1940s, many for an unproduced musical, *Be Yourself*)
Henry Creamer (approximately forty songs, including songs for two unproduced musicals, *Teddy* and *Sissy*)
Arthur Porter (with whom Blake wrote BLUES WHY DON'T YOU LEAVE ME ALONE?* and AS LONG AS YOU LIVE)
Jack Scholl (with whom Blake wrote LOVING YOU THE WAY I DO)
F. E. Miller (with whom Blake wrote songs for Irving C. Miller's *Brown Skin Models,* 1954, and *Hit the Stride,* 1955)

Among Noble's other collaborators were:
Harry Revel, Will Vodery, and Edgar Battle

VI

EUBIE BLAKE PIANO ROLLOGRAPHY

Dates shown below are months in which the rolls were released for sale to the public, as indicated by lists issued by the various roll companies. Actual recording dates are unknown but would normally have preceded the date of release by a month or two. Unless otherwise noted, artist credits in each case read "Played by Eubie Blake." Most of these rolls appear in reissue form on Biograph long-playing records (Biograph BLP 1011Q and BLP 1012Q). Rolls preceded by an asterisk (*) have not been located yet. In most cases, data shown come directly from the roll labels or catalogues.

1917
CHARLESTON RAG (Eubie Blake) Ampico 54174-E
Played by Composer 1.25

This may be Eubie's first issued piano roll. The exact release date is uncertain but may have followed shortly after CHARLESTON RAG was copyrighted, on August 8, 1917.

January 1918
* RAIN SONG (Will Marion Cook) Rythmodik J19124
1.00

The January supplement described this roll as follows: "This is an arrangement of one of the negro songs in the nature of a 'spiritual.' It is folk music of the colored race, and this interesting number has created a sensation wherever it has been heard." Unfortunately, no surviving copy of this roll has been found by collectors, nor have copies of the other rolls that are asterisked.

February 1918
* EV'RYBODY'S CRAZY 'BOUT THE DOGGONE BLUES Rythmodik X101103
(Creamer and Layton) .85
Fox Trot Key of A flat

SOMEBODY'S DONE ME WRONG (Skidmore) Rythmodik X101113
Fox Trot Key of B flat .85

August 1919
* MIRANDY (Europe, Sissle and Blake) Rythmodik J103843
Fox Trot Key of F 1.00
Played by Eubie Blake; assisted by Edwin Williams
"This number, the last written by Lieutenant Jim Europe before his lamented death, is a typical Southern melody and an ideal fox trot."

GOOD NIGHT, ANGELINE (Europe, Sissle and Blake) Rythmodik J103933
Fox Trot Key of G 1.00
Played by Eubie Blake; assisted by Edgar Fairchild

"Eubie Blake, who played this number, had also a hand in its composition. It is a typical Southern number with a touch of 'blues.' "

GOOD NIGHT, ANGELINE was also released later, presumably the same arrangement and performance, on a reproducing Ampico roll 200743F ($1.50) but the month of release is uncertain. This version has not turned up yet, however.

* SAVE YOUR MONEY, JOHN (Copeland and Rogers)
Fox Trot from *Ziegfeld Follies,* 1918 Rythmodik J104323
Key of C 1.00
Played by Eubie Blake; assisted by Edwin Williams

Sometime, probably during 1919, Eubie took a train from Boston to New York. A man on the train recognized him and invited him to stop off in Meriden, Connecticut, to make rolls, which Eubie did. Apparently Eubie recorded at this time for the Artrio-Angelus label, rolls for which were made by the Wilcox & White Co. in Meriden. An Artrio-Angelus roll catalogue dating from about 1922 lists six of these early Blake rolls, only two of which have actually been found. Two of the remaining four are rumored to exist, but as of this writing they have not surfaced.

1919 (?)
* ZIEGFELD FOLLIES, 1919 Selection Artrio-Angelus 8036
(Dave Stamper) 2.00
Introducing: (1) Shimmie Town; (2) A Pretty Girl Is Like a Melody; (3) Sweet Sixteen; (4) Syncopated Cocktail; (5) Mandy; (6) Tulip Time

Dave Stamper was the "official" composer of the *Follies,* but most of the above songs are by Irving Berlin.

* GOOD NIGHT, ANGELINE (Lieutenant Jim Europe, Lieutenant Noble Sissle, and Eubie Blake) Artrio-Angelus 8037
1.75

* CHINESE LULLABY *East Is West* Artrio-Angelus 8038
(R. H. Bowers) 1.75

* GREENWICH VILLAGE FOLLIES Selection Artrio-Angelus 8039
(A. Baldwin Sloane) 2.50
Introducing: (1) I Want a Daddy Who Will Rock Me to Sleep: (2) My Little Javanese; (3) The Message of the Cameo; (4) Red, Red as a Rose; (5) My Marionette; (6) I Want a Daddy Who Will Rock Me to Sleep

SCHUBERT [*sic*] GAIETIES OF 1919 Selection Artrio-Angelus 8048
(Jean Schwartz) 2.00
Introducing: (1) I've Made Up My Mind to Mind a Maid Made Up Like You; (2) Cherry Blossom Lane; (3) Beal [*sic*] Street Blues; (4) I'll Be Your Baby Vampire; (5) My Beautiful Tiger Girl; (6) I've Made Up My Mind to Mind a Maid Made Up Like You

Eubie has heard this roll and claims it is not his playing. He feels it is a bootleg issue. Indeed, the roll does not sound like Eubie's style. We can only guess why Wilcox & White would have put his name on a roll medley he did not actually play. It is possible that Eubie played these numbers out of his characteristic style or recorded the tunes while practicing them the first time, not knowing the machinery was on, recording what he was doing. The company may have been satisfied enough with the result to issue the roll, even though Eubie, if he did play it, did not grant his approval of the finished product. However, even "Beale Street Blues," which Eubie surely would have been playing prior to 1919, does not come off sounding like a Blake performance.

GEE! I WISH I HAD SOMEONE TO ROCK ME IN THE CRADLE OF LOVE (Blake) Artrio-Angelus 8049
1.50
Eubie has listened to this roll and confirms that it definitely is his recording. The roll sounds like Eubie, too.

Eubie's remaining rolls were made for the Mel-O-Dee label, which was first introduced by the Aeolian Corporation in January 1920. Mel-O-Dee rolls were word rolls or song rolls, with the words printed along the right-hand edge of the roll. Eubie remembers being recognized and approached one day as he walked along Broadway by George H. (Jack) Bliss. Bliss asked him if he'd like to make some piano rolls, and Eubie said sure. Bliss had been with QRS since 1914 and joined Mel-O-Dee in April 1920. By October he was General Manager. This street contact with Eubie probably took place in late 1920, based on the dates of Bliss's employment with Mel-O-Dee, the timing of Eubie's first release, and the opening of Mel-O-Dee's new factory in New York.

Many of Eubie's Mel-O-Dee rolls are heavily edited with extra notes which either Eubie or some anonymous arranger added after the initial recording to give the rolls a jazzy, fuller sound. Rolls like these apparently attracted sales and gave credence to the rave notices that Mel-O-Dee issued about Eubie's "world-famous" artistry. Bliss clearly saw Eubie as Mel-O-Dee's trump card and used him to show up the other major companies, notably QRS. QRS countered a few months later by announcing that James P. Johnson was recording exclusively for them. Several James P. rolls were released by QRS in May 1921 and may be heard on Biograph BLP 1003Q.

The *Music Trade Review,* in its January 15, 1921, issue, reported that "Mel-O-Dee has just issued two new bulletins, one devoted exclusively to 'Blues,' and including a list of all the Mel-O-Dee records made to date by Ubie [*sic*] Blake, the noted interpreter of blues, and by other specialists in that class of music. . . ."

January 1921
BROADWAY BLUES (Morgan) Mel-O-Dee 4153
Fox Trot Key F 1.25
Played by Ubie [*sic*] Blake (per the roll; "Eubie" per the January 1921 bulletin)

February 1921
CRAZY BLUES (Bradford) Mel-O-Dee 4199
Fox Trot B flat 1.25

"Crazy Blues, as interpreted by the new Mel-O-Dee artist, Eubie Blake, is doing very well in the Southern cities," said the *Music Trade Indicator,* January 15, 1921. "The most popular 'blues' we have had for several years," said the February bulletin.

STRUT MISS LIZZIE (Creamer and Layton) Mel-O-Dee 4241
Fox Trot B flat 1.25

During this period, the Wilcox & White company was issuing certain rolls of popular tunes for a new word roll series on their Artrio-Angelus label. STRUT MISS LIZZIE, the only Blake recording to so appear, was released on Artrio-Angelus 2035 in May 1921, but it is the identical recording issued by Mel-O-Dee. The Artrio version, however, includes extra expression perforations along the edge and was designed to reproduce on Artrio-Angelus players.

Most of the rest of Eubie's rolls were assigned "S" serial numbers. Apparently this signified rolls of special-interest music and meant that the rolls were not automatically shipped on standing orders from Mel-O-Dee dealers. Dealers had to order these rolls specially to get them.

IT'S RIGHT HERE FOR YOU (Bradford) Mel-O-Dee S2948
Fox Trot Key F 1.25

HOME AGAIN BLUES (Berlin and Akst) Mel-O-Dee S2949
Fox Trot Key G 1.25

" 'Home Again Blues,' written by Irving Berlin and Harry Akst of the Mel-O-Dee recording staff, has attained unusual popularity. The Mel-O-Dee roll is played by Eubie Blake, the popular Mel-O-Dee 'Blues' pianist. Blake is one of the few colored men whose professional work has gained approval and success. He is a big-time vaudeville artist as well as a star member of Jack Bliss's Mel-O-Dee recording staff." (*Music Trade Indicator,* February 5, 1921)

FARE THEE HONEY BLUES (Bradford) Mel-O-Dee S2950
Fox Trot B flat 1.25

March 1921
THE GOOD FELLOW BLUES (Blake) Mel-O-Dee S2959
Fox Trot Key F 1.25

DON'T TELL YOUR MONKEY MAN (L. Johnson) Mel-O-Dee S2966
(Monkey Man Blues) 1.25
Fox Trot E flat

BOLL WEEVIL BLUES (Hess) Mel-O-Dee 4259
Fox Trot Key G 1.25

"The rolls played by Eubie Blake, the famous 'blue' player, are meeting with great demand (in the South). . . . A special shipment is being rushed on 'Boll Weevil Blues' played by Eubie Blake"—*Music Trade Indicator,* February 5, 1921. A nearly identical announcement appeared in the *Phonograph and Talking Machine Weekly,* February 16, 1921. In that release Eubie was referred to as "the *world's most* famous 'blue' player"!

April 1921
IF YOU DON'T WANT ME BLUES (Brabford) [*sic*] Mel-O-Dee S2980
Fox Trot Key C 1.25

WANG-WANG BLUES (Mueller, Johnson and Busse) Mel-O-Dee S2985
Fox Trot Key F 1.25

ROUMANIA (Williams) Mel-O-Dee S2988
Fox Trot E flat 1.25

NEGRO SPIRITUALS Duo Art Song Roll 10091
Go Down Moses 1.75
I'm a-Rolling
Nobody Knows de Trouble I See, Lord
I Got Shoes

Played by Ubie [*sic*] Blake

The misspelling of Eubie's name on this, his only Duo Art roll, compares to the misspelling of his name on the first Mel-O-Dee roll, issued in January. It is possible, then, that both rolls were among the first he recorded, with the erroneous spelling following the Duo Art master roll all the way through production until final issuance several months later, in April 1921.

The following description of NEGRO SPIRITUALS appears in the April 1921 Duo Art bulletin (under the category "Popular Salon Music"), as well as in the company's 1924 and 1927 catalogues, in which "Ubie" becomes "Eubie."

> *"Especial interest attaches to the unique record-roll of 'Negro Spirituals,' in which the talented young pianist, Ubie Blake, has skilfully arranged and played a group of four of the best-known folk-songs of his race in America. 'Go Down Moses' was a sort of song-prayer much sung by the 'darkies' of the South in slavery days, and the tune is still regarded as sacred to the black race. 'I'm a-Rolling' is a typical work-song and has long been sung in the cotton fields. 'Nobody Knows de Trouble I See, Lord' is also a work-song; while the last of the group, 'I Got Shoes,' is a 'jubilee' song, formerly called 'jube' by the negroes, and is frequently sung by the traveling negro quartets of today. Its words constituted the poor slave's way of explaining the difficulty of getting into Heaven."*

The roll is sometimes listed as Duo Art 100917, the last digit meaning the size and price of the roll.

May 1921
MEMPHIS BLUES (Handy) Mel-O-Dee 4371
Fox Trot Key F 1.25

"A new arrangement of this favorite blue song," said the May 1921 bulletin.

September 1921
DANGEROUS BLUES (Brown) Mel-O-Dee 4427
Fox Trot (Blues) Key F 1.25

November 1921
ARKANSAS BLUES (Lada) Mel-O-Dee 4549
Fox Trot Key F 1.25

December 1921
THE DOWN HOME BLUES (Delaney) Mel-O-Dee S3001
Fox Trot—Blues Key C 1.25

UNCONFIRMED BLAKE ROLLS

Two rolls not listed above may have some connection with Eubie. One is a Rythmodik roll, MY SWEETIE, which is listed in the company's catalogues as having been issued on Rythmodik G100703, played by Al Sterling and Victor Arden. The tune is a fox trot credited to Irving Berlin as composer. It was the American Piano Company's (Rythmodik's) practice to copyright their rolls during this time to prevent unauthorized duplication by other firms. To do this, application cards were sent to the Library of Congress, where they are still on file today. The card for MY SWEETIE shows the artists as Sterling and Arden, in pen, but someone has crossed these names off and written "Eubie Blake" over this entry. The roll has not been located, so until it is and can be heard, we can't be sure whether or not it's a possible Blake recording. Possibly two versions of the roll were cut for consideration by the Rythmodik recording manager. The Blake roll may have been the one that was issued, but through a clerical error the credit in the catalogues was given to Sterling and Arden. The penned correction at the Library of Congress may have been an attempt to set the record straight.

The other roll is a Mel-O-Dee number. In the 1923 Mel-O-Dee catalogue, Mel-O-Dee roll S3003 is shown as having been issued as TEN LITTLE FINGERS AND TEN LITTLE TOES, played by Eubie Blake. A copy of the roll has been found, and the artist credit shown is "Played by Phil Ohman." Indeed, the roll doesn't sound at all like Eubie. To further compound the confusion, the *Music Trade Indicator* for November 12, 1921, in listing the December Mel-O-Dee rolls, shows DOWN HOME BLUES as by Blake in the special-number series, and then lists TEN LITTLE FINGERS, also in the special-number series, but with no artist shown. The puzzling part is that this was a regular popular tune of the day, and there was no apparent reason to issue it on the "S" series unless it was a Blake performance that might offend straight ears. Here, too, maybe both Blake and Ohman recorded the roll, with the Ohman master being the one that was issued but with credit going to Blake in the catalogue. Unless a copy credited to Eubie on the label turns up someday, we will have to conclude that DOWN HOME BLUES was Eubie's last issued piano roll.

Compiled by Michael Montgomery

VII

PIANO ROLL REISSUES ON RECORDS

Twenty-two of Eubie Blake's thirty known piano rolls have been located; all twenty-two were reissued in early 1973 on long-playing records. They may be ordered directly from their producer, Arnold S. Caplin, Biograph Records, P. O. Box 109, Canaan, New York 12029, if they cannot be obtained from record stores.

EUBIE BLAKE VOLUME I BLUES & RAGS
Biograph BLP—1011Q (Stereo)
His Earliest Piano Rags 1917–1921 including CHARLESTON RAG

Side 1
CHARLESTON RAG (Eubie Blake)
SOMEBODY'S DONE ME WRONG (Skidmore)
GOOD NIGHT, ANGELINE (Europe, Sissle and Blake)
SCHUBERT [*sic*] GAIETIES OF 1919 Selection (Jean Schwartz)
(1) I've Made Up My Mind to Mind a Maid Made Up Like You; (2) Cherry Blossom Lane; (3) Beal [*sic*] Street Blues; (4) I'll Be Your Baby Vampire; (5) My Beautiful Tiger Girl; (6) I've Made Up My Mind to Mind a Maid Made Up Like You
GEE! I WISH I HAD SOMEONE TO ROCK ME IN THE CRADLE OF LOVE (Sissle and Blake)

Side 2
BROADWAY BLUES (Morgan)
CRAZY BLUES (Bradford)
STRUT MISS LIZZIE (Creamer and Layton)
IT'S RIGHT HERE FOR YOU (Bradford)
HOME AGAIN BLUES (Berlin and Akst)
FARE THEE HONEY BLUES (Bradford)

EUBIE BLAKE VOLUME II 1921
Biograph BLP—1012Q (Stereo)
Rare Piano Rolls of Early Blues and Spirituals

Side 1
THE GOOD FELLOW BLUES (Sissle and Blake)
DON'T TELL YOUR MONKEY MAN (MONKEY MAN BLUES) (L. Johnson)
BOLL WEEVIL BLUES (Hess)
IF YOU DON'T WANT ME BLUES (Bradford)
NEGRO SPIRITUALS
(1) Go Down Moses; (2) I'm a-Rolling; (3) Nobody Knows de Trouble I See, Lord; (4) I Got Shoes

Side 2
WANG WANG BLUES (Mueller, Johnson and Busse)
ROUMANIA (Williams)
MEMPHIS BLUES (Handy)
DANGEROUS BLUES (Brown)
ARKANSAS BLUES (Lada)
THE DOWN HOME BLUES (Delaney)

VIII

EXPLORATORY DISCOGRAPHY OF NOBLE SISSLE, EUBIE BLAKE, AND JAMES REESE EUROPE

This is an exploratory list of the known recordings of Noble Sissle and Eubie Blake and of their colleague and mentor, James Reese Europe. This compilation, by Michael Montgomery and Robert Kimball, was taken from a number of sources—from the labels of the records and from the evidence furnished by the records themselves; from trade magazine listings of the period in which the records were issued; from record catalogues; and from data originally published in *Record Research Magazine* (Brooklyn, New York) and in the works of Brian Rust and others.

Obviously, this is a preliminary effort in an area where scholarship is still relatively new. Therefore, what follows is in some instances fragmentary and incomplete. Nevertheless, we offer it as the most comprehensive and accurate survey we can make from the limited information available.

Braces indicate that catalogue numbers apply to both titles.

1. JAMES REESE EUROPE'S SOCIETY ORCHESTRA, 1913–1914

EUROPE'S SOCIETY ORCHESTRA
Recorded in New York City, December 29, 1913.
TOO MUCH MUSTARD (Cecil Macklin)
DOWN HOME RAG (Wilbur C. Sweatman) Victor 35359

AMAPA—MAXIXE BRASILIEN (J. Storoni)
EL IRRESISTIBLE—TANGO ARGENTINE (Lozatti) Victor 35360

Recorded in New York City, February 10, 1914.
YOU'RE HERE AND I'M HERE (Kern)
CASTLE WALK (Europe) {Victor 17553, HMV B–258 *

CASTLE HOUSE RAG (Castles in Europe)
CONGRATULATIONS WALTZ (Lame Duck) Victor 35372

Recorded in New York City, October 1, 1914.
FIORA WALTZ
FOX TROT {Victor rejected (unissued)

2. SISSLE AND BLAKE, 1917–1918 (Pathé)

NOBLE SISSLE (with Blake?), tenor
Recorded in New York City. Released *c.* April 1918(?).
CAN'T YO' HEAH ME CALLIN', CAROLINE (Roma)
LITTLE ALABAMA COON (Starr) Pathé 20194
(One source shows this to be dated May 1917.)

"NOBLE SISSLE, tenor, with Orch. Accompaniment"
(a Pathé house band under the direction of Dominic Savino, and including Eubie Blake on piano)
Recorded in New York City, probably in the summer or fall of 1917. Released early in 1918.

These recordings must have been made prior to Noble Sissle's departure for France in late 1917. Thus the dates listed below are issue dates.

MAMMY'S LITTLE CHOC'LATE CULLUD CHILE (Sissle–Blake) Pathé 20210

GOOD NIGHT, ANGELINE (Sissle–Europe–Blake)
SOMEBODY'S GONA [GONNA] GET YOU (Morgan) Pathé 20226

A LITTLE BIT O' HONEY (Jacobs-Bond)
STAY IN YOUR OWN BACK YARD (Udall) Pathé 20233

THERE IT GOES AGAIN (Jentes) Pathé 20267 (*c.* January 1918)

HE'S ALWAYS HANGING AROUND (Sissle–Blake)
THAT'S THE KIND OF A BABY FOR ME (Egan) Pathé 20280
(from *Ziegfeld Follies of 1917*)

MANDY LOU (Cook) Pathé 20295 (*c.* March 1918)

EUBIE BLAKE TRIO—Piano Duo with Drums
Eubie Blake, piano, with another unknown piano (possibly Elliott Carpenter) and unknown drums (possibly Buddy Gilmore)

Recorded in New York City, c. August 1917. Released in April 1918.
HUNGARIAN RAG—One Step (Lenzberg) Pathé 20326

AMERICAN JUBILEE—Fox Trot (Claypoole) Pathé 20326, 5389

SARAH FROM SAHARA—Oriental Fox Trot (Frey) Pathé 20358, 5389 (*c.* May 1918)

BLAKE'S JAZZONE ORCHESTRA
Eubie Blake (piano) with unknown group.
Recorded in New York City. Released *c.* August or September 1918.
THE JAZZ DANCE (W. Benton Overstreet) Pathé 20430

From *Record Research Magazine,* Vol. 1, No. 1: The *Eubie Blake Trio* and *Jazzone Orchestra* recordings are in the realm of mystery. Eubie Blake only dimly recalls the trio sides. He conservatively commented that Buddy Gilmore may be the trio's drummer. However, he wasn't sure. The same vagueness applied to the Jazzone group. Since pertinent information is lacking, this discography would like to present some interesting excerpts from a 1918 Pathé supplement about these organizations.

Concerning the Eubie Blake Trio—HUNGARIAN RAG and AMERICAN JUBILEE: "The Eubie Blake Trio comprises an organization of three extremely clever colored musicians whose talents in entertaining the '400' and ultra-fashionables of N. Y. C. are extremely in favor and much sought after. As exponents of real 'jazz' and 'ragtime' piano work, two of its members are 'King pins.' Member number three is the 'sassiest' drummer you ever saw. He's a bunch of smiles and nerves, with most dexterous fingers, and when these colored gentlemen begin to play, Oh lawdy. Well, just hear these two recordings and we will leave the verdict to you. They're simply great. The two selections are happily chosen and afford fine opportunity for display of real 'down south' ragging both on the piano and in the drummer. The dance tempo in each number is perfection itself."

Concerning *Blake's Jazzone Orchestra:* "No matter where one goes to dance the moment the sound of 'jazz' dance music is heard it arouses the greatest interest, especially when well played and in characteristic 'jazz' style, as appears in the rousing selection, now very popular, upon this record. Blake's Jazzone Orchestra, a colored organization, is a N. Y. sensation."

3. EUROPE'S BAND, 1919

From the *Phonograph and Talking Machine Weekly,*
April 30, 1919, page 32:
ANOTHER BIG SCOOP FOR PATHÉ!
LT. JIM EUROPE
THE "JAZZ KING"

and his famous 369th "U. S. Infantry" Hell Fighters Band are now recording exclusively for Pathé records the music that put pep into our boys over there, who put pep into the war and settled it.

This famous overseas band is now making a two-year triumphal tour of the country, from Maine to California, playing every matinee and evening to packed houses in every city. Everybody is wild about the lively jazzing and syncopated rhythm, played as only Jim Europe's band can play it. When you hear the wonderful music you can't sit still. Your head and shoulders have to sway. "It's Jaz as is!"

Lt. Noble Sissle, the finest colored tenor in America, and Creighton Thompson, popular colored baritone, two of the band's favorite soloists, are singing the latest ballads and song hits; the Singing Serenaders and the Hell Fighters' Double Quartet harmonize real Southern jubilee songs.

Jim Europe's Hell Fighters Band and its famous soloists are now making records exclusively for Pathé. The first of these remarkable records, to be released on April 20th, will include:

LT. JIM EUROPE AND HIS FAMOUS 369TH U.S. INFANTRY ("HELL FIGHTERS") BAND
Recorded in New York City, February 1919.
HOW YA GONNA KEEP 'EM DOWN ON THE FARM? (Donaldson) Pathé 22080 10 inch .85
Vocal refrain by Lt. Noble Sissle
ARABIAN NIGHTS (David–Hewitt)

DARKTOWN STRUTTERS' BALL (Brooks)—Medley Pathé 22081 10 inch .85
INDIANOLA (Oniwas)

BROADWAY "HIT" MEDLEY, introducing (1) I've Got the Blue Ridge Blues, (2) Madelon, (3) Till We Meet Again, (4) Smiles Pathé 22082 10 inch .85
JA-DA (Carleton)

MOANING TROMBONES (Bethel) Pathé 22085 10 inch .85
MEMPHIS BLUES (Handy)

LITTLE DAVID PLAY ON YOUR HARP—Negro Spiritual
Lt. Noble Sissle and Lt. Jim Europe's Singing Serenaders Pathé 22084 10 inch .85
EXHORTATION (Cook)—Jubilee Song
Creighton Thompson and Lt. Jim Europe's 369th U.S. Infantry ("Hell Fighters") Band

These are going to be the record sensations of the year. Everyone will crowd around to get them, just as they rush to pack the theatres when the Hell Fighters play.

Wire in your order today. Double the largest order you have ever placed and you'll still run short.

Pathé Frères Phonograph Company
20 Grand Avenue E. A. Widmann, President Brooklyn, New York

LT. NOBLE SISSLE Accompanied by Lt. Jim Europe's 369th U.S. Infantry ("Hell Fighters") Band—Tenor Solo
Recorded in New York City, March 1919. Release date unknown.
ON PATROL IN NO MAN'S LAND (Sissle–Europe) Pathé 22089
MIRANDY (Sissle–Europe–Blake)

ALL OF NO MAN'S LAND IS OURS (Sissle–Europe) Pathé 22104
JAZZOLA (Robinson–Morse)

JAZZ BABY (Sissle–Europe–Blake)
(Creighton Thompson and Hell Fighters) Pathé 22103
WHEN THE BEES MAKE HONEY (Sissle–Europe)
(Lt. Noble Sissle and "Hell Fighters")

LT. JIM EUROPE'S SINGING SERENADERS
Recorded in New York City, March 1919.
HAUNTING BLUES Pathé 22086
PLANTATION ECHOES

LT. JIM EUROPE'S 369TH INFANTRY ("HELL FIGHTERS") BAND
Recorded in New York City, c. March 1919.
ST. LOUIS BLUES (Handy) Pathé 22087
RUSSIAN RAG

LT. JIM EUROPE'S 369TH INFANTRY ("HELL FIGHTERS") BAND
Recorded in New York City, April 1919. Release date unknown.
DIXIE IS DIXIE ONCE MORE (Turner–Kard)
Lt. Noble Sissle and Lt. Jim Europe's 369th U. S. Infantry ("Hell Fighters") Band Pathé 22146
THAT'S GOT 'EM (Sweatman)

MY CHOC'LATE SOLDIER SAMMY BOY
Sissle and Band Pathé 22147
MISSOURI BLUES

LT. EUROPE'S 369TH INFANTRY ("HELL FIGHTERS") BAND
Recorded in New York City, April 1919.
THE DANCING DEACON Pathé 22167
CLARINET MARMALADE

4. PATHÉ, 1920

LIEUT. JIM EUROPE'S FOUR HARMONY KINGS
Unaccompanied
SWING LOW, SWEET CHARIOT (Jubilee Song) Pathé 22187
ONE MORE RIBBER TO CROSS (Jubilee Song)

NOBLE SISSLE—Tenor with Orchestra
Trumpet, clarinet, and/or flute, saxophone, trombone, violin, drums, tuba, with piano by Eubie Blake.
Recorded in New York City. Released *c.* April 1920.
I'M JUST SIMPLY FULL OF JAZZ (Steele [*sic*]–Blake)
(correct credit is Sissle–Blake) Pathé 22284
AIN'T CHA COMING BACK, MARY ANN, TO MARYLAND (Sissle–Blake)

(INSTRUMENTATION UNKNOWN)
Recorded in New York City. Released *c.* July 1920.
MELODIOUS JAZZ (Merrill–Jerome) Pathé 22357
JAZZ BABIES' BALL (Bayha–Pinkard)

NOBLE SISSLE—Tenor with Orchestra
Probably a Pathé house band, with Eubie Blake, piano.
Recorded in New York City. Released *c.* September 1920.
MAMMY'S LITTLE SUGAR PLUM (Davis–Erdman) Pathé 22394
GEE! I WISH I HAD SOMEONE TO ROCK ME IN THE CRADLE OF LOVE (Sissle–Blake)

NOBLE SISSLE—(with Blake? with orchestra?)
Released *c.* November 1920.
MY VISION GIRL (Sissle–Blake) Pathé 20463

NOBLE SISSLE—Tenor with Orchestra
Probably a Pathé house band with Eubie Blake on piano.
Released *c.* December 1920.

GEE I'M GLAD I'M FROM DIXIE (Sissle–Blake) AFFECTIONATE DAN (Sissle–Blake)	Pathé 20470
PICKANINNY SHOES (Sissle–Blake)	Pathé 20475 (*c.* January 1921)

NOBLE SISSLE—Tenor with orchestra (Instrumentation similar to Pathé 22284—April 1920)
Recorded in New York City. Released *c.* February 1921.

GREAT CAMP MEETIN' DAY (Mikell–Sissle) CRAZY BLUES—Dance Rhythm (Bradford)	Pathé 20484, Actuelle 020484

NOBLE SISSLE AND HIS SIZZLING SYNCOPATORS
Same instrumentation as Pathé 22284, April 1920.
Recorded in New York City. Released *c.* April 1921.

ROYAL GARDEN BLUES (Williams–Williams) LOVELESS LOVE (Handy)	Pathé 20493, Actuelle 020493

5. SISSLE AND BLAKE, EDISON, 1921

SISSLE AND BLAKE
With orchestra?
Recorded in New York City. Released January 11, 1921.

CRAZY BLUES	Edison 50754, Edison Blue Amberol 4264 (cylinder)

6. SISSLE AND BLAKE, EMERSON, 1920–1922

The following text appeared in a full-page trade advertisement taken by Emerson in the March 16, 1921, issue of the *Phonograph and Talking Machine Weekly:*

Noble Sissle Will Hereafter Record Exclusively for Emerson Records

Oh, yo' Noble Sissle Man,
Yo' sure has der stuff,
W'en yo' sings it's simply gran'—
Cannot get enough.
Syncopated melody,
"Broken time" dat BUBBLES!
Joyous, happy harmony,
Takes away mah troubles.

PUTS MAH MONEY DOWN TO BET
IS YO' AIN'T DER BESTEST YET!

Sissle is without doubt the greatest tenor of his Race.

As popular with white audiences as with colored ones, he cemented his claim to fame in the late war as soloist with the celebrated "367th."

Indeed, it is related that Sissle was an especial favorite of the great French General, Gouraud.

The records of very few artists—white or black, equal Sissle's in demand.

He does not strain for his effects. His renditions are typically his own, yet happily natural and spontaneous in their interpretations of the music of his Race.

While his first Emerson records are of the popular hit type, it is our intention to record him later in a group of negro "spirituals," in the singing of which he is unexcelled.

Two selections which Sissle and his side partner, Blake, have recorded for Emerson and which are selling especially well are:
CRAZY BLUES—Emerson Record No. 10326
BROADWAY BLUES—Emerson Record No. 10296

NOBLE SISSLE
Vocal, accompanied by Eubie Blake, piano.
Recorded in New York City, c. September 1920. Released *c.* December 1920.

BROADWAY BLUES—Blues Character Song (Swanstrom and Morgan)	Emerson 10296, Medallion 8246, Regal 911 (as by "Leonard Graham" and "Robert Black")

Vocal, accompanied by Eubie Blake, piano.
Recorded in New York City, December 1920. Released *c.* March 1921.

CRAZY BLUES—Blues Character Song (Perry Bradford)	Emerson 10326, Medallion 8252 (as "Willie Black and Ruby Blake"), Medallion 8305 (same), Paramount 12007 (as "Sissle & Blake," released 1922), Regal 911 (as "Leonard Graham" and "Robert Black")

NOBLE SISSLE AND HIS SIZZLING SYNCOPATORS
Sissle, vocal; Frank de Broite (?), trumpet; Frank Withers (?), trombone; Edgar Campbell, clarinet; Nelson Kincaid, alto sax; Herbert Wright, drums; Eubie Blake, piano.
Recorded in New York City, February 1921. Released *c.* May 1921.

ROYAL GARDEN BLUES—Blues Novelty Song (Clarence and Spencer Williams)	Emerson 10367, Emerson 10604, Medallion 8286 (as "Willie Brown and His Sizzling Syncopators")

Recorded in New York City, March (2?), 1921. Released *c.* July 1921.

THE BOLL WEEVIL BLUES—Blues Novelty	Emerson 10357, Emerson 10627 (rel. 7/23)
LOVELESS LOVE—Blues Ballad	Emerson 10357, Emerson 10605 (rel. *c.* 5/23), Regal 946 (as "Leonard Graham and His Jazz Band")

Recorded in New York City, April 1921. Released *c.* June 1921.

LOW DOWN BLUES—Blues Character Song	Emerson 10365, Emerson 10627 (released *c.* July 1923), Regal 946 (as "Leonard Graham and His Jazz Band")
LONG GONE—Blues Character Song (Handy)	Emerson 10365 (released *c.* June 1921), Emerson 10574 (released *c.* February 1923), Medallion 8279
MY MAMMY'S TEARS—Blues Song (Coslow–Ringle–Schaffer)	Emerson 10367

Recorded in New York City, April–May 1921. Released *c.* August 1921.

BALTIMORE BUZZ—Blues Character Song from *Shuffle Along* (Sissle and Blake)	Emerson 10385, Emerson 10574 (released *c.* February 1923)
IN HONEYSUCKLE TIME (When Emaline Said She'd Be Mine)—Blues Ballad from *Shuffle Along* (Sissle and Blake)	Emerson 10385, Regal 9102 (as "Leonard Graham and His Jazz Band")

NOBLE SISSLE
Vocal, accompanied by Eubie Blake, piano.
Recorded in New York City, June 1921.

LOVE WILL FIND A WAY—Ballad (Miller and Lyle [*sic*]—Sissle and Blake)	Emerson 10396, Emerson 10604 (released *c.* May 1923), Regal 9107 (as "Leonard Graham and Robert Black"), Symphonola 4361
ORIENTAL BLUES—Blues (Miller and Lyle [*sic*]—Sissle and Blake)	Emerson 10396

EUBIE BLAKE
Piano solos.
Recorded in New York City, July 1921. Released *c.* October 1921.

BALTIMORE BUZZ — Medley — Introducing: "In Honeysuckle Time" from *Shuffle Along* (Sissle and Blake)	Emerson 10434
SOUNDS OF AFRICA—One Step (Eubie Blake)	Emerson 10434, Symphonola 4360, Paramount 14004 (a reissue made in the 1950s, labeled "African Rag" by "Unknown Rag Pianist"—this was made from a blank-labeled Emerson test pressing)

Reissued on Columbia album SOUNDS OF HARLEM 3-Col C3L-33. This is Eubie's earliest *phonograph* recording (that we know of) of his famous classic "Charleston Rag," and it permits interesting aural comparison with his 1917 piano roll made for Ampico of the same number. Eubie remembers Will Marion Cook thinking up the title "Sounds of Africa." Two different masters of "Sounds of Africa" were issued. Look for "41886–4" or "41886–6" in the wax between the labels and grooves.

SISSLE AND BLAKE
Recorded in New York City, August 1921.

I'VE GOT THE BLUES (BUT I'M JUST TOO MEAN TO CRY) (Parish–Young–Squires)	Emerson 10443, Emerson 10605 (released *c.* May 1923), Regal 9137 (as "Leonard Graham and Robert Black")
ARKANSAS BLUES—Down Home Chant (Williams–Lada)	Emerson 10443, Emerson 10605 (released *c.* May 1923)

EUBIE BLAKE
Piano, with Irving Kaufman, vocal
Recorded in New York City, September 1921. Released *c.* December 1921.

SWEET LADY—Medley (Johnson–Crumit–Zoob) from Musical Production *Tangerine*	Symphonola 4360, Emerson 10350, 10450, Regal 9130 (as "Billy Clark accompanied by Robert Black")
MA!—Fox Trot (Con Conrad)	Emerson 10450

Eubie listened to this recording in May 1972 and said his broken right-hand chords on the record represented Hughie Wolford's style of playing.

SISSLE AND BLAKE
Recorded in New York City, October 1921.

I'VE GOT THE RED, WHITE AND BLUES—Blues (Clarence Gaskill) I'M A DOGGONE STRUTTIN' FOOL—Blues (Ryan–Pinkard)	Emerson 10484, Regal 9158

Recorded in New York City, January 1922.

BOO HOO HOO—Blues Novelty (Nelson–Link–Aaronson–Lentz)	Emerson 10512, Regal 9180
I'M CRAVING FOR THAT KIND OF LOVE (from the Musical Production *Shuffle Along*) (Sissle and Blake)	Emerson 10512, Regal 9203

EUBIE BLAKE AND HIS ORCHESTRA
Similar to personnel for the Victor session for July 15, 1921.
Recorded in New York City, February (11?) 1922.

CUTIE (from the Musical Production *The Blue Kitten*) (Rudolf Friml)	Emerson 10519, Regal 9198
JIMMY, I LOVE BUT YOU	Emerson 10519, Regal 9199

7. SISSLE AND BLAKE, VICTOR, 1920–1921

NOBLE SISSLE
Vocal, accompained by Eubie Blake, piano.
Recorded in New York City, April 9, 1920.

GOOD NIGHT, ANGELINE SIMPLY FULL OF JAZZ	Victor tests (unnumbered)

FLORENCE EMORY
Vocal, accompanied by Eubie Blake, piano.
Recorded in New York City, April 15, 1920.

AFFECTIONATE DAN GEE! I WISH I HAD SOMEONE TO ROCK ME IN THE CRADLE OF LOVE	Victor tests (unnumbered)

EUBIE BLAKE
Piano solos, with unknown alto (and banjo *).
Recorded in New York City, June 30, 1921.

BANDANA DAYS I'M JUST WILD ABOUT HARRY BALTIMORE BUZZ *	Victor tests (unnumbered)

Recorded in New York City, July 11, 1921.
Broadway Jones (vocal) added

BALTIMORE BUZZ DAH'S GWINTER BE ER LANDSLIDE	Victor tests (unnumbered)

EUBIE BLAKE AND HIS Shuffle Along ORCHESTRA
William Hicks, Russell Smith (trumpet), Carroll Jones (trombone), Johnson (clarinet), Vess Williams (alto sax), Yearwood (flute), Noble Sissle (violin), Eubie Blake (piano), Vandeveer (banjo), John Ricks (brass bass), George Reeves (drums).
Recorded in New York City, July 15, 1921. Released *c.* October or December 1921.

BALTIMORE BUZZ (Sissle–Blake) —Introducing "In Honeysuckle Time" BANDANA DAYS (Sissle–Blake)—Introducing "I'm Just Wild about Harry"	Victor 18791, HMV B-1297, HMV Victor 18789

8. SISSLE AND BLAKE, PARAMOUNT, 1922

ALBERTA HUNTER
Vocal, accompanied by Eubie Blake, piano.
Recorded in New York City, early July 1922. Released *c.* fall 1922.

I'M GOING AWAY JUST TO WEAR YOU OFF MY MIND (Warren Smith–Clarence Johnson–Lloyd Smith) JAZZIN' BABY BLUES (Jones)	Paramount 12006, Para. 12043 (*c.* Jan. 1923)

SISSEL [*sic*] AND BLAKE
Solo and piano accompaniment.
Recorded in Chicago (?), *New York City* (?), 1922 (?).

IF YOU'VE NEVER BEEN VAMPED BY A BROWNSKIN YOU'VE NEVER BEEN VAMPED AT ALL (Sissel [*sic*] and Blake)	Paramount 12002 (two takes used: 1114-1, 1114-2)
BANDANA DAYS (Sissel [*sic*] and Blake)	Paramount 12002 (take 1115-3)

9. SISSLE AND BLAKE, VICTOR, 1923–1924

NOBLE SISSLE
Vocal, accompanied by Eubie Blake, piano.
Recorded in Camden, New Jersey, May 25, 1923.

WAITIN' FOR THE EVENIN' MAIL (Sittin' on the Inside, Lookin' on the Outside) (Billy Baskette)	Victor 19086, HMV Victor 19086
DOWNHEARTED BLUES (Hunter–Austin)	Victor 19086, HMV Victor 1986, HMV B–1703

Recorded in New York City, August 17, 1923.

DON'T LEAVE ME BLUES (Sissle and Blake) DEAR LI'L PAL (Sissle and Blake)	Victor rejected

Recorded in New York City, August 23, 1923.

DON'T LEAVE ME BLUES DEAR LI'L PAL	Victor rejected

Recorded in New York City, January 18, 1924.

DEAR LI'L PAL	Victor rejected
SWEET HENRY (The Pride of Tennessee) (Benny Davis–Harry Akst) OLD-FASHIONED LOVE (from the Musical Comedy *Runnin' Wild*) (Cecil Mack–Jimmy Johnson)	Victor 19253

Recorded in New York City, March 7, 1924.

MANDA (Sissle and Blake) JASSAMINE LANE (Sissle and Blake) DIXIE MOON (Sissle and Blake)	Victor rejected

Recorded in New York City, October 22, 1924.

DIXIE MOON (from the Musical Comedy *The Chocolate Dandies*) (Sissle and Blake) MANDA (from the Musical Comedy *The Chocolate Dandies*) (Sissle and Blake)	Victor 19494

MANDA was reissued on the RCA Victor long-playing album, ORIGINALS: MUSICAL COMEDY—1909–1935 LPV-560.

10. SISSLE AND BLAKE, EDISON, NEW YORK AND LONDON, 1925–1926

Recorded in New York City, May 27, 1925.

BROKEN BUSTED BLUES (J. Edgar Dowell and Henry Troy) YOU OUGHT TO KNOW (Sissle and Blake)	Edison rejected

Recorded in New York City, June 10, 1925.

BROKEN BUSTED BLUES (J. Edgar Dowell and Henry Troy) YOU OUGHT TO KNOW (Sissle and Blake)	Edison 51572, Edison Blue Amberol 50141 Cylinder

Recorded in London, England, c. January 1926.

WHY? (Sissle and Blake) OH, BOY! WHAT A GIRL	Edison Bell Winner 4337 (British)

Recorded in London, England, c. February 1926.

UKELELE BABY UKULELE LULLABY	EBW 4356
I WONDER WHERE MY SWEETIE CAN BE (Sissle and Blake) THERE'S ONE LANE THAT HAS NO TURNING (Sissle and Blake)	EBW 4371

Recorded in London, England, c. March 1926.

PICKANINNY SHOES (Sissle and Blake) DINAH	EBW 4402
A JOCKEY'S LIFE FOR MINE (Sissle and Blake) YOU OUGHT TO KNOW (Sissle and Blake)	EBW 4417

11. SISSLE AND BLAKE, 1927

Recorded in New York City, February 5, 1927.

'DEED I DO EV'RYTHING'S MADE FOR LOVE	Okeh 40776, Parlophone E-5796

CRAZY BLUES — Okeh—rejected

PICKANINNY SHOES — Okeh 40917, Parlophone R-186

Recorded in New York City, February 8, 1927.
MY DREAM OF THE BIG PARADE (Dubin–McHugh) — (Victor) Vitaphone VA–464–3
ALL GOD'S CHILLUN GOT SHOES

The two tracks listed above are on the same side of a very rare 16-inch record that plays at 33⅓ r.p.m. On PARADE, Noble Sissle sings and recites a special dramatization. Eubie and an orchestra play behind Sissle. This record was obtained by James O. Taylor of Detroit, who presented the record to Eubie recently when he was in Detroit (1969 or 1970). The disc is marked "2/8/27 VA-464-3 Rec 97 Vol. +5 Recorded by and Property of the Vitaphone Corp., NY, NY—Pressed by the Victor Talking Machine Co. Camden, NJ"

To play it, a large turntable is needed and the needle is placed on the inside and travels out to the edge as the record plays. It was apparently issued as a soundtrack to a film short that has not been found. On the second title, SHOES, there is no orchestra; Sissle and Blake sing, and Blake plays piano. Both selections last a total of eight minutes. Until the film that goes with this soundtrack is found, we won't know to what extent Sissle and Blake are in the picture themselves. This item is included in the listing of records for chronology's sake at this point, even though this is not a commercially available recording.

Recorded in New York City, May 10, 1927.
SLOW RIVER
HOME, CRADLE OF HAPPINESS — Okeh 40894, Parlophone R-3368

12. NOBLE SISSLE, 1927–1929

Accompanied by Rube Bloom, piano.
Recorded in New York City, July 26, 1927.
SOMETIMES I'M HAPPY
HALLELUJAH! — Okeh 40859, Parlophone R-3428, Odeon 193069

Recorded in New York City, August 15, 1927.
HERE AM I—BROKENHEARTED — OK 40877, Par R-3449
JUST ONCE AGAIN — OK 40877, Par R-3507

Accompanied by Andy Sannella, clarinet, and one steel guitar; Rube Bloom, piano.
Recorded in New York City, August 17, 1927.
GIVE ME A NIGHT IN JUNE — OK 40882, Par R-3449
ARE YOU HAPPY? — ——— Par R-3507

Accompanied by Rube Bloom, piano.
Recorded in New York City, September 6, 1927.
SWEETHEART MEMORIES — OK 40917, Par R-186
WHO'S THAT KNOCKIN' AT MY DOOR? — Par R-3471

Accompanied by Murray Kellner, violin; Rube Bloom, Eddie Lang, guitar; others.
Recorded in New York City, September 7, 1927.
KENTUCKY BABE — OK 40964, Par R-3471
LINDY LOU — ——— Par R-337
Sissle is known as "Lee White" on Okeh 40964.

Accompanied by his own Special Orchestra: Harry Revel, piano, and others.
Recorded in London, England, February 1928.
SINCE YOU HAVE LEFT ME
WESTWARD BOUND — Par R–101

I'M GOING BACK TO OLD NEBRASKA (Sissle–Revel)
I'M COMING VIRGINIA — Par R–3522

Recorded in London, England, May 29, 1928.
WHAT DO WE CARE?
LIMEHOUSE ROSE — Par R–128

GUIDING ME BACK HOME
SUNNY SKIES — Par R–129

NOBLE SISSLE AND HIS SIZZLING SYNCOPATORS, including Harry Revel.
Recorded in London, England, May 29, 1928.
JUST GIVE THE SOUTHLAND TO ME
SUNNY SKIES — Par R–125

AGAIN (Waltz)
LOVE LIES — Par R–126

NOBLE SISSLE,
accompanied by his own Special Orchestra, with Harry Revel, piano.
Recorded in London, England, June 12, 1928.
OL' MAN RIVER
WHY DO I LOVE YOU? — Par R–145

WHEN THE CLOCK STRIKES TWELVE (waltz)
JUST KEEP SINGING A SONG — Par R–146

Recorded in London, England, June 13, 1928.
HOW CAN YOU FORGET? — Par R–164

NOTHING HAS CHANGED — Rejected

BROKEN-HEARTED DOLL — Par R–164

HELPING HAND — Par R–337

LUCKY IN LOVE
GOOD NEWS — Par R–206

With Barry Mills, piano, and others.
Recorded in London, England, October 1928.
GET OUT AND GET UNDER THE MOON
DAKOTA — Par R–219, Ar 4308

SINCE YOU SAID YOU LOVED ME — Par R–220, Ar 4310
JUST LIKE A MELODY OUT OF THE SKY — ——— Ar 4308

NOBLE SISSLE,
accompanied by his Sizzling Syncopators.
Recorded in London England, December 8, 1928.
GREAT CAMP MEETIN' DAY
MIRANDA — Par R–251

Recorded in London, England, December 13, 1928.
FOR OLD TIMES' SAKE (waltz)
ALL BY YOURSELF IN THE MOONLIGHT — Par R–252

SHOUT HALLELUJAH! 'CAUSE I'M HOME
COLOMBO — Par R–259

NOBLE SISSLE AND HIS ORCHESTRA: Buster Bailey and others.
Recorded at Hayes, Middlesex, England, September 9, 1929.
KANSAS CITY KITTY — HMV B–5731

CAMP MEETING DAY
MIRANDA — HMV B–5709, R–14274

Recorded at Hayes, Middlesex, England, October 11, 1929.
I'M CROONING A TUNE ABOUT JUNE — HMV B–5731

RECOLLECTIONS (waltz) — HMV B–5723
YOU WANT LOVIN' AND I WANT LOVE — HMV B–5723

13. EUBIE BLAKE, 1929

EUBIE BLAKE
Piano solos, with Broadway Jones (vocal).
Recorded in New York City, December 3, 1929.
MARCHING HOME
MY FATE IS IN YOUR HANDS — Victor—tests

HOUSE RENT LIZZIE
DISSATISFIED BLUES — Victor—rejected

14. NOBLE SISSLE, 1930–1931

NOBLE SISSLE AND HIS SIZZLING SYNCOPATORS
Recorded in London, England, December 11, 1930.
DAUGHTER OF THE LATIN QUARTER
SUNNY SUNFLOWER LAND — Columbia CB–192

YOU CAN'T GET TO HEAVEN THAT WAY
CONFESSIN' — Columbia CB–193

With Sidney Bechet, soprano and baritone saxophone, and others.
Recorded in New York City, January 24, 1931.
GOT THE BENCH, GOT THE PARK — Brunswick 6073, 01117, A–9049, Supertone S–2173

LOVELESS LOVE — As above plus Melotone M–12444, Perfection 15649

Melotone as THE GEORGIA SYNCOPATORS; Supertone as MISSOURI JAZZ BAND.

Recorded in New York City, April 21, 1931.
BASEMENT BLUES — Brunswick Br 6129, A–9149, A–500124

WHA'D YA DO TO ME? ROLL ON, MISSISSIPPI, ROLL ON	Br 6111, 01158, A–9073

15. EUBIE BLAKE, 1931.

EUBIE BLAKE AND HIS ORCHESTRA
With Dick Robertson, vocal.
Recorded in New York City, c. February 1931.

PLEASE DON'T TALK ABOUT ME WHEN I'M GONE	Crown 3090, Broadway 1448 (as "John Martin and His Orch.")
I'M NO ACCOUNT ANY MORE	Crown 3090
WHEN YOUR LOVER HAS GONE	Crown 3086

Recorded in New York City, c. April 1931.

TWO LITTLE BLUE LITTLE EYES	Crown 3111, Broadway 1460 (as "John Martin and His Orch.")
NOBODY'S SWEETHEART	Crown 3130, Varsity 8046 (as "Dick Robertson and His Orch.")
ONE MORE TIME	Crown 3111
ST. LOUIS BLUES	Crown 3130, Varsity 8046 (as "Dick Robertson and His Orch.")

Recorded in New York City, June 3, 1931.

THUMPIN' AND BUMPIN'	Victor 22737
LITTLE GIRL	Victor 22735
MY BLUE DAYS BLEW OVER (When You Came Back to Me) (Seymour–Rich)	Victor 22735

Recorded in New York City, c. September 1931.

BLUES IN MY HEART	Crown 3197, Varsity 5056 (as "Dick Robertson and His Orch.")
LIFE IS JUST A BOWL OF CHERRIES	Crown 3193, Imp. 2628, Varsity 6017
SWEET GEORGIA BROWN	Crown 3197
RIVER, STAY 'WAY FROM MY DOOR	Crown, 3193, Varsity 6017

16. NOBLE SISSLE, 1934–1938

NOBLE SISSLE AND HIS (INTERNATIONAL) ORCHESTRA
Recorded in Chicago, August 15, 1934.

UNDER THE CREOLE MOON (Noble Sissle, vocal)	Decca 153
THE OLD ARK IS MOVERIN' (Billy Banks, vocal)	Decca 153, Br 01861
LOVELESS LOVE (Lavada Carter, vocal)	Decca 154, Br 01861
POLKA DOT RAG	Decca 154, Br 02511

Recorded in New York City, March 11, 1936

THAT'S WHAT LOVE DID TO ME (Lena Horne, vocal) YOU CAN'T LIVE IN HARLEM (Billy Banks, vocal)	Decca 778
I WONDER WHO MADE RHYTHM (Billy Banks, vocal)	Decca 766, Col DB–5032
'TAIN'T A FIT NIGHT OUT FOR MAN OR BEAST (Noble Sissle, vocal)	Decca 766, Col FB–1493
I TAKE TO YOU (Lena Horne, vocal)	Decca 847, Col DB–5032
RHYTHM OF THE BROADWAY MOON (Noble Sissle, vocal)	Decca 847, Col FB–1493

Recorded in New York City, April 14, 1937.

BANDANA DAYS I'M JUST WILD ABOUT HARRY	Variety 552
DEAR OLD SOUTHLAND ST. LOUIS BLUES	Rejected

NOBLE SISSLE'S SWINGSTERS: Sidney Bechet, others
Recorded in New York City, April 16, 1937.

OKEY-DOKE CHARACTERISTIC BLUES (Billy Banks, vocal)	Variety 648, Vocalion 3840

With Neil Spencer, vocal.
Recorded in New York City, February 10, 1938.

VIPER MAD (Neil Spencer, vocal)	Decca 7429, 3521, Br 02652
BLACKSTICK WHEN THE SUN SETS DOWN SOUTH (SOUTHERN SUNSET)	Decca 2129, 3865, Br 02702
SWEET PATOOTIE (Neil Spencer, vocal)	Decca 7429, Br 02652

17. EUBIE BLAKE, 1951

At the urging of the great composer-pianist James P. Johnson, Rudi Blesh and Harriet Janis interviewed Eubie Blake for their now classic study, *They All Played Ragtime.* It had been Johnson himself who had picked up the phone and arranged the interview, for Blesh and Janis were not aware that Blake was still alive. In his new book *Combo: USA* (1971) Rudi Blesh relates how he and Harriet Janis recorded Eubie in 1951:

On January 7, in the apartment of the author of this book, Eubie jammed there with the Conrad Janis Tailgate Jazz Band and, with the Janis rhythm section, he recorded "Maryland, My Maryland" and "Maple Leaf Rag" on an old Steinway square grand, c. *1865. "Maple Leaf" was issued as part of a 10-inch Circle LP, "Jamming at Rudi's No. 1." (Circle L–467 LP)*

No other companies, major or minor, rushed to record the great ragtime pioneer, so Circle (a company consisting of Harriet Janis and this author) took an engineer, Peter Bartok, and portable equipment to Eubie's Brooklyn home the following May and taped thirteen numbers. Among these were Eubie's rags: "Charleston Rag," 'Dicty's on Seventh Avenue," "Black Keys on Parade," "Troublesome Ivories," and "Chevy Chase," as well as Jess Pickett's "The Dream" and Ben Harney's 1896 ragtime song, "Mr. Johnson Turn Me Loose" and the Joe Jordan song, "Lovie Joe," that, in the 1910 Ziegfeld Follies, *gave Fannie Brice her first big hit.*

Circle retired from business the following year without having issued the projected Eubie Blake 12-inch LP album. Later acquired by Jazzology, it is scheduled for eventual release.

In a recent conversation Rudi told the authors of this book that with the help of Terry Waldo these recordings would be released during 1973.

18. SHUFFLE ALONG OF 1952

One fortunate result of the ill-fated production was that RCA Victor asked Eubie to conduct an orchestra with vocalists, doing four songs from the original 1921 *Shuffle Along.* The recordings were issued on "45 Extended Play" as well as on "33 Long Playing" as part of the RCA Victor *Show Time* Series.

SONGS FROM *SHUFFLE ALONG* RCA VICTOR LPM–3514, EPA–482

Orchestra directed by the composer, Eubie Blake

LOVE WILL FIND A WAY (Vocalists—Louise Woods and Laurence Watson)
I'M JUST WILD ABOUT HARRY (Vocalists—Thelma Carpenter and Avon Long)
BANDANA DAYS (Vocalist—Avon Long)
GYPSY BLUES (Vocalists—Thelma Carpenter and Avon Long)

19. EUBIE BLAKE, 1958–1959, TWENTIETH-CENTURY FOX

In 1958 and 1959 Eubie was featured artist on two Twentieth-Century Fox recordings which, regrettably, are out of print and very difficult to locate.

Twentieth-Century Fox 3003 THE WIZARD OF THE RAGTIME PIANO. Buster Bailey (clarinet), Eubie Blake (piano, vocal), Bernard Addison (guitar), Milt Hinton/George Duvivier (bass), Panama Francis/Charles Persip (drums), Noble Sissle (vocal).

JUBILEE TONIGHT
EUBIE'S BOOGIE RAG
MAPLE LEAF
MOBILE RAG
I'M JUST WILD ABOUT HARRY
SUNFLOWER SLOW DRAG
THE DREAM RAG
MISSISSIPPI RAG
RAGTIME RAG (This is really "Troublesome Ivories")
CARRY ME BACK TO OLD VIRGINNY
MARYLAND
CAROLINA IN THE MORNING
THE RAGTIME MILLIONAIRE
MY GAL IS A HIGHBORN LADY
GOOD MORNING CARRIE
BILL BAILEY, WON'T YOU PLEASE COME HOME

Twentieth-Century Fox 3039 MARCHES I PLAYED ON THE OLD RAGTIME PIANO. Buster Bailey (clarinet), Eubie Blake (piano, vocal), Kenny Burrell (guitar), Milt Hinton (bass), Panama Francis (drums).

STARS AND STRIPES FOREVER
GREETING TO BANGAR
DUNLAP COMMANDERY
OH, BRAVE OLD ARMY TEAM
RAGTIME POLISH DANCE
HIGH SCHOOL CADETS
OUR DIRECTOR
RAGTIME TOREADOR
CHARLESTON RAG DANCE
SEMPER FIDELIS
SONG WITHOUT WORDS
KING COTTON
RAGTIME PIANO "TRICKS"

20. EUBIE BLAKE, 1962

In 1962 Eubie was reunited with Joe Jordan and Charley Thompson and, with "Ragtime" Bob Darch, as producer and master of ceremonies; the three performed on an LP titled GOLDEN REUNION IN RAGTIME Stereoddities *c.* 1900.

MEET ME IN ST. LOUIS	Blake, Jordan, and Thompson
BUNCH O' BLACKBERRIES	Blake, Jordan, and Thompson
MAORI	Blake, Jordan, and Thompson
LOVIE JOE (Jordan)	Jordan with Blake and Thompson
LILY RAG (Thompson)	Thompson and Blake
MEMORIES OF YOU (Razaf–Blake)	Blake
TEASIN' RAG (Jordan)	Jordan and Blake
OLD BLACK CROW	Jordan with Blake and Thompson
WAITING FOR THE ROBERT E. LEE	Thompson, Jordan, and Blake
THAT'S JELLY ROLL	Blake
UNTIL (Jordan)	Jordan
DELMAR RAG (Thompson)	Thompson and Blake
DORA DEAN	Blake, Thompson, and Jordan
DICTY'S ON SEVENTH AVENUE	Blake
BROADWAY IN DAHOMEY	Blake, Jordan, and Thompson

Since the album does not indicate who plays which selection, we have listened as carefully as possible and submit the above as a probably correct listing.

Stereoddities also issued a two-LP package complete with verbatim script ("for easy cueing") for use as a one-hour radio show. It contains only three numbers that are on the LP as released for general use. Music contained on these LP's includes:
MEET ME IN ST. LOUIS—waltz tempo and in ragtime
ALEXANDER'S RAGTIME BAND
FUNERAL MARCH—demonstration
RAGTIME FUNERAL MARCH MUSIC
WON'T YOU COME HOME, BILL BAILEY?
SWEETIE DEAR—played by Jordan
TRICKY FINGERS—played by Blake
BUFFET FLAT BLUES—played by Jordan
MOROCCO BLUES—played by Jordan
BLUE THOUGHTS—played by Blake
LOVIE JOE—played by Jordan
BROTHER-IN-LAW DAN—played by Jordan
WAITING FOR THE ROBERT E. LEE
JUDGE FOGARTY—played by Blake

21. EUBIE BLAKE, 1968–1969

THE EIGHTY-SIX YEARS OF EUBIE BLAKE
Columbia C2S 847

This album, produced by John Hammond after three historic recording sessions in late 1968 (December 26) and early 1969 (February 6 and March 12), was conceived as a kind of retrospective of Blake's long career. Instead, the album launched Eubie on an entirely new phase of activity as a concert artist, television performer, lecturer, and spark plug of the ragtime revival. With Sissle present to join him on some of the numbers and to lead a rooting section of many of Eubie's friends, Eubie responded, as he always does to the presence of an audience, with a magnificent effort. The album includes:

Record One

Side One—Blake, piano with occasional vocal
DREAM RAG (Pickett—arranged by Blake)
CHARLESTON RAG (Blake)
MAPLE LEAF RAG (Joplin—arranged by Blake)
SEMPER FIDELIS (Sousa—arranged by Blake)
EUBIE'S BOOGIE (Blake)
POOR JIMMY GREEN (Blake)
TRICKY FINGERS (Blake)

Side Two—Blake, piano with occasional vocal
STARS AND STRIPES FOREVER (Sousa—arranged by Blake)
BALTIMORE TODOLO (Blake)
POOR KATIE RED (Blake)
KITCHEN TOM (Blake)
TROUBLESOME IVORIES (Blake)
CHEVY CHASE (Blake)
BRITTWOOD RAG (Blake)

Record Two

Side Three
MEDLEY: BLEEDING MOON—UNDER THE BAMBOO TREE (Cole and Johnson—arranged by Blake)—Blake, piano
IT'S ALL YOUR FAULT (Sissle, Nelson, and Blake)—Sissle, vocal; Blake, piano and vocal
SHUFFLE ALONG MEDLEY (Sissle and Blake)—Sissle, vocal; Blake, piano and vocal
BANDANA DAYS
I'M JUST SIMPLY FULL OF JAZZ
IN HONEYSUCKLE TIME
GYPSY BLUES
IF YOU'VE NEVER BEEN VAMPED BY A BROWNSKIN
LOVE WILL FIND A WAY
I'M JUST WILD ABOUT HARRY
I'M JUST WILD ABOUT HARRY (Sissle and Blake)—Original waltz version—Blake, piano
SPANISH VENUS (Roberts—arranged by Blake)—Blake, piano
AS LONG AS YOU LIVE (Porter and Blake)—Blake, piano and vocal

Side Four
MEDLEY OF JAMES P. JOHNSON SONGS (arranged by Blake)
CHARLESTON
OLD-FASHIONED LOVE
IF I COULD BE WITH YOU—Blake, piano
(While playing CHARLESTON, Eubie snapped a string on the piano, which happened to be Vladimir Horowitz's favorite piano in Columbia's 30th Street studio. The snap can be heard on the record.)
YOU WERE MEANT FOR ME (Sissle and Blake) Sissle, vocal; Blake, piano
DIXIE MOON (Sissle and Blake)—Blake, piano
BLUES, WHY DON'T YOU LET ME ALONE (Porter and Blake)—Blake, piano and vocal
BLUE RAG IN 12 KEYS (Blake)—Blake, piano
MEMORIES OF YOU (Razaf and Blake)—Blake, piano

22. EUBIE BLAKE, 1972

In early 1972 Eubie Blake established his own record company, Eubie Blake Music. Three records produced by Carl Seltzer have already been issued, and others will be released during 1973. They can be obtained from Eubie Blake Music, 284A Stuyvesant Avenue, Brooklyn, New York 11221.

EUBIE BLAKE, VOLUME I: FEATURING IVAN HAROLD BROWNING, EBM 1

Side One: Eubie Blake, piano and vocals
DICTY'S ON SEVENTH AVENUE (Blake)—Blake, piano
FIZZ WATER (Blake)—Blake, piano
SUGAR BABE (Cole and Johnson)—Blake, piano and vocal
MELODIC RAG (Blake)—Blake, piano
RAGTIME MERRY WIDOW (Lehár—arranged by Blake)—Blake, piano
NOVELTY RAG (Blake)—Blake, piano

Side Two: Browning and Blake
(Eubie Blake accompanying vocals by Ivan Harold Browning)
LITTLE GAL (Dunbar and Johnson)
GOOD NIGHT, ANGELINE (Sissle and Blake)
JUNGLE NIGHTS IN GAY MONTMARTRE (Browning and Starr)
SOME LITTLE BUG IS GOING TO FIND YOU (Hein, Burt, and Atwell)
LOVE WILL FIND A WAY (Sissle and Blake)
ROLL THEM COTTON BALES (Johnson and Johnson)
MY LINDY LOU (Strickland)
DE GOSPEL TRAIN (Traditional, arranged by Blake)

EUBIE BLAKE: FROM RAGS TO CLASSICS, EBM–2

Side One—Eubie Blake, piano and vocals
CHARLESTON RAG (Blake)—A 1971 Performance—Blake, piano
CHARLESTON RAG (Blake)—A 1921 Performance—Blake, piano
CAPRICIOUS HARLEM (Blake)—Blake, piano
RUSTLE OF SPRING (Sinding—arranged by Blake)
YOU'RE LUCKY TO ME (Razaf and Blake)—Blake, piano and vocal
YOU DO SOMETHING TO ME (Porter—arranged by Blake)—Blake, piano

Side Two—Eubie Blake, piano
RAIN DROPS (Blake)
PORK AND BEANS (Roberts—arranged by Blake)
VALSE MARION (Blake)—Written in 1972 for Marion Blake
CLASSICAL RAG (Blake)
SCARF DANCE (Chaminade—arranged by Blake)
BUTTERFLY (Blake)
JUNK MAN RAG (Roberts—arranged by Blake)

EUBIE BLAKE AND HIS FRIENDS: EDITH WILSON AND IVAN HAROLD BROWNING, EBM–3

Side One—Eubie Blake, piano; Edith Wilson and Ivan Harold Browning, vocals

HE MAY BE YOUR MAN (BUT HE COMES TO SEE ME SOMETIMES) (Fowler)—Edith Wilson, vocal; Eubie Blake, piano

THERE'LL BE SOME CHANGES MADE (Overstreet–Higgins)—Edith Wilson, vocal; Eubie Blake, piano

BLACK AND BLUE (Waller, Razaf and Brooks)—Edith Wilson, vocal; Eubie Blake, piano

JOSHUA FIT THE BATTLE OF JERICHO (Traditional—arranged by Blake) —Browning, vocal; Blake, piano

GO DOWN MOSES (Traditional—arranged by Blake)—Browning, vocal; Blake, piano

IN THAT GREAT GETTIN' UP MORNING (Traditional)—Browning, vocal; Blake, piano

EXHORTATION (Cook–Rogers)—Browning, vocal; Blake, piano

MEDLEY FROM *Shuffle Along* (Sissle and Blake)—Browning, vocal; Blake, piano
IF YOU'VE NEVER BEEN VAMPED BY A BROWNSKIN
IN HONEYSUCKLE TIME
I'M JUST WILD ABOUT HARRY

Side Two—Eubie Blake, piano and vocals

EUBIE DUBIE (Guarnieri and Blake)—Blake, piano

I CAN'T GET YOU OUT OF MY MIND (Reddie and Blake)—Blake, piano and vocal

MEMPHIS BLUES (Handy—arranged by Blake)—Blake, piano

CORNER CHESNUT AND LOW (Blake)—Blake, piano

WHEN DAY IS DONE (DeSylva and Katscher—arranged by Blake)—Blake, piano

IX
LIST OF SISSLE AND BLAKE FILMS

SISSLE AND BLAKE'S SNAPPY SONGS, *c.* 1923, A Lee DeForest short subject, one of the earliest sound films. Sissle and Blake perform their own AFFECTIONATE DAN and the traditional ALL GOD'S CHILLUN GOT SHOES.

There is a possibility that Sissle and Blake appeared in a Vitaphone short subject *c.* 1927, in which they may have performed Dubin and McHugh's MY DREAM OF THE BIG PARADE and the traditional ALL GOD'S CHILLUN GOT SHOES. No copy of this film has been located.

HARLEM IS HEAVEN, 1932, Lincoln Pictures Inc. Full-length sound film. According to dance film historian Ernest Smith, "Bill Robinson performs tap routines with chorus line to the music of Eubie Blake and his Orchestra. He also performs his famous Stair Dance to the tune of 'Swanee River.' "

PIE, PIE BLACKBIRD, 1932, Warner Bros. A one-reel short subject. Sound. The Nicholas Brothers dance to music of Eubie Blake and his Orchestra.

THAT'S THE SPIRIT, 1933, Vitaphone Corp. One reel. Sound. Cora La Redd tap-dances to music of Noble Sissle's Orchestra.

(PHOTOGRAPHS BY MARY VELTHOVEN)

Afterword

Sissle and Blake are old now. At this writing Noble is eighty-four and Eubie eighty-nine. Shuffle Along *opened fifty-one years ago, seventeen years before the older of the authors of this book was born.*

The recent ragtime revival has carried on its wave the still nimble rag-piano of Eubie Blake, perhaps now the sole active survivor of the early years. Eubie's playing seems even to improve with age. Noble performs rarely these days. On June 22, 1972, however, we, our editors at Viking, and Mary Velthoven Kopecky, an editor and photographer for the Viking staff, were privileged to glimpse some of the old Sissle and Blake magic. At Bob Kimball's apartment, only recently moved into, we were surrounded by packing cases, cardboard boxes, and furniture still in crates. Alan Williams hand-held the one available lamp to help Mary take her pictures. There were still streamers on the windows from Bob's recent wedding.

Eubie sat down at Bob's piano and began to warm up the keyboard. Somehow, tunes from Shuffle Along *emerged from the stream of notes, and Noble's face began to light up. Soon we were being treated, incredibly, to "On Patrol in No Man's Land," the number in which, fifty-three years ago, Noble slid across the floor to duck the "Minnenwurfer." "Don't try it, kid!" Eubie yelled back to Noble, who sat behind him on the other end of the piano bench. Noble didn't, but he still could draw, with his eyes, his hands, and that pearly-precise diction of his, a rueful and good-humored picture of World War I as seen by Lieutenant Sissle and long-gone Jim Europe. Other songs followed, some from* Shuffle Along, *others from their other shows and vaudeville routines. The machinery, the timing, the magic still worked; one sensed a complex and finely polished theatrical world, still there, still radiant.*

And absolutely unique.